MASSIVE >

MASSIVE ›

**An everyday tale of drugs, devil
worship and Geordie leek-growers.**

› **MICKEY
HUTTON**

JOHN BLAKE

Published by John Blake Publishing Ltd,
3, Bramber Court, 2 Bramber Road,
London W14 9PB, England

First published in paperback in 2003

ISBN 1 903402 92 1

British Library Cataloguing-in-Publication Data:

A catalogue record for this book is available from the British Library.

Design by ENVY

Printed in Great Britain by Bookmarque, Croydon

1 3 5 7 9 10 8 6 4 2

Papers used by John Blake Publishing are natural, recyclable products
made from wood grown in sustainable forests. The manufacturing processes
conform to the environmental regulations of the country of origin.

To my mam and dad Ellen and Bill Hutton
and my nana and grandad Nell and Vince Curran.
Any similarities the characters in this book have to
you lot are wholly intended. You're weird!

1 〉

George and Nellie Creedy could read minds. They knew they could communicate with each other by thought as soon as they met. Now most of us, if we'd been given the gift of mind-reading, would have thought, That's a result, turned to a life of crime and ended up ruling the world with an iron hand. The whole population of the Earth would have to bow to our might and those who didn't would be flung into giant vats of crocodiles, lions, tigers and nippy crabs. And we would laugh like scary giants: 'HA! HA! HA!' we would say.

But not George and Nellie. You see, being a mighty ruler of the planet didn't enter your mind when you were brought up in Wallsend, a small town just outside Newcastle-upon-Tyne. You didn't desperately want to draw attention to yourself, like an ex-*Big Brother* contestant opening a fast food restaurant in Slough, or a nobody fat-ankled 'It' girl with a drug problem. George and Nellie were quite happy just getting on with their lives simply and quietly.

was a great relief when they found each other, though. Up until then, neither of them had any idea what was happening. At first they didn't realise the voices they could hear in their heads were other people's thoughts. How scary is that? Each was vaguely aware that the other existed, because every now and then their minds would connect, like radios being tuned to the right station, and when that happened they felt they weren't alone.

Before they met, they had both been very quiet and introverted. They had been like this all their lives. This was because they knew they were different and had the good sense to keep their skills to themselves, which gave them both a reputation for being moody and not much fun. When they finally found each other it was as though their brains connected as one; the radio waves tuned in and the whole world looked clearer and brighter. Even better, they had someone to talk to about 'The Thing', which is what they both called their mind-reading gift.

George and Nellie met at 'The Hoppings', an annual funfair on Newcastle's town moor that goes on to this day. It was 1948. Nellie was 18 and George was a very mature 23. He'd always been a bit of a loner had George, so his job as a welder suited him fine: he didn't have to talk to anyone when he had his mask on. He would have liked to wear his mask all the time, but even George knew lasses didn't like you much if they couldn't see your face. And what a face George had. He looked like a movie star, and could have been one if Hollywood had been in Newcastle.

George enjoyed his job and had enjoyed living at home with his mam. His dad had been gassed in the war so he had never really known him. When I say gassed, he had been having a fling with a French lass when he was over there in the army. She'd put the oven on to keep them warm while they were on 'manoeuvres', the flame had blown out and they'd gone to sleep. For good. The army thought it best to keep it hushed up.

George's mum, Meg, worried about him so much she never even told him she had 'the cancer'. She didn't want to worry him. Although George knew there was something up he would never use 'The Thing' to find out what was happening to his mam. He had done that once before and nearly threw up when he realised she fancied the coal man. His mother thinking about other men like that! Young George was stunned. He grew up a bit that day. And he certainly grew up when she died, which sent him further into himself. He had hardly crossed the threshold since then, going out only to go to work or get groceries.

Of course, in a tight-knit community like Wallsend, George was doted on by all the women. They had, after all, grown up with his mam, but they also just thought he was bloody gorgeous and would drop him off little treats just to look at him. The fact he never smiled or spoke seemed to make him more attractive to the lasses. The reason George never smiled or spoke to anyone was that he didn't want to make friends. He knew he was weird and didn't want anyone else to find out. He was always desperately trying not to read other people's minds, but when he did he would say odd things and he was worried that if he did this too much people would shut him out completely.

So George just carried on with his work and when he wasn't working he read all the gardening books his dad had left in a battered old suitcase. He read them again and again, until he knew them all off by heart and would quite happily have re-read them once again if the Hoppings, a big man in a too-small monkey suit, and a little dog hadn't stepped in.

young, beautiful, orphan George woke up to a gorgeous Saturday morning in July and lay there wishing he could go to work so he could keep his mind occupied. It had been exactly a year to the day since his mam had died and he really missed her. He was dragged from his miserable thoughts by a frantic banging at the front door. Pulling on his work trousers, George miserably stamped downstairs to see what all the commotion was about. Is there anything more attractive than a miserable, stamping, good-looking man?

He pulled open the door and was nearly sucked off his front step by the intake of breath from the three girls who stood in front of him. He had no idea of the effect that he, standing shirtless, muscular and barefoot, with tousled, just-woken-up hair, was having on the three teenage Dodds sisters, who lived next door to him. To George it appeared that they were fighting for breath: opening and closing their mouths, their eyes round and bright like car headlights.

'Well?' barked George.

'M ... m ... m ... m ... m ... mmm,' the youngest sister stuttered.

'M, m, m, m, what, man? Monsters comin' te get wi?' said George, making himself appear more mean, moody and gorgeous.

'Mam says do you wanna come to The Hoppings with us this afternoon, 'cos wa aall gannin?' the eldest, prettiest and gingerest of the three girls managed to stammer out.

'Eh, nah thanks, lasses, I'm not really very good company the day,' said George, and with that he slowly shut the door on the girls who stood stunned, staring at the wood for a good three minutes until they came to and staggered off. The effect was the same as if, today, the Brad Pitt Quintuplets had walked into a posh girl's school naked.

It wasn't until later on that morning, as George was re-

reading Henry Littleton's best-selling book, *Greener Grass, Larger Leeks*, that he realised how rude he'd been. The lasses had only been trying to cheer him up and he'd virtually slammed the door in their faces. What would his mam have said? But George knew exactly what she would have said. She would have said nowt; she'd have given him a good kick up the arse.

Right, thought George, standing up and throwing Henry Littleton on to the threadbare settee. I'm gannin to the Hoppings an' I'm ganna apologise to them lasses an' win them some presents.

Little did he know he would be coming back with more than cheap fairground tat.

So that's how George ended up at the Hoppings on that hot June afternoon and he was thoroughly enjoying himself. Although not jumping up in the air and clicking his heels, he was taking great pleasure from the sights and sounds of his surroundings. It was then that he witnessed the attack.

At first he couldn't quite believe what he was seeing, but staggering towards him was a monkey. A big monkey. A big drunk monkey. It looked terrible. Its skin was stretched tightly across its body, it was wearing tiny, round, thick-lensed glasses and it was talking to itself: 'Fucking monkey suit. I'll give him fucking monkey suit,' the monkey slurred.

Now being a shipyard worker, George was used to bad language. But he wasn't used to hearing it come from a monkey, wearing glasses, with a thick Geordie accent. He couldn't help himself, he began to laugh, and the more the monkey swore the more he laughed. Soon he was bent double laughing, hands on his thighs, and because he hadn't laughed for so long his body seemed to be giving him double helpings of laughter. George was helpless with mirth. Tears were running down his face; snot was running out of his nose.

He straightened himself up and wiped his eyes on the palms of his hands only to find himself looking straight into the glasses of the big stretched monkey.

'And what the fuck are you laughing at, Snotty?' said the monkey, enveloping George in a cloud of alcohol. George tried to keep his face straight but it wasn't possible. He laughed in the monkey's face. Well, more of a splutter really. Which, as everyone knows, is the worst thing you can do to a monkey, what with them being so sensitive. By now they had gathered a bit of a crowd, which, finding George's laughing contagious, was giggling and pointing, sending the drunken monkey into a fury. So incensed was the big monkey that he took a swing at George, just as George doubled up again. The monkey punch missed George completely, the monkey spun around three times and fell flat on his monkey bum.

At this point a little running-on-three-legs-wipe-yer-bum-on-the-grass Jack Russell, who had been observing the proceedings, ran up to the sitting-down monkey and began to nip and bite it. The monkey leaped up and grabbed the dog by the throat and screamed at the crowd.

'Whose fucking dog is this?'

It's mine, said a tiny voice.

George was stunned. It was as if someone had poured warm water over him, then hit him with wind chimes. He couldn't believe a voice could sound so beautiful. But the weirdest thing of all was George had heard it in his head and not his lugs.

He turned and looked into the eyes of the girl he knew he was going to marry, Nellie. It was as if a big bubble of lovely stillness had descended on the young couple, and their thoughts were streaming into each other's minds. So this was the person each of them had been connecting with all these years. Luckily, both Nellie and George had found a way to block out other folks' thoughts.

The moment was shattered by the monkey screaming, 'I'm going to fucking strangle this fucking little bastard!' Which is not the most welcome of background noises for those eyes-across-a-crowded-room moments. The monkey's big hairy hands were tightening around the Jack Russell's throat, its tongue was sticking out and its eyes were bulging. George heard a tiny gasp of fear from the dog's owner and his bride-to-be.

So he did the honourable thing. He knocked the monkey out with a punch that probably travelled just four inches. The monkey's eyes went back in their sockets, its legs buckled and it fell over. Out cold. It lay there for 15 minutes, until a bunch of kids rolled it into the main road and it was arrested for obstructing the traffic. It was fined £5 and ordered never to be a monkey again. The dog was unharmed but when it was released from the monkey death grip it came over all peculiar and bit an ice-cream man.

George ended up taking Nellie home to Byker, where she lived with her mam, Mary. Her dad, Vince, had been shot in the war by his sergeant, a man called Maurice Rice. One night, after drinking stolen brandy, he got so drunk that he made a puffy pass at Vince. So Vince hit him. The sergeant, coming all over all 'I'm-not-a-puff-really', shot Vince through the head and then tried to shoot himself. Unfortunately he was so drunk he missed his mouth and shot a horse standing next to him, which collapsed and fell on him due to the bullet in its horsey head.

Maurice died later in hospital from gangrene, which had infected the compound fracture in his leg, caused by the wounded horse falling on him. The horsey recovered, but was tragically killed a year later when, returning home to

Norfolk on a boat, it fell overboard and was eaten by a whale. The army hushed it all up of course and Nellie's mother was awarded a generous pension. The horse's mother didn't get a thing.

A year after the Hoppings, George and Nellie were married. A year after that their only child, Neville, was born.

Now after fifty years of marriage, the Geordie couple found they could sit in what appeared to others to be a companionable silence, when in actual fact they were having a right old mental laugh together.

It was a far cry from their young days when they never spoke to anyone. George and Nellie never stopped talking. It could get a bit embarrassing, because Nellie was a bit of a giggler and George would always try to set her off. If he could create a snot-from-the-nose moment, it really would make his day.

They certainly never would have told a soul about their skills when they first met. In those days telling folk stuff like that could get you put away, and anyway no one wanted to be different. It wasn't just the mind-reading they could do. They could do other spooky stuff as well. Just little things like moving objects around a bit, but they didn't really like doing that, it was a bit scary.

Although it was handy once, when a young lad tried to break into their house one night. Obviously not realising he was essentially breaking and entering the *X-Files*, he got a shock when he was thrown out of the Creedy's garden and into the allotments next door. He was even more surprised when he marched himself down to the police station, gave himself up, and then asked for ten other burglaries to be taken into consideration.

Every now and then George found he had X-ray vision (which Nellie didn't like at all), and Nellie found she could levitate. One New Year's Eve, Nellie had a bit too much to drink and levitated to the ceiling in the living room. When George came in, she swooped down on him like a vampire. Gave him a bit of a turn that did. That was a snot-from-the-nose moment for Nellie.

The mind-reading came in especially handy if they wanted to get out of awkward situations. Situations that usually involved their only son, 'Cheeky-faced Neville', as he was known to the mums in the area. It wasn't as if George and Nellie disliked their son, or that Neville was a bad lad, it was just that they had absolutely no idea where he came from. It had always been the same. Even when he was born, Nellie had been sure he was surveying his new surroundings with complete disdain. And as he grew older there was no doubt about it: Neville was a snob.

Then, one Christmas Eve, everything fell into place.

Neville was three at the time, and one of the first words he had learned to say was 'dog'. He said it all the time, whether there was a dog in sight or not, and every time he saw a dog in the street he rushed over and made a big fuss of it. He never called his parents 'mamma' or 'dadda': to him they were both called 'dog dog', or sometimes 'god god'. He even said that as though his mum and dad were below him.

Both George and Nellie had tried to probe Neville's mind to find out about this dog stuff, but it made him cry and they didn't want to hurt him, so they never did it again. It appeared he just liked dogs, although why, when he called parents 'dog dog', he should have his cheeky-faced look on, neither George nor Nellie had any idea.

With Christmas coming up, the Creedys decided to buy their odd son what he seemed to want most in the world: a dog. George went out to the cat and dog shelter on Christmas Eve and bought the daftest-looking dog he could find. It appeared to be a cross between a beagle, a badger and a squirrel. It had black and white stripes, a big fat bum, connected to a short stubby tail and long floppy ears; its front paws were longer than its back paws and it had two goofy front teeth. It would've looked as if it was smiling if only its tongue wasn't hanging out licking everything in its path.

The perfect pet for the bairn, thought George, as he carried the daft mutt under him arm through the slush, back to his family.

As George, dog in arms, had turned the corner into their street, Neville, who had been sitting quietly, colouring in, jumped up and started banging on the front door shouting, 'Dog God!' at the top of his voice. Nellie sent George a mental warning that he should go to the back door, but as soon as she did this Neville immediately ran to the back door and started banging and screaming, 'Dog God!'

Nellie ran over, picked him up and tried to soothe him, but he wouldn't have it and squirmed out of her arms and ran back to the back door screaming, 'Dooooooog!' as loudly as he could.

George could hear all the commotion from the garden and asked Nellie if he should go, but she told him that they might as well give Neville his present now to calm him down, so George went into the little house carrying the bundle of fur and tongue.

As George walked into the living room and held the damp dog out for his son to see, the pup shot out of his arms and, slowly twisting, hovered in the air at a height of four feet.

George and Nellie stood stunned, but not as stunned as the dog, as it was now doing loop-the-loops. An ecstatic Neville who was jumping up and down shouting, 'Dog, Dooooooooog!'

Then it happened. Neville leaped into the air to try and

touch the dog and didn't come down. He too was hovering. Neville and the dog shot up to the ceiling in a flying dog/child ballet. George thought it was one of the most beautiful things he had ever seen.

Suddenly, the dog and the boy seemed to lose control. The mutt dropped from te sky and hit Neville in the chest, knocking him into the hearth. Nellie screamed. The dog leaped up, shook itself and ran to Neville, who lay still, blood pouring down his ashen face.

Shaking, Nellie ran to her son and gathered him up into her arms. Tears were streaming down her face. Neville had a bad cut above his right eye and it was quickly turning purple. Trying not to panic, George gently lifted Neville away from his mam so he could inspect the damage. George had seen enough cuts to realise that it in itself wasn't life threatening. However, he didn't know just how serious the damage inside his son's head was, and he knew he had to get the boy to hospital quickly. George carried him towards the front door. They would go next door to their neighbour, Bobby Blackburn, and ask him if he'd drive them to hospital.

When Bobby opened the door to the strange procession, he acted as if he had these sort of visits every Christmas night. A very pale George, carrying his unconscious bloodied son, and Nellie sobbing, carrying a puppy that was howling like a squeaky wolf.

'I thought it might have been the three wise men but it's that daft family from next door,' said Bobby putting on his cap and shouting over his shoulder to his own family, who were preparing for Christmas. 'I think we'd better be getting the lad to hospital, eh, George?'

Neville opened his one good eye, said, 'Spinny Dog', and fell unconscious again.

If there's a more depressing place to be on Christmas Eve than a children's ward, I reckon the Devil is keeping it under wraps.

Bobby Blackburn's ambulance arrived at the Royal Victoria Infirmary with its cargo, and Neville, Nellie and George were ushered straight into casualty. It wasn't very busy at that time; a bit too early for all the daft lads in the Bigg Market to realise it wasn't such a good idea to drink their mam's weight in lager and then fight each other.

So Neville was seen straight away. The young, grim-faced lass doctor examined Neville from top to toe but even she found it hard to suppress a smile when Neville opened his eyes and shouted, 'Spinny Dog, Spinny Dog,' and then burst into tears. The dog, which was sitting outside the cubicle, being petted by a policeman, burst in, started yapping at everyone and tried to climb on to the bed. But it was restrained by the copper. The pup was called Spinny Dog from then on, although after a few months its name was shortened to plain Spinny.

'Well I think he's going to be fine,' said the doctor, 'but I do think we should keep him in for observation, I know it's Christmas and that, but I think it's wise.'

Neville was unaware of all this as he was quite happily singing to 'Spinny Dog', who had crept back into the cubicle and sat watching his new master.

So the Creedys spent a miserable Christmas Eve in a children's ward. Nellie was on a bed next to her son, George and Spinny Dog on a couch in the corridor. They didn't wake up until the carol singing started at 8 o'clock the next day.

'Glor-o-o-o-o-or-o-o-o-o-o-or-o-o-o-o-o-o-or-o-o-o-o-o-or-o-o-o-o-o-o-ooria, Hosanna in excelsis!' is not the best thing to hear when waking up in hospital. You think you've died and gone to heaven, or on seeing the big, fat do-gooder women who are singing it you may think you've died and gone to hell, which is enough to give anyone a heart attack.

This is what woke George up on that fateful Christmas Day, and he would've leaped straight up to see how his son was doing if he hadn't had a sleeping, snoring, dribbling dog on his chest. So, tucking the pup under his arm, George tentatively opened the door to Neville's ward and was greeted with a sight he would never forget. The two people he loved most in the world tucked up together: dribbling, bubbling and snoring gently.

After a good checking over by the lass doctor, who was dressed as one of Santa's elves, it being Christmas Day, young Neville was pronounced fit as a fiddling flea and was told he could go home and enjoy all the presents Santa would surely have left him. So the Creedys – Neville, with a big bandage on his damaged head, squirming in his mam's arms; the dog squirming in George's arms – set off home to celebrate what was left of Christmas Day.

Bobby Blackburn, who had phoned the hospital earlier that morning, was waiting for them as they pushed open the doors of the hospital. He had put cardboard reindeer horns on the front of his car and covered it in fake snow and holly. He himself was dressed as Santa Claus, and a very fine festive sight it was that greeted the Creedys. Bobby was even doing a little Santa song and dance. It was a sort of cross between a donkey stamping its feet and the twist, as he sang 'Good King Wenceslas', which he didn't really know the words to, so there was a lot of humming and ahhhing. A twinkly-eyed ambulance driver asked Bobby if he wanted to see a doctor, which made Nellie and George laugh even more.

When Bobby Blackburn's ambulance finally returned them all safely home (Bobby Blackburn was known to be the slowest driver in Wallsend), the neighbours were out in force, enquiring after young Neville, who by now had recovered sufficiently to run up and down the street with his new pet. George and Nellie were exchanging worried looks and thoughts. They had no idea what the reaction of their neighbours would be if Neville and his dog suddenly shot up into the air like super baby and super daft puppy. Thankfully, feet and paws stayed safely on the ground and, while Nellie kept Neville busy, George nipped into the house and put up the lad's Christmas stocking.

It seemed as if last night had never happened as Neville excitedly opened all his presents and then showed them to Spinny Dog to see if he approved. Spinny Dog particularly liked the Action Man, which he grabbed by the head, and dragged off around the room being pursued by Neville. When the dog wee'd on the Etch-a-Sketch, Nellie decided the dog should go into the garden while Neville opened the rest of his presents.

The rest of the day carried on as every other Christmas Day. Neville forgot about his presents and demanded Spinny Dog be let back into the house, and they all ate far too much, even Spinny, who ate anything anyone didn't want, including, much to Nellie's annoyance, Action Man's arms. George and Nellie also drank a bit more than they normally did. Part of it was relief that their only son seemed unharmed and part of it was that they both knew the time was coming for them to test their son to see if he could still do 'The Thing'. It had appeared to both Nellie and George the bairn couldn't just do 'The Thing' but he could do it better than them.

They kept Neville up late that Christmas Day, trying little experiments with him to see exactly what it was he could do. They had seen him levitate himself and the dog, they assumed he had X-ray vision and he could certainly read minds as he had proved when George had approached the house earlier with the dog. But it appeared Neville had forgotten all about yesterday and seemed to have no idea what his mum and dad were talking about. Just as Nellie and George were re-enacting yesterday's flying scene by pretending to fly Neville and Spinny around the room, Neville fell asleep in his dad's arms. So they tucked him and Spinny up in their beds. They went to bed shortly after but lay talking late into the night about the consequences of bringing up, in a small north-eastern town, a son who was not only as weird as them, but probably had an extra helping of weirdness on the side.

Boxing Day was approached with caution in the Creedy house. George and Nellie had finally fallen asleep at dawn and didn't wake up until ten in the morning. They both woke at the same time and sat up as if stung, expecting to hear some sort of commotion going on in the little terraced house. They were both of the mind that, after the shock of what happened and the excitement of Christmas Day, Neville might start to remember what had happened to him and how to do it again.

They jumped out of bed, dressed quickly and tiptoed into the living room. There was no sign of anything untoward. It looked quite festive with the tree and all the decorations up. They were using all their mind-reading skills but they couldn't get through to their son. George accidentally tapped into Spinny Dog's head, a trick he had never managed before and didn't wish to repeat, since all he heard was a load of bleating and baahing.

They approached Neville's room and pushed open the door and couldn't believe what they saw. Nowt. There was Neville fast asleep with his arms around Spinny's neck, the dog's big fat tongue hanging out. It was the last, most normal thing they had expected to see. Nellie and George exchanged a glance and breathed a mental sigh of relief.

About half an hour later, a sleepy-eyed Neville wandered into the living room, with Spinny dog behind him. Spinny seemed to be in awe of his new young master. Neville's eyes quickly lost their sleepiness when he saw all his Christmas presents scattered around the room. With a whoop, Neville and Spinny hurled themselves back into their make-believe world of the day before. It turned out to be a fairly uneventful day. George and Nellie tried to coax Neville into displaying some of the talents he had shown on Christmas Eve, but he seemed completely uninterested, just wanting to play with his new cars, guns, fort and Etch-a-Sketch – which wasn't working very well. Mainly, though, he wanted to play with Spinny Dog.

This he did from then until he went away to university, sixteen years later. That Christmas Eve was never mentioned again and Neville never ever again demonstrated his strange talents to George and Nellie.

So Nellie and George's life with their strange son and his daft dog galloped on, like a fat old dobbin not even stopping for a bit of hay. As he grew up, Neville always had that air of superiority about him. He was even trying to lose his Geordie accent. They had heard him practising talking posh late at night in his bedroom. Another time they heard him speaking like Ponch, the star of the American motorbike cop show *C.H.I.Ps*. He sounded ridiculous. Good name for a show set in Newcastle, though.

A couple of times Nellie had caught George looking sideways at her with a 'Maybe he's not mine' look, but she had given him such a mental tongue-lashing that he had to run out of the room, his head spinning.

Nellie told all her friends that the reason Neville was so odd was down to the fact that they'd had him so late in life. She was 40 and George was 45 when he was born. This started some ribald conversations between George's cronies at work, who were all drinking pals, most of them married to Nellie's mates. Not that George's mates would've ever let George know they were talking about him like that. George knew it was happening since the conversation always stopped dead when he went to fill his mug up with hot water to make his tea at work in the morning.

Nellie wasn't so coy about her and George's physical relationships with her bingo cronies. She once stopped a game when she whispered out loud to her mates, one of whom was waiting for a single number for a full house, that between the sheets George was like an on-heat, cap-wearing, orang utang, sex stallion, and that she loved it. In the ensuing screams, laughter and tutting, the friend's full house – and consequently the chance to pay off debts, put back eviction and avoid the divorce – went by unnoticed.

2〉

So as Neville started to grow up, the perpetual 'I'm above
all this' look stayed. This was fine and dandy when he
was at home in the tiny council house they all shared, but
once he went out on the street or to junior school that look
earned him many a good kicking from the kids in the area.
If there's one thing tough Geordie kids don't like it's
someone thinking they're better than they are.

Even George, who was a welder in Swan Hunters shipyards, as tough as they come and of the 'a few beatings will
harden kids up for life' school, was worried by the number
of times his son would come home with a bloodied nose or
broken tooth. Neville could fight back; it was just that, as he
was fighting, the look on his face was so haughty it drove his
opponent into a complete fury.

George even had to go around to see the parents of the
kids who were beating up his son and reason with them.
These were people he had grown up with and who he

respected: men who he worked long hard shifts with. They always apologised profusely, as George was known locally as a bit of a hard case, but he would always agree with the dads later that night over a bottle in the Coronation Club when they said, 'Whey, man, ah'm sorry, man, George, it's just that yer bairn has such a look on 'is face ye cannit help but te want te knock it off.'

Of course he would never have told Nellie he agreed with the dads, in the same way Nellie would never tell George she secretly agreed with the mams when they said to her, 'Eee, I'm sorry, pet, ah knaa he's yer only bairn an' that, but if one of mine had that look on his face I'd give him a clout every day an' twice on Sunday.' The conversation usually ended there as some of the mothers who were slightly more religious than the others said, 'Maybe they should pray for the Lord to give Neville a bit of a slap.' But no mother, no matter how cheeky looking their bairn is, wants their kid to be hit by Jesus. I mean he could have a thunderbolt or a plague of frogs or a fridge in his big holy hands, and that has to hurt.

Even George had tried to knock the look off Neville's face years before, when he thought he was being lippy, but he soon found out it just made Neville worse. So George and Nellie brought up their son as best they could. They tried to keep him out of trouble and out of hospital, but they both often joked they had been given the wrong child at birth. They thought they had been given the child of a member of the royal family. Of course they both knew members of any royal family are seldom born in Wallsend, and they were both sure enough of their local history to know there hadn't been a king in Wallsend for a couple of years.

Things at home became a bit better when Neville passed his eleven plus and won a place at the local grammar school, St Cuthbert's. This meant that Neville was now mixing with kids who, it seemed to George, all had the same look as his son. He even started to make friends. Not, of course, that he would ever bring his new friends to George and Nellie's house. On one memorable night, Neville proclaimed he couldn't possibly bring any of his classmates to their little terraced house, as some of their fathers were doctors. Nellie saw the way George was gripping the arms of his chair and hustled Neville out of the room, narrowly saving her son from the beating of his life.

George and Nellie's belief that their son was a king was slowly changing into the suspicion that he was a queen. Not that George and Nellie would ever have used that expression. Homosexuality wasn't even frowned upon in Wallsend, as people had more things to worry about than whether you liked dying your hair blond and kissing blokes. As George once said, 'Some of the hardest blokes I knaa are puffs, man.' It was just that if their only son were gay they wouldn't get any grandbairns.

However, the fear their lad would be saying 'Shut that door' for the rest of his life was laid to rest one Sunday night in the Coronation Club. There was a meat draw and dancing that night, so George and Nellie were out together having a whale of a time. One of George's workmates, Jimmy Barnes (actually a gaffer, so technically George's boss, not a mate, so they didn't really mix what with gaffers being a cut above), sent a couple of drinks over to their table.

This, of course, started a nudging and whispering competition among the wives and workmates at George's table. George and Nellie had no idea why they should be getting free drinks. It wasn't until later on, in the toilet, that thing became clearer, when Jimmy started chatting to George, which in itself was unusual as most blokes in toilets, especially working men's club's toilets, get in, stare silently at the wall, then get out as quick as possible. Not Jimmy, not tonight.

'So,' he said, 'wha ganna be related soon then?'

George, who'd had a couple of bottles and had exactly no idea what Jimmy was on about, said, 'Eh?'

'Wha ganna be related, man,' said Jimmy. 'Hasn't your lad told ye?'

By now George thought Jimmy was talking in a foreign language but that's what he usually thought, what with Jimmy being from Sunderland.

'Jimmy, man, what ye taalking about, man?' said George. 'How can we be related?'

'Through marriage, man,' said Jimmy, as if talking to a child, which is how he talked to most of the blokes under his charge anyway.

'Howay, man, Jimmy. I can't marry you,' said George. 'I'm already spoken for.'

If the conversation was being studiously ignored by the rest of the blokes in the toilet, they let themselves down now as they all burst out laughing. There's nothing they liked more than seeing a gaffer, especially a gaffer like Jimmy Barnes, being the butt of a joke.

'No, man, man,' said Jimmy carrying on through the catcalls. 'Ah'm taalking aboot your Neville and wor Ellen tyin' the knot.'

So shocked was George by this unexpected news, he felt light-headed and to steady himself he put his one free hand on Jimmy's shoulder, which just confirmed to the rest of the blokes there that George and Jimmy had indeed fallen in love.

So that's how, one Saturday night, George and Nellie found themselves sitting in the front room in Mr and Mrs Barnes's bungalow in Westerhope, just outside Newcastle. Westerhope is a place where people show how posh they are by having ruched curtains and nick-nacks on show on the window sill. It's where gaffers live.

As George sat there eating stale cake and drinking weak tea, he marvelled at the pace of events over the last few weeks. He had gone from being George the welder, to his mates, to being George the gaffer's in-law.

It's not right, man, thought George.

You're right there, pet, butted in Nellie with a thought, *and look at that swirly carpet, I'm glad you're not a gaffer.*

It was then that young love in the shape of Neville and Ellen entered the room.

And what a shape she was, thought George. Trying to be as fair as he could to the lass, George thought Neville's bride-to-be looked like a pit pony. A pit pony on a diet of pies and chips. And even though Nellie tried to see the best in people at all times, even she thought George was doing a disservice to big, fat, ugly pit ponies. Spinny Dog came bounding in, much to the obvious annoyance of Ellen.

'All right, man, Spinny?' said George, as he pushed the daft dog to the floor, where it sat panting and looking like a cartoon version of a dog. Spinny always got on George's knee. They would sit there watching the news together, Spinny's head resting on George's chest.

'All right, Nev?' said George to his son.

'It's Neville,' said Ellen firmly. The only thing that stopped George explaining to Ellen in shipyard terms just why he would carry on calling his son what he wanted was the arrival of Mr and Mrs Barnes.

Once, thought George, Jimmy Barnes just looked like a bloke who worked in the yards, wiry and weather-beaten. Even when he was wearing his best suit, you just knew he could weld. But it was different when you were sat in their house eating their cake, looking at their nick-nacks and discussing wedding plans concerning your bloody weird son and their big gallumphing daughter. He didn't look like a bloke from the yards then. No, he looked like you: he looked like a relative.

Which was more than could be said for Mrs Barnes. George was convinced her nearest relatives were a pit pony and one of those big elephant seals. She even had the moustache. Although even George, with his limited knowledge of animal breeding habits, knew it was impossible to cross an elephant seal with a pit pony. For a start, how could they have possibly met? Unless some freak accident happened, like an elephant seal had fallen out of a plane while being delivered to a zoo and miraculously fell down a mine shaft and came to rest near a pit pony who was looking particularly sexy that day.

Mind you, pondered George, if he himself had fallen out of a plane and survived no doubt even Mrs Barnes would look quite fanciable.

All Nellie could think of as she looked Mrs Barnes' best frock up and down was, Where does she get all the material?

Mr Barnes brought them all back to the real world with a clap of his hands.

'Right, everyone. I'd just like to bring this meeting to order.' The fact Jimmy Barnes was now talking his equivalent of posh, which just sounded ridiculous, and he had used the phrase 'Bring this meeting to order', caused George and Nellie to glance at each other. This did not go unnoticed by Neville, who managed to curl his lip at them and look lovingly at Ellen at the same time, giving him a very attractive Quasimodo Elvis look.

'Now,' Jimmy Barnes continued, 'as we all know, our two little love birds here would like to get married this summer, and Elizabeth and I [at this point Jimmy clasped his wife's hoof/flipper in his hand] would like to give them the best wedding the area has ever seen. No expense spared.'

George cleared his throat.

'Dad,' warned Neville. But George was not to be stopped. Even less so when he heard the tone Neville had used saying 'Dad'.

'Well, Jimmy, Liz …' began George.

'Elizabeth,' corrected Ellen sharply.

George studiously ignored her. '… its grayt the bairns aall wanna git married an that …'

Nellie stared at her husband. She had never in all their years of marriage heard him speak in such a broad Geordie accent. She knew it must sound like chalk down a blackboard to the Barneses, in their front room with their nick-nacks and their ruched curtains. She pulled her cardigan around her and settled in for a bit of entertainment. Eee he can be a bad 'un, that George Creedy, she thought, which is exactly why she married him in the first place.

'… but, an this is what am worried aboot, Nev,' said George.

'Neville,' corrected Ellen.

'Aye, pet,' said George to Ellen, with a look on his face that would've made a hungry shark think twice about attacking him, even if George had been wearing a bacon and sausage wet suit.

'You see, Nev,' George stopped and looked at Ellen, who opened her mouth in protest but thought the better of it and slammed it shut. 'You see, Nev,' George continued, 'ye've aalways said yer gannin te university. So how are ye ganna de that if ya ganna get married?'

'Weeell …' began Neville.

'Ye see, son, ah'm aall for ye getting married. Especially to a lovely looking lass like Ellen.' Both Ellen and her mum preened at this point; Jimmy gave a slight shudder.

'But why not give it a few years, man? Gan te university

next year. Get a degree, a good job and ye winnit have te live from hand te mooth like me an' Jimmy here.'

At this Nellie spluttered into her tea, which was a good distraction as Liz and Ellen were about to get on to a very high horse. Poor horsey; it would never race again if those two climbed on its back.

To his surprise, George found he had an unlikely ally in Elizabeth Barnes.

'I think George is absolutely right,' she said, pulling herself to her full height, which was about 4 foot 10 in all directions. 'Getting an education is the only way to better oneself. Isn't that right, James?' she added, pointedly looking at her husband. George thought it wise not to point out that him and Jimmy had both left school at 14 and were about as educated as snowmen.

'I mean, who knows?' continued Mrs Barnes. 'Neville could be a doctor or a lawyer or a vet, then he could come and live here in Westerhope.' She beamed at the room like a Buddha, as if she had just handed down some great wisdom and they should all be grateful. The moment was shattered when George dropped his plate on the floor, firing bits of cake across the room like shrapnel, which Spinny wolfed down. Later on he told Nellie it was her fault because she had slipped into his mind and told him that Liz Barnes even had a fat voice.

So it was settled. It was as easy as that. Neville went to London University to study law. Ellen, on the other hand, stayed in Newcastle, failed all her exams and ended up working in a chip shop. She became fatter and fatter, because not only was she eating massive portions of chips, but she was also getting a portion from one of the customers, Dougie Kinnie, a painter and decorator from Consett, who got her pregnant. They were married and had six more kids. Needless to say poor Dougie's life was a living hell, what with Ellen and her mother, but Dougie was too stupid to know.

Ellen never saw Neville again. Which was only slightly less than George and Nellie saw their son.

Oh and Spinny Dog died happily in his sleep, dreaming he was a sheep, which was what he had always done. That's what made him so daft. He was a sheep trapped in a dog's body.

Neville looked as though he thought he was better than everyone else because he was. He did love his parents, but he had absolutely nothing in common with them. They just didn't understand him. On another memorable Christmas Eve, he had even asked them if he was adopted, but they had just laughed and told him not to be so daft, he was their little treasure. Nevertheless, Neville had always known what they thought of him. He never told them he could read their minds and that on a good day he could sort of read other people's minds as well. He was practising really hard at this.

He also had flashes of X-ray vision, he could levitate and sometimes he could shoot flames from his fingers. But when he tried any of his skills he always felt tired out afterwards, so he mainly stayed with the mind-reading. He was clever enough to keep all this stuff to himself, because he felt as though he was being pulled through time and that someone somewhere had big plans for him. He just had to learn as much about life as possible so that when the day came he would be ready.

Neville had known from an early age he was destined for bigger things, but not what they were, which is why he had latched on to the dreadful Ellen. He was far too inexperienced to know about the big world outside of Wallsend, and had thought that, because her dad had a better job than his dad, if he married her it would somehow give him a leg-up in the world. He was quite relieved when his dad had insisted he wait until after university until they got married. He had never really fancied Ellen, and when he saw her mum he realised that education was probably the way forward.

University changed Neville for good. Even though he was a very clever lad, his arrogance stopped him from opening his eyes to what went on outside his tiny world. He thought he knew it all. He soon realised when he arrived in London how little he did know, but he was a keen scholar and excelled at his lessons. He was desperate to be a lawyer, because he had read somewhere that lawyers could make a lot of money. In actual fact, the article he had read was about a lawyer who had swindled his client out of millions of pounds but was caught due to his playboy lifestyle. This had set Neville thinking: what if he was a lawyer and swindled people out of all their cash but was never caught? He could live that life until the call came to tell him of his destiny.

As plans go it wasn't a bad one.

After the meeting at the Barnes's house, Neville went home and George and Nellie went in to the Coronation Club to celebrate the putting back and hopefully the putting off of the marriage. George had a little too much to drink with Davey Viney, a slinger, the bloke who loads the cranes up in the shipyards.

Which was how the accident happened. You see, the next day at work, Davey, who was still a bit groggy from the night before (even the inhalation of pure oxygen from the welder's bottles had failed to clear his head), had slung a bottle of propane so badly it had fallen from its cradle and hit George Creedy on the shoulder, narrowly missing his head (which would certainly have killed him). Normally, George was quite conscientious about safety, but he was feeling as delicate as Davey and failed to hear the shouts of warning as the bottle fell.

So George ended up being pensioned off with a big wad of compensation, and although he couldn't use his left arm properly again, he knew he'd rather spend the rest of his time at home with Nellie than be able to do a Mexican wave.

Neville was finding it wasn't just his coursework he was excelling at. The girls at the university found him absolutely gorgeous. He had lost his cheeky-faced look and grown into his face. He looked a bit like his dad had at his age, with a touch of his mother thrown in. So, all in all, he was a bit of a lass magnet. And he played it to the hilt. It also helped that his mind-reading was getting a bit better. While not being able to read minds completely, he could find out enough about a girl from her thoughts. Luckily for Neville, he still had enough of his mam and dad in him at that time not to exploit the situation completely, or he would have ended up in prison at the age of 18. His telekinesis and madness were still to come.

So George spent his time at home with Nellie and they had a nice bit of cash to allow them to enjoy their old age. Neville was off at university in London and forgot about his parents and, of course, Ellen. He did go home every now and again, but these visits gradually became fewer and fewer. He didn't even tell them he had graduated or that he had been offered a job in a prestigious law firm, or that he had bought a flat and was having a high old time with some high old people. And, strangely enough for a northern couple with a posh son, George and Nellie weren't too bothered. He may have been their son but they hadn't liked him much in the first place. And unknown to Neville they could keep track of him by just thinking about him.

George and Nellie really enjoyed their time together, since they really did like each other. The reason their son was so strange was that they were quite strange themselves, it was just that they could hide it better. Strangeness was the first thing they saw in each other when they met all those years ago, although it took them years to realise quite how special they were.

But back to weird Neville. One of the many reasons Neville's visits home to his parents dwindled was that he knew he now didn't fit in there at all. When he visited, he was amazed that he could have been brought up in the tiny cramped council house. He sensed that at first his mam and dad were quite pleased to see him, but after a couple of days he could tell they would rather be in their own company. He couldn't tell what they were thinking any more and when he tried to read their minds he just drew a complete blank. Anyway, he enjoyed his days and nights in London much more than his days in Wallsend.

He had moved out of the student halls of residence and rented himself a tiny flat above a record shop on the Edgware Road. As ever, Neville's desire to learn everything about everything meant he was soon a regular customer at Ronnie's Records and, after a couple of months, was an expert on every form of music from Beethoven to Judas Priest.

Of course, all this new-found musical knowledge made him even more attractive to the opposite sex.

And then he learned to dance.

Neville took up dancing in the way that he took up everything: with grim determination. He had to be the best at it; and the best he certainly was. At first he had shyly gone to a little dance school called Miss Bracken's Danceteria on Bell Street, just off Edgware Road. His impression was that

Miss Bracken had tried to jazz up her dance school in the sixties by calling it a 'Danceteria', and the now fading sign had stayed.

In the dusty front window there were some faded photographs of Miss Bracken, he assumed, dancing with a rather fey, good-looking young man; and a pair of old ballet shoes. When he pushed the door open he was acutely embarrassed to find he had walked straight in to a dance class in mid-rehearsal.

'Yes, can I help you?' said a voice, and Neville found himself looking into the amazing sightless blue eyes of Miss Bracken. Yup, blind as a bat, she taught dance by the sound of feet on the floor. She was probably the worst dance teacher in the world, but her pupils seemed to teach themselves; it was more of a social thing, really. She was always Miss Bracken. Neville never found out what her first name was.

'I'd like to learn to dance,' said Neville, feeling completely out of place.

'Well, join the class,' said Miss Bracken.

At first Neville was disconcerted to see he was the only man in the room. Until he had a really good look at his fellow pupils. They were a strange bunch. There were young trendies who lived in the Peabody Trust flats around the corner, mums from the housing estate across the road in big jumpers and leggings, posh mums from Lisson Grove in matching eyeshadow and jewellery, a couple of Chinese women who couldn't speak English, one person who had definitely had a sex change, and not a particularly good one at that, four African women who were putting their own interpretation on Miss Bracken's lessons and two Arab women in full metal face plates and black Burkas. Neville sensed they were all there for the company, not least Miss Bracken who must be aged at least ... well, Neville had no idea how old Miss Bracken must be. So he joined in and was, as he knew he would be, bloody good.

So there they were, George and Nellie, after all that had gone on. Just the two of them together. The more time they spent in each other's company the more they got to like each other, and their mind-reading was really good now.

They started to live life to the full. They went out on trips in their old Vauxhall Viva down to Whitley Bay or over to the Metro Centre in Gateshead. They couldn't get enough of that, and were always amazed at how fast technology was leaving them behind. They even went into one of those internet cafes for a cup of tea and were doing quite well surfing the net until George whispered he had to go to the internetty and Nellie laughed so much she spit cake all over the computer screen. From the looks on the faces of the pale-complexioned youths in there you'd think she'd sworn in church, so they left holding each other up, giggling like a pair of teenagers.

They still regularly went down to the Coronation Club and were always the first to put their names down for any dancing competitions. Their big love, though, was their garden, and if it was fine weather they'd both be out in it, Nellie planting vegetables and George sitting in a deckchair smoking skinny roll-ups, reading and occasionally helping with a bit of digging and a bit of slapping of Nellie's bum. He was always amazed at how fit and supple she was, and how she never seemed to suffer from any of the ailments she should at her age. Mind you, he always felt pretty sprightly too and Nellie told him it was down to the juice she gave him. About ten years ago she had invested in a juicer and started juicing up her herbs, vegetables and fruit; some he'd never even heard of. Most of them tasted delicious but occasionally they tasted like mud. Still, if they were what was keeping them both healthy then George would carry on drinking them.

A strange thing had happened about five years before, which had convinced George the juices were good for them. One of the local bairns, Lily, from down the road, actually one of the Dodds sisters' grandbairns, had been diagnosed with cancer. It was terrible, a little lass like that wasting away. But Nellie had gone to visit her, regularly taking the bairn some of her juice. Within two months little Lily was up and running around. Now the doctors said it was the medicine and treatment they had been giving her, but George thought surely treatment that makes your hair fall out and causes you to throw up blood can't be good for a little bairn. A few other people in the area must have thought the same thing because they always had visitors popping in for a sup of Nellie's juice. Come to think of it everybody who drank Nellie's juice seemed to be pretty fit. Well, thought George, I suppose it's better to be drinking the juice than to be eating chips.

Now one day as George sat in the garden reading the racing results he was suddenly drawn to the name of one of the trainers; his name was Henry Littleton. George was immediately catapulted back to the days after his mother died, when he would sit alone reading gardening books. A real sadness came over him, which caused Nellie to turn and look at him with a worried frown on her face. She was concerned to see George staring into space with a far-away look.

'Are you all right, pet?' said Nellie.

'Oh aye, sorry, love.' He gave her a big smile. 'You know what I'm ganna de?'

'What, pet?' said Nellie.

'I'm ganna grow leeks,' said George. 'The biggest leeks in the area. They're ganna be massive.'

Neville had really thrown himself into the dancing at Miss Bracken's, even though it wasn't really the style he felt he needed to learn. He had really wanted to be able to impress the girls at university with his hip hop, trip hop, drum 'n' bass, r 'n' b, hard house, hector's bloody house – dance floor moves other than the tangos, waltzes and quicksteps he was being shown. Oddly enough, though, he loved learning all the old stuff and realised he could easily change the steps to fit whatever music he was dancing to.

The rest of the dance pupils at the tiny old-fashioned school loved having Neville there, mainly because he was the only man they had to dance with. On a few occasions he found himself being held just a little bit too tightly, even by the Arab women who, he could tell even through their heavy black burkas, were obviously young, fit and attractive. Not that they were at the school for long, after he joined. When someone that Neville assumed to be one of their brothers came to pick them up and saw there was a man in the class they were never seen there again.

Neville really hit it off with Miss Bracken, and even though she tended to ramble she was a very amusing and, for her age, whatever that was, a very sexual woman. All in all Neville had dancing lessons for six months. In that time he became rather too attached to one of the posh housewives, Rosie Ward, with whom he regularly tangoed, whether they were at the club or not. She wasn't, as Neville had first thought, from Lisson Grove. She wasn't even in fact a housewife. She owned a clothes shop in Covent Garden and had been introduced to the lessons by her sister who was a housewife from Lisson Grove. Rosie had a rather flash apartment above the shop that she shared with her husband, who rather handily spent a lot of time away from home, what with him being dead. So Neville spent quite a lot of time at Rosie's. Well they had a

lot in common like their shared interest in all things dance
and mad shagging.

It was while Neville was heading back to university after a
frenzied afternoon session with Rosie that he took a shortcut
down Denmark Street and there, in one of the many musical
instrument shops, he saw something that changed his life
completely: a blue sparkle custom Gibson Flying V guitar. It
was without doubt the sexiest thing Neville had ever seen in
his life. He couldn't play a note but he had to have it. It had
to have him. He went into the shop and, using one of the
credit cards Rosie had kindly given him, he bought it. After
that day Neville Creedy was never heard of again.

3〉

Luckily George had kept all of his dad's old gardening books and they were still in the battered old suitcase his dad had put them in. With a load of huffing and puffing, George climbed into the cupboard under the stairs to retrieve the books. As we all know, there's not a grumpier creature in the world than a bloke trying to find something in the dark on a hot day, in a confined dusty space, but he managed to find them and dragged the suitcase into the garden. There he pulled out a book, and set about making himself the crown king of leeks.

It was hard for George to read the books at first because they brought back all the unhappy memories of his past. His mum dying, his shyness and the loneliness he felt at the time. Of course Nellie knew exactly what he was thinking, so to cheer him up she squirted him with the hose.

With a roar, George leaped up and started to chase her around the garden while she kept him at bay with some well-placed squirts. George finally managed to grab her and they rolled around the garden laughing and giggling. It wasn't until they heard a child's voice say, 'Are you going to strangle her, Mr Creedy? 'Cos if you are can you hurry up 'cos I'm on me way to get me special sweets?' that they realised they were not alone. The wrestling couple looked up into the faces of little Lily, who was, by now, well recovered from her illness; her teenage sister Holly, who like all teenagers was frowning at the thought of old people having fun; and their Nana Jean who was shaking her head and smiling at how daft they were acting.

George and Nellie jumped up. 'I'll tell you what,' said a drenched George to the visitors, 'I'm gannin in to phone the police. She's mad that wife. Look at me, I'm drenched, I could catch me death. I'm 104, you know.' And with that, George disappeared into the house to get out of his wet clothes.

'You two are like bloody kids,' said Lily's nana Jean, 'and he was a right miserable so-and-so in his young days, ye knaa. Bloody gorgeous though.' She sighed, remembering how she would watch a young George come home from work all dirty and dishevelled and would want to help him wash the muck off.

The older women started laughing in the comfortable way old friends can.

'Was he really gorgeous?' said an incredulous Holly, who, of course, thought old people had always been old.

'Oh aye, pet,' said Nellie. 'All the lasses really fancied him, especially your nana. But I got him 'cos I was beautiful and your nana was a right old witch.' This made the woman laugh again, while the younger girl looked on, amazed that old people could possibly think they had a sense of humour.

'Well, what can I do for you, my little angel?' said Nellie, as she grabbed Lily in a big cuddle, which made her squirm and giggle.

'We just thought we'd pop in and make sure you're not dead,' said Nana Jean.

'Nana!' gasped Holly.

'Its OK, pet, that's just one of your nana's daft jokes. She's never been funny. That's why no one likes her and she took to drink and lost her looks,' laughed Nellie.

'Oh, I don't know,' said nana Jean, patting her hair and doing a little dance. 'I reckon I could take your Georgy off you any time I wanted. I've still got it, ye knaa.'

'Well, if you've still got it I wish you'd take it somewhere else,' said a freshly changed George as he ran into the garden with his best scary monster face on and pulled Lily into his arms.

'And where are you off to, me little darling?' said George to the giggling mass of arms, legs and curls.

'I'm going to get me special sweets,' replied a breathless Lily.

'Special sweets, what are those?' said a concerned Nellie, who thought maybe it was another name for medicine.

'Well, Holly's going to a concert tonight and I can't go 'cos I'm too little, so I'm getting special sweets instead, so I won't cry.'

'Yeah, that makes sense,' said George.

'Who are you going to see Holly?' said Nellie.

'A load of bloody noisy rubbish, if you ask me,' said Nana Jean.

'Awwwww, Nana, man, you don't know anything about music so leave him alone!'

'Yeah, leave them alone, Nana, man,' said Nellie. 'Us kids are talking.'

'Who is it you're going to see, Holly?' said Nellie to the girl.

'Luscious,' said Holly.

'Eh?' Nellie blinked. There was a sudden buzzing in her head.

'Luscious. He's on at the City Hall tonight. He's from America and they're the loudest band in the world ever and he sings about the Devil and death and evil and they're fantastic and the lead singer Luscious is the most beautiful man in the world so can we go now, Nana, 'cos I'm going to be late!' All of this came out as one word.

'Hmm,' said George. 'I think I'm going to need some special sweets as well.'

About a year later, it appeared that George really was the king of the leeks and Luscious had the biggest band in the world. Actually the Luscious thing had become a bit of a joke between Nellie and George. Every time they went shopping in the centre of Newcastle – Nellie for clothes for them both, George for leek stuff – they would always see groups of very serious teenagers dressed identically in oversize Luscious sweatshirts, trainers and jeans in various shades of black, hanging around looking pale and … well, if you had to be really honest, boring.

Every now and again, George and Nellie would hear snippets of 'Luscious Sect' as they were dubbed, conversation, which usually went along the lines of how they were so individual and how nobody understood them, especially their parents. As a joke, Nellie even bought George a Luscious CD that they played once and then gave to Holly as a birthday present.

It wasn't as if Nellie and George were musical snobs, it was just that they were a bit too old to enjoy a rich rock star like Luscious screaming, against a minor key backdrop, about how great the Devil was and how we should all worship him. As a matter of fact, they had a right laugh at the naïvety of the lyrics. They even had a competition between the two of them to see if they could write better lyrics than Luscious. The lyrics were so daft, though, that, much to their annoyance, they couldn't.

One of their favourite games was the 'crowbar Luscious into any conversation' game. If ever George and Nellie were out with friends, invariably in the Coronation Club, they would always try and get the name Luscious into the conversation, whether it had anything to do with the topic in hand at all. Which is, I suppose, how all the trouble started.

It had become a bit of a joke among the local gardening fraternity that George had sold his soul to Satan, like the guitarist Robert Johnson, to become the king of the leek growers. Although Mr Johnson had become an inspired guitar player who could play as if the Devil was on his tail, George had merely been able to grow the biggest leeks anyone had ever seen. You see, the growing of leeks, especially giant leeks, is seen as a bit of a science. You can't just say to everyone, 'Right, that's it, I'm growing big leeks,' and then do it. It takes years of work and study, and the making of secret potions whose recipes have been handed down from generation to generation. It's top-secret stuff. So you can imagine how miffed everyone was, when, from nowhere, George Creedy started showing up with massive leeks.

At first the leek club had refused to recognise them, thinking it was George having a bit of a joke (well, they knew how daft George and Nellie could be), but they had to admit they were big leeks, and if they were big leeks, where had they come from? It was only when a delegation from the leek club went down to visit George's leek troughs in his allotment that they were forced to believe what they were seeing with their own leek expert eyes.

The older members of the leek club were fine about this new big leek competition, after all, most of them had grown up with George and they knew he was an honest man. It also helped that in his young day he had been known as quite a handful. But it was the younger members of the club who

took it most to heart. After all, they had been growing leeks
for years, so why should they hand the prize money over to
someone who had been in the game for five minutes. I mean,
sometimes the prize money could be as much as £30. What
the younger members failed to ask themselves was what they
were doing growing leeks in the first place. Even the older
members thought that maybe these youngsters should be
going out and meeting girls and stuff. That's what they would
have been doing, not standing on some cold allotment with
mud in their fingernails and big leeks on their minds.

Now George's big leeks weren't exactly the Devil's work,
but they certainly were the work of a higher power, or
whatever it was that enabled George and Nellie to
communicate without talking. George only discovered his
new leek-growing power one morning when he went into his
greenhouse to look at his first crop of leeks, only to find they
were tiny – without doubt the smallest leeks he had ever
seen. He was in a right strop when he stormed back over to
the house to have a bit of a moan at Nellie about why he had
failed to produce the superleeks he had expected. Nellie,
who was in the middle of pulling up some carrots to make
some of her juice, explained to George that what she did was
talk to her vegetables and give them a bit of a stroke every
now and again.

'What you should do, George,' said Nellie, 'is treat your
leeks as if they were pets. Give them love and they'll love
you back and get really big.'

'I'd like to do that, Nellie,' said George, with a straight face,
'but you see I'm not soft in the bloody heed!'

Luckily the carrots Nellie threw at George missed him as
he left the garden to go back to tend his new 'pets'.

George didn't really know what to say to the leeks when he
went into the greenhouse. He just mumbled a quick, 'All
right, leeks?' as he took his cap off, and then held it all

scrunched up in his hands as he asked them how they thought the Toon would do on Saturday. 'This is bloody ridiculous,' said George out loud.

'What is?' said a voice behind him, as Big Fat Squinty Bill squeezed himself into George's shed. Big Fat Squinty Bill, as he was known for short, had been a mate of George's since they were kids, and had been Big and Fat and Squinty all his life. He, of course, was given his nickname when he was a kid – we all know what little bastards kids are. Even his wife was called Mrs Big Fat Squinty Bill, and when they were out together they were called the Big Fat Squinties. Big Fat Squinty Bill called his wife 'love' and she called him 'Big Fat Squinty Bill'. They weren't bothered by the nickname; they'd had it for so long they couldn't really remember their real names.

'Well,' said Big Fat Squinty Bill, 'what's ridiculous, man?'

'Oh just these bloody leeks, man, Big Fat Squinty Bill,' said George. 'I mean, look at the size of them. They'll never win owt and the leek show's on in four weeks.'

'Aye, yer right there, George,' said Big Fat Squinty Bill, stroking the leeks with a pudgy paw and giving them a squinty once over. 'They're like courgettes, man, I divent knaa why ye want to grow leeks, man, ye knaa nowt aboot them, man.'

'Well, it's something I've aallways wanted te do. And ye knaa that me dad grew some monster leeks, man, plus it gives us something to do. I mean, I cannot hang aroond Nellie aall day, she might chuck us oot,' said George.

'Aye, I suppose,' said Big Fat Squinty Bill. 'You haven't any biscuits, have ye? I'm gannin to feed the ducks.'

'Well, there's two things I have to point oot to ye then, Big Fat Squinty Bill,' said George 'Number one, ye've never given away any food in yer life, and number two, the ducks aren't there any more. There's a load of building work going on on the tip. They're flattenin' it, man, putting up some sort of warehoose thing.'

George had never seen Big Fat Squinty Bill move so fast. He leaped up. To be fair he wasn't really sitting down, he was sort of lounging against the wall but that kind of movement was like running a marathon for Big Fat Squinty Bill. 'They cannit de that, man, George! Me an' ye spent wor childhood there! It's an area of natural beauty, it's like a nature reserve,' spluttered Big Fat Squinty Bill. 'I'm surprised David Attenborough hasn't been down there discoverin' stuff.'

'The only thing David Attenborough would discover if he went doon to the tip is how quickly he could be eaten by the rats,' said George, taking a pull on his skinny roll-up. 'Have ye seen the size of them, man? They're like bloody corgies. They'll take yer hand off.'

'Well I'm gannin, doon there to see what's gannin on,' said Big Fat Squinty Bill. 'It's our childhood, man, our childhood. Ah've many happy memories of me runnin' aroond the tip in just me short pants. Well, I'm gannin' ower to pay me last respects, like.'

And with that, Big Fat Squinty Bill lumbered out of George's greenhouse.

'Watch the rats diven't get ye mind,' shouted George to his mate as the big old lad carefully picked his way out of the allotment. 'They'd be eatin' ye for weeks.'

The next day started out the same as any other day in the life of George and Nellie Creedy. Later on, though, when George thought of all the events that the day triggered off, he thought of that day as day one.

The Creedys had never been the type to sleep in and were always up and about by seven. Nellie bustled around making the breakfast, while George lit up a healthy skinny roll-up and headed out to the newsagents to get his papers.

'How's yer leeks gannin, George?' said Wheelie Billy Carr the newsagent, as George entered the tiny shop, which was stacked high with anything that could be sold.

'They're not,' said George.

'Aye, I'd heard as much,' replied Billy, trying not to grin at the look of exasperation on George's face.

'Ah divvent knaa. Yer cannit de out aroond here withoot everyone knowin yer business. Ye should be a spy not a newsagent, man, Billy,' said George, as he picked up his papers and an ounce of tobacco.

'I think I'd make a good spy, me,' said Billy, filling up a jar with sherbet flying saucers. 'All they do is fly aroond the world knacking people an' that. It can't be that hard, can it? And then there's aall them lasses in skimpy frocks what hang aroond spies when they're in the casinos findin' the bad blokes. They're lovely them lasses. Funny though, innit, George, how the bad blokes are always in casinos, you'd think with all their money an' lasers an' that they'd try an' be a bit more secretive like, ye know, maybe get a secret underground lair. That's the first thing I'd do if I was a baddie bloke. Get me own underground lair.'

George had been in this situation many times with Billy and he still couldn't get to grips with how a little crippled Indian newsagent in a wheelchair could talk so much shite. George supposed, with so much time on his hands sitting behind the counter doling out boiled sweets and newspapers, Billy's mind ran riot and once he started he couldn't be stopped.

'I'll tell ye what, Billy,' said George. 'I'm going past the job centre later on, I'll nip in an' see if there's any spyin' vacancies on the go.' And with that, George squeezed out of the shop to the sound of Billy firing an imaginary machine gun at imaginary baddies. 'I'd be careful if you're a Russian spy, missus,' George said to an old lady as she entered the shop. 'He's armed an' dangerous.'

With his papers tucked firmly under his arm, his tobacco safely in his pocket and a skinny roll-up compressed between his lips, George began to stroll home.

Just as he was passing the allotments he decided he would pop in and see how his bloody leeks were doing. Not that he had much hope for them. And even though he knew he was in for a right mickey-taking from all of the other leek growers, he thought he'd go and see them anyway and then throw the useless things at anyone who dared to say anything to him about the quality of his vegetables.

It's not often you hear shouting, swearing and singing at 7.15 in the morning on an allotment in Wallsend, well not unless the owner has been thrown out of his house for being drunk and spending all his wages in the betting shop, and has just woken up face down in the soil. So the other gardeners were a bit surprised to be confronted by George Creedy running out of the allotment, stopping only once to point at the other blokes tending their leeks and telling them they could all, 'Stick their titchy leeks up their arses,' before running off towards home.

Mind you, they weren't as surprised as Nellie, when George came crashing into the house shouting to her to come at once to the allotment to see what he'd grown. Nellie, who had been sitting quietly, sipping her juice, was in the middle of telling George the only thing he'd grown was dafter, when she found herself being dragged out of her chair, thrown over his shoulder and carried down to the allotment. Nellie wasn't bothered, it was cheaper than a taxi, but she was glad she had her good knickers on.

George put Nellie down as soon as they reached the top of the path. Well, he was an old man. Nellie was a bit miffed at this and tried to climb back on, but George was obviously in no mood for daft carry on and said, 'Howay, man, Nellie, man, you have to come an' see this,' and then shot off towards the allotment with Nellie in hot pursuit. They caused a bit of a commotion when they galloped into the allotment and all the other growers decided to have a look at what was going on in George's greenhouse. It had to be good to cause all this excitement. So, with George leading, a crocodile of people made their way down the narrow pathway and then crowded into his greenhouse.

'Da Daa!' shouted George, like a magician performing a trick.

His fellow leek growers exchanged glances and then burst out laughing.

'Whey they're tiny, man, George,' said one man.

'I thought you were going to show us monsters, man,' said another.

They all wandered away shouting at George over their shoulders. There was only one of them who stayed, staring at George's leeks with what appeared to be awe: Big Fat Squinty Bill. He'd squinted at the leeks the day before, and while they couldn't be classed as world beaters yet, they were four times the size they were yesterday.

'Er, what am I supposed to be looking at, George?' said Nellie to her excited husband.

'There, man, woman, man, me leeks, man,' said George.

'I can see they're leeks, George,' said Nellie, 'but they're not exactly world class yet. Whey, man, they're not even Byker class. So what's all the fuss aboot, man?'

'They were four times smaller yesterday, Nellie,' said Big Fat Squinty Bill.

'They can't have been,' said Nellie, looking from her husband to Big Fat Squinty Bill. 'That's impossible.'

'No, man, pet, man. I followed your advice, man, Nellie, about treating them like pets and talking an' strokin' them an' that, and now look at them, man. They're four times the size,' said an incredulous George.

'Well, that's lovely, pet. You're a right Alan Titchmarsh,

but can we have our breakfast now? I'm starvin.' And she shoved her way out of the shed and set off back to the house, leaving Big Fat Squinty Bill staring through the glass at the leeks and an ecstatic George running after his wife.

'It's great, isn't it, man, Nellie?' said George, as they walked up the path arm in arm.

'It is,' said Nellie. 'It's just, well, I think you should be a bit careful, pet.'

'Why's that, pet?' said George, frowning, as they entered their kitchen.

'Well,' said Nellie, bustling around preparing breakfast, 'I know you're talking to them leeks an' all that. An' it might give them a bit of a jump in the growing stakes, but I think we both know what's made those leeks get bigger and it certainly isn't that muck you're feeding them.'

'Ah,' said George, suddenly realising what his wife was talking about, '"The Thing",' he said.

'Exactly. "The Thing",' replied Nellie. 'I thought it would work, it always has on my vegetables.'

'But why should I be careful, Nellie, man?' said George.

'Well, look, George, you're only deein' this as a hobby,' replied Nellie, 'but you knaa what them leek lads are like with their secret formulas and their mixtures. They take it deadly seriously, man, especially when there's money involved. If you just go waltzin' in there winnin' aall the shows, questions will be asked. An' they can get a bit rowdy that lot. Remember what happened to that lad who started winning that last time. What was he called again? He had them big lugs, er, little Steven Sloper?'

'Could I have some fried bread, pet?' said George, changing the subject.

Later that day George was in his shed reading his paper and chatting to his leeks about this and that. He was going to tell them what had happened to little Steven Sloper, but thought tales of folk getting their ears cut off might scare the little leeks. After all, they were only young. He found he liked chatting to his new green mates. He could talk about whatever he wanted, as long as it wasn't too violent or smutty, and they always agreed with what he said. It's probably because I'm so interesting, thought George.

He was just in the middle of explaining to the leeks how to drive a car, when he heard a tiny squeak from the leek trench. George sat up suddenly. Oh no, they're not going to start answering bloody back, I hope, thought George, and with his paper scrunched up in his hands he peeped into the trench to see what was happening.

What he saw caused him to leap up in shock and bang his head on the shelf above. Luckily he was wearing his cap. The leeks were growing as he watched, but since he had stopped speaking their growth rate had slowed down. 'Bloody hell,' breathed George, which caused all the leeks to give a little spurt of growth and caused George to snap his mouth shut. George stood stunned, gawping at his leeks. They were twice as big as this morning.

The moment was shattered as the door behind George opened and the booming voice of Big Fat Squinty Bill called out, 'A million bloody quid, George. A million bloody quid!' Big Fat Squinty Bill squeezed himself into George's shed, and assumed by the shocked look on George's face he knew what he was talking about. 'I know it's amazing, innit, George. A million bloody quid. Imagine what you could buy with that. I'd buy, I'd buy ... well, I don't know what I'd buy but ... '

'What are you talking about, Big Fat Squinty Bill?' snapped George, but he realised he'd made a mistake opening his mouth as soon as he heard the tiny squeaks behind him.

'The new garden centre, man, the leeks, the million quid.

Haven't you heard?' George thought it wise to keep his mouth shut and to drag Big Fat Squinty Bill out of his shed, out of earshot of the squeaky leeks.

'How, man, George, yer nippin us, man, ye've got me skin,' whined Big Fat Squinty Bill as George dragged him out of his shed by one podgy arm.

'Well, you've got plenty skin to gan roond, haven't ye?' chuckled George, his eyes watering as the smoke from his skinny roll-up drifted into his eyes. 'Now what's all this shite yer talking about a million pounds? Who has a million pounds and what's it got to do with leeks?'

'It's the new garden centre,' said Big Fat Squinty, massaging his nipped arm. 'I'll tell you what, George, you've a grip like a vice, I'm surprised me arm hasn't fallen off what with having the blood flow cut off for so long. I'm definitely ganna have a bruise. Imagine when I strip off the neet for our lass, she's ganna be put right of us, now me perfect beauty has been marred by your violence.' The look on Big Fat Squinty's face was so pathetic and his acting so good George couldn't help but burst out laughing.

'Come on, daft lad, I'll take you down to the club and get one of the trained bar staff on the case,' said George. 'I'm sure we can save your arm.' And they left the allotment to pay a mercy mission to the club to save Big Fat Squinty Bill's arm.

'Now tell me what yer gannin on about, Big Fat Squinty,' said George, as he handed Big Fat Squinty his drink, which made him look even more ridiculous than he already did. Big Fat Squinty Bill only drank Sea Breeze, and he insisted he have a straw and a little umbrella in it. He thought it made him look sophisticated, which is the equivalent of putting a top hat on a pig so it looks posh. But the thing about Big Fat Squinty Bill was he really didn't care what anyone thought of him, which is why he was so popular.

'Right,' said Big Fat Squinty, taking a long pull on his

drink. 'You knaa I went down to the tip to see what they were doing?'

'It was only bloody yesterday, I'm not senile yet,' replied George, looking at his pint and wondering if he'd get told off by Nelly for drinking in the afternoon, decided he wouldn't and took a long swig. Of course she knew exactly what he was up to.

'Well, I went down and started chatting to the foreman on the job. He's Eric Cowie's grandson. You remember Eric? He made that sleigh, tied all those dogs to it and they pulled him into the road and he was hit by a tram?'

'Eh yes,' said George, shaking his head and laughing. 'It's not every day dog sleighs get hit by trams aroond here. He was lucky not to get himself killed.'

'Aye, he never rode on a tram again, though,' said Big Fat Squinty, staring into the distance. 'Anyway,' he said, snapping back from his dog-sleigh-tram memories, 'Eric Cowie's grandson told me the reason they're digging up the tip is because they're ganna build one of those giant garden centres there. They're ganna be employing hundreds of people.'

'What and pay them a million pounds each?' said George, with a cheeky look in his eyes.

'Ahh, divent be bloody daft, man, George. Who gets paid a million poond?' said Big Fat Squinty Bill. 'Probably only the Queen and she's not ganna be working in a garden centre, is she? She's enough gardenin' of her own to do at yem. No, man, what happens is when one of these garden centres moves into an area it holds a competition to win a million poonds. And each area has a different competition. For instance, when they opened up in Edinburgh they held a competition to see who could grow the biggest turnip and when they opened in Birmingham it was to see who could grow the biggest carrot and when they opened up in London it was to see who could grow the biggest ...'

'Soft puff?' said George, winding up the big man.

'Don't be daft, man, George, man,' squinted Big Fat Squinty Bill, supping his drink and holding his little finger out all posh.

'Ye diven't grow puffs, man, they're made in secret laboratories by the brainy scientists that the government employ. Everyone knaas that. No, in London it was something to do with flowers or something. Anyway, what Eric Cowie's grandson reckons is that the competition up here is ganna be for the biggest leeks, an a'll tell ye what, George, the way you're gannin with your leeks you could win the million easy. An' then you can buy me one of them Furryrarri sports cars.'

'I'll tell ye what, George, if there was a million-pound prize for who could talk the most shite that Big Fat Squinty Bill would walk away with it every time,' said Nellie Creedy later that day when George told her of the conversation he'd had with his big mate.

'What? So you don't think this new garden centre place will be doling out the cash then?' said George.

'Why would anyone give you a million pounds for big leeks?' replied Nellie. 'It doesn't make sense, man, pet. And even if it were true you certainly couldn't enter the competition. How are you going to suddenly explain your leek-growing expertise? Especially to those daft gets in the leek club. You know what they're like. It's like being in the freemasons. I'm sure I saw that big one, what's he called Ally or Abby?'

'Albie,' said George.

'Yeah him,' continued Nellie, 'giving one of those other big daft gets a secret handshake, or he certainly passed something to him. There's just something not right with those leek lads. I mean you can understand it about the older ones, they've been doing it for years. But the younger ones, why aren't they out meeting girls? There must be some girls who like fat cave men with tattoos.'

'Aye, I knaa, they're aa'll thick, pet,' George began, 'but I'll tell ye what. It'd be nice winnin' a million poond. We could, we could ...'

'We could what, George?' snapped Nellie. 'Buy a plane and a sports car. Eeh, I know what we could buy. We could get matching monkeys to carry us down the shops. Yeah, that would come in handy.'

'Ah yer just being daft now, Nellie. What about giving some of the money to our Neville?' said George, although he regretted bringing up the subject immediately, but he couldn't help it. The words died on his lips. 'I bet he'd like a few bob.'

'George,' said Nellie, turning away from her husband so he couldn't see the tears in her eyes, although he could most certainly hear the little catch in her voice, 'we haven't heard from our Nev for years. Who knows where he is?'

'Ah come on, man, pet,' said George, standing up and putting a comforting arm around his wife's slim shoulders. 'You know as well as I do that our Neville's all right. I can feel it, and if I can so can you. I only wanted to enter the competition to see if I could win. But you're probably right. Big Fat Squinty Bill is probably talking a right load of old shite. Come on, get yer coat, I'll take ye doon the club for a drink. Apparently there's a good turn on the night.'

'Is there? Who?' said Nellie, knowing full well George was lying just to cheer her up.

'Oh,' said George, his eyes wide and innocent as a cuddly baby's, 'it's the Ping Pong Girls from Patpong, and I think we should encourage youngsters in sport.'

Now Nellie had been absolutely right about the blokes in the leek club. When it first started, most of the blokes did it just to get out in the fresh air and to take their minds off the back-breaking toil of the mines or the shipyards. They were very proud of their leeks and a friendly rivalry had started between the growers, but they still went for a pint together after their meetings. After all, they had worked together for years, so they were hardly going to let a few vegetables come between them. Then, when unemployment hit the north-east hard, the founder members' sons had more time to spend in the allotments and less money to spend on pints after their meetings. They also found that they could pick up a few extra quid by entering and winning leek competitions. Although it was still friendly, the rivalry became a bit more intense, and older members were dismayed to find that some of the sheds were now kept locked and the sharing of tips and tools didn't happen any more.

Then the grandsons of the original members became involved and that was when things really changed. These kids were younger and rougher and had never held down a job. They didn't have any loyalty to anyone but themselves, and leek growing became the most important thing in their lives, perhaps because it made them feel as though they were men, as though they had some sort of job to do. For many it was the only thing in their lives. They may have been rough and tough, but when it came to leek growing they were the best, and when they competed they competed aggressively.

The most aggressive of all the leek growers was Albie Donnelly. He'd been taken to his first leek show at the age of five by his dad who then won first prize. Albie had never forgotten his pride at being on the front page of the local newspaper sitting in the cup his dad had won. He'd also never forgotten the shame a week later, when the same

picture was shown again with a picture of his dad, who had
gone on a drink bender with his prize money and beaten a
man to death with the same cup. His father had died in
prison two years later and something snapped in Albie. He
thought if he could grow big leeks he'd somehow get his dad
back. His mother wasn't really bothered about her husband's
death and she took up with a female falconer called Angela.
Albie and Angela never really hit it off. They hit it off even
less fifteen years later when Albie realised his mother and
Angela were living together as wife and wife; which caused
him to throw himself into his leeks even more.

All in all, Albie was a particularly unstable character, but
as everyone in the area agreed, he may have been a nutter,
but he was their nutter, and he had brought a bit of fame to
that part of the world with all the prizes he'd won for his
leeks. He'd even been interviewed by Alan Titchmarsh, and
it doesn't get bigger than that. And because of his tiny
amount of fame, he had attracted hangers on who were
happy to agree with everything he said and, every now and
then, to intimidate other leek growers.

Although no one really believed it, the gossip about the
million-pound leek prize soon spread. These were the same
people who bought a lottery ticket every Saturday afternoon
and prayed they would win so they could show off their bad
taste in spectacular fashion.

There was certainly a garden centre being put up on Big
Fat Squinty Bill's beloved tip. He and George would wander
down to the site and watch the men at work. The youngsters
from the area would watch too, although since they wouldn't
know work if they saw it, they had no idea what the strange
actions that the men performed every day were. Of course,
everyone had ideas about the garden centre and how it
would be spread out, especially when the locals found out it
was an American company called 'Big Trees'.

It wasn't just a garden centre, of course, it had a DIY section, a pet care section and a timber section; everything, in fact, for the budding home improver. 'Big Trees' had centres all over the world and was a very successful and growing company. The head of the company was a man called Clancy Tree. At a rugged 6 foot 4, the 76-year-old Clancy Tree looked just like one of the rugged redwoods in his home state of California.

An ex-farmer, Clancy had started work in his father's shop 50 years ago, selling nails, screws, barbed wire and animal feed to the local farmers. The shop, due to the young Clancy Tree's business acumen and hard work, had quickly expanded. So he bought another, and another. After his wife, Dilly, had died 30 years ago, he had worked even harder, and he now had fifty stores in America and was easily a billionaire. His business plan was this: always open a new shop in an area where there is high unemployment but where there are hardworking men. His plan was to give them jobs, lots of jobs and try to regenerate the area. This, in turn, meant that folks would want to better themselves and their homes, so they would buy things from him. This was fine if you were opening shops across America, where people tended to fall for that sort of bollocks, but his plan didn't seem to be working too well in Blighty. The stores did OK, but not as well as he would have liked and that was why he had started giving away millions of pounds to men of the soil. They were his people and he wanted to help them and he didn't do too badly out of all the publicity either. Publicity was uppermost in his mind when he paid a visit to Wallsend, to see how his new 'corner shop' was coming along.

4 〉

The local paper, The Evening Chronicle, could hardly contain itself. It had the news of the wealthy American's arrival spread over five pages. It listed all of his accomplishments and what he had achieved for areas of high unemployment in the States and announced that it was a great opportunity for the people of the north-east. The paper had lots and lots of photographs of Clancy Tree collecting various awards, and told the story of how his beautiful pregnant wife had been tragically killed when her Porsche convertible had spun out of control and hit a tree. Luckily she wasn't killed instantly and she lived long enough to give birth to a son, Clancy Jr. The baby was only six weeks premature when it was born, but, on seeing the child, a grief-stricken Clancy Tree could only gurgle, 'It looks like a fucking fat rat.'

Whether or not children can remember anything from their birth is debatable, but Clancy Jr had only ever known hatred for his father. The young Clancy boy was the exact opposite of his pater. Where his dad was effortlessly tall and muscular, Clancy Jr had stopped growing at 5 foot 3, and if any of his limbs stopped moving they immediately became covered in a layer of fat. Young Clancy never stopped exercising and always carried with him on their trips around the world a running machine, a step machine, a ski machine and various other items of torture to try and stop himself turning into a lardy ball. Clancy had once retained the services of a private trainer, but he was sure he was laughing at him, so Clancy killed him with a dumb-bell and buried his body on their ranch. 'Eight hundred calories burned,' he noted in his diary later that day.

Where his father was a natural speaker and could get on with anyone, from a beggar to the leader of a country, Clancy Jr couldn't even look at anyone without blushing. He had inherited these traits from his mother, who, although a lovely, kind woman, was also very shy. That's why she drank and that's why she was killed.

In all the photographs there were always pictures of old man Tree striding purposefully off a plane or flashing his winning smile while shaking a senator's hand, but in the background there always seemed to be lurking a little fat shadow, a sort of chubby ghost.

'Of course we're gannin to see him,' said George, in reply to Big Fat Squinty Bill's question of whether he and Nellie were going down to the site to see Clancy Tree.

'Our Nellie thinks he's bloody gorgeous,' George continued. 'She's always had a thing about Yanks. She loves that new bloke, what's he called? George Clooney. And as for that Brad Pitt, she reckons she'd chuck me for him. Can you imagine that, eh, Big Fat Squinty Bill?' chuckled George. 'A lass fancying an American over a Geordie, whey, it's not right, man, it's against nature.'

'Aye, yer right there, George,' said Big Fat Squinty Bill, with his most indignant face on. 'Our lass reckons Brad Pitt's got a better belly than me! Can you imagine that? Who wants one of those little skinny bellies with six little lumps on them when you can have one big lump like what I have. Aye, women, man, I'll never understand them, man.'

'But that's because you don't understand anything, Big Fat Squinty Bill,' said Nellie, pulling on her coat and joining her daft husband and his even dafter mate in their small back garden. 'Come on, let's go. I want to hear what gorgeous Clancy Tree has to say for himself. Isn't Missus Big Fat Squinty Bill coming?'

'Coming! She's been queueing up since this morning! She thinks he looks like bloody Elvis!' said Big Fat Squinty Bill, as he strode out in front rather irritably.

There was quite a big turn-out at the site when Nellie, George and Big Fat Squinty Bill arrived. A stage area had been erected, along with a small PA system.

'Eeeeh, what's gannin on hinny?' said an old fat woman wearing her nightie under her threadbare coat and staring at the stage. 'Is it the Rolling Stones?'

'Aye, that's right, missus,' said Big Fat Squinty Bill, as he squeezed past, looking for Mrs Big Fat Squinty Bill.

'Eeeeh, I'd better be careful then, that Mick Jagger might get us,' replied the old woman, trying to pull the coat closed in front of her as if at any moment Mick Jagger might swoop down and drag her off.

'There she is!' shouted Big Fat Squinty Bill, pointing to where his wife was standing, in front of the stage. Hearing her beloved husband's voice, Mrs Big Fat Squinty started waving, forgetting she had a '99' in her hand. Surprisingly, the ice cream stayed put, but the chocolate flake shot out and nearly blinded one of the young lads who was making the final adjustment to the PA system. What started as, 'One two, one two,' ended up as, 'Ow me fucking eye, me fucking eye!'

No one in the crowd batted an eyelid. It was a shame flake-eye hadn't batted his.

A bit of a revelation was Mrs Big Fat Squinty Bill. Everyone assumed she would be fat like her husband, but no. She was a slim blonde woman, about the same age as Nellie. Needless to say she drank Nelly's juice all the time.

'Eeeh, hello, pet,' said Mrs Big Fat Squinty Bill, giving her husband a big hug. 'You're just in time. It's about to kick off.'

'Isn't Clancy Tree lovely, Mrs Big Fat Squinty Bill?' said Nellie, as her and George squeezed in beside their friends.

'Aye, he looks like a film star,' replied Mrs Big Fat Squinty, and with that the two older women fell into giggles like two teenagers at their first pop concert.

Feed back howled from the PA and the north-east got its first glimpse of Clancy Tree.

The north-east nearly didn't get a glimpse of Clancy Tree at all. Father and son had been up arguing into the early hours of the morning. And it was about the same old thing. As soon as they had landed, Clancy Jr had exercised for two hours, then disappeared into Newcastle to sample the nightlife and whatever else he could get his hands on. But not for him the corporate delights of strip clubs, casinos or whores. Clancy lived for rock'n'roll. Well, not real rock'n'roll, but death metal or black metal or anything with a white face and leather trousers that was loud and sang about the Devil. Clancy Jr had heard Newcastle was the heavy metal capital of Britain and he had intended to savour all of its haunts and vices.

Of course his father hated this and tried to stop him from going out and getting all 'frantic' as old man Tree called it when his son got messed up on coke. Clancy Jr was unaware that his father even knew he was taking drugs, you don't get to be as wealthy as as Clancy Tree without knowing exactly what was going on in your world. When he was in America he could easily afford and obtain the best cocaine his father's money could buy, and since it wasn't 'cut' he tended to get less frantic than in this country, where he was sure the cocaine was cut with chemicals he'd never even heard of. Here, it seemed to make him go even madder than he already was, and now he was trying to score drugs in Newcastle, a place where, to his ears, they couldn't even speak English.

While not exactly dreading the effect of the unknown coke, he did wonder what the effect of the latest cut crap would be, as he left his hotel dressed in his usual night-time attire of black leather jacket, black T-shirt, black jeans, Chrome Hearts jewellery and heavy biker boots, into which he had tucked a very small handgun.

Then Clancy Jr had a stroke of good luck. There, directly opposite the hotel, was a poster featuring the biggest and his favourite black metal band of them all: Luscious. The poster was over a year out of date for their concert at Newcastle City Hall, but it did give the address of their local fan club, which was based in a pub called The Bonny Lad, whatever that meant, in the centre of town. He jumped into a cab at the rank and told the driver to take him there. The driver was quite impressed at having someone in his cab who wasn't from Newcastle, although he had no idea where he could be from. He suspected south of the river. When he tried to ascertain just where his fare had been born, he was met with a blank stare that only a spoiled rich American can give a Geordie taxi driver who sounds like an inarticulate Gazza.

Poor man, they both thought, as Clancy Jr climbed out of the cab.

As soon as Clancy entered The Bonny Lad he felt at home,

if a bit underdressed. Some of the clientele were in full Luscious dress: white face, eyes heavy with black eyeliner, thick red lipstick smeared across their lips, hair teased into blond dreadlocks. Some of them were even built like their hero: wiry and muscular, so that the leather and lace outfits they wore looked right. But the majority had had far too many pints and late-night kebabs, so the pub looked as though it was full of chubby demons. Clancy loved it.

He elbowed his way up to the bar and, in a loud voice, making sure he overplayed his accent, asked for a large Jack Daniels. The effect he was after was spoiled by the barmen shouting back, 'Aye, all right, John Wayne. It's happy hour. Two for the price of one!' Clancy Jr didn't realise that everyone in the bar affected an American accent to be more like their hero. Picking up his drink he pushed his way over to a small table being vacated by two ugly girls that turned out to be two pretty boys.

'Eh, we're not gannin' yet, mate, but you can sit there till we get back,' said the smallest, prettiest boy, winking in the direction of the toilets. They returned wiping their noses and sniffing loudly, and in his opinion a bit too dramatically, and Clancy knew he had found what he wanted.

When the two lads found out Clancy Jr was a real American who had seen Luscious twelve times and had even met the charismatic front man, he found he had made friends for life. They were even sort of impressed at who his dad was, although gardening didn't really feature very highly in their young lives. They even offered him a line of their coke, but he declined, telling them he'd like to buy some of his own. The young lads made a couple of phone calls on Clancy Jr's mobile phone, and assured him 'The Man' was on his way.

As usual with this type of deal, 'The Man' turned out to be a spotty kid in an oversized tracksuit, who looked completely out of place in the busy pub, although he seemed to be known by many of the people in there. He made his way straight over to the trio and started to tell the tale of how he had the best stuff, blah, blah, blah. His confidence was somewhat dented when Clancy asked for two ounces. 'The Man' had six 50-quid wraps on him, and Clancy Jr loved watching the cocky, cokey smile slide from his face as he placed his order.

'Two fucking ounces?' spluttered The Man.

'Is that a problem?' smiled Clancy Jr, his small, perfect, white teeth accentuating the fact that his smile never reached his eyes.

'Eh, no, not a problem, like, it's, eh, well I'll have to make a call, like,' said The Man.

'Go ahead,' replied Clancy Jr, pushing his small, expensive mobile across the beer-soaked table.

'It's OK. I've me own,' said The Man indignantly, and pulled out what to Clancy looked like a brick. It was then the American knew he was dealing with an amateur. No drug dealer in America would be seen dead with the piece of shit this kid was calling a phone.

'Look, I'll have to go outside,' said The Man, glancing nervously around him.

'No problemo, baybeee,' said Clancy Jr, trying to keep the conversation light and easy, although his eyes were now flashing a dangerous black. 'I'll come with you.'

He picked up his phone, drained his drink and strode off into the crowd, followed by The Man, who was already mentally counting the profit he'd make from this stupid American midget.

As they left the crowded pub, The Man was already speaking into his antique phone, gesticulating the way people do when they're on the phone in the street. As The Man stuck his arm out once more to make a point, Clancy Jr grabbed his hand and spun him face first into the window of the shop next door. Unluckily for The Man, the shop, an 'Everything For A Pound' store, had its security grille down, and his scrawny face was forced through a gap, skinning the side of his head and nearly ripping off both ears. The force of the throw meant the grill was now behind his jug lugs, so he was stuck fast. The only way Clancy Jr could stop him screaming was by punching him in the back of the neck until he was unconscious.

'That must've been about 300 calories,' smiled Clancy Jr to himself as he reached around the unconscious body and relieved The Man of his drugs.

While he was doing this he was aware of a tinny voice somewhere in the background of the violence. He looked at his feet and smiled as he picked up The Man's discarded mobile.

'There's been a change of plan,' he shouted into the mouthpiece, before cramming the big old-fashioned phone into his jacket pocket.

The change of plan involved getting wasted on coke and Jack Daniels in a different pub. Although there was no one around when he attacked the young drug dealer, he thought it wise to be away from the immediate vicinity. It had taken just two minutes from leaving the pub to walking quickly away with six grammes of coke.

Clancy Jr arrived back at the hotel at 4am. The coke hadn't been very good. Every time he did a line, he shook his head and coughed, 'What the fuck is this cut with?' But he still managed to do three grammes, which would have been about the same strength as one in America. As he walked into the foyer of the hotel, he suddenly found himself travelling a mite faster than he wanted to. This was due to his father's big hand on the back of his neck, dragging him towards the lift. Clancy Tree Sr virtually lifted his son above his head and threw him to the small, mirrored elevator.

'Where the fuck do you think you've been, Devil boy?' snarled his father, towering over his son.

'Fuck you,' spat Clancy Jr, from his position as a crumpled heap on the floor. Before he knew it he had pulled the tiny handgun from his boot and was pointing it straight at his father's face. With a grunt, Clancy Snr kicked his son hard in the face, turned left out of the lift, strode across the foyer and stopped at the stairs. There he turned to look at his son and said quietly, 'You'd better be there tomorrow, boy.'

He took the stairs three at a time.

'Hello and Howay The Lads,' were the first words Clancy Tree uttered to Wallsend.

Now I don't know what sort of accent you have, but if you've an accent, like I have, you'll know how annoying it is when people try to imitate it. And us accented people never say anything, we just laugh hollowly and lift our chins slightly. If you are a person who thinks it's funny to imitate other people's accents, DON'T.

So Clancy Tree had made a bad start, and he knew it when no one clapped or cheered. They just stared. Clancy Tree assumed it was because they hated him, but it was partly that they were thinking, He's a billionaire! Not one person there could comprehend just how rich that was. Most of the women were thinking, Oooh, he's lovely for his age, although there was one person who was thinking, Eeeeh, ah hope that Mick Jagger doesn't get us.

Clancy Tree hadn't made his billions by being daft, though, and he went on to make a speech that would have had the assembled crowd marching on Downing Street, although what they would have done when they got there is anyone's guess. Of course, being the old campaigner that he was, he kept the best bit of news until last. He was going to hold a leek-growing competition, he said, and the person who grew the biggest leek would win … £2 million.

The crowd went silent. Then the noise started at the back of the crowd. It was like an old car starting up on a cold morning, which, in a way, it was. It was the old leek growers coughing in astonishment at what they had heard. Two million pounds. The journalists present began to shout down their mobile phones at their feature editors, which seemed to shatter the spell. Suddenly, everyone on the site of Big Trees was shouting and laughing in excitement. If the Big Tree home improvement store had been open then they would have completely sold out of gardening equipment.

'Well, I'm definitely entering,' said Big Fat Squinty Bill to his wife and George and Nellie as they took their seats in the Coronation Club later that night.

'Don't be daft, man, Big Fat Squinty Bill, man, pet. You've more chance of growing horns than you have of growin' a two-million-poond leek,' laughed his wife, as she arranged her ten bingo cards into an order.

'Well, I've more chance of winnin' money with a leek than I have of winnin' the lottery,' replied Big Fat Squinty, taking a thoughtful sip of his sophisticated Sea Breeze. 'Stands to reason, doesn't it? Rules of the competition says you can only enter if you live in Wallsend and there's only about, well, I haven't counted them all, but there's not many people live here and most of them won't be entering, so that cuts the odds right down.' Which was the exact same thought everyone in Wallsend, young and old, was having at that moment.

'Anyway,' continued Big Fat Squinty Bill, 'I've got a secret weapon.'

'Ah knaa but I've never knaan ye keep it secret,' cackled his wife.

'No, man,' said Big Fat Squinty Bill seriously, tapping his

nose and squinting in his most inscrutable way. 'It's Georgie boy here. His leeks virtually grow as you watch them.'

'No no no, my George isn't entering any daft leek competition,' said Nellie Creedy to Big Fat Squinty Bill. She didn't know what it was but there was definitely a feeling of menace in the club that night. There were lots of people huddled at tables talking about the prize-money, how they were going to win it and what they were going to spend it on. They all seemed to have leek-growing recipes their great granddad had handed down to them and they were all sure they were going to win the money. It just didn't feel right to Nellie, and she knew when folk were that desperate to win money people could get hurt.

'Eeh, why not, man, Nellie?' said Mrs Big Fat Squinty Bill, selecting her lucky bingo pen from her bag full of lucky bingo pens. 'Imagine what you could get with two million quid. You could afford anything you wanted from the catalogue. You could even buy stuff you didn't need, just to have it. That's what them rich people do what live in that London. Whey, man, they just buy expensive nick-nacks an' leave them lyin' aroond the hoose. If I had loads of money ye wouldn't be able to get moved in wor hoose for expensive nick-nacks.'

'Well, that'll make a difference 'cos we cannit get moved for cheap shite at the moment,' laughed Big Fat Squinty Bill, enveloping his wife in a big bear hug. 'It'll be heartwarming to knaa that whatever I break in future will be worth more than wor hoose.'

There wasn't much cuddling going on in the Tree family at that moment. While his father had been making his impassioned speech, Clancy Tree Jr had been lurking at the back of the stage planning how he could kill him. Some of the audience noticed Clancy Jr, but because of the way he was dressed assumed he was something to do with the PA. From where they were standing they couldn't see he was wearing make-up to conceal his bruised face. Clancy Jr would like to have gone the whole hog and worn full Luscious make-up but his father would've had a heart attack trying to strangle him. Mind you, he thought, that's not a bad way to go.

He hated his father and every corporate thing he stood for, but the main reason he hated him so much was that he kept him on such a tight leash. Fair enough, he'd fucked up a few times, but you were allowed to when you were a kid, weren't you? OK, so he'd once been so out of it he'd shot some animals. That could've happened to anyone. The beating he'd received from his father was more than made up for by all the money his dad had paid the zoo in compensation. Fuck, it was only a couple of deer. He'd been looking for the pandas. He would love to have seen their fat lazy bamboo-filled asses full of holes. But the six guards overpowered him before he could get a Chi Chi in his sights. He had one rough moment when the biggest of the guards, with tears streaming down his face, started screaming that they should throw him in the lion cage. They probably would've done it too if the real cops hadn't arrived at the right time. Oh, Lordy, that had cost his daddy some hush money. Oh yes.

The fact that he managed to keep cool and not pull his gun from his boot and start blasting when he heard his father say he was going to give away £2 million made him feel proud. He felt like screaming, 'You see, big fucking Daddy? I do have some self-control!' On the way back to the hotel in his car he couldn't help saying to himself under his breath, 'Two million fucking pounds,' over and over, until it came out as one word, like steam escaping from a split pipe. The chauffeur kept glancing back nervously. He didn't really know what to make of the young man in the back of the car wearing pale make-up. He did k̶ incredibly rich and could knock out a g̶ seemed to have a bad cold.

'Two million fucking pounds,' whispere̶ eyed and pale-skinned, as he bent over and to̶ of coke, dipping the long nail on his little fin̶ white powder and forcing it up his clogged nose.   ̶at will I get? Fucking revenge is what I'll get.'

'Ah come on, man, George, you have to enter the competition, you'll win easily, man,' said Big Fat Squinty Bill for the twentieth time that night, as they sat in the Coronation Club. He'd said it so often he'd started to attract the attention of some other members of the leek club who were sitting at nearby tables. A couple of them had seen George's tiny leeks when he'd got all excited a few weeks ago and started to rib him good-naturedly.

'Ah ye should enter, man, George,' said the oldest member of the leek club, a man called Trinder Dogg. 'Ye never knaa, we might aa'll drop doon deed an' your titchy little things could walk away with the two million poond. Or what happens if a big strong giant leek thief breaks in and carries off aall our lovely leeks to put in a big leek pie. Ah, man, the money would be yours, man, George.'

The good-natured ribbing halted abruptly when the high-pitched, spiteful voice of Albie Donnelly cut across the banter: 'Well, nee body had better gan near my leeks if they knaa what's good for them.' Albie's three cronies, the Taylor twins, Lawrence and Derrick, and Pudgy Gee, sniggered behind their drinks. Albie was at his most dangerous and bullying when he was like this. Just the right side of drunk and carrying big punchy fists.

'There's only one person ganna win the money. An' that's me. Isn't that right, lads?' His lads nodded their assent. 'So

yourself as a leek grower, eh, George?' said Albie,
ng to look at his newest rival.

'Aye, I grow leeks, son,' said George, 'but I don't think I'm
in your league yet.'

As this exchange was going on, Nellie was flashing
thoughts to her husband, warning him to be careful – which
was completely lost on George. If there was one thing he
hated more than anything else in his Wallsend world it was
a bully. Which is exactly what Albie Donnelly was. A big, fat
cowardly bully, and if he wasn't careful with his mouth
George was going to put him down right now.

'No, you're no competition for me, granddad. I'm ganna
win the money and fuck right off from this shithole.'

Nellie saw the flash in George's eyes. She knew
something was going to happen and, even though she was
worried for George, she knew she wouldn't let anything
happen to him. And part of her wanted to see Albie
Donnelly slapped down.

'Watch the language, son,' said George, taking a
nonchalant sup of his pint. 'Yer not on yer allotment now.'

'I'll speak the way I fucking want, granddad, and you'd
better keep it buttoned if ye kanaa what's good for yer,' said
Albie, his face flushed red as he stood up.

The whole bar had suddenly gone silent.

'Sit down, you silly little lad,' said George, matching
Albie's stare.

It happened in a split second. Albie, who was towering
over George, pulled back his fist and it never stopped going
back. It appeared as though he'd been dragged over the bar
by an unseen hand, but everyone knew that couldn't
happen. Albie must've just toppled over.

The crash of the bottles and glasses as Albie landed broke
the moment, and everyone was on their feet shouting. The
concert chairman of the club, Dougie Moss, probably the

most miserable man in the world due to the fact that he was a gay cancan dancer trapped in a 6 foot 5, fat, northern bloke's body, picked Albie up and dragged him out of the club as easily as if he were a helium-filled hen.

'Yer barred,' he growled, as Albie landed in a stunned heap in the disabled parking bay outside the club, 'and unless you're in the possession of a disabled badge you can't park yer fat arse there.' And with a dusting off of his hands he turned and slammed the door shut.

As a stunned Albie was being carried away by his three friends, the bar in the club settled down.

'Eeeh, ah diven't knaa,' said Mrs Big Fat Squinty Bill. 'These young kids are as mad as old Joe Malone.' The explanation of who exactly Joe Malone was and why he was so mad was halted by the return of the Albie-tossing Dougie Moss, who came straight over to George.

'I'm sorry about that, George,' said Dougie. 'He's a bloody nutter that Albie, just like his dad. He won't be getting back in here again in a hurry.'

'It's OK, man, Dougie,' said George, standing up and trying a couple of karate chops. 'I reckon I could take him any time. I've got a black belt, ye knaa.'

'Aye, it holds yer suit trousers up. Come on, you, Bruce Lee. Home,' said Nellie, taking her husband by the arm and guiding him out of the club through all the bottles and glasses that had been smashed by the flying Albie Donnelly.

'Be careful, mind, George. Albie Donnelly might be hangin' around,' said Big Fat Squinty Bill looking worriedly at his mate.

'Whey, I'm not scared of him,' said George over his shoulder, but his view was blocked by Dougie Moss.

'Look, George, do you want me to come with you?' said Dougie. 'He's a wicked spiteful bloke that Albie.'

'Thanks, Dougie,' said George, 'but I've our lass here to

protect me.' And with a wave George and Nellie stepped out into the night.

'Nice work, pet,' said George to Nellie when they were clear of the club. 'I haven't seen you throw someone over a bar for a long time.'

'I really enjoyed it too,' said Nellie. 'He's a horrible bully is Albie Donnelly, and I knew if I left it up to you you'd probably get all dramatic and levitate him and his three mates, so I went for a quieter, more controlled method of stopping a bully.'

'Aye, that's right, pet, good move,' said George, eyes twinkling in the night. 'I don't think anyone in the club noticed at all.'

Nellie grabbed George's arm, and the pair giggled into the night at the memory of Albie Donnelly's shocked face as he was thrown over the bar.

'Glad someone's having a happy time,' said an American voice behind the giggling pair.

'Howdy, partner,' said George, smiling up at the northeast's newest benefactor, Clancy Tree.

'Oh hello, Mr Tree,' said Nellie, who was in a giggly mood anyway, but, surprisingly for a 71-year-old with super mental powers, meeting Clancy Tree meant she now turned into a giggling teenager. This made George laugh even more.

'You been out celebrating something?' said a bemused Clancy Tree, seeing the laughing couple were nearer his age than he first thought, although they seemed remarkably well preserved.

'Well, we haven't,' said George, 'but everyone else in the neighbourhood has been celebrating the fact they're all going to win your £2 million.'

'And what about you?' said Clancy Tree. 'Don't you fancy yourself as a millionaire?'

'Yeah, I might give the leek growing a go,' began George, but he was cut off by his wife.

'George, you are not entering that stupid competition. It's too dangerous!'

'Dangerous?' laughed Clancy Tree. 'How can growing leeks be dangerous?'

'People take their leek growing very serious around here,' said a solemn Nellie.

'So what you doing walking around here, Mr Tree?' said George, changing the subject.

'Call me Clancy, please,'

'Ooh, hey you hear that, Nellie? I'm on first-name terms with billionaires, me. Elton Bloody John will be calling me up next and asking me to sign him in the club.'

'Shut up, George,' said Nellie, deadpan. 'So what are you doing around here, Clancy?'

'Well, I had a car to take me back to the hotel, but it appears my good-for-nothing son has taken it. I don't mind. I can walk back. I quite like to get a feel for the surroundings.'

'Aye, well, there are a few people around here who might like to get a feel for your wallet,' said George. 'Anyway you can't walk back, it's four bloody miles.'

'Oh, that's all right,' said Clancy Tree. 'I walk six miles a day when I'm at home.'

'That's as maybe,' said George, 'but you don't have to walk through Byker when you're at home.'

'He's right, Clancy. There's some bad 'uns around,' said Nellie. 'Come on back to our place. We'll order you a taxi.'

And Nellie linked her arm through Clancy Tree's and steered him towards home and a nice cup of tea.

Clancy Jr leaped out of the car and ran straight up the hotel stairs to his room. Even though he would have loved to exercise, he had more pressing things on his mind, like where to get more drugs. As he entered the room his thoughts were shattered by the ringing of a phone.

He instinctively pulled out his mobile from the inside pocket of his leather jacket. 'Hello, hello!' he shouted at the mouthpiece. No answer. 'Piece of shit,' shouted Clancy Jr as he snapped it shut and threw it on the table. There was a phone ringing somewhere.

Clancy Jr picked up the nearest land line.

'Who the fuck is this?' he screamed, coke paranoia now kicking in big time.

The line was dead and the phone was still ringing.

'Fuck,' shouted Clancy Jr, pacing the room. 'What the fuck?'

And then he saw it. The big brick of a mobile he'd taken off that cheap prick of a so-called drug dealer. He'd used it to wedge open the door of his bathroom, so he could watch the Luscious special that had been on MTV the night before, and it was still there. Obviously the fucking lazy maid had missed it. But as he tried to pull the ringing phone from under the door he realised it was stuck fast. He had to lie down with his head on the floor next to the phone to answer it.

'What ...' he shouted into the mouthpiece with his feet stretched into the bathroom, '... the fuck do you want!?' he continued.

'Is that you, Russell?' said the voice on the other end.

'No,' snapped Clancy Jr. 'Who the fuck is this?'

'Fuck you!' said the voice, and hung up. Clancy Jr leaped to his feet and was about to kick the phone around the room, when he suddenly realised he had no drugs. And what was wedged under his bathroom door was a drug dealer's phone. Even in his frazzled state he knew there must be some interesting numbers in there. He just had to get the fucking phone out of the evil clutches of the door.

Right! he thought, his brain racing. Tools are what I need. Phone-retrieving tools. And with that he snatched up the ironing board and started smashing it into the door, while repeating the special phone-releasing rhyme, 'Get the fuck from under the fucking door you fucking stupid fucking phone fuck!'

Well, the magic rhyme must have worked because, with a final crunch, the door slammed into the wall and the phone shot across the bathroom floor. It wasn't until the noise had died down that Clancy Jr realised there was another phone ringing. Snatching the mobile from the floor he screamed, 'Yes?' into the mouthpiece. It was then that he realised it was the phone in his room. He picked it up and threw it through the window, followed by the TV and the ironing board. Rock and fucking roll! he thought, as he passed the security men in the hallway rushing to his room.

'You'd better call the fire brigade!' he screamed at their backs as he stepped on to the fire escape and began to leap down the stairs, six at a time.

'So what do yer reckon, Clancy? This must be a home from home for you,' said George, showing Clancy Tree into the tiny house he shared with Nellie.

'You'd be surprised, George. I wasn't always a rich man,' said Clancy Sr. 'As a matter of fact I grew up in a house about the same size as this, although we had a bigger yard and a horse.'

'A horse?' said Nellie, entering the room with cups of tea on a metal tray that had a picture of a zebra on it.

'Nellie has always had a soft spot for those stripey horses,' George would tell his mates in the club. He preferred his horses to run fast around a racecourse.

'What was it called?' said Nellie.

'Er, it was called, erm, Charlie,' said a bemused Clancy Tree. 'My father and Charlie used to deliver horse-feed to the other farmers in the area. That's how I first started in this business. I noticed the farmers wanted other supplies delivered so I'd try to oblige. Business suddenly became pretty big. There was one man though, a farmer called Willie Maysborough, who always wanted us to deliver a woman to him. A woman – can you imagine?' Clancy gave a throaty chuckle. 'Maybe I should have had a line in loose women. I would've been a wealthier man than I am now.'

The three of them laughed together in a way that old people who have seen a bit of the world can.

'It's not all about money though, is it, Clancy? What about your son?' said Nellie.

'My son?' said Clancy Tree, the humour leaving his eyes in a snap. 'My son hates me, always has, always will, and I have no idea why. I've given him everything he's ever wanted and he gives me nothing back. Do you have any children?' said Clancy to George and Nellie. He realised this was the wrong thing to say as soon as he saw Nellie's face and the way George put a comforting hand over Nellie's.

'Aye, we have a son. Haven't seen him in years. We know he's OK, it's just that, well, he's never been in touch for a long time.'

'Hmm,' said Clancy Tree. 'Well, in my experience sometimes it's best you don't know what your kids are up to. It makes you worry even more.'

If Clancy Tree had known what his son was up to at that precise moment he would certainly have been worried. Clancy Jr had set fire to the bed, the fire alarm had been activated and, using the panic of the other guests as cover, he sprinted up to his father's penthouse apartment and, without a by-your-leave, kicked the door in. After his dealings with the phone-trapping door in his own room, Clancy Jr had a big down on doors.

He knew exactly what he wanted from his father's room. He moved quickly across the penthouse pushing over lights and ornaments, just because he was bad, and arrived at the wardrobe. Ripping the flimsy, louvred door off its hinges he started to key in the number that would open the safe. Silly old fuck always used the same number 26970, thought Clancy Jr. My birthday.

The safe clicked open and Clancy pulled out the wads of new notes, about ten grand in pounds and dollars, and stuffed them into the pockets of his jacket. Right at the back he saw something that made him laugh out loud: a picture of him as a baby. Ahh, he thought, how fucking sentimental. He grabbed the polaroid photograph, ripping it up and throwing it into the air, then instantly forgetting what he'd done as the pieces fell into his hair.

Because it was then he saw the gun. It was resting upright against the side of the safe, nozzle pointing away from him, angled towards the back of the safe and the floor. A big magnum like the one Clint Eastwood used in those stupid cop movies. Only his fucking father would have a big macho gun like that. His father didn't realise that no matter how small the gun was it could kill you. How fucking gloriously fitting that would be, sticking his father's own gun into his face and then blowing it off. Blowing his fucking corporate face off his fucking skull. Oh, how he would enjoy that. This was turning out to be a perfect day. Grabbing the gun he turned and fell into a shooter's stance, both hands gripping the butt. He felt like the fucking FBI.

'Freeze!' he shouted at the room. The room froze – it didn't want to be shot. 'You're under arrest, motherfucker!' screamed Clancy Jr. The room threw up its hands. It knew its life of crime was over.

Laughing, Clancy ran from the room, before re-entering and setting the bed on fire.

Thankfully, the beep of the car horn outside stopped any more talk of wayward sons.

'That'll be your cab,' said Nellie, standing up and signalling to the cab driver through the window.

'Well, thanks for the hospitality,' said Clancy Tree. 'I hope I can repay it some day.'

'Ah, that's all right, pet,' said Nellie. 'You're more than welcome here any time.'

'Hey, I'll tell you what you could do, though,' said George. 'How about fixin' it so I win yer two million poond with me titchy leeks?'

'Why don't I just hand you the two million now?' said Clancy Tree, his eyes twinkling. 'I always carry that much around in loose change.'

'Why don't you just go home and stop encouraging daft lad here?' said Nellie, taking Clancy by the arm and steering him towards the front door.

'Erm, I couldn't ask you one more favour?' said Clancy Tree sheepishly.

'Anything, pet,' said Nellie.

'Could you lend me £10? I have no cash on me.'

'Nee wonder you're a bloody billionaire,' said George, pulling the cash out of his wallet, a big smile on his face. 'You never bloody spend owt.'

'Thanks, George,' said Clancy Tree. 'I'll make sure you get it back.'

'Ah knaa yer will, kidda, ah knaa where ye live,' said George.

The taxi beeped again and Clancy Tree opened the front door and stepped into the street.

'Tara, pet,' said Nellie, waving.

'Aye, tara, you money-grabbing scrounger,' said George, laughing.

'The Delmont Hotel, please,' said Clancy Tree to the cab driver, as he climbed into the car.

'Ye'll be lucky,' said the cab driver, looking at his passenger in the rear-view mirror.

'You do know,' said Nellie to her husband after waving off their rich visitor and closing the front door, 'that you're not entering the leek competition.'

'Oh ah knaa that, yer wicked old woman,' said George, putting his wallet back in his pocket. 'But I'm ganna have to grow something to eat. He took aall our money. We can't afford to buy food.'

'Burned down! What do you mean burned down?' said an incredulous Clancy Tree to the back of the cab driver's head.

'Aye, it's been on the news aall night,' said the cabbie, turning in his seat and dislodging a half-eaten pastie he had resting on his lap. 'Apparently it was arson,' he continued, as he reached down to retrieve his dislodged dinner. Clancy Tree was too shocked by the news to realise that the cab had mounted the kerb. The people at the bus stop looked shocked at what appeared to be a driverless cab rushing towards them, but when he'd located his pastie the cab driver managed to get his car under control.

'Arson!' said Clancy Tree.

'Aye, that's right,' said the cabbie, his face wrinkling as he took a bite of his now hairy pastie. He put it on the seat next to him. He'd brush it off later.

'I drove past there before. It's like a war zone, man.'

'Was anyone hurt?' said Clancy, hoping his son wasn't at the hotel.

'Eh, I don't think so,' said the cabbie. 'It said on the news everyone managed to get out safely. Do you want a fruit pastille?' he continued, offering the sweets over his shoulder. Clancy politely declined.

The cab driver had eaten all the fruit pastilles and a packet of fruit polos, and was starting on the hairy pastie again as they pulled up to the hotel. Clancy Tree was relieved to see that the cab driver's account that the hotel had been burned down was an exaggeration. The building was surrounded by fire engines and police cars, but all the guests had been allowed back into their rooms. After handing over the £10 note and telling the munchie cab driver to keep the change, Clancy Tree entered the hotel and was immediately stopped by hotel security.

'Mr Tree,' said the small Italian head of security, who had no idea how he had ended up doing this job.

'Yes?' said Clancy Tree, seeing the security badge pinned to the man's well-tailored suit before he saw him.

'Could you follow me, please?'

Clancy Tree followed the small, neat Italian, who turned and walked neatly through a door marked 'Hotel Security'.

'I'm just going down the paper shop, pet,' said George to Nellie as nonchalantly as he could. He had learned many years ago that even without her mind-reading skills Nellie could see straight through him. Nellie stuck her head out of the kitchen and gave him that look that must be handed down from mother to daughter. They keep it for those special occasions when blokes are trying to pull the wool over their eyes and, of course, blokes, being as daft as a shop full of brushes, immediately crumble when confronted by said laser look.

'All right, all right, I'm going down the allotment. But I'm just goin' to see me leeks. I'm not entering them in any competition or owt. I mean, I'm not that stupid ...' George didn't really stop speaking here, he just stammered to a halt as if his mouth had run out of petrol.

'Oh, that's all right, pet,' said Nellie, a smile spreading across her face. She always thought he looked about ten when he was like this. 'You go and have a look at your daft leeks. But, George ... bring us back a present.'

Nellie disappeared back into the kitchen and the sound of the juicer started up.

George couldn't quite put his finger on it, as he strolled down to the allotments. It wasn't until he stopped at the newsagent's to buy his paper and tobacco and found he was standing in a queue that he realised what it was. There were people around. Normally it was quiet at this time of day, but there were people about and they seemed to have some sort of purpose, as if they had jobs to go to.

'Eeh, I'm rushed off me wheels,' said Wheelie Billy, as he brought his wheelchair to a halt in front of George. 'It's the leeks money, you see, George. They've all gone leek mad. I've never stopped. I've hardly any time to look after me own leeks.'

'You're growing leeks?' spluttered George. 'Get away, man, Billy, man. How can you grow leeks? You don't even have an allotment, you daft get.'

'You don't need an allotment,' said Wheelie Billy. 'Here, have a look at this.'

Wheelie Billy pulled aside the curtain that separated the shop from his living room at the back of the house. There, arranged around the walls of the room, were deep plastic boxes filled with soil and small leeks. It smelled like a greenhouse. 'You can't grow leeks here, man, Billy, man,' said George, a look of 'you're bloody mad, you' on his face.

'I can if I'm ganna win two million quid,' said Wheelie Billy. 'When I win I'm ganna buy one of those electric wheelchairs. But I'm ganna have a really big engine put in it so I can do about a hundred miles an hour an' mebbe some rockets an' …'

Because the shop was so full Wheelie Billy had no time to carry on telling George how he was going to spend the £2 million he was going to win, but without missing a beat Billy just carried on the same conversation with the next customer.

So, with his newspaper tucked under his arm and skinny

roll-up jammed between his lips, George strolled down to his allotment.

He wasn't surprised to find there were a lot more people there than normal working away in their greenhouses, willing their leeks to grow. A few of them waved in his direction, but most of them were studiously digging or mixing up some secret potion to apply to their leeks. George unlocked his greenhouse door and shouted a hello to his leeks. He half-expected them to squeak back.

Taking a drag of his roll-up, eyes watering from the smoke, George glanced into the trench.

His leeks were gone.

5〉

For the first time in his life, Clancy Jr had a lot of cash on him. Cash he'd worked for. Well, that was the sort of work he preferred doing: kicking in doors and setting fire to things. He wondered if anyone had been killed in the fire. He hoped so. Shame his father hadn't been in his bed when he'd set it alight.

Now he had more pressing things on his mind: drugs – and where to get them. He was sitting in a park somewhere in the centre of Newcastle. He had no idea where he was and he didn't care. He hated this place but he had a plan: a plan that could get him money and get him away from his father. That meant it was a good plan.

But first of all, drugs. He had The Man's phone; he just had to scroll through the numbers until he found a likely name. Something like D. Dealer would be good. As it happened it was even easier than that. There was only one number in the phone. There wasn't even a name. Just the letter A.

'Fucking piece of shit,' he said as he hit the dial button.

The phone on the other end rang and rang and rang. Clancy Jr could feel his brain bubbling with anger. His fist tightened on the phone, although his grip wasn't too tight as he could hardly get his hand around it. Just as he was about to throw it at a passing car, a voice snapped at him down the earpiece.

'Yes?' it barked.

'I believe we could do business,' said Clancy Jr into the mouthpiece, surprising himself with how smooth and confident his voice sounded. He must've learned something from his father after all.

'What do you mean, do business?' the voice on the other end snapped back.

'Weeell, I took this phone off a silly little boy the other day when I was trying to do a little deal. I assume he was talking to you. So I want to do business with you and not some fucking SCHOOLKID.' Clancy Jr screamed the last word and this calmed him down. He heard a hand go over the mouthpiece at the other end. He heard a mumbled conversation, one person shouting and some men laughing.

The voice came back on the line.

'Meet in The Bonny Lad in half an hour. Bring some cash, big-shot.'

The phone went dead.

Clancy Jr closed his eyes and tilted his head back and, oblivious to anyone else in the park, started singing, 'I'm gonna suck the eyes right out of your head, baybee, because you love me too much.' It was his favourite Luscious song. There had recently been a court case in America where a 15-year-old boy, a Luscious fan, had tried to suck his girlfriend's eyes out. Luckily, he only managed one before she stabbed him up the nose with the aerial of her mobile phone, tearing his nose up the nostril. Her parents were blaming Luscious and the song. The singer was being sued for millions of dollars.

'We don't really know what to make of it, Mr Tree,' said Ellen Difford, the hotel manager. She knew she was on very dodgy ground. It wasn't every day you had to tell a billionaire, a very litigious American billionaire, that his son had gone missing, and he was suspected of carrying out the arson attack on the hotel.

'Do you think it could've been some sort of robbery gone wrong?' said a clearly concerned Mr Tree. He had already been on the phone in the hotel security office demanding his team of American lawyers get their fat asses over here to this tiny out-of-the-way island *now*. And at this moment she was sitting in the security office trying to be as calm as possible. On her left was her head of security Luis, looking as calm and collected as ever with his skinny hips and handmade suits. She knew he supplied prostitutes to the guests, if only she could prove it. On her right was Chief Inspector Biddy of Newcastle CID. He was very friendly with Luis and she knew why. If only she could prove it. They all seemed to looking at her in an accusing manner. As if it was her fault Clancy Tree Jr, who was, in her opinion, mad as a cat, had gone missing. It was she who had been fending off complaints from the rest of her well-heeled guests for the last five days. She knew just what Clancy Jr was like. She'd been up to his room trying to calm things down precisely seventeen times. Once she was even called from home at 3am to sort him out. God, she hated this mad kid.

'Hmm, it could be,' said Ellen, having no idea which way the conversation would go next. They'd already been through the possibility of a terrorist attack. Her head was pounding and her feet were killing her. Worst of all, she had no bloody knickers on. She'd met her boyfriend for a quickie in one of the rooms, when all hell had broken loose. She'd only just had time to get her shoes on when, luckily, the stampede of the guests leaving the hotel had concealed her whereabouts. If she'd been caught with him in an empty hotel room she would've been dismissed instantly. She shouldn't have a bloody boyfriend anyway. She should be happily married with children. She was 52, for God's sake. What was she doing hanging out with a 29-year-old rapper? She laughed uproariously inside at the idea of a Geordie rapper. He couldn't even rhyme. He had once tried to get all romantic and rap something to her. She would have preferred something other than: 'I'm the big daddy/And when I'm good and ready (see what I mean about the rhyming?) /I'm gonna scratch your itch bitch.' But it wasn't the rhyming she wanted him for. It was, well, she was 52 she would never get a boyfriend that gorgeous again. That stomach, and that …

'So I think it has to be a kidnapping,' said Clancy Tree to the assembled group, bringing Ellen back from wherever she was.

'Kidnapping!' she squeaked, before taking a glass of water in her shaking hand. 'I don't think it's a kidnapping.' That was the last thing she wanted, guests in her hotel, rich guests in her hotel, being snatched willy nilly. The shareholders and her bosses would take a dim view of that. She could even get the sack, and where would she get such a well-paid job at her age? She needed the money to keep herself looking good, so she could attract young rappers. She was a rapper slapper – a thought that, in her highly strung state, nearly made her laugh out loud.

'No, I do think it is kidnapping, Miss Difford,' said a confident Clancy Tree.

('Miss!' she hated 'Miss'.) 'But how can you be so sure?' she said.

'Oh there are certain signs there, which aren't visible to the layman's, sorry layperson's, eyes,' chuckled a patronising Chief fucking Inspector Biddy of Newcastle CID.

Luis, of course, nodded in agreement. She had the

impression the three men had started the meeting before her. Actually they had, due to the fact that she had been on the phone reassuring her boyfriend (urgh, she hated that) that, yes, she'd rescued his precious trainers from the room. But there was something more. It was as though they'd all decided to agree with whatever Clancy Tree said. Well, a kidnapping would certainly get her the sack, but on the other hand …

'A robbery. That's what it was,' she blurted out.

'You really think so?' said Clancy Tree, fixing her with his pale blue eyes.

'Yes. Definitely a robbery. And we should get on the case straight away.' She looked around the table at the three men, looking like a woman who was on the edge of, well, something.

'Do you know, I think you're right, Ellen,' said Clancy Tree, smiling more to himself than to them, she thought. 'I think it was a robbery. A robbery gone wrong. You're very clever, Ms Difford.'

Was she just imagining it or had she just been played like a violin? Or am I going mad? she thought, as she slipped her hand on to Clancy Tree's knee. Ah well, if she was going mad she might as well try and bag a billionaire on the journey.

'Ah don't know, Nellie. Is nowt sacred aroond here?' exploded George once again. He kept brooding about his leeks, then started shouting about it all over again. 'I mean they were just bairn leeks. They weren't ganna win any prizes. They were only little!'

'Well, I think it was a warning from Albie Donnelly,' said Nellie. 'Ye showed him up in the club, man.'

'Me? It wasn't me showed him up. He showed himself up. Fancy attacking an old man like me. What's the world coming to? Any road up, it was ye what threw him ower the bar, Nellie,' said George catching Nellie's eye. They burst out laughing.

'Ah divent knaa what your laughin' at,' said Big Fat Squinty Bill, levering himself into the Creedy's small kitchen and helping himself to a handful of Hob Nobs. 'I mean they were your pride and joy them, George,' continued the big man, spraying Hob Nob crumbs around the room in his indignation.

'Now someone's going to take your bairns and grow them up into superleeks and win the £2 million, whey, it's a tragedy, man, especially for me.'

'Hold on. I though you were going to win the two million pound,' said Nellie to Big Fat Squinty Bill as she mopped up moist crumbs.

'Er, slight problem there, Nellie,' said a very sheepish Big Fat Squinty Bill, squinting at Nellie.

'Oh aye. What's that then?' said George, his whole face twinkling in anticipation of a Big Fat Squinty Bill story.

'Well, you knaa I had a little leek trough in the living room. Ye knaa, like Wheelie Billy.'

'Well, I didn't,' said George, although he did suspect Wheelie Billy had showed quite a few people his front room greenhouse and they'd all copied his idea. He also suspected the wives and partners of the home leek growers wouldn't object too much to this ridiculous idea if there were £2 million in the offing. 'But carry on,' he continued.

'Well, it was that bloody *Changing Rooms*'s fault.'

George and Nellie were completely lost. They stared at Big Fat Squinty Bill.

'*Changing Rooms*, man,' said Big Fat Squinty Bill. 'Ye knaa. That Scottish lass off the lottery gans aroond changing people's homes into palaces for two quid or something.'

'Oh yes,' said Nellie, realising what Big Fat Squinty Bill was rambling on about.

'Carol Smillie, man, George,' said Nellie. 'You know *Changing Rooms*. They change people's homes about. You know, you're always shouting at it when it's on the telly.'

'Oh aye,' said George. 'So that Carol Smillie lass has been to your house?'

'Don't be stupid, man, George. The only way she could make our house look any better is by blowing it up, man. No, man. Me and our lass were watching *Changing Rooms*. We watch it every week. But I hate that long-haired Lawrence Llewelln la-de-da fop bloke. An' he was talking such a load of old shite about paint an' stencils an' that, that I threw me leek trough at the telly. I couldn't help it, man. He drives me mad.'

'Fair enough,' said a straight-faced George, before he and Nellie fell into each other's arms laughing.

'It's not funny, man,' said a sad-faced Big Fat Squinty Bill. 'There's mud up the walls an' on me Ronald MacDonald head. Our lass has gone ballistic. And now I have to decorate. I tell you it would've been easier to get *Changing Rooms* around to do it.'

'Ah well, at least your living room will look nice, and you can't blame Mrs Big Fat Squinty Bill for being annoyed. No one likes mud up their walls and on their Ronald MacDonald head,' said Nellie, trying to keep a straight face.

'It's not that though, Nellie,' said Big Fat Squinty Bill. 'It means I'm not ganna win the two million poond with me leeks an' our lass won't get her expensive nick-nacks. That's what she's annoyed at. She quite likes the new mud pattern on the walls. Thinks she saw it in one of those posh design magazines when she was in the dentist's the other week. I was on me way over to ask George here if he'd buy our lass some expensive nick-nacks when he wins the two million poond. Ye knaa, just something small in precious gems. Just to keep her happy. But then I find out your leeks have been stolen. So it's pointless asking you now, George. Our lass is ganna have to go without her nick-nacks. We are going to be a nick-nack-free house and it's all because of *Changing Rooms*.'

Big Fat Squinty Bill looked to the lino, a tear trickling down his fat cheek.

'Well, we can't have that, can we, Big Fat Squinty Bill?' shouted George, standing up and slapping his hand on his thigh, and looking and sounding like Robin Hood's granddad.

'We must win Mrs Big Fat Squinty Bill her nicks and her nacks, and I'm just the one to do it. Let's away to the allotment now, my fine fellow-me-lad.'

If Nellie hadn't been able to read George like a book she would have thought all of this was planned, but even Big Fat Squinty Bill wasn't that good an actor.

'All right, enter the competition, daft lad. But if you win I want you to give money to charity as well,' said Nellie, clapping her hands and laughing at her husband's antics.

'I will, my darling,' said George, pulling out his cap from his trouser pocket. 'But is there any better cause than Mrs Big Fat Squinty Bill's nick-nack charity?'

With a theatrical flourish, George exited through the back door nimbly, while Big Fat Squinty Bill lumbered out. Nellie stood for a while, smiling and shaking her head. She'd protect her daft husband and his nick-nack-winning leeks from anyone.

The voice on the other end of the phone may have thought it a very clever idea to keep Clancy Jr waiting, but it was a very bad idea indeed. The voice didn't realise it wasn't dealing with its own type. It could handle people from its own area. It understood them. But it certainly couldn't handle a deranged drug-ravaged, murdering, arsonist American, carrying two guns, whose brain was boiling at the indignity of being kept waiting. He'd already drunk four double Jack Daniels when four big blokes entered, spotted him sitting in the corner of the dingy pub and walked over to him. Because Clancy Jr was wearing mirrored shades, the newcomers didn't even know if the American was looking at them as they stood around his table.

'So you want to do business?' said the one standing closest to Clancy Jr, in a high-pitched, spiteful voice. It was Albie Donnelly.

'How do you know I'm me?' said Clancy Jr, staring at the four strangers, completely unafraid; confident he could kill them all and escape the pub easily.

'You've been identified,' said Pudgy Gee, trying to sound hard. The Taylor twins just looked fat. As a gang they weren't exactly *Reservoir Dogs* standard. If they had been in that movie they would've had nicknames like Mr Gormless, Mr Shaving Rash and Mr Belly. No, they didn't intimidate Clancy Jr at all.

'And who identified me, ladies?' said Clancy Jr, smiling his shark smile. At that the four apprentice thugs parted to reveal The Man. Clancy couldn't help it – he laughed out loud. In front of him stood the young drug dealer. He was still wearing the same tracksuit, thought Clancy Jr incredulously. It was covered in blood. But what made him really laugh was his head. It was swathed in bandages. He was looking through a tiny slit. Clancy Jr could hear his laboured breathing coming through the hole for his mouth. He didn't look well at all. If the gang had been expecting to intimidate Clancy Jr with the appearance of The Man, they were off-message. It was they who were now feeling threatened, standing there under the mirrored gaze of the laughing American.

'Fuck! Mummy boy!' laughed Clancy Jr. 'You look terrible. You should be in hospital, my man.'

'I was,' stammered The Man through the bandages.

'He discharged himself so he could identify you,' whispered Albie, trying to look threatening. Which usually worked when he was dealing with people he understood, but his hardest glare had no effect whatsoever on Clancy Jr.

'He got blood poisoning from that fucking grille you pushed him through. Could've died,' said one of the Taylor twins.

Clancy laughed even harder.

'Ladies, ladies, sit down and join me. We have business to do and then we can send that back to the hospital or fucking Egypt or wherever it is he comes from,' said Clancy Jr, pointing and laughing at The Man, who glared at him through the bandages.

'Not here,' hissed Albie Donnelly. 'We've a car outside.'

'Ooh lovely, are we going on a date?' said Clancy Jr, standing and walking towards the exit.

'I do love a first date. All that expectation,' he continued, as he leaped up the stairs. It all happened so fast that Albie and his gang didn't know what was going on, and it took them a second to realise that the American was leaving.

'Hurry up!' spat Albie to the rest of his cronies. Their exit wasn't helped by The Man being disoriented, walking into the girls' toilet and having to be rescued by the Taylor twins. It was lucky they managed to get out of there sharpish, or they might have found themselves on the receiving end of a good kicking by the delightful young ladies who were in there.

When the gang exited they were surprised to see that, far from escaping into the night, Clancy Jr was lying on the bonnet of a brand new BMW parked at the kerb outside the pub.

'Well, ladies, come on, let's go,' shouted Clancy Jr at the gang.

'Oi, what the fuck do think you're doing, sonny?' shouted a large shaven-headed man coming out of the amusement arcade across the road from The Bonny Lad.

'What's wrong, Butch?' said Clancy Jr to the shaven-headed man.

'I'll tell you what's wrong. That's my fucking car Stevie fucking Wonder,' said the man, as he reached Clancy Jr and dragged him off the bonnet by the front of his jacket.

'Oh,' said Clancy camply, as he pulled his tiny gun out of his boot and shot the angry man once in the face. Everyone froze. All except The Man, who was so disoriented and in pain that he was wandering off up the street. The gang could not believe what they had seen. The gun had hardly made a sound. Not one of the few people around had noticed anything amiss. Apart from the moaning mummy weaving up the street. One of the Taylor twins started to cry. Albie Donnelly was rooted to the spot, his face frozen and his small, spiteful mouth forming a perfect letter 'O'.

Reaching into the man's inside pocket, Clancy Jr took his wallet and then pushed the falling body out of sight under the car.

'So where is your car, gangsters?' said Clancy to the gang.

A stunned Pudgy pointed to an old Ford Transit on the other side of the street.

'Well, I suggest we make a quick getaway, ladies,' said Clancy Jr calmly, as he walked towards the van.

'Oh and you're all accessories now,' he added over his shoulder.

These must have been the magic words, because the moment was broken and they scattered towards their getaway vehicle.

Clancy Tree hadn't batted an eyelid at Ellen Difford's manicured hand sliding up his leg under the table. He'd had many women come on to him over the years. He knew he cut an imposing figure. He'd always been a good-looking man and he knew he looked good for his age. But that was precisely the problem. He looked good for his age. He was under no illusion that all of these women came on to him because of his looks. Why would an attractive young woman, and let's face it they were all young compared to him, want to get a pensioner into their bed? Well, there were billions of reasons and he knew it. That was the good thing about being so rich, you could do exactly as you wanted, he mused, as he watched Ellen Difford slink off to her own office across the hotel foyer.

He had, of course, gently rebuffed her advances by completely ignoring her. She looked dangerous to him; a woman on the edge of, well, something. But the policeman and the security officer he could deal with. He'd offered them £25,000 each as soon as they stepped into the room. He could tell by their greedy eyes that they'd take it. He'd told them the conditions in ten seconds, as they were waiting for Ellen Difford to arrive. All they had to do was take his lead and accept whatever he said. The Italian just kept his mouth shut, which was a good thing, but the policeman was very good at elaborating and backing up his story, which led Clancy Tree to suspect he wasn't a novice when it came to accepting bribes. He'd have to be watched.

Neither was his son a novice when it came to causing mayhem, and it was easier, quicker and cheaper to bribe the main players than to waste time and money going to court and paying off everyone who suffered because of the consequences of his son's actions. Over the years Clancy Sr had been sued by and countersued a lot of people. He'd once been sued by a dog, for Christ's sake. Snippet, a highland terrier, was being taken for its daily constitutional by its owner, 47-year-old Bradley Boohewn – Boo Hoo to his friends and co-workers down at the Spotted Hankie cocktail bar and notorious gay pick-up joint.

Just as Boo Hoo passed Clancy Jr's car, a ridiculous bright

red AC Cobra which was idling at the kerb, if such a car can really idle, because even when they're sitting in a garage quietly minding their own business, maybe doing a crossword or reading *Playcar* magazine, they look as though they're travelling at 100 miles per hour. Anyway, as Boo Hoo and his dog minced past, Clancy Jr snapped an AC/DC CD into the player. 'Whole Lotta Rosie', surely one of the best guitar riffs ever written, blasted out from the stationary, growling vehicle and Boo Hoo was so surprised he leaped back pulling the dog and twisting its little doggy neck. It had to be taken to the vet to have its spine realigned and, according to Bradley Boohewn, it was severely traumatised and off its doggy food and seemed to be listless. No doubt Snippet wouldn't have been so traumatised and listless if its owner hadn't clocked the car, recognised Clancy Jr and decided to go for a fast buck. The case was thrown out of court by the judge because of a technicality. Because, technically, married judges weren't supposed to be photographed in bed with waiters from the Spotted Hankie. That had cost him dearly. Although it was worth it just to see the judge, an old friend of Clancy Tree's as it happened, wearing leather hot pants. He was 67! 67! Everyone knows you shouldn't wear leather hot pants past 60.

So Clancy Tree was in Newcastle bribing people again to keep his son out of jail and his company out of the headlines. Now he just had to find his mad son before he did any more damage to himself or his father's company. Now he would do what he always did: get his hired bloodhounds over from America to find his son and keep him locked up.

'You see,' said George to Big Fat Squinty Bill, 'to grow big leeks you have to love them as if they were …'

'Budgies?' said Big Fat Squinty Bill, butting in his big face innocently.

'Er, yeees, budgies,' said George, wondering if the

throwing of his leek trench had somehow unhinged him. 'But like long green budgies that live underground and have no feathers.'

'Hmm,' said Big Fat Squinty Bill, concentrating hard. If he'd had a pencil he would have licked the end and started taking notes.

'So is there, like, special leek seed you have to give them then, George?' said Big Fat Squinty Bill. 'Or is it cuttlefish? Or how about a mirror? I bet them leeks would love to look at themselves to see how lovely and big and fat they're getting, or what about ...'

'Er, no,' said George, quickly stopping Big Fat Squinty Bill before he got further into one about budgies. 'What I mean is you have to talk to them and pet them and give them encouragement. So they grow.'

'Ahhh,' said Big Fat Squinty Bill. 'Makes sense.'

'Right. Let's get started,' said George, pulling the leek seed from his pocket. He'd had some given to him by Wheelie Billy the newsagent when he'd found out about George's disappearing leeks. Of course, Billy told George they were magic seeds and, if you planted them, lush naked lasses would sprout up from the soil. George managed to snatch them from Wheelie Billy's hand before anyone in the shop tried to get them. The way folk were acting at the moment, they'd believe anything.

'Now what we do is we plant these seeds in this special secret compost,' continued George, knowing everything he said now was going to be a pack of lies. Why would he need special secret compost? He could make his leeks grow with a bit of a chat. Big Fat Squinty Bill watched as if he was being told how to turn lead into gold. George poked his finger into the soil and threw in a seed. He repeated this six times. He lightly covered the seeds with soil and rubbed his hands together.

'Right, that's it,' he said, grabbing his cap from a nail in the door. 'Let's go to the club and drink to us getting Mrs Big Fat Squinty Bill her nick-nacks.'

Big Fat Squinty Bill was astounded.

'Is that it?' he said. 'Don't you have to say prayers or anything over them, or sacrifice a chicken or something?'

'Whey, no, man,' said George. 'That's for amateurs, man, and anyway chickens are budgies' cousins. No, we just leave them and tomorrow we'll come back and see how they look.' George gave Big Fat Squinty Bill a weak smile as he squeezed out of the greenhouse, beckoning to him to come with him as if they'd just put a baby to bed. As George was waiting to lock up, he noticed his friend was uncharacteristically quiet.

'What's wrong, Big Fat Squinty Bill?' said George, placing his hand on his mate's beefy shoulder.

'Well, I couldn't see much budgie care going on there, George,' said Big Fat Squinty Bill, squinting.

'Oh sorry, I forgot,' said George, pulling the door open and tapping the side of his nose conspiratorially. 'I do have one little thing I like to do. Who's a pretty boy?' he shouted at his leek trench, feeling like a right divot.

'Ah ha,' whispered Big Fat Squinty as if he was in church.

If he had been listening hard enough he would have heard the leek seeds give a little squeak.

'Fuck! Fuck! Fuck!' shouted Albie Donnelly in his high-pitched voice as he gunned the Transit away from the kerb, narrowly missing The Man, who had wandered into the road. He didn't stop to see if the young drug dealer was OK. Albie's eyes were wide with terror. That would've been because he was terrified. He had just seen a man killed in cold blood and the fucking maniac who had killed him was sitting right next to him, singing at the top of his voice. Fuck! he thought. What's he going to do now?

He was surprised to see both Lawrence and Derrick, who he had been in many a fight with, so he knew he could depend on them, sitting bolt upright next to the maniac and sobbing. Pudgy was rolling about in the back of the van shouting, 'No!' over and over again. Mind you, thought Albie, *he'd* be shouting 'No!' if he was in the back of the van. It was covered in compost and smelled like a horse's arse. Albie knew he had to keep calm if they were to get out of this and his gang certainly didn't look as if they would be any help.

'Shut the fuck up!' Albie suddenly screamed at the little American who was sitting next to him. 'Shut the fucking fuck up!'

The silence in the speeding van was so overpowering it seemed as if the clapped-out engine was holding its breath.

'Hey, don't you like Luscious?' giggled Clancy Jr, tapping Albie on the side of the head with the big magnum he had pulled out of his pocket. He had slipped his small gun back into his boot. He figured his new compadres would be more impressed by a gun they had seen in the movies.

'That wasn't fucking Luscious,' said Albie Donnelly, taking his eyes off the road and staring down the big black barrel of the gun. He found it hypnotic and it wasn't 'til Clancy Jr pointed the gun towards the windscreen that the spell was broken and Albie pulled the van hard to the left, narrowly missing a people carrier full of kids coming towards them. At that moment the woman driving the other vehicle was much more scared than everyone in Albie Donnelly's van.

'Oh, you're a Luscious expert, are you?' sneered Clancy Jr, stroking Albie's face with the gun.

Albie snorted, threw back his head and started singing, 'Baybeee, you wanna leave me, but if you do you're gonna be dead.'

'Stop the fucking car!' screamed Clancy Jr. The van fishtailed to a halt. The drivers in the cars behind them leaned on their horns.

'Do that again,' hissed Clancy at Albie, keeping the gun pressed against his head.

'Baybeee you wanna leave me, but if you do you're gonna be dead,' sang a terrified Albie Donnelly, expecting to be dead at any moment. He was astounded when Clancy Jr came in exactly on cue and sang the next line in perfect harmony with him: 'Cos baybeeee you try an' leave me, I'm gonna kill you in your bed. Hey baby, baby gonna kiiiill you right there in your bed.'

The silence in the van was absolute. The twins stopped crying and Pudgy stopped rolling around in horse shite.

'No one knows that song,' smiled Clancy Jr.

'Well, it looks like I do,' said Albie, returning Clancy Jr's stare. It was weird. The little American reminded him of someone.

'Hmm,' said Clancy Jr. 'Let me tell you a little story. You see, Luscious wrote that song for me.'

'Oh fuck off,' said Pudgy, from the back of the van. He was scared, tired, an accessory to murder, covered in horse shit and about to die. He didn't care any more.

'Why the fuck would Luscious write a song about you? And if he did, why didn't he call it fat, dwarfy, murdering, American psycho.'

Now normally if faced with this kind of outburst, Clancy would start firing indiscriminately. He'd once shot four skiers in Idaho because he thought their ski suits were too loud. But he was so surprised that anyone knew the lyrics to one of Luscious's lesser-known songs it put him in a remarkably good mood. He turned and smiled at Pudgy Gee who was now standing up in the back of the van, although a little hunched up.

'Have you ever heard the phrase, "Man who smells like shit talks like shit"?' said Clancy Jr to Pudgy, who by now was hunched up against the doors of the van under the scary smile of the scary American. Albie Donnelly giggled. Who the fuck did the American remind him of?

The Taylor twins didn't know whether to laugh or cry.

'Yes, I am very proud to say,' continued Clancy Jr, 'that I am a true disciple of Luscious. I was lucky enough to meet him when he first started the cult and I really am a true believer.'

'True talker of shite, if you ask me,' said Albie, starting the van and pulling away from the kerb. He didn't even check to see if there was anything coming, he just shot out into the traffic. He enjoyed hearing the screech of brakes and the blaring of horns. He felt invincible. It was as though, because he hadn't been shot by the crazed American sitting next to him, nothing else could touch him. There was an electricity flowing through him. He wondered if the others felt the same way. He took a sideways glance and found himself looking straight into the eyes of Clancy Jr. They were blacker than any gun barrel.

'Are you a believer?' said Clancy Jr to Albie.

'A believer in what?' said Albie. He was getting sick of this game.

'In Luscious, of course,' said Clancy Jr, the last two words coming out as a whisper between his fat wet lips.

'He's a fucking popstar, what's to believe in, man?' said Albie Donnelly, deliberately trying to wind up the American.

'Pull in over there,' said Clancy Jr, pointing to a row of empty parking meters. They were empty because they stood outside Leagreen, a small park known as a notorious hang-out for all the lowlifes in the area. The van and its occupants fitted in perfectly. 'And I will explain to you the cult of Luscious,' he smiled, giving each person in the van a hard, hooded-eyed stare.

6 >

Clancy Tree Sr was glad his new suite was just as good as his old burned-up one. There hadn't really been any damage done to the hotel, as the sprinklers had kicked in as soon as his bed had been lit, but he'd had to throw away all of his clothes. He knew from bitter experience that he'd never get the smell of smoke out of them. He'd quite enjoy shopping for more, though. He might even take Ellen Difford with him. He did enjoy having women flirt with him. It made him feel younger.

But far more pressing was the need to find his son. Clancy Tree had no idea where he could be. Normally he came running back when his money ran out, but this time he had more money than he was usually allowed. Clancy Sr was well aware that his son knew the code to his safe and had stolen his money. He had been doing that for years. But the canny Clancy Tree usually put just enough in there so that his son would have to come back at some stage. It was a game they had been playing for years, but this time the old man had slipped up. Stupidly, he had forgotten to empty the safe, so his son had emptied it for him. But the most worrying thing was that Clancy Jr had the gun.

'We're ganna win the money, nee problem, eh, George?' said Big Fat Squinty Bill later on in the Coronation Club.

'Er, whey aye, man, Big Fat Squinty Bill, man,' said George, nervously looking around the club. 'Look, keep yer voice down, man, I divvent want that Albie bloody Donnelly to knaa ah'm growin' leeks, an' I certainly don't want him payin' me a visit again.'

'Oh aye sorry, George, man,' said Big Fat Squinty Bill, squinting around the club. But no one was taking any notice of George and Big Fat Squinty Bill.

Most of the club members were talking about what they were going to do with the prize money. George had heard it all, from fast cars to helicopters. One bloke had even wanted to buy the Turin Shroud. The Turin bloody Shroud! At least you could do something with a car or a helicopter, but what were you going to do with a bloody shroud? Use it as a bedspread? Oh and another bloke wanted to buy two camels. Apparently his wife, whose only experience of animals was watching *Animal Hospital*, really liked the look of them, but thought they should get two so they could keep each other company and wouldn't miss the sand and cactuses and whatever else they had in the desert. This was also the same woman who assumed camels eat sand the way cows eat grass. So it wasn't as if their new humpy pets were going to have a long and prosperous life.

They all wanted the money so badly and they were all so confident they could win. The problem, mused George, as he looked around the club at the people he had known for most of his life, was that they didn't realise they'd have to put some work in with the actual growing and tending of the leeks. They all had a plan, an easy way of making a fast buck. But then, was he as bad as them? Nah, surely not. He was doing it purely for ... what?

Well, he supposed revenge. Revenge against Albie Donnelly. Was that worse than greed? Probably. Ah well, he might as well win the two million and decide then.

'What you smiling at, Georgie boy?' said Big Fat Squinty Bill to his mate.

'Weeell,' said George, looking around the club conspiratorially, 'I think we should start getting nick-nack catalogues sent to us from around the world. Can you imagine some of the nick-nack delights Mrs Big Fat Squinty Bill could get in the nick-nack department from, say, Brazil? Her nick-nacks would be the pride of the area. She could probably enter the world nick-nack championship they hold every year in Los Angeles. She'd be bound to win that. Even though she'd be up against stiff competition with the likes of Cher and Samuel L Jackson exhibiting. I'm sure she could at least come away with a commendation rosette.'

Big Fat Squinty Bill was beaming.

'George,' he said, looking at his mate with a soppy grin on his face, 'I think I'd better take you home. You've gone all Alzheimer's on me, you daft owld get.'

Clancy Jr led the way confidently into the small park. The gates had been pulled off years ago. Once, young mothers would bring their kids here to play on the swings or on the climbing frame or in the sandpit. There had even been a life-size concrete donkey standing on one side of the play area watching over the kids. Someone had stolen it. The effort involved in getting a concrete donkey out of there must have been Herculean. Everyone thought the concrete donkey rustlers thoroughly deserved their donkey prize.

Now the park was decaying and overgrown. On one side of the play area there was a forest of dense bushes. About ten homeless people had a little village in there. The village didn't appear to have woken up yet. Clancy Jr sat on the patchy overgrown grass on the other side of the play area, facing the forest of homelessness.

'Gather round close, ladies,' giggled Clancy Jr, making himself comfortable. 'Except you, shit boy, you can sit over there in the stinky person's area,' he said, pointing to a patch of soil about four feet from the rest of them. Why that should be the stinky person's area, Pudgy never asked. There certainly wasn't a sign up or anything. Albie Donnelly was staring at Clancy Jr. The three of them could easily take him now as he sat on the grass, but then what? Make a citizen's arrest? Turn him into the police? Or they could just kick him to death. But Albie realised he was having the most fun he'd had in a long time. He thought he'd go along with the mad American for a while longer; see what happened. And anyway he was a fan of Luscious so he couldn't be all bad.

The Taylor twins sat down facing Clancy Jr, their backs to the forest. Albie sat to their right, midway between them and the stinky person's area, where Pudgy Gee was now lying stretched out, his hands behind his head, eyes closed. Albie could smell him from where he sat. He didn't mind the smell. It was his smell after all. The smell of the compost he'd invented for his leeks. The smell that was going to win him £2 million. That was if he could get away from this fucking lunatic and get back to his allotment.

'So, my new gangster friends,' said Clancy Jr, sitting cross-legged, his black jeans pulled up, revealing more of the heavy boots he was wearing, and a Luscious logo which was a skull with criss-crossed Gibson Flying V guitars underneath it, imprinted into the expensive, looking leather, noted Albie. Fuck, this bloke really was a fan. 'First of all I want drugs, then I will tell you all about Luscious, who is soon to arrive in this shitty little country,' continued Clancy Jr. He actually felt quite relaxed, possibly because he hadn't had any drugs. 'So who's holding?'

No one answered. Clancy pulled out the big gun. They all stared at it, mesmerised.

'You wouldn't want me to get angry now, would you, my daaaarlings?' whispered Clancy Jr, as he pointed the gun at each of them in turn.

'They're not here,' blurted the Taylor twins. They often said the same thing at the same time. This was one of the rare times there were no swear words in the sentence.

'Not here?' said Clancy Jr, his eyebrows raised like a camp panto baddie.

He's Luscious, thought Albie Donnelly, stunned. That's who the little American reminded him of. It was staring him in the face, but because Clancy Jr was a little, fat, ugly bloke and Luscious was tall skinny and good looking, not that Albie would ever admit to thinking Luscious was good looking, it hadn't connected straight away. He does what Luscious does on stage. This fucking nutter acts like Luscious all the time, thought Albie, but at least I now have a handle on the fat dwarf.

Albie was a big fan of the American singer. He had seen him five times and had all his videos, so he knew what he was talking about. For some reason this made the American even more scary. 'So where are they, baybeees?' said Clancy Jr, a half-smile on his thick lips. Fucking hell, he was good, thought Albie Donnelly.

Derrick Taylor was staring at Clancy Jr. Lawrence was staring at Albie.

'In the leeks,' they blurted out at the same time.

Clancy Jr's face went bright red. If it had been possible for steam to come out of his ears he would have looked like an old steam train with lugs. He jumped up, walked straight across to the twins and hit them both hard with the butt of the big gun. 'Don't you talk about fucking leeks! Don't you fucking laugh at me with your fucking leeks,' spat Clancy Jr. Lawrence was unconscious, blood streaming down his face from a cut to his head. Derrick was scrunched up with his arms covering his face. He wasn't cut but his face was badly bruised.

'We're not laughing,' he screamed.

Clancy Jr stood over them, the gun panning from one to the other.

'The drugs are in the leeks, man. You fucking nutter,' said a calm voice. Clancy Jr spun around. He stared hard at Albie, who was now standing up, his big arms hanging by his sides. He was breathing heavilly.

'Don't you fucking start, boy,' warned Clancy, pointing the big gun straight at Albie. Pudgy Gee was asleep and was missing all the excitement.

'Look, baybeee,' said Albie, mimicking Luscious, although his heavy Geordie accent and beer belly meant he would never be coming through the steamy doors on *Stars In Your Eyes*.

'That's where I keep all me drugs, man. That's where I grow some of them. I'm a fucking dab hand as well. So if you want drugs I'll take you to them. But put yer fucking big daft gun down, you daft get, and calm down. And what do you have against leeks, man? I'll tell you what, they're ganna make me a fortune,' said Albie, nodding his head as if he had won the leek prize money already. Clancy Jr let the gun drop, and his hard stare turned into a smile, which turned into a hearty laugh, which was cut short by the shouts of Lawrence as a mad old homeless person from the forest brought him round by pissing on his head.

'Any word on the robbery, Ms Difford?' said Clancy Tree

into the phone. He was sitting in his son's new suite. He had no idea where his son was, but he had to keep up the pretence that he was around and about. He'd had some of his son's clothes sent over from the States. That was easy, since Clancy Jr always wore the same things. Except when his father forced him into a suit, which happened less and less now.

He had taken Ellen Difford out shopping with him. She had proved to be very good company, if a little too sarcastic, and she did have a good eye for clothes. Clancy was heartened to see she wasn't disappointed when he didn't buy her anything. So he bought her dinner. And she proved to be excellent company at the dinner table too and she didn't seem too disappointed when he went back to his room alone.

'The police are still investigating,' said Ellen Difford, as if reading from cue cards. 'I spoke to Chief Inspector Biddy this morning and he says they're confident of making an arrest soon.' She swore she could hear him smile on the other end of the phone.

'Hmm, good,' said Clancy Tree, distracted. He wished he could hand over the prize money and go back to America, but he had interviews to do to promote his company. He had to find new sites for other shops. But he did have one idea about the competition. He thought he should hurry it along a little and he had just the plan. But first, he thought, a little bit of fun.

'Would you like to have lunch, Ellen?' said Clancy Tree into the mouthpiece. It was Ellen Difford's turn to smile into the phone.

'You're not going anywhere till you've drunk your juice, daft lad,' said Nellie Creedy to her husband, as she bustled around the kitchen preparing their breakfast.

'Ah, man,' said George, looking like a petulant 10-year-old.

'I'm gannin doon the allotment, man, woman, man, me leeks need us. I haven't time for juice.' The look Nellie gave her husband ensured he would indeed be drinking his juice and in fact doing anything else she wanted doing around the house.

'And I'm coming down to the allotment with you,' said Nellie, trying not to laugh at her husband, who was drinking his juice in great gulps like a child.

'What do you wanna come doon there for, man, woman?' said George, his top lip now coloured orange from the carrots Nellie had put together with the apples and ginger in the blender. 'You'll only get covered in mud.'

'I'm coming down to have a look at your superleeks,' said Nellie. 'I'm planning what to spend our winnings on. Mind you, I could always dump you and get a toyboy.'

'Nee body would have ye, man, woman,' said George, suppressing a smile. 'Yer too cruel. Look what you're doing to me, a poor old man, making us drink yer juice, yer a witch, man, woman, a witch.'

'Well, you won't be wanting this,' said Nellie, putting a plate down in front of her husband. 'It could be poisoned.'

'I'll just have to take that chance, witchy,' said George, as he tucked into bacon, sausage, egg, beans and fried bread.

'You couldn't make some of that poison for me, Nellie, pet?' said Big Fat Squinty Bill, squeezing into the kitchen. 'Ah'm starvin'. Our lass has put me on a diet. It's not right, man. I'm wastin' away. I'm surprised the Red Cross don't send parcels to our house.'

'Sit yourself down, slim,' said Nellie. 'There's plenty more.'

'Ow,' shouted Big Fat Squinty Bill, as George stabbed him in the hand with his fork. It was his own fault – he had been trying to nick one of George's sausages.

Luckily Nellie put a plate of food down before poor starving Big Fat Squinty Bill faded away completely. Then she sat down at the table with a glass of her juice: beetroot, apple, carrot, ginger and celery. It was her favourite. She tried to keep away from the munching men who had their heads down and were tucking into their breakfasts. She hated being splashed with bean juice.

'This is champion, man, Nellie,' said Big Fat Squinty Bill, waving his fork in the air to show just how pleased he was.

'Don't speak with your mouth full,' said Nellie, taking a sip from her glass. George always wondered how she never got a juice moustache like he did.

'I'm dyin' to see yer leeks, George,' said Big Fat Squinty Bill, a sausage sticking out of the side of his mouth making it look as if he was smoking a cigar made of meat.

'Well, let's go, then,' said George, as he wiped his mouth, stood up, had a satisfying stretch, pulled his cap from his pocket, jammed it on his head, snatched his jacket from the back of his chair and headed for the door, with Nellie in hot pursuit. Big Fat Squinty Bill was astounded to suddenly find he was alone in the small kitchen with a plate of uneaten fried food, so he picked up his plate and followed George and Nellie down to the allotment.

The people they passed made no comment on the fact that Big Fat Squinty Bill was eating breakfast while walking along the street. They had long ago become accustomed to his ways, including the time he had a fight in the street with the mayor, who was wearing full mayoral garb. The mayor gave Big Fat Squinty Bill a right kicking even though she was a woman and Big Fat Squinty Bill's sister. There was another time when Big Fat Squinty Bill had managed to get his head stuck in the mouth of a Ronald MacDonald litter bin, and had ended up pulling the head off Ronald's body and walking home with it stuck firmly on his head. Mrs Big Fat Squinty Bill had removed it by covering his head with lard and slipping it out of Ronald's mouth. Needless to say

Ronald's head now took pride of place in their living room. If Mrs Big Fat Squinty Bill didn't want to know how he came to get his head stuck in Ronald MacDonald's mouth, the people he passed in the street certainly weren't bothered about why he was eating a full English breakfast in the street.

There was quite a stream of people heading down to the allotment. Most of them had the look of gold prospectors in the gold rush: grim determination and desperation. It's the same look you see on people's faces now when they are buying lottery tickets they know they can't afford.

The trio thought they would give Wheelie Billy's packed shop a miss. As they passed the front door they were just in time to hear Billy asking any of his customers who would listen if scientists had invented a helicopter wheelchair yet because that's what he was going to get one day.

When they finally reached the allotment the three of them were out of breath. None of them had realised just how quickly they were walking in their excitement to see how big the leeks were, but also if the leeks were still there. Nellie in particular was worried about the vegetables being missing, because if they were she would know Albie Donnelly really had it in for them, and her hot-headed husband would have something to say to him about that. George reached the greenhouse first, and snapped the lock open with the key, Nellie followed him in and Big Fat Squinty Bill looked over their shoulders, the way Joe Pesci did over the shoulders of Mel Gibson and Danny Glover in the posters for *Lethal Weapon 3*.

'Bloody hell, it's massive,' was all they could say at the sight that greeted them in the greenhouse.

'Bloody hell, what's massive?' said a voice behind them.

'Shut the fuck up,' said Clancy Jr, as he stopped dead before entering the allotment. He had both his arms spread out, stopping his 'gang' from proceeding any further. The fact he had his father's big gun in his right hand was enough of a deterrent. 'Follow me,' he spat, as he turned and pushed past the four big men and climbed back into the van.

'What's up?' said Albie Donnelly.

'Here, that's that rich American, isn't it? The one who's giving away the two million quid?' said Pudgy Gee, staring into the allotment. His hair was still damp from having the tramp's cider-smelling shower. The tramp hadn't known how lucky he was, as Pudgy would certainly have killed him if he had caught him, but as he tried to get up he had slipped in the tramp's piss, causing a muddy, pissy globule to be flicked down his throat. He really thought he was going to choke to death, but the quick thinking of Clancy Jr had saved his life, using the Heimlich manoeuvre, although this nearly didn't happen at all what with Clancy laughing so much at the tramp scene. It took a couple of seconds for the American to get his breath back and realise what was going on and use his first aid skills to save the fat Geordie bloke. When Pudgy could stand upright and had stopped coughing and being sick, he frantically searched the area for the pissy tramp, but he had disappeared. Luckily for trampy. That would certainly been have the last time he pissed on anyone's head.

When Pudgy returned from careering through the bushes, where he had made a very good job of shouting, swearing and swinging his fists at imaginary foes, he found the rest of the group still laughing at what they had witnessed. The bloodied Taylor twins were holding on to each other and giggling, Lawrence obviously hadn't been hurt too badly and both of their cut heads had stopped bleeding. Albie was doubled up laughing in the high-pitched breathless way he did and Clancy Jr was bellowing heartily, all his chins keeping time with each other. The fact that Pudgy was still so angry and smelled so bad made them all laugh even harder, until even he had to admit it was funny. And that's how they bonded. They were now a gang.

And that gang now sat in the van, watching what was going on in the allotment.

'Yup, that's that American bloke,' whispered Clancy Jr.

'But who's he with?'

'George fucking Creedy, that's who,' said Albie, still smarting from the scene when he was thrown over the bar. He didn't quite know why he was blaming George Creedy, but he knew he would get his revenge.

It hadn't even been him who had stolen George's leeks. That had been another jealous competitor, Organ Rob, who played keyboards in the Coronation Club and who had been disappointed to discover that without George's tender loving care the leeks had shrivelled up and died. His wife was annoyed because her plan was to take the £2 million to America for a new face and life with her lover, Bass Bob, who played in Organ Rob's band. The drummer was just called 'Drums'. He preferred the single moniker.

'What they deein' together?' said the Taylor twins in unison.

'I don't know,' said Clancy Jr. 'But whatever it is it can't be good news.'

7 ›

The news wasn't good. Well, it wasn't good for George's competition. Big Fat Squinty Bill knew it was good news for him and his quest for posh nick-nacks and a quiet life. The voice they had heard which surprised them so much had, as observed by Clancy's gang, belonged to Clancy Tree Sr.

'So?' repeated Clancy Tree inquisitively, his eyebrows raised in amusement. 'Bloody hell, what's massive?' Trying to imitate their accents but, of course, failing dismally.

'Er, nothing, Clancy,' smiled Nellie, quickly gathering her senses and forcing everyone out of the greenhouse, closing the door behind her. 'It's just our leeks are doing quite well. Thought we might be in with a chance of taking your money off you.'

'Well, as it happens, that's exactly why I'm here. To give you money.'

Big Fat Squinty Bill was squinting more than he'd ever squinted before. He had no idea how his two friends could be acquainted with the rich American. And he was going to give them money! Surely he couldn't have seen what they'd all just seen in the greenhouse. Clancy Tree pulled out the skinniest wallet Big Fat Squinty Bill had ever seen and from that he extracted two crisp £5 notes and handed them to George.

'I should ask you for interest,' laughed George.

'Well, you could try,' countered Clancy Tree. 'Why don't you speak to my lawyers?'

Big Fat Squinty Bill's head was spinning. Why was Clancy Tree giving George and Nellie ten quid? Luckily, when Big Fat Squinty Bill found himself in the presence of people with money, he found himself struck dumb. Which meant whenever he left Wallsend he was never his normal boisterous self, but was quiet and self-effacing. Mrs Big Fat Squinty Bill had known this for years, so sometimes she would tell her husband someone was rich just to get a bit of peace and quiet. Big Fat Squinty Bill never questioned how his wife could know the earning potential of quite so many people.

'That's not the only reason I'm here,' continued Clancy Tree.

'I've decided to bring forward the date of the leek judging. It's going to be four weeks from today. So you'd better tell those leeks of yours to start growing, my friends.'

Clancy Tree had no idea just how close to the truth he was.

'In four weeks' time the biggest leeks will win £2 million, no matter how small they are.'

Smiling, he turned to leave.

'I'm definitely walking back to the hotel this time,' said Clancy Tree over his shoulder. 'And I don't care what you say about Byker.'

'He's gannin'. The yank's leaving,' said Albie, as they all watched Clancy Tree step around the gardeners who were now clustered at a sign pinned up on the allotment hut. Most of the gardeners were so interested in reading what it said they didn't see the man who left it.

'Bye bye, Daddeee,' sang Clancy Jr in a high falsetto. 'Bye bye.'

Albie, who thought Clancy Jr was once again imitating his hero, Luscious, suddenly became very interested in their new companion when Pudgy Gee suddenly blurted out, 'I fucking knew it! I knew ahh fucking recognised ye, Yank! You're his fucking son!' Suddenly it all went quiet in the stinky Transit as everyone stared at Clancy Jr, who started to laugh.

'Well, are you his son, clever shite?' said Albie, shaking his head. He couldn't take in just why someone who was so wealthy would want to throw it all away the way Clancy seemed to want to. Albie knew if he had the chance of having so much money, there is no way anyone would get it off him and he could live the life he should've had. Which is why he was going to win the £2 million leek money.

'I am,' giggled Clancy Jr, stepping from the van. 'Come on, gang, show me your leeks and your drugs. It's quite safe now Daddy's gone.' He started towards the allotment. 'Well, come on,' he shouted back, 'don't you want to know what happens next?'

George, Nellie and Big Fat Squinty Bill could hear the shouting, but they weren't taking much notice of what was going on around them, because they were all staring back into George's greenhouse. 'Bloody hell, it's massive,' they all said, once again, in unison.

They were looking at the biggest leeks anyone had seen anywhere. Ever.

'George' said Big Fat Squinty Bill. 'You know you said leeks were like budgies?' George knew he had, but he kept quiet because he could feel the look Nellie was giving him.

'Well, if I was ye, I wouldn't breed budgies,' continued Big Fat Squinty Bill. 'They'd probably take over the world, and imagine how loud a budgie that big could shout? Ye would hear it shoutin', "Who's a pretty boy?" for miles, man. The neighbours would gan mad.'

The leek was enormous: at least six foot by two foot. There was only one of them left from the six seeds George had planted. It was as if this giant leek had destroyed the others, the way animals in the wild decide on the survival of the fittest. Needless to say George and Nellie were conversing madly, mentally, on what was going on. Blissfully unaware, Big Fat Squinty Bill just stood and gaped and mentally calculated the size of his new nick-nack cupboard. He was going to need a lot of wood.

I hope Albie Donnelly doesn't see this, thought Nellie to George. It's going to cause a right load of trouble if this gets out.

Ah we'll be all right, pet, man, thought George. Divvent forget you've superpowers man. Ye'll easy knack him.

'What ye ganna de, George?' said Big Fat Squinty Bill. 'Do ye think it's safe to leave it here? Someone might pinch it.'

'It'll be safe,' said George. 'As long as no one blabs about it.' George looked meaningfully at Big Fat Squinty Bill, who became all flustered.

'Well, ye knaa ye can depend on me, George,' stuttered Big Fat Squinty Bill. 'Discretion is my middle name.'

'I thought your middle name was pie-eater?' said a high-pitched voice behind them.

Nellie, George and Big Fat Squinty Bill had been so engrossed in their conversation about the leeks they hadn't noticed Albie and his gang come up behind them. The trio stared at the five newcomers. Even Clancy Jr was surprised at how fearless the threesome appeared. He wondered how they'd react if he pulled his gun out. But even he realised that would be a very stupid idea when surrounded by so many witnesses. Clancy Jr always appeared to be on the edge of madness, but he had a very calculating, cunning mind.

'Aye, that's very funny, cup boy,' said Big Fat Squinty Bill.

When you've been called Big Fat Squinty Bill all your life name-calling ceases to have any effect on you. Clancy Jr was amazed at the effect being called cup boy had on his new friend, however. Albie ran towards the fat man and tried to grab him by the front of his extra-large donkey jacket, but there was the not-so-slight matter of Big Fat Squinty Bill's stomach being in the way, and Albie Donnelly wasn't exactly slimline. They looked like sumo wrestlers on a day out to the garden centre. Big Fat Squinty Bill wasn't even fazed by Albie's attack. He might be a big fat squinty bloke but he could take care of himself. And Albie seemed suddenly distracted. He was looking over Big Fat Squinty Bill's shoulder at George. His eyes widened in shock before he was batted away as if he was a big fat fly.

Albie screamed at his gang to get the fat bastard, but they were surprised to find they couldn't move. That was a little trick of George's, who didn't think he would be able to pull it off because he was a bit rusty in 'The Thing' department. Clancy Jr was nodding, while staring at Nellie and George with a knowing smile on his face. George released the four thugs and three of them were catapulted forward. They landed on Albie in a mass of flailing arms and legs, each one of them trying to punch the other one. Even Clancy Jr joined Nellie, George and Big Fat Squinty Bill in laughing at the ridiculous sight.

'Get up now,' screamed Clancy Jr, in a voice that seemed far too deep for his fat little frame. This attracted the attention of the other gardeners working in the area, who were by now all staring at the scene. Two of the gardeners picked up shovels and started walking over to the heap of men.

'Ye all reet, George?' shouted one of the gardeners, a bloke called Charlie Nolan, who had served his apprenticeship with George before going on to serve four years for grievous bodily harm. He was staring hard at Albie Donnelly. He'd known him since he was a bullying boy and was looking for an excuse to give him a good hiding.

'Nah, I'm all reet, Charles,' said George. George always called him Charles, ever since Charlie's mum had asked him to on his first day as George's apprentice in the shipyards.

'Albie's just leavin', aren't ye, son?' continued George as he watched Albie untangle himself from the twins and Pudgy, and stomp over the allotments towards, his own greenhouse. Clancy Jr looked from Nellie to George and whispered, 'I think we'll meet again,' before strolling nonchalantly after his four gang members.

'Ah'm bloody nails, me,' said Big Fat Squinty Bill, brushing himself down and trying to look like Clint Eastwood.

'Nails!' said Nellie. 'I think you've a screw loose. That mad man could've killed you.'

'Whey, no, man, Nellie, man, pet, he's as soft as clarts,' said Big Fat Squinty Bill. 'Even his gang couldn't move. I tell you they were terrified of me. Like I say. Ah'm bloody nails, me.'

Nellie looked at her husband. She was shaking her head incredulously.

'And there's no way we can leave that massive leek here tonight,' said Nellie. 'Albie an' his gang will have it away as soon as we're gone.'

'I divvent think so, pet,' said George, scratching his chin. 'I think some of the leek growers are now staying here over night to protect their own leeks. Albie wouldn't dare try owt with them here.'

'I think yer right, George,' said Big Fat Squinty Bill. 'Him and his gang are far too chicken to try owt here. Hey, did you notice Albie has a new mate. The one with a funny accent. Do you think he's from Sunderland?'

'Sounded more like South Shields to me,' said George.

'He's American,' said an exasperated Nellie. 'Can't you tell?'

'Eh, no,' said George and Big Fat Squinty Bill together.

'Are ye sure he's a Yank, Nellie?' said George.

'Not only is he an American, he's Clancy Tree's son,' said Nellie to her bewildered husband and an even more bewildered Big Fat Squinty Bill.

'What the fuck happened there?' shouted Albie Donnelly to his three oldest and only friends as they reached the far side of the allotment where his greenhouse was located.

'Donnelly's End', as it was known, was by far the biggest plot there, because it had been owned by three generations of Donnellys. The greenhouse was also the most secure on the allotment. It may have appeared to be a haphazard construction made from bits of old doors, but this was exactly the impression Albie wanted to give. The whole structure was, in fact, held together by RSJs welded together and concreted into the ground. To the casual observer, it looked like any other greenhouse, but if you looked closer there were odd additions. For instance, the windows, which were scratched, dirty and covered in cobwebs, had a tiny kite mark in each corner. This would have informed anyone in the know that they were, in fact, double-glazed and reinforced. There were electronic contacts on the front door, which was reinforced with steel; and just visible, in two dusty corners, were the blinking eyes of burglar alarm sensors. But perhaps the most disturbing additions there were two tiny cameras hidden in the roof. These all-seeing eyes permanently watched over Albie's prize leeks, which were arranged around the walls in their troughs. The cameras were connected to cables that ran to Albie's house, over a quarter of a mile away. It had taken him a month and a mile of cable to install the cameras because he had to do it late at night and run the cable through his neighbours' gardens. All this so he could look at his leeks any time day or night. Sometime he just lay in his bed surrounded by posters of his hero Luscious, staring at his prize vegetables. He kept some compost in his bedroom to give it that authentic greenhouse smell.

Albie Donnelly had never been in the same room as a naked lady.

But it wasn't just his leeks Albie was watching over. There was his other business: drug dealing. Albie had become a dealer by accident, really. He'd been given some marijuana seeds and thought he'd try and grow them, just to see if he could; and if there was one thing Albie was good at, it was growing stuff. Pretty soon he had a crop of twelve healthy 10-foot dope plants in his greenhouse, and he had no idea what to do with them. Plus they were starting to stink. A couple of the older, well-travelled gardeners had taken to calling him Bob bloody Marley, although Albie had no idea why. It was Pudgy Gee who suggested they should sell his crop, and it took many days on the internet to find out how to turn their plants into ready cash. They soon realised they'd have to increase their yield if they wanted to make a lot more money. But how could they do that without attracting the attention of everyone else on the allotment? Even the most unobservant of gardeners would want to know what the smelly new plants growing all over the place were.

So Albie and Pudgy went underground. They simply dug a room under Albie's greenhouse. It took them six months and they had to get the help of the Taylor twins, but by the end of all the digging, stealing of materials and fitting out, the foursome had a home from home, unobserved, beneath Albie's greenhouse. Albie's original structure was 18 foot square. The new room was slightly smaller, at 16 foot square, but it was 7 foot deep. On the ceiling they had installed powerful lights to give the impression of daylight and there was an electronic watering and feeding system, which ensured their precious plants received all the nutrients they needed. There was also a ventilation system, which meant every now and then the gardeners on either side of 'Donnelly's End' got a blast of the West Indies.

So, with his new partners, Albie had taken to selling a bit of dope around and about. Mainly in the area of Newcastle called the Big Market, where all the kids go out and party hard and where the inevitable stag or hen night ends up. Out-of-towners usually end up there too. Mainly to gawp at some of the drunken behaviour and to tell all their friends back home that it's absolutely right what they say about Geordie women; they hardly wear any clothes no matter what the weather.

One Saturday night, Albie and his gang were in the Big Market selling little bits of their home-grown here and there, when they fell into conversation with one of the doormen who they had done a bit of business with. The doorman, Stormin' Normin' as he was known to three of his girlfriends, suggested to Albie he could make a lot more money if he moved into selling harder drugs, namely cocaine, and before you could say 'Henry Hill', Albie, Lawrence, Derrick and Pudgy were sitting in the back office of a well-known Newcastle nightspot discussing drug business with Frankie Younger, an infamous entrepreneur and bad lad.

At first the gang started small, buying a half an ounce of coke, just to see how they would get on. And get on they did.

The party animals that danced the night away in the nightclubs and bars couldn't get enough of the drug, and pretty soon Albie was having a cocaine-filled car tyre delivered to his greenhouse once every two months. Albie tried to build up a network of petty dealers but they fell away, mainly because they kept getting high on their own supply. The only person who had managed to stay the course with the gang was The Man, who, at that very moment, was sitting in his mother's council house nursing his fat-infected head. His mother told him she would look after him, but only if he went back to school – oh, and gave her a couple of free grammes every weekend.

You would've thought Albie and his gang could've made a bit of cash out of their dealing, but they had one thing going against them. They were stupid. The Taylor twins liked to spend all of their cash on matching designer clothes and strong lager, which also ensured they ended up giving a lot of their cocaine away. They had a lot of 'really good close friends', because of that. They hadn't seen their mother for ten years and had never met their father.

Pudgy Gee put his money under a loose floorboard in his bedroom at his parents' house, where he still lived. Unfortunately his parents knew this and made sure the cash went to a good home: Scottish and Newcastle Breweries. Then, of course, there was Albie. He never really liked the actual drug-dealing side of the business. He liked the growing of the plants. He was never too comfortable with the gang's branching into cocaine. He didn't really understand how it was made, although he knew there were plants involved somewhere. He spent all his money and time on his leeks.

There were many complex reasons for Albie being like he was. His father and the shame of his arrest was, of course, the main reason; the fact his mother was a lesbian was another. But the main reason he was such a fuck-up was that, deep down, Albie was a complete wanker.

'Yer fuckin' wankers. You could've given me a hand with the fat get,' shouted Albie to his three friends, as he deactivated the alarm on the front door of his shed. You had to look really, really closely at the top of the doorjamb to see the little recess there, covered by a slip of steel about the size of credit card. Behind this there was a keypad. When Albie keyed in the correct series of numbers there was a sound of electronic bolts sliding back and the door swung open on its well-oiled hinges.

The foursome stepped in the greenhouse.

'I mean we're supposed to be mates, aren't we? An aall ye could de was to fuckin' stare. Ye fuckin' wankers.'

'Ah couldn't move, man! Me legs felt aall heavy an that, man! I thowt ah was havin' a heart attack, man!' said Pudgy Gee, massaging his meaty thighs.

'The reason yer fucking legs felt heavy is because you're a fat chicken get!' said Albie, angrily pulling aside a tattered old carpet on the floor, which revealed a trapdoor set into the floorboards.

'He's right though, Albie,' said the Taylor twins in unison. 'We had fat legs annaall. We couldn't move either, man.'

Shaking his head, Albie twisted a brass handle recessed into the floor, and the trapdoor swung down revealing a set of sturdy metal stairs in the bright light.

'Fuck me, a James Bond bad guy lair. Maybe you guys aren't the bunch of retards I first took you for,' said Clancy Jr, as he stepped into the greenhouse, pulling the door closed behind him.

Big Fat Squinty Bill was deep in thought as he left the allotment with his friends. All this thinking caused him to walk even slower than he normally did. Nellie used to say that watching Big Fat Squinty Bill walk down the street was like watching a big sleepy squinty bear on wheels. It looked as if he was rolling not walking. One day she expected his brakes wouldn't work and he'd keep on rolling until he hit something. So it took Big Fat Squinty Bill five more minutes to arrive at Nellie and George's house and by that time his eyes were virtually closed from all the deep-thinking squinting he was doing. By the time he arrived, Nellie had the tea and Hob Nobs on the kitchen table, which caused Big Fat Squinty's eyes to open, though not by that much.

'Look, George,' said Big Fat Squinty Bill to his mate as he sat down and took two Hob Nobs off the plate in front of him. 'There's something gannin' on here, an' you have to tell me what it is.' The last bit of the sentence was almost unintelligible, due to Big Fat Squinty Bill slurping his tea down and eating two Hob Nobs at the same time.

'What ye taalking aboot, man?' said George, laughing. 'The only thing that's gannin on is us winnin' the two million poond, an' your lass getting a house full of nick-nacks.'

'It's just that,' Big Fat Squinty Bill started, 'ah've a bad feeling aboot aall the gannins on, ye knaa, with the big leeks an everybody getting greedy. There's a funny feelin' aroond here at the moment like, er, like an evil feeling.' Big Fat Squinty Bill stopped talking and looked embarrassed. Northern blokes very rarely talked about feelings, especially evil feelings.

'What do you mean, pet?' said Nellie, as she sat down next to the big man. 'Evil?'

'Well,' continued Big Fat Squinty Bill, 'ever since this leek thing started ah've noticed that folk have stopped taalkin' to each other an' they've started to be all secretive and that. Ye know I even heard little Bumpy MacItyre an' his wife have split up over the leek money.'

'Never!' said Nellie, shocked. 'They've been together forty years. Even when she found out he was having an affair with that blue-veiny-legged woman from the next street, the one who always wore that cardie with a pocket missing, that didn't split them up, so why would a leek competition?'

'Money,' said Big Fat Squinty Bill. 'They wanted to win so much they both started growing leeks in separate parts of the garden, man. Before they knew it they were accusing each other of spying on each other's leeks, man. Well, she's only upped and left. Living at her mother's she is.'

'Did she take her leeks?' said George.

'George!' said Nellie sharply, although she wanted to know the answer. It's one of those things lasses have to do when their husbands say stuff they want to say.

'Aye, she did,' said Big Fat Squinty Bill, 'and she's saying that when she wins the prize the first thing she's ganna dee is get rid of little Bumpy an' shack up with a Brazilian air steward. It's not right, man. Anyway how's she ganna meet a Brazilian air steward? She doesn't even knaa where Brazil is. People are gannin' mad, man. There's something in the air. I cannit help it, man, but I think something awful's ganna happen.'

Nellie was stunned. In all the years she had known Big Fat Squinty Bill this was the longest speech she'd ever heard him make without it having some sort of daft joke in it. Even George, who had been trying to make light of everything that had been going on, knew there was something up. Him and Nellie both sensed there was something coming, but neither of them could say what it was.

8 ⟩

Something was coming, and it was just about to land in Britain as Big Fat Squinty Bill was giving his speech.

That 'something' was Luscious.

The rock star was just about to start his British tour. It was only seven dates, but those dates were at Wembley stadium and each night had completely sold out. It was unheard of for any act to sell so many tickets so quickly, but his fans were so fanatical that some of them would buy tickets and give them away to non-fans so that they too could appreciate the Luscious experience. Every one of those non-fans after seeing him became not just a fan but a convert, and followed his every move. Just like Clancy Tree Jr and Albie Donnelly. Every other music act in the world hated Luscious for his success. Luscious landing in Britain was big news. His arrival featured on every TV channel and in every tabloid.

The *News Of The World* ran a 'Should We Keep This Devil-Worshipping Beast Out Of The Country?' campaign, following it up the next week with a, 'You Too Can Look Like Luscious,' feature, showing the readers how to get the Luscious 'look' but cheaper. It was hard for most people to get the Luscious look, mainly because the singer was six foot tall, weighed about nine stone and had blond dreadlocks which reached to his waist. Luscious was a singularly good-looking man, with high cheekbones and piercing blue eyes. His fans of both sexes would gladly have done anything he wanted. Luscious took advantage of this whenever he could.

As the Luscious entourage touched down at Heathrow airport in the Luscious 747, painted completely black, his trademark skull with two flying V guitars underneath it painted on the side, it was met by 20,000 screaming fans. The tabloids hit on a very clever comparison with the Beatles, in the same way that they always bring up the 1966 world cup final when talking about the England football team.

Luscious watched the pandemonium at his arrival from the top of the jumbo. His entourage called it his lair and could only enter if they were summoned. They dreaded the call. Luscious had some very odd ideas on how he should treat his staff, although they were completely devoted to him. Luscious always travelled with four people.

One of these was Enya, his Russian hair and make-up artist, who looked like the little girl in the movie *Leon* and never appeared to get any older, although she was the same age as Luscious. She had been his girlfriend many years ago when he first appeared in New York, and it was she who had first persuaded him to wear make-up and start colouring his hair. There was his manager, Scooby Breasly. Scooby had always worked with Enya and Luscious. At first he was their pimp when they worked the village in New York. Nothing much had changed in their relationship. He literally knew where the bodies were buried. Next there was his PA, Fairy Flowers. She looked like a miniature version of Luscious, the same slim figure, the same blonde dreadlocks, and she too had been with him from the start and probably had the hardest job of all, since she was the one who had to keep the stories about him out of the press.

Most of the tales about Luscious were so outrageous that his fans and the rest of the world treated them as if they were another chapter in a made-up story. It brightened up their dreary days. In actual fact these stories were the ones she herself had leaked. If anyone ever found out what the rock singer really got up to they would all end up in prison, and in some states of America the electric chair.

Finally there was his bodyguard, Junior. Junior had only been with Luscious for four months. He had been recommended by Luscious's last bodyguard, who had mysteriously disappeared. The reason Luscious only needed one bodyguard was that he could afford to hire the best, which is precisely what Junior was. If Luscious ever brought out an album which was all about Junior he would have to call it *Probably The Best Bodyguard In The World. Ever!*

Standing at just over 6 foot 4 and weighing a trim 14 stone, Junior would discourage the most determined of Luscious's fans from trying to get a piece of his boss with just a look. And being ex-Special Forces, Junior had seen combat in most countries in the world. Countries he shouldn't really have been in. So all in all, Junior was quite handy, but there was one thing he didn't share with the rest of Luscious's staff. He couldn't stand Luscious or his music. To Junior he was just doing a job, and it certainly beat hanging around jungles killing people with his bare hands.

There were two planes on the Luscious tour: one for him, and one for his six-piece band, although the singer hardly had any contact with the musicians apart from when they were on stage. The only musician he had any contact with was his guitarist Jimmy Gold, who was Enya's brother and the musical director. He gave the band Luscious's directions about the way the music should be sounding. Jimmy Gold was one of the finest guitarists in the world, but when Luscious played he made Jimmy look like an amateur.

The band much preferred Jimmy doing the arrangements. Even though they were a rock band and had all the rock band vices (vices which Luscious wholeheartedly encouraged), they never liked being in the same room as their boss and tried not to get too close to him. Sammy Blue, the bass player who also sang backing vocals, was the only one in the band to endure physical contact with the singer. Sometimes, in the middle of a show, Luscious would run across to Sammy's mic, fling his arm around Sammy's shoulder and sing harmonies with him. Sammy told the rest of the band that if he wasn't so full of cocaine and Jack Daniels he would run off the stage and never come back. Being touched by Luscious, he said, was like being touched by a dead snake. The rest of the band took the piss mercilessly, but they were glad Luscious ignored them most of the time. Only the Drummer, Kid Mikey, knew that before he joined Luscious's band Sammy Blue had been a teetotal Christian.

As the plane rolled to a halt and the fans at the airport screamed even harder, a bell rang in the plane. This was Enya's cue to join Luscious in his lair and get him ready for his public. As she climbed up the stairs to the top of the plane, Junior noticed there were tears streaming down her face.

Luscious may have had his lair soundproofed, but the rest of the passengers on the plane flinched as they heard Enya's pathetic screams from behind the locked door.

When the foursome had descended into what Clancy Jr had

called the James Bond bad guy lair, Albie, who quite liked being thought of as a James Bond bad guy, pulled aside another tattered carpet revealing a heavy safe concreted into the ground. Quickly spinning the combination into the lock he pulled back the door to reveal the contents of the safe.

Although it wasn't the most cocaine Clancy Jr had ever seen in his life, it was surprising to see so much of it in an allotment in Wallsend. There were four bags weighing about a pound each. Ideally they should have looked the way they do in the movies, when the gangsters finally reveal their stash. Unfortunately, two of the bags were Tesco bags, one was a Netto bag and the other had a picture of a duck on it. The duck was saying 'Happy Birthday Bernie'. Laughing, Clancy Jr bent down and pulled the duck-wrapped cocaine out of the safe.

'Fuck! Bernie's going to be disappointed he's not getting his present,' said Clancy Jr as he threw the parcel on to a table and pulled out a penknife. Albie noted it had the Luscious logo on it. Clancy split open the bag with the knife, scooped up some coke with the blade, took a hit and a big smile spread over his fat features.

'What the fuck,' said Clancy Jr shaking his head, 'do you guys cut this stuff with?'

The foursome looked at each other, incomprehension written all over their faces.

'Cut?' said the Taylor twins.

'Yes, cut,' said Clancy Jr, as he licked the coke off his fingers. Albie noticed Clancy Jr's left eye had begun to twitch.

'What do you add to the cocaine to make it go further, so you can make more of a ...' Clancy Jr's voice trailed off as he realised his gang had no idea what he was talking about. 'You don't cut it with anything, do you?' he said, shaking his head in amazement at their naivety. One of his eyes was watering. 'You don't fucking cut it with anything,' he laughed, slapping his hand on the table and causing a little puff of coke smoke to rise up from the slit bag. Clancy Jr tried to bite it.

'Do you realise you could have been making double your money if you'd been cutting it?'

'What do you mean cutting it?' said Albie, clearly getting very annoyed at being laughed at.

'You're supposed to cut the coke with something else to make it go further, so you can sell more of it, you dipshit fucks!' said Clancy Jr, now clearly agitated and swatting at imaginary flies.

'But what the fuck do we cut it with, man?' said Pudgy Gee, trying to see what Clancy Jr was swatting at.

'Anything,' said Clancy Jr. 'Sugar, flour, fucking rat poison, ground fucking glass, as long as those babies are getting their "stay up all night" they don't give a fuck. We could make a fortune out of all this coke,' he continued, as he stuck his penknife back into the bag.

'That's if ye divven't de it aall first, ye greedy fucker!' growled Albie, as he slammed Clancy Jr's hand into the tabletop. Then he snatched up the bags of coke, slammed them into the safe and slammed the door.

'But I've an idea how we could make a million. Well, two million to be exact.'

'I would normally kill someone for doing that,' smiled Clancy Jr, 'but you seem to have a secret plan and I would like to subscribe to your newsletter, so tell us the tale, Albeee baybee.'

It was only Albie who realised why Clancy Jr spoke the way he did, Pudgy and the Taylor twins thought he was a reader's wife short of a *Razzle*.

'We win the leek money,' said Albie, as if it was the most obvious thing in the world.

Clancy Jr pulled out the big gun and shot Pudgy Gee in the face.

Junior looked up from the book he was reading when he heard the door to Luscious's lair click open. Enya stood framed in the door. She looked unsteady on her feet. Her expression was glazed. She swayed on her high heels and, just when it looked as if she was about to fall over, she regained her composure and stepped out of the darkened room. As she walked down the stairs, Junior noticed she was limping. She seemed to be just about holding herself together. Even though she was staring down at the carpet, Junior could see she had bite marks on her face and the ends of her fingers. When she turned to walk away from him he could see her ribs through her ripped T-shirt and blood trickling down her back.

It was not the first time Junior had seen Enya hurt by Luscious. All of Luscious's staff seemed to get beaten regularly, even Scooby, who looked and acted like a New York hood. Junior seemed to be the only one Luscious left alone. Funny that. But even though he was making ten grand a week, Junior knew that if Luscious put one finger on him he'd cut it off and make him eat it. And he hadn't done the making-a-person-eat-his-own-digit thing in a long time.

The moment was broken by the plane doors being opened by the cabin crew. There were two of them: big fat men who were about as tall as Junior and were crammed into their black uniforms. They never spoke any language but Spanish and never took their mirrored shades off. Junior only ever saw them on the plane. The same was true of the flight crew, who were slimmer versions of the cabin crew. When they stood together they looked like brothers. What Junior didn't realise was that, apart from being real brothers, the five men were in fact ordained priests, but it would take a lot more than having their fingers fed to them to reveal which church they belonged to. If it was revealed who they worshipped, eating their fingers would be the least thing they would have to worry about.

Junior watched as the customs officers came on to the plane. That was the good thing about being so rich and famous, mused Junior, people came to you. But it was always a cursory inspection. No matter what country they went to, customs always wanted to facilitate Luscious in any way they could. Sometimes they seemed to be in the employ of his boss too.

Which was handy as it meant the entourage could bring in anything that they wanted. While the musicians took advantage of this by bringing in their own personal stash of drugs, Junior had a few things he liked to carry with him just to make his trips around the world a little more comfortable for him and his boss. In a shoulder holster he carried a Swiss 12-shot 228 pistol. He had the same gun strapped to both of his ankles. Not for Junior the tiny pearl-handled girl's guns most people had in their ankle holsters. His reckoning was that if you have a man's ankles, strap a man's guns to them. He liked to feel the weight against his legs. Around his neck, Junior wore a heavy silver necklace he had taken off a German paedophile in South America. The German had thought Junior was in that nightclub on that night because he had the same ten-years-of-age tastes as he did. Unfortunately for the German he started bragging to Junior about just what he liked to get up to with his 'dates'. Junior smiled and nodded and told him he liked his necklace as he planned ways to kill him.

Junior had actually been there to kill a drug baron. This he did quite spectacularly, by shooting him with a silenced Berretta from 50 feet, causing him to fall over a balcony on to a table below. In the confusion, Junior managed to stab the paedophile in the throat with a knife he had snatched up from the bar. It must have been a really painful way to die; the barman had been using the knife to cut limes – that's got to sting. The blow to the throat severed the necklace, so Junior assumed the German wanted him to have it. Snatching it up he quickly left the club. Junior thought of the killing of the paedophile as a little present to himself for a job well done.

Later, back at his hotel, he managed to fix his new necklace. It was heavy silver, and had blue stones set into each link. Just next to the catch there was a tube, and when Junior unscrewed it found to his annoyance it was full of pure heroin. So emptying it into the sink, he replaced it with strychnine, which he happened to have lying around from an earlier job and thought might come in handy in the future. When he tried the necklace on he thought it really suited him, it just needed one more tiny adornment. He attached a six-inch, lightweight, throwing knife to the back of it, so it hung down the back of his neck. It occurred to him that the necklace could be a lure for other paedophiles, but this didn't unduly worry him – at least then he could try out his new knife.

Junior touched the necklace, for luck, as he always did, as he saw his boss come down the stairs.

'Hey, Junior, baybee, you gonna look after me, baybee? I'm your boss man, my baybeee, which means you belong to me,' sang Luscious as he sashayed down the stairs. His accent today was fucked-up New Orleans. He was fully made up: jewellery, death-white face and full red lips. He was wearing skintight leather trousers and heavy biker boots. Slung low on his skinny hips was a heavy leather belt. It had a silver buckle in the shape of a snake. His T-shirt, although ripped and sewn back together, obviously cost a fortune. He glows, thought Junior, as he stood up to greet his boss. Must be a rock star thing.

'Yeah yeah, boss man, gonna look after yo skinny white ass,' said Junior, laughing, as he took his familiar place on Luscious's right side. Luscious had explained that was his blessed side, since, being a left-handed guitar player, his right hand must be protected at all times. Junior could've quite happily chopped his right hand off, there and then.

'So, baby, Junior, waddya reading?' said Luscious, as he glanced at the book on the seat Junior had vacated.

'Oh it's about crazy stuff you probably don't know about, boss rock star,' said Junior, trying to keep the conversation light but also trying hard not to kiss ass.

'Oh and what don't I know about my big black bodyguard bear?' said Luscious, as he turned his mirrored gaze on his minder.

Junior felt his knees buckle slightly. The plane must've moved, he thought.

'You,' said Junior, trying to see his boss's eyes through the mirrors that covered them, 'know nothing about joinery and neither do I. That's why I'm reading about it.'

Junior snatched the book up from his seat and showed it to Luscious.

'I've just bought a new house and I'm gonna do it up as soon as we finish this tour. Do you wanna borrow it, boss? I can tell you're a bit of a DIY person,' Junior continued, a cheeky smile sliding across his big face.

The entourage was held spellbound by the conversation. No one talked to their boss like that, innocuous as the conversation was.

Luscious took the book out of Junior's hand. Junior noticed his knuckles were bleeding. Luscious smiled languidly.

'You'd be surprised, Junior, my man, at the things I do know. I even know about joinery. Why don't you ask my man Scooby here? We built crucifixes with our own fair hands in the early days. Isn't that right, Scoooooooby bayybeeee?'

Scooby nodded distractedly.

'Used to be a lot of folk liked to get hung up and whipped oh yes, oh yes, oh yes.' Luscious licked his red lips and turned his eyes to Enya, who was leaning against a seat for support. She shivered under Luscious's gaze.

'You know?' said Luscious. 'I will borrow this book. Come, let's go and meet the world.' And with that he turned and strode from the plane, Junior at his right side and his entourage trailing behind.

Albie Donnelly's world was turned upside down. The noise of the gun in the confined space turned them all instantly deaf. What Albie had at first thought was bells ringing was, in fact, a high-pitched screaming in his ears. The horror of what Albie had seen happen to his oldest friend was so acute he thought the outside world would've momentarily come to a standstill. He expected the people working in the allotment to come streaming down the stairs into the basement to rescue them from the crazed American. Surely they must've heard the gunshot.

Everything had not, as Albie would've expected, moved in the clichéd slow motion the way it did in the movies. If anything, everything had speeded up like a cartoon. Even the colours seemed brighter, but that may have been due to the flash from the gun. One moment they were all standing there, as normally as they could given the situation, the next the American had shot Pudgy Gee. But shot was too small a word for what happened to Albie's oldest friend. His head had been blown right off. Everyone in the room was covered with blood and brains, and for a second Pudgy stayed standing, as if not sure what had happened. Then a geyser of blood erupted from the hole in his shoulders where his head had been and the body crumpled to the floor. It didn't even twitch and Albie remembered thinking, That's not how it happens. A body with its head shot off should twitch. That's how it happens in the movies. Then, with a sudden comprehension, he realised that all the movies he had been hiring from the local video shop had been lying to him. Bodies don't twitch when they have their heads blown off.

The screaming in his ears seemed to be getting louder as he wiped the gore from his face. Clancy Jr was standing exactly where he had been when he shot Pudgy, although he was now swatting imaginary flies with the heavy gun. Albie realised the screaming in his ears was the Taylor twins. They were lying on the floor holding each other, the way they had held each other in their mother's womb. The reason they had held each other so tightly inside their mother was that they were usually drunk. Throughout her pregnancy, Mrs Taylor never saw fit to moderate her intake of whisky or cigarettes. Even as tiny foetuses the twins were always drunkenly hanging on to each other, each telling the other that he was his 'beshht mate'. Now they lay on the floor, holding each other tight, their eyes screwed tight shut, covered in blood, screaming the way they had when as tiny children they had tried to protect each other from the violence of one of their mother's many boyfriends.

Clancy Jr stared at them as if suddenly realising they were there. He skipped over to where they were lying and began to dance around the twins, wiggling his fat little hips. Even though Albie couldn't hear the words to the song, he instinctively knew it was by Luscious and it was called 'Bury My Baby, Baby'. Albie knew the song well and he fast forwarded it in his head. Just as he reached the chorus, where Luscious sang, 'And then I killed the twins,' he rushed forward. But it was too late. Clancy Jr pulled out his tiny handgun and shot the twins through the head. That ended their screaming and their suffering.

Albie collided with the American, knocking him to the floor. Even though Albie was twice his size, he had no strength in his body at all. He wanted to kill the American and would have if he could've raised his fists, but he just lay there next to Clancy Jr, great, wracking sobs exploding from deep in his chest. Albie had never cried this bad, not even when his father had been sent to prison. Now he lay there, curled up, while next to him Clancy Jr started doing sit-ups, the hands behind his head still clutching his tiny gun.

At that precise moment, Clancy Tree Sr had his hands behind his head too, but they were neither bloodstained nor holding a gun. He had the same look of concentration on his face, though, as he surveyed the two men in front of him. One was his lawyer, Ivan Cresswell, although his birth certificate had said his name was Ivana. Only Clancy Tree Sr knew this. The other man was a private detective called Michael Satriani. Clancy Tree had used him many times in connection with his son and while he didn't trust him completely he trusted him enough, but then again he was being paid a lot of money. There was another man waiting outside who was a colleague of Mr Satriani. If he had a name it was never offered and he never spoke. Not even Clancy Tree knew who he was but he suspected he and Satriani were lovers. Straight men could not be that good looking.

'I don't believe you can't find him,' said an exasperated Clancy Sr.

'Look at the size of this place. My ranch in Idaho is bigger than this whole town. Shit! The toilet on my ranch in Idaho is bigger than Wallsend and it's cleaner and with more amenities!' This got a laugh from the two men sitting opposite Clancy Sr, although laughs were not what he wanted. What he wanted was his crazy son back before he did any more damage.

'There's not a trace of him,' said Michael Satriani. 'I've been all over Wallsend and the burgh next door, er ...' he looked at his notes, 'Newcastle-upon-Tyne. I even drove over the river and had a look around. But ... well, to be honest there's not much there. Then there's the language problem.'

'They speak English,' said Clancy Sr, shaking his head.

'Do they?' said Satriani. 'Well, can someone tell them? I have no idea what they are talking about most of the time and they all think I'm from a place called Sunderland, whatever that is. Someone even called me a monkey hanger and that was the only bit I could understand. Why would I want to hang a monkey? When I explain I'm from America they start laughing and doing John Wayne impressions. A bunch of young women asked me if I knew Michael Jackson and one of the ladies in the group asked me if she could see my American cock to see if everything in America was as big as they say.'

'And did you show her?' said Ivan Cresswell, who up to then hadn't tasted the delights of Newcastle-upon-Tyne and the surrounding areas and was taking what Satriani said with a handful of salt, although he'd never known the good-looking, hard-bitten detective to exaggerate before.

Satriani burst out laughing.

'Yeah, yeah, of course I did. I got my big American dick out in the street,' he said, wiping his eyes. 'Hell, I wouldn't even get my dick out for of these girls if we were alone in a hotel room. They have a look in their eyes I haven't seen since I was in active combat.

'Jesus,' breathed Ivan Cresswell, who couldn't imagine any woman anywhere asking him to get his dick out.

'As much as I'd love to carry on a conversation about your

pricks, you pricks,' said Clancy Tree, 'is there any chance we could get back to the matter in hand?'

'Well, I do have one bit of news I picked up from around and about,' said Satriani.

'Yes?' said Clancy Tree, placing his elbows on the highly polished table in front of him.

'Luscious,' said the detective.

'Fuck!' shouted Clancy Tree and Ivan Cresswell at the same time.

'He's not here, is he?' said Clancy Tree.

'No, he's in London,' continued Michael Satriani. 'He's doing seven nights at Wembley stadium, and from what I can gather that's quite a feat.'

'Yes, you can't go anywhere in the world without seeing his made-up face leering down at you. Well, if we can't find Clancy Jr here, we certainly know where we will find him: with his hero, Luscious. I wonder if he's changed at all since we last met him.'

'I wonder how his bullet wounds have healed,' said Michael Satriani, deadly serious.

Luscious's bullet wounds had healed up very well indeed. In fact, they would've killed anyone else who had taken them, but now Luscious boasted four scars: two very small entry wounds on his chest, but two very large exit wounds on his back. The scars on his well-muscled back always received the most attention, as fans always said one of them looked like God and one of them looked like the Devil. Before he died, American comedian Bill Hicks said he thought they both looked like Phil Collins, who in his opinion had done about as much for modern music as Luscious had. Bill's belief had been captured on a live bootleg album and you can hear him being cheered most vociferously for this opinion.

Anyway, both bullets had missed Luscious's heart by centimetres. Although they had gone through both his lungs, somehow he had survived. Of course, this all added to his allure. An attempt on a rock star's life makes him even more appealing. The attack on Luscious had made every TV station and newspaper in every country in the world and the sight of a good-looking, muscular rock star fighting for his life did wonders for his record sales. Even journalists that would normally have nothing to do with his type of music or would ridicule the type of life Luscious led, began to write about how misunderstood he was and the irony of his lyrics. Lyrics from songs such as 'I'm A Nazi and I'm Gonna Eat Your Kids'.

Pretty soon, Luscious was the biggest thing in the world. His 'irony' was loved by everyone, which was why there were so many people here to greet him as he touched down on British soil. There were a few detractors in the awaiting throng but not many media folk took much notice of 'Lesbians against Devil Worshippers' or 'Christian Anorexics against Satan'. The latters' banner originally read, 'Christian Anorexics against Stan', until a helpful policeman pointed this out to them and they managed to change it using lipstick and felt pen.

So with Junior at his right hand, Luscious stepped off the plane to be greeted by the world's press. If there was one thing Luscious was good at it was manipulating the media. As soon as the flashbulbs started popping, Luscious grabbed on to Junior for support, as if he was suffering from some life-threatening illness. He pretended to stagger at every step. This, coupled with the fact he was clutching a book called *Joinery For Beginners*, had his fans all over the world trying to fathom the mystery that was Luscious. Fashion editors around the world sent their minions off to find the book and all copies were sold out within weeks, which was nice for the author, Andy Carr, a presenter on a little-known cable TV show called *Change Your House*. With the royalties from his book, he not only changed his house but his wife and his mistress.

Junior alone knew just how healthy Luscious was, as he could feel every muscle and sinew move against his body. The only time Luscious came alive was when a young girl broke away from the cordon and ran towards her hero. Luckily she was carrying nothing more threatening than a bunch of flowers, so Junior was able to quite gently fend her off, but he felt Luscious's body flex and he knew then his boss was aware of everything that was going on around him. Junior half-carried, half-dragged Luscious to his waiting limo as the entourage fussed behind them and the local police did all the real work. Still they enjoyed the overtime and most of them were fans of Luscious and would have worked for free anyway.

The Mercedes driven by Junior sped down the M4, away from Heathrow and towards the centre of London. Behind them followed the entourage in an identical Mercedes and the band, which travelled in a luxury tour bus which was much more comfortable than the car their boss was travelling in. They were followed all the way by the paparazzi, who were on powerful motorbikes, and fans who were driving everything imaginable but took dangerous chances trying to keep up with their idol. Junior was well qualified for this type of driving and kept his passenger safe. The roads actually became safer the closer they got to London as the amount of traffic meant they had to slow down. The photographers abandoned their bikes when they hit a traffic jam and rushed up to the limo, trying to get a shot through the window, which was impossible as they were so heavily blacked out. Some of the fans who left their cars and attempted to peer in at their hero were left behind as the traffic began to move again and had to rush back to their vehicles, dodging cars and bikes and insults thrown by irate London drivers who had no idea what they were up to.

All the way down the motorway Luscious kept up a running commentary on the sights and sounds which were unfolding before them. Junior was surprised at just how knowledgeable Luscious was on Britain, as he had considered himself quite an expert. He had been in Britain and Ireland many times working, although most of that time had been spent so undercover that he was living in fields and bushes.

Luscious and his entourage weren't actually staying in London but a little further north in a mansion he had hired. There was enough room for him and his band but the most important thing was they had privacy. So when Junior reached the turn-off for the North Circular, he accelerated up the exit ramp and joined it at the Hangar Lane roundabout, to a background of Luscious voiceover. Just before they reached the turn-off for the M1, Luscious shouted for Junior to pull over. As he did so, to a chorus of beeping horns from the cars they had cut up by swinging across the lanes, a beaten-up rusting Fiat 126 pulled up behind them on the hard shoulder. Junior was instantly on his guard.

In one cat-like jump, Luscious was out of the car and running towards the Fiat, quickly followed by Junior, his hand inside his open jacket. Luscious reached the car, pulled open the driver's door and dragged out the motorist, a pale blonde girl whose skin was so white she seemed transparent. Luscious picked her up and carried her to the limo. The entourage hadn't even caught them up yet. Junior guessed correctly they'd been caught at the lights at the last slip-road. Luscious and the now giggling girl climbed into the limo followed by Junior, who gunned the engine and sped off into the traffic. All of this had taken five seconds.

Junior at first doubted it had even happened until he glanced in the rear-view mirror and watched the smoked privacy glass slide up. He saw the blonde girl staring rapt into Luscious's eyes. He was licking his lips as if he was about to devour her.

When Albie woke up he had no idea where he was. He must've been asleep a long time because all his muscles were cramped, and that fucking dream. Albie was instantly awake. He shot up. He had been lying under some black bin liners. There was blood on them. 'Fuck, fuck, fuck!' he shouted, staring wide eyed around the room for his dead friends. The bodies were gone but there was blood everywhere. Much more blood than he remembered. There was a neatly folded pile of clothes in the corner. Fuck, he was going mad. And talking of mad, where was the crazy American?

'Fuck indeed,' said a voice above Albie's head. He spun around to see the American looking down at him from the trapdoor, a big grin on his face. He was covered in mud and blood. He looked hideous.

'I've been doing a little gardening,' said Clancy Jr. 'A little planting, but let's hope those babies don't pop out in the spring.' He began to giggle at his own joke.

'What have ye done, ye crazy fucker?' shouted Albie at the American as he climbed down the steps. Albie could now see how filthy the American was. He was also completely naked.

'Well, I had to get rid of the bodieeees, didn't I? So I planted them,' said Clancy Jr, one muddy eyebrow raised archly. 'You're gonna have to hose me down. That'll be fun for you. It'll be like a first date.'

Albie threw up with retching gasps, mainly at the thought of the American burying the bodies, but there was a bit of him that was repulsed at having to hose down his fat little body. He threw up again. He had one arm against the wall. He was sweating and throwing up whatever else he had in his stomach. Which wasn't much. When he recovered he wiped his mouth with the back of his hand. The smell in the room was repellent. Blood, vomit and shit. Pudgy would've said it smelled like his last girlfriend, but Pudgy was dead. Great wracking sobs suddenly exploded from Albie and he fell to his knees, saliva hanging in great strands from his quivering lips.

'Ye fuckin' killed them, ye fuckin' killed them. Ye fuckin' killed me mates,' sobbed Albie.

'No, no, no, my darling,' said Clancy Jr, unconcernedly picking mud from his flabby chest. 'I will tell the police we both killed them and chopped them up together. They don't like that sort of thing, you know. That's one thing I do know. That killing folk, chopping them up and burying them thing is a no no.'

Albie had his head in his hands, sobbing pathetically.

'What do you mean chopped them up?' said Albie, speaking through his fingers and staring straight at the American, his tears drying on his face.

'Well, how do you think I managed to get the bodeeeees out of here?' whined Clancy Jr, staring at the ceiling. 'I couldn't carry them, they were far too heavy for little old me. So I chopped them into itsy-bitsy pieces and planted them all over your lovely allotment.'

Albie threw up again and it really hurt his chest. No wonder there was more blood than he remembered. It must have been like a butcher's shop. A thought flashed through Albie's mind: he was in the presence of a serial killer – a real American serial fucking killer. It was like being in a movie. Albie wondered if they'd make a movie about all this. Of course they would, everyone loved serial killer movies. But who would they get to play him? He hoped it wouldn't be some fucking nancyboy like Brad fucking Pitt. Albie wanted Stallone, Schwarzenegger or, at a push, Bruce Willis to play him. Mind you that *Gladiator* bloke would be quite good too.

Albie burst out laughing. He couldn't hold it in. He lay on the floor gasping for air, laughing like he'd never laughed before. He was going mad, he thought. Clancy Jr surveyed all this as if it was the most natural thing in the world. When you go around killing people and chopping them up, I suppose it is.

'I'm glad you find it also amusing, my darling. Now what's a girl got to do to get a shower round here?' said Clancy Jr, doing a little dance on the spot. This caused Albie to laugh even harder, especially when Clancy began to climb up the steps and his fat arse was jiggling about. Albie rolled into a ball and roared with laughter.

The Luscious entourage had caught up with their boss by the time they reached their exit off the M1. Luscious had rolled the privacy screen down and was giving Junior directions as they sped down country roads. The blonde girl was curled up asleep on the seat like a tiny white cat, her impossible blonde hair fanning out from her head. Even though Luscious's directions were quite difficult to follow because he insisted on singing them, Junior managed to keep up which was more than could be said for the vehicles following them, whose drivers obviously hadn't had Junior's training. Junior was driving particularly fast on purpose to see if he could make his boss a tiny bit frightened. This was because, as the little blonde girl woke up and stretched, Junior noticed she had bite marks on her. Although he had killed many people in his life, including women, Junior abhorred unnecessary violence, so he took great delight in watching his boss flinch when he pretended to lose the car on a tight bend.

Luscious indicated to Junior he should take the next left and he swung the big car into what looked like a solid wall of leaves; however these parted to reveal a gravel drive winding uphill. Junior gunned the car and it shot forward throwing gravel and stones out from under the wheels. As the car reached the summit, Luscious told Junior to stop, and as the car rolled to a halt the house below was revealed. When Luscious had told Junior they would be staying in a mansion he wasn't too impressed. He had stayed in quite a few luxurious places over the years. Even his own home was pretty impressive and his friends jokingly called that 'the mansion', but nothing had prepared Junior for this. Across a lake and set in hundreds of acres of land stood a massive building with no redeeming features at all.

Junior had expected it to be a massive gothic horror-type place. It looked like a cross between an office block and a hospital. Junior pushed open the door and climbed out of the car. As he stared down at the appalling building he heard his boss come up behind. He didn't turn around.

'Fucking horrible, isn't it?' Luscious whispered in his ear.

'Sure is,' said Junior. 'Why would someone build this here, and why are we staying here, surely there's better places than this?'

'Ah, my darling builder boy,' said Luscious camply, he still had Junior's book in his hand, 'it was built by an Arab, er, friend of mine. He needed to lose some money quickly and he really had no idea about architecture. The reason we're staying here is that it's probably the most secure building in Britain. Very touchy about security was my Arab friend, very touchy. He's dead now. Drowned in that very lake.'

Luscious grabbed the pale-skinned girl's hand. She had

crept up on them when they had been talking, although Junior knew she was there. Lucious began to run downhill towards the house, dragging the girl behind him. Junior heard the other vehicles enter the property so he climbed into the Mercedes and drove down to the front of the house.

As he pulled up he realised that there was no front or back to the house. It was the same on every side. It had been built using sandstone bricks and it was ten storeys high. He was surprised it couldn't be seen from the road. Every side of the structure was covered in massive windows that were impossible to see in through as they were blacked out like all of the Luscious cars. Once again Junior climbed out of the car. He tried the front door and found it was locked. He would just have to wait for Luscious. He sat down on one of the two stone seats that were on either side of the door and began to trace patterns in the gravel with the toe of his shoe. He had unwittingly drawn the Luscious logo, and was just asking himself why he had done that when the other two vehicles pulled up. Scooby climbed out of his car first and greeted Junior.

'I hate this fucking place and where's our fucking star?' said Scooby, flicking away a cigar butt into the shrubbery and not waiting for an answer from Junior. 'Why can't the fucking country be in the city? Make it easier for all of us.' Scooby pulled a six-inch tube out of his pocket, tugged at either end, Junior heard a click and the tube grew in length like a car aerial; it had doubled in length. A light glowed at one end. Scooby approached the door and inserted the tube into a tiny hole at about eye height. He compressed the tube and there was the sound of tumblers turning, as if a giant safe was being opened. The door swung silently open.

'Welcome to the dungeon,' said Enya, as she walked, stoop-shouldered, into the building. Junior saw she had cleaned up the blood on her back and that carefully applied make-up hid her bruised face. Fairy, ever serious, was talking in Dutch on her tiny mobile as she followed Enya. Scooby came right up to Junior.

'So where's the fucking rock star?' he said, covering Junior's lapels in a fine spray of saliva.

'He went for a little walk,' said Junior, looking down at Scooby with disdain.

'Walk, my ass,' said Scooby, who hadn't even noticed the look Junior had given him. 'Hunt more like. Hey, guys, you're staying around the back next to the studio,' Scooby shouted at the musicians who were climbing off their bus. Junior saw instantly what their vices were as some of them appeared very sleepy and some of them were wide-eyed and wired.

Now that must be an interesting combination, thought Junior, and made a mental note to himself not to get into conversation with any of the band members or spitty fucking managers for that matter. There was the sound of another powerful engine driving at speed down the drive. It was a truck from the airport carrying their luggage. The heavy lorry was blaring its horn as it careered towards the building. The radio was on full blast – a Luscious song was playing. It screeched to a halt, sending loose gravel shooting across the driveway. Scooby began to scream at the driver as he pulled open the door. There, sitting in the driver's seat was Luscious, giggling like a schoolboy. The driver of the van and the pale blonde girl were nowhere to be seen. Scooby immediately stopped his tirade and stomped off to the main building, cursing fucking spoiled rock mutherfucking stars as he left. The musicians had slunk away around the corner to where they were staying. Enya and Fairy, who had stuck their heads out of the main door when they heard the commotion, realised what was going on and turned on their heel back into the main building.

'Nice drivin', skinny,' said Junior to Luscious as he approached him. They were the only two left standing in the massive driveway.

'Hmm,' said Luscious. He was clearly distracted by something, he was picking at his fingernails. Junior saw there were specks of blood on his hands and on his face. Luscious looked straight at Junior as he pulled his mirrored shades off. The bodyguard had never seen Luscious's eyes look so blue. A big smile spread across his beautiful face.

'Your book's in the cab, baybee,' said Luscious, pointing over his shoulder as he sashayed past him and into what was to be home for the next month.

9 >

Now all this talk about sex and drugs and rock and roll is all very well, but what you really want to hear about is leeks.

George's leek was now bloody gigantic. It was half the size of his shed. He and Nellie both knew they couldn't show it. It was just too big and it could talk. Well, not talk in the recognised sense, but it could certainly squeak, especially as it was getting bigger. There was no way they could show it to anyone. It was too much of a freak. He couldn't just tell the leek show judges he got big leeks by talking to them and stroking them as if they were puppies – they'd think he was a nutter. And if he told them he'd invented some sort of secret potion they'd want to see it, of course. No, he'd have to destroy 'the Big Fella' as he had taken to calling him. At first Nellie thought George was talking about getting rid of Big Fat Squinty Bill in case he let it slip there was a monster in their greenhouse, until George reminded her that Big Fat

Squinty Bill was always telling folk tall stories and a monster leek would surely be taken with a large pinch of salt, and some vinegar and some fish and a double portion of chips, with a pickle and some bread and butter, if Big Fat Squinty Bill had anything to do with it.

But, of course, Nellie and George had forgotten about Mrs Big Fat Squinty Bill and the promised nick-nacks. When Big Fat Squinty Bill had got home later that night he had told Mrs Big Fat Squinty Bill all about the giant vegetable which was going to bring untold nick-nacks to their council house. They would be the envy of the area. Mrs Big Fat Squinty Bill was so excited she decided she and her husband should pay a visit to George and Nellie the next day to see the veggie beast. So that's how the Big Fat Squinty Bills happened to be in George and Nellie's kitchen at 8 o'clock the next morning. Big Fat Squinty Bill was most put out because Nellie had insisted he drink some of her juice before they all went down to the allotment. He had to admit he did feel a lot better for it, although he did ask for a bacon sandwich to take the healthy taste away. George and Nellie didn't have the heart to tell them both they were going to get rid of the massive leek, they thought they would cross that one when they came to it.

'Come on then, let's go,' said George, draining the last of his tea and putting out a skinny roll-up in the ashtray. 'Let's gan and see the monster.' He said the last word in a deep scary trembling voice. 'In an allotment no one can hear you scream,' said George, warming to his scary voice thing. 'Just when you thought it was safe to go back into the …'

'All right, George, we get the drift,' said Nellie, laughing. They trooped out of the kitchen. As Nellie was locking the back door she looked over her shoulder at her husband.

'George,' she said.

'Yes, my darling,' he replied.

'The force is strong in you today, Skywalker.'

George made a sound like a light sabre and they all carried on their way. Mr and Mrs Big Fat Squinty Bill had no idea what their daft friends were going on about and they didn't care, they were going to see a big leek with the promise of unlimited nick-nacks.

'Eeeh, look at her nets,' said Mrs Big Fat Squinty Bill, keeping up a running commentary on the state of their neighbours' houses, especially how clean their net curtains were. Most older women in Wallsend equated dirty nets with getting up to no good.

'I mean,' said Mrs Big Fat Squinty Bill, lips pursed, 'one minute ye've got dirty nets man, the next you're selling yourself on the street. Take Hitler for instance ...' Mrs Big Fat Squinty Bill's observations on Hitler's dirty nets and his descent into street walking was thankfully cut short by Wheelie Billy rolling out of his newsagent's.

'Hoy, man, George, man,' shouted Billy as he shot across the road without using his green cross code. He was dressed from head to foot in Ferrari racing overalls and was making a noise like a racing car as he approached his friends. George didn't know which was worse, Mrs Big Fat Squinty Bill's commentary or Wheelie Billy's rambling. He decided to make a run for it. They'd never catch him. He'd get plastic surgery and set up a new life for himself in Morocco.

And what about me? Nellie flashed into his thoughts.

Curses. Foiled, smiled George back at his wife. Wheelie Billy screeched up to the foursome.

'What's aall this ah hear aboot ye havin' a monster leek, man, George, man?' said Wheelie Billy, keeping his engine running.

'Can't a man keep owt secret aroond here?' said George, turning to give Big Fat Squinty Bill a hard stare. Big Fat Squinty Bill suddenly found something very engrossing down by his feet.

'Can ah see it, man, George, man, canna?' said Wheelie Billy. 'Go on, man, canna? You wouldn't not let a poor cripple not see yer big leek, would ye, George? Who knaas it might heal me. It might be a miracle leek and I could walk again. That's what it says in the Bible, ye knaa, George, "and verrily the little Paki lad was saved by the magic leek and he didst cast away his wheelchair and started playin' for the Toon and lo many lasses wanted to lay with him". That's true that, ah, come on, man, George, lerrus see yer massive leek.'

'I don't believe this,' said George. 'Look, man, Billy, man, can't ye wait till the competition?'

'Ye just divent want me te waalk de ye George, cos ye knaa I'm a better dancer than ye,' said Wheelie Bill, shouting the last sentence. The other people in the street who were heading down to the allotment and their own big leeks were starting to become interested in what was going on with the strange-looking fivesome. A couple of them looked as though they were going to come over and join their group.

'Keep yer voice doon, man, Billy, man,' hissed George.

'Well, can ah see it, man, George, man, caaaaan I?' said Billy. His engine wasn't running any more; he must've stalled it.

'All right,' said George exasperatedly, 'but ye've got to keep yer gob shut, all right?'

'On the honour of my forefathers,' said Wheelie Billy, suddenly adopting an Indian accent which he'd never had in his life, what with him being born in Gateshead.

'Come on, an' try not to draw attention to yerself,' said George, as he led the group down towards the allotment and the 'Big Fella'. 'I want a word with you,' said George to Big Fat Squinty Bill as he passed him.

When they reached George's shed, he stopped them all and told them to keep calm and not start shouting when they saw the leek. It was probably the biggest vegetable they

would ever see in their lives. He also warned Wheelie Billy
not to go throwing himself on it trying to get saved. If he did,
George had said, he would personally break both his arms so
he wouldn't be able to wheel himself home, never mind
deliver the papers the next day. They all solemnly promised.
George opened the lock and flung open the door. The leek
give a little squeak. It now filled three-quarters of the shed.
Big Fat Squinty Bill, Mrs Big Fat Squinty Bill and Wheelie
Billy all shouted in unison, 'Bloody hell, it's massive!' Then
Wheelie Billy tried to throw himself on it. In all the
confusion none of them noticed they were being watched.

'What the fuck's this? The annual old retard and cripple
meeting?' giggled Clancy Jr to Albie as they peered around
into Albie's shed like a couple of naughty schoolboys.
Clancy Jr was now fully clothed, his wet hair plastered to
his head. Albie had hosed the blood off the fat American,
stopping only once to throw up when he realised there was
some brain in his own hair. He tried to hit it out the same
way a girl would if she thought there was a spider on her
head. Clancy Jr, who thought all of this most amusing,
simply took the hose off him and hosed Albie's big head
until the 'bits o' brain', as Clancy Jr called them, were gone.
Albie was drenched. He also knew he must be clinically
insane. How else could he be holding himself together after
all that had gone on? All of his fucking friends had been
slaughtered, chopped up and planted in the fucking
allotment by a psycho, for fuck's sake. Surely that's enough
to send anyone mad? But if he was mad, how come he felt
completely calm? And how come all he could think about
was massive leeks? Yup, that proved it for him. He was now
madder than a box of caffeine-filled cats. Ah well, thought
Albie, I suppose I might as well enjoy me madness. It looks
like it might be the last bit of fun ah'm ganna have.

'It's his big leek what they've all come to see, man,' said Albie to Clancy Jr, in a surprisingly calm voice.

'Don't start that fucking leek stuff again,' hissed Clancy, his giggling ceasing immediately.

'Well, your fucking dad started it,' replied Albie. 'Hey, imagine if your daddy hadn't opened one of his shops here, me an' you would never have met, baybee.'

Clancy Jr stared at Albie. Then he burst out laughing. He sounded just like Luscious. Hey, for the first time in his life Clancy Jr had a friend. A friend who was as mad as him.

'Do you wanna go see the big leekee weekee, Albie baby?' said Clancy Jr to Albie, in his best baby-talk voice.

'Not now, dozy bollocks,' said Albie. 'Not with that fucking circus there. We'll wait 'til it's dark then take a peep. But until then let's go and take drugs.'

Clancy Jr's eyes lit up at the suggestion and the pair skipped off hand in hand singing a merry song. The last bit's not true but that's how happy they were.

George had dragged Wheelie Billy out of his shed by the scruff of his neck – which wasn't hard as he weighed the same amount as a skinny man in a wheelchair – and managed to lock the door again.

'What did ah tell you, man, Billy?' said George to the little Indian bloke.

'Sorry, man, George,' said Billy. 'I divent knaa what come over us, man. I think your leek might be possessed.'

'Aye, ah've read about that sort of thing before, ye know, George,' said Big Fat Squinty Bill, not wanting to be left out of the conversation. 'Possessed vegetables, it's quite a common occurrence. It's always in the papers an' on the news an that.' Mrs Big Fat Squinty Bill was nodding her head in agreement. George and Nellie were staring at their friends as if seeing them for the first time.

'Always in the papers?' George finally managed to stammer out. 'What paper do you read then? News of The Shite, because that's what yer talking, man. It's only a big leek, man. Ah'm not ganna get Father Moloney oot to exorcise it.'

'Eee, you should, ye know, George,' said Mrs Big Fat Squinty Bill. 'It could be the Devil's leek, ye never know, do ye? I mean look how Wheelie Billy acted. An' they say Asians an' that have that second sight.'

'I knaa one thing,' said George. 'Ye lot are all bloody mad. An' he's not bloody Asian, he was born in Gateshead. He can't even speak the language. I worked with his dad, man. Anyway, I thought ye wanted me to win the competition so I could buy ye all stuff?'

'Well, that's very nice of ye, ah knaa, George,' said Big Fat Squinty Bill. 'But I wouldn't want to see ye in eternal damnation because of a possessed leek.'

'Eh, I think he'll be all right,' said Nellie. 'If anyone's ganna throw my George into the fires of hell they'll have to get through me first.' She was trying to act as if having a massive leek in their shed was the most natural thing in the world, although she was astonished at the turn the conversation had taken.

She and George were having a fast and furious conversation with each other, though of course their friends couldn't hear them. They agreed that the reason their friends had gone a bit odd was seeing such a big leek for the first time. It was enough to send anyone a bit odd. Well, odder than they already were. George and Nellie made up their collective minds they would get their friends away from the allotment, then George would come back later that night and get rid of the leek.

'Right, you lot,' said George. 'You've all seen the massive leek an' you can see I'm ganna win, so come on, let's gan doon the club an' have a drink on me.'

George knew the offer of a free drink would mean his friends would go anywhere he wanted them to, and he quite fancied a drink himself after all the excitement. He grabbed Wheelie Billy by the wheelchair and began to manoeuvre him out of the allotment, which was no mean feat.

George's concentration was being severely tested as he tried to avoid the mud, ruts and vegetable patches that make up an allotment, as Billy kept up a monologue that seemed to George as though it was actually in Indian. Plus he could hear Mr and Mrs Big Fat Squinty Bill airing their views on everything from possessed vegetables to how they would spend their nick-nack money wisely. Then there was the added distraction of Nellie, who was keeping up a mental conversation with him. However when she shouted into his head, 'Hey, Georgy. Nice arse!' George lost concentration completely and pushed Wheelie Billy into a trough of courgettes, which would normally have gone unnoticed, but the bloke who had grown them was off work that day, due to the fact that his girlfriend had just had a baby. This in itself would have been no big deal, but he was 63 and his girlfriend was 17, and he'd met her at the school where he'd been headmaster – which he wasn't any more. Neither was he married any more what with headmasters' wives not being that impressed with husbands who get schoolgirls pregnant, especially when the schoolgirl is their youngest son's girlfriend.

So the ex-headmaster was just sitting quietly in his shed, musing on the fact that mad sex with a 17-year-old-doesn't compare with a bacon sandwich from a wife and companion of forty years, when a crippled Indian suddenly ends up face down in his prize courgettes; the only things in his life that didn't judge him. Something snapped in the ex-headmaster. He picked up a handy hoe and charged towards the courgette killers, determined to wreak his revenge.

George, who was trying to get his daft Indian newsagent

mate back into his wheelchair, which wasn't an easy task
what with all that slipping about on courgettes and the
talking of shite, didn't even see him coming. Luckily Nellie
did though. Just as the teenager-shagging-new-dad-ex-
headmaster reached George and Billy, hoe held in the killing
position, Nellie mentally catapulted him into a tree at the
edge of the allotment. There should have been a 'Who has
the most surprised face?' competition going on at that
moment, as it would've easily have been a draw between
everyone who was on the allotment.

The teenager-shagging-new-dad-ex-headmaster wasn't
suspended for long though, since Wallsend firemen are
considered the best in the world at getting headmasters out
of trees. He was returned to the ground but he never
recovered from his ordeal and spent his last few years in a
home for headmasters who have been levitated into trees.
His girlfriend married a rich circus owner and his son went
on to be one of the finest lion tamers in the world, although
his fame brought him a heroin habit and he was eaten by a
lion after a show in Milan.

Our five heroes entered the Coronation Club that night
and ordered two pints of Exhibition, a Sea Breeze, a white
wine and an amaretto. Wheelie Billy had loved amaretto
ever since he had spent two weeks in Taomina, Sicily, which
is probably the worst place in the world for anyone in a
wheelchair to go on holiday, what with it being virtually
made of steps. Mind you, it does mean they can spend their
days in the hotel drinking amaretto with the locals. Wheelie
Billy was determined to put as much amaretto away as
possible that night; he thought he deserved it, after all the
excitement he'd been through.

'Well,' said Big Fat Squinty Bill to the others, 'I'd like you
to raise your glasses to the man whose going to win us the
competition. Our very own George Creedy.'

'George Creedy!' said everyone in return, even Nellie who was doing it as a wind up.

'Keep yer voices down, man,' said George annoyed. 'Everyone'll wanna see the Big Fella.'

'To the Big Fella!' said Big Fat Squinty Bill, laughing at George's discomfort. None of them knew they would never see the 'Big Fella' again. They all had a really good night in the club that night and Nellie won the bingo.

'I hope you weren't cheating, lass,' George mentally said to his wife, 'or you're in for a beating.' Everyone in the group thought Nellie must be a bit drunk, what with her laughing at nothing. Nellie announced that because she was virtually a millionairess since she had won the bingo, £30 to be exact, she'd treat them all to fish and chips, although she pronounced it finch and chimps.

It was 10.30 when they left their friends at the chippy, which was late for them. They all went their separate ways, although they knew exactly where Wheelie Billy was, because they could hear him singing as he headed home to the next street. They even heard what happened when he wheeled into the wrong garden and was attacked by a dog. He seemed to get away unscathed because after the initial barking and shouting Billy resumed his singing, although now he was singing something about how tough he was because he had defeated a mighty wolf.

Nellie and George smiled at each other as they listened to their daft mate's voice recede into the distance. 'Eeh, I haven't had fish and chips for ages,' said George, who was carrying their supper parcel under his arm, which is the only way to carry fish and chips.

'Aye, an' ye need yer strength, George,' said Nellie, her eyes flashing in the streetlight. 'You've gotta get rid of yer leek, before it gets rid of us.'

'Aye, yer right, Nellie, pet,' said George. 'Shame, though,

I've grown quite attached to it.' Nellie reached into her handbag and pulled out their front door key and let them into their tiny house. George put the chip parcel down on the table, while Nellie went to get the plates, salt, vinegar and tomato sauce. He loved tomato sauce did George. That was one thing 'The Thing' came in handy for: coaxing sauce out of the bottle.

When their fish and chips were served up, George and Nellie sat in companionable silence enjoying their meal.

'He does lovely chips that lad in the chip shop,' said Nellie. 'I think he's got a gift.'

'Aye, his fish is lovely an' aall,' said George, covering the big battered cod in sauce.

Both of them knew they were just making conversation because George had to go out again and get rid of his prize and it was making him unhappy. When they had finished Nellie got up and took the plates away and George lit a skinny roll-up. He hadn't even taken his jacket and cap off. Hardly worth it, really, he just had to go out again. Nellie came back into the room, sat in front of George and clasped his hands across the table.

'You will be careful, pet,' said Nellie, staring into her husband's strong blue eyes.

'Course I will, man, pet, man,' said George, smiling at his wife. 'I'm only gannin' to knack a leek, it's not ganna bite us.'

And with that George stood up, leaned across the kitchen table, kissed his wife on the tip of her nose and walked out of the front door. Nellie sat staring at the chair George had been sitting in. She felt something was up. Something very bad indeed.

Just as George was walking through the darkened streets of Wallsend, skinny roll-up stuck between his lips, on his way to assassinate the 'Big Fella', Junior was padding quietly around the mansion getting his bearings. For a big man he could move in complete silence. Sometimes when he was on a job he would give the impression he was clumsier than he was, knocking things over, stepping on people's feet and talking in a loud voice. That way it was more of a surprise later on when he popped up and, say, strangled or suffocated someone.

He would always have a little chuckle to himself when he remembered the surprised look on Little Joey Barzini's face when he appeared from the darkness of Joey's well-guarded office and pushed a Mont Blanc ink pen through his eye and into his brain. The reason Mr Barzini, a well-connected Mafia don, was so surprised was that all day he had been calling Junior a big clumsy dumb faggot, albeit in Italian, one of the many languages Junior was fluent in. Junior had been playing his part, that of a clumsy, camp interior designer to the hilt as he showed Barzini how he could transform his tasteless New York mansion into the height of sophistication. The don was doing all of this decoration because his wife had found out he had been cheating on her with her cousin. Barzini might be a big tough mafia bloke but so was her father. So to appease her he sent her away for plastic surgery and promised her their New York house would be so posh they could invite the Queen of fucking England around for fucking tea and fucking crumpets.

As Junior minced, cooed and knocked things over, he worked out ways of getting close enough to Barzini to send him to the big Mafia graveyard in the sky. When Mr Barzini left the room to take a call, Junior quickly went into the garden and stealthily climbed a sheer 40 feet to the Italian's office, killed two of his guards, broke in through the balcony doors and secreted himself in the shadows behind a lifesize, though rather slimmer version, statue of Barzini. All of this was within 30 seconds of Barzini leaving the room. Junior wasn't even out of breath.

Barzini had entered the room and picked up the phone on his desk. As he preened himself in the mirror above the desk, waiting for his call to be answered, Junior suddenly appeared in the reflection. Barzini was so surprised he hardly realised he was dead. Junior minced out of the mansion without a second glance but he did consider going back to kill some of Barzini's henchmen who had been whistling at him and making crude comments in Italian. Sensibly he didn't. Junior was thinking about the Italian because he had entered the part of the mansion that had an Italian theme. He could see the paintings and statues were genuine works of art, and was surprised he hadn't seen this part of the house before, since he hadn't had much to do the last couple of days but snoop. The one thing he had found out about the house was that it may look like a big plain mirrored box from the outside but inside it was a maze of corridors and rooms. There were also security cameras everywhere, not that anyone would realise unless they had Junior's training.

He was just about to retrace his steps – he had an idea he would like to find the room that controlled the cameras – when he heard music. It wasn't the music of the band rehearsing, which went on day and night, this sounded like opera. It seemed to be coming from the walls. Junior stepped forward and placed his palms flat on the expensively papered wall in front of him. It was vibrating with the sound of a choir singing in a minor key. The music was barely audible through the soundproofing, He had found out that every room in the place was soundproofed.

Junior did what every other well-trained operative would do in this situation. He stepped into the bedroom opposite, snatched an expensive cut glass from the bedside table and held it against the wall. He wished at that moment that he had some sort of James Bond-type thingy; some sort of snoop-o-scope with him, which would enable him to hear what was going on. He knew he looked ridiculous standing against the wall, his ear up against the glass. Surprisingly, he could hear remarkably well. He could make out the choir, there was some chanting, what sounded like a rough sea washing up on a pebbly beach, and alternate laughing and high-pitched screaming. He had no idea what was going on or where the noise was coming from.

He felt his way along the wall and found there was a tiny gap running up to the ceiling, although when he investigated further he realised that what he had found was actually a concealed door and it was a masterpiece of construction. Junior had heard experts say that the Egyptians were the finest builders ever to have lived, and that their creations were even better than today's. Junior thought this was nonsense; give him modern techniques any day. The door he was examining now was a work of art. He was so engrossed in it he didn't realise the odd noises had stopped. Suddenly there was an electric hum and the door vibrated slightly. Junior decided it was time to leave. He melted silently into the shadows. He would be back.

George reached the allotment and pushed open the gate. It was pitch black in there now, quite spooky, really, but it held no fear for George, who had been going in there since he was a kid. All the gardeners had gone home hours ago, although some of them had left lights burning in their greenhouses, the way parents do for small children. It wasn't just George who was fond of plants. He picked his way through the corridors of darkened plants towards his greenhouse. He could see it silhouetted in the distance. George loved the smell of the allotment at night. It seemed more earthy – more alive. He fancied he could hear the plants talking to each other now they were alone, but when he tried to pick out single noises they suddenly shut down as if they knew he was listening.

You're getting as daft as Big Fat Squinty Bill, he thought to himself, shaking his head. George flicked his skinny roll-up into the darkness and pulled out the keys to his shed.

He was always amazed at how big the leek was every time he saw it. It had grown even bigger in the last few hours. It was a real shame he had to get rid of it.

Ahh, well, thought George, I better get on with it. It's ownly a vegetable not a bloody puppy.

George hung his cap up on the nail and was just taking his jacket off when the shed door opened behind him. He had been so engrossed in the leek, his mental radar had been down. Albie Donnelly stepped into the shed and punched George hard in the face. George dropped to the floor. It had been a long time since he had been hit so hard. Half a mile away, Nellie screamed and fell to her knees.

Albie kicked George twice in the ribs. The old man was going in and out of consciousness, there was blood running down his face, and one arm was twisted behind his back where it had got caught in his coat as he fell. Albie would probably have killed George there and then, but he was distracted by the giant leek.

For a moment Albie thought his mind was playing tricks on him; no leek could possibly be as big as that. But now as he stared open mouthed at the giant vegetable in front of him he was like a child meeting Father Christmas.

'How the fuck?' said Albie, as he stroked the leek. His hand was shaking, partly because he was in awe of what he was seeing, but mostly because he had taken so much cocaine he was vibrating like a plucked guitar string.

'How the fuck?' he kept repeating. He had to find out how

this old man had grown such a massive leek. Remembering George was there, Albie turned and kicked him once again. A low moan escaped from George's swollen lips.

Quarter of a mile away Nellie, who had felt everything, stopped her old lady running and leaned against a wall for support. Saliva ran from her open mouth as she bent over, gasping for breath. She watched, wincing, as the runny spit trickled on to her slippers, darkening the fur. She never went out in her slippers and without her coat, she thought. Instantly she snapped back to reality. 'George!' she cried and staggered on to rescue her husband.

Back in the shed, Albie picked up George by the front of his shirt. His hands slipped on the blood and George fell back to the ground, his head hitting the floorboards with a dull thud and then falling on to the right side of his face, the blood chanelling across his cheek to drip on to the floor. Albie grabbed George by the jacket, which twisted George's arm further around his back. Pain shot through the old man's body. He shivered, teeth chattering, his eyes snapped open and he stared straight into the twitching face of Albie. The big man smiled madly at George and touched his face gently. He was just about to say, 'Nice leek, man,' when George mentally threw him across the shed. He had never used 'The Thing' in anger before. It felt fantastic, better than sex. So all in all George felt pretty good.

Albie was hurled against the big leek. It exploded like a bomb. It didn't even have time to squeak.

The pair were covered in leek guts. Albie mewled like a kicked cat. The massive leek was dead, and in a minute George would be too. Albie hated cruelty to leeks, especially leeks that were going to win him two million quid. The younger man was scrabbling and slipping around in the green goo. There was leek juice in his eyes; he thought of it as leek blood. He wiped his face with the back of his hands and pulled himself up using the two by twos which ran in parallel down the shed walls. George had managed to get up on to his knees, his twisted arm hung limply by his side, his jacket hung from his hand. The blood on his face now mixed with leek blood. He was staring hard at Albie. I'm going to kill him, thought George, and a flush of happiness spread through his body.

He smiled at Albie. Albie smiled back, and then threw a plant pot at George. It was so slippery and Albie's hands were shaking so much it missed completely and went harmlessly through the window. Not that it would have hit George anyway. He could feel 'The Thing' building up inside him. He felt as if he had a force-field around him. He felt invincible but incredibly peaceful. Albie, being coked out of his head, felt exactly the same way as he pulled a spade off the wall where George had neatly stacked it. Being a gardener, Albie appreciated neatness. 'A place for everything and everything in its place,' as his father used to say. But the place where Albie certainly shouldn't be was floating in the air, his back touching the rough ceiling.

Albie Donnelly could not comprehend what was happening to him at all. He had taken so much coke his brain was boiling and now he was floating. Surely this must be some sort of hallucination. If it was it was a very good one. He must remind himself to do that much coke again. He wondered why he was holding a shovel, then remembered George and the dead leek. There was a sudden flash as if someone was taking a photograph. If only Albie could swim down towards the old man he would bash his brains in. The fact he couldn't swim didn't unduly worry him as very few people had drowned in the air.

What should have worried him was George. His brain was boiling too, but it was with the power of 'The Thing'. George was going to make Albie Donnelly explode like the giant leek. He wanted to see his blood and guts mix with the leeks. He would, in fact, enjoy killing the fat bully. George's head dropped to his chest; he was breathing heavily. He could only just lift his eyes so he could see the fat bully floating in his shed. Albie couldn't see George's eyes – they were lost in the shadow of his forehead, which was now shiny with the sweat of concentration. It was a good thing for Albie that he couldn't see George's eyes, they were the eyes of a man who could make other men explode at will, which on the whole makes them pretty evil peepers. Albie suddenly started to scream like a baby, his voice getting higher and higher. His internal organs began to vibrate and expand; blood poured from his eyes, nose and ears; an eardrum popped at the same time as one of his eyes; his whole body was vibrating like the cheapest effect on a bad horror movie, but this was real life for Albie, so it hurt. His skin bulged like a bursting sausage; you could see the blood running through his overfilled veins.

'George!' screamed Nellie, as she rushed into the shed. George fell to the floor. Albie fell from the ceiling on to Nellie, breaking her frail old lady's neck in an instant. The three of them lay on the leek, like smashed toys. Blood and mud covered the floor.

'Ooh, look. Someone's been having fun,' giggled Clancy Jr as he stepped into the shed and surveyed the carnage.

10〉

'**S**o how you enjoying the countryside, baybee?' whispered Luscious into the ear of Junior as he sat watching the band rehearse in the studio. The singer had tried to creep up on his bodyguard, unaware that the big man knew exactly where his boss was at all times. It would have appeared to anyone who was watching that this was very nearly the last thing Luscious did, as Junior instinctively spun around and grabbed the singer by the throat. He enjoyed the look of fear which flashed across the star's handsome features, but it was gone in an instant as the singer immediately recovered his composure and smiled his hundred-watt smile at the big black man.

The only person who noticed what had happened was Enya. Her eyes widened when she saw Junior grab her boss, and, as she started towards them, Junior noticed she put her hand behind her back as she took her first step, as if going for a weapon. He stored this interesting piece of information. Enya stopped when she saw Luscious grinning, and to cover her embarrassment at her overreaction she pulled a tiny mobile phone from the pocket in the front of her Levi's and began to punch in a number. Not that she would be able to hear anyone she called over the noise of the band.

The lead guitarist had just taken a solo, his old Les Paul sounding just like an old Les Paul should when cranked up through a Marshall amp: fat, round and funky, as if it was being sucked through a tube. The skinny-hipped guitarist leaned back, the low-slung guitar hard against his hip, his hair falling down his back, his slim fingers wringing big fat vibrato heavy notes from the Sunburst guitar. Without missing a beat, Luscious untangled himself from his bodyguard, leaped on to the stage and, in a movement that to Junior seemed all arms, hips and lips, launched into the chorus. Pretty impressive, thought Junior, as the singer preened, postured and stuttered across the tiny rehearsal stage.

Luscious looked straight into the bodyguard's eyes as he flipped the bottom of the mic stand into the air with his right foot. It pivoted on the joint where the mic clip met the stand so the singer was still able to sing into the microphone. It was an old trick but it still looked impressive, especially to younger fans who had never seen Led Zeppelin or Free, although the song the band was playing, their hit single 'Hey You Die', was much darker and louder than anything even Led Zeppelin had ever done. The singer sang the chorus one more time and threw the mic stand into the air. With perfect timing he caught it in his right hand just as the song crashed to a halt. The music had been so loud Junior fancied he could still hear it even though he was wearing earplugs; the pathetic noise of Enya applauding her boss sounded ridiculous.

Rehearsals were over for the day. The band were handing their instruments to roadies and good-naturedly taking the piss out of each other. Luscious, followed as ever by Enya, walked over to where Junior was sitting and sat his skinny butt down next to him.

'So waddya think, Junior baybee?' said Luscious, not looking at his bodyguard but watching the band clown around as they made plans for that evening. When Junior turned to look at the singer he noticed there was a wistful look on his face. Surely Luscious couldn't envy his band, who were all hired hands?

'Yeah I think you're pretty good. Who knows? You could even become quite popular in a Flock-Of-Seagulls-type way,' said Junior seriously, as he watched Enya talking quietly into her mobile.

Luscious burst out laughing. 'Yeah, yeah, you're right, we could even get a few club gigs around town, eh?' said the singer. 'Although I don't think I could ever be as good as that Flock Of Seagulls singer.' He continued laughing. 'What was his name again?'

'Who cares?' said Junior, which caused Luscious to laugh even harder.

'Hey, Enya,' Luscious shouted at his assistant. Her head snapped up, all her attention on her boss. 'What was the name of the lead singer from A Flock Of Seagulls?' She shook her head, her brow wrinkling. She was distracted by a tinny voice from her mobile phone.

She spoke into the mouthpiece. 'He wants to know who the lead singer was from A Flock Of Seagulls,' Enya said to the person on the other end. Her eyes followed the bass player out of the room. She looked back at Luscious.

'Scooby says: "That's showbusiness".' She looked confused. Luscious burst out laughing once again. Even Junior raised a smile.

'He's right, right, the pussy cat's right,' sang Luscious, getting up from his seat. 'C'mon, kids, let's play.'

Just before he reached the door he turned and looked hard at Junior, then said: 'Hey, Junior, you got everything you want?'

'Yeah, we get treated pretty good here.' Junior shrugged.

'No, I mean in life,' said Luscious, walking back to the big man.

'Yeah, I'm pretty happy,' said Junior wondering which way the conversation was going. He hadn't seen Luscious take any drugs that day but that meant nothing.

'Let's take a drive,' said Luscious, and he slunk out of the room like a cat.

'Take a drive where?' said Junior, catching up with the singer.

'Don't you want to see the beautiful English countryside?' said the singer, pulling on an expensive leather jacket.

'It's dark,' replied Junior.

'Come on, we'll 'ave a larf,' said Luscious, imitating a London accent badly. 'Enya, darlin',' said Luscious, continuing with his Dick Van Dyke impression, 'could ya bring the motor round, love?' Luscious and Junior were walking down the corridor that lead to the front door. 'Do you like Italy?' said the singer, out of nowhere.

'Yeah, it's all right,' said Junior, trying to hide the fact that he'd been caught off guard.

'There's an Italian part of this house, you know?' continued Luscious.

'Hmm,' replied Junior trying to sound non-committal. 'Is there?' By now they had reached the front door and Junior opened it for his boss. Luscious stepped out into the night.

'I love this time of day,' said Luscious taking a deep breath. 'The countryside seems to come alive. Reminds me of when I was a kid.'

Junior's reply was cut off as an old Ferrari Dino sped round the corner and skidded to a halt in front of them. Junior was surprised because he had never seen the car before, but he noticed it was left-hand drive and had Californian plates so he assumed Luscious had had it brought over from the States. He was shaking his head at this rock star excess as Enya leaped out of the vehicle.

'I love that car,' she said, handing the keys over to Luscious.

He grabbed her and kissed her hard on the mouth. 'Thank you, my darling,' he said dramatically.

Junior moved towards the driver's door assuming he would be chauffeuring his boss, but Luscious waved him away. 'Hey, big man,' said the singer, 'let me drive you for a change.' Junior stopped and looked at the singer. There was a light in his eyes he had never seen before.

Great, thought Junior. I'm going to die in a blazing Ferrari in fucking England. Ah well, he thought as he wedged himself into the leather bucket seat.

Luscious leaped into the car like a cat, rubbing his backside down into the seat. Junior hardly had time to close the door before the car shot off down the driveway towards the main gate, slowing only marginally when it reached the road. Luscious could see what was coming either way via two big mirrors that were placed on either side of the hedge. He skidded into the road and hit a button on the CD player in a single move. His new album blasted from the hidden speakers as he put his foot down. The engine roared, the car seemed to hunker further down on to the tarmac and they leaped forward into the darkness of the country roads.

This is the perfect soundtrack for us both frying in a hedge, thought Junior as he stared at the dark road snaking out in front of them, but much to Junior's surprise Luscious was a very good driver. He even slowed right down for a couple of female joggers, giving the two women his best rock star smile as he slowly passed. When they realised who it was they screamed and tried to catch up with the car; a waste of millions' worth of Ferrari development money if they had succeeded.

'So you're a happy boy?' shouted Luscious over the music, not taking his eyes off the road.

'Yup,' replied Junior, shifting uncomfortably in his seat. He hated fucking sports cars.

'How many people have you killed?' continued Luscious, without missing a beat.

Junior turned his head and looked at the singer, who was looking straight out of the windscreen, a slight smile on his lips. The bodyguard turned back to the road without saying a word. Luscious snapped off the music.

'Weeeeell?' wheedled Luscious. 'How many you wasted, killer?' He made the sound of a gun being fired.

'Look what the fuck is this about, rock star?' said Junior quietly. He hated this question. It was usually asked by the rich businessmen he was sometimes hired to look after – the type who bought *Guns and Ammo* and paid to kill tame animals on game reserves. They got a kick being in the company of a real killer.

'Well, if you've killed people you are going straight to hell, brother,' continued Luscious, dropping down a gear but keeping his foot on the accelerator as he took a tight turn. 'Imagine that. I don't think hell can be very nice, do you?' he said, laughing as the big man sitting next to him shook his head as if dealing with a child.

'Oh, I don't know,' said Junior, staring at the skinny singer. 'I think I've seen hell. I think I can handle it.'

'Oh, do you?' giggled Luscious. He was staring at some lights in the distance trying to work out what they were. He was delighted to see they belonged to a quaint country pub and it was still open. 'Hey let's have a drink, baybeeee.'

He swung the car expertly into the pub's car park. It was packed with cars. 'Ooh, looks busy,' said Luscious as he leapt out of the car and started towards the quaint looking inn without even looking back. A sign above the door squeaked its welcome. There was a peeling picture of a chicken standing on a pigs back. The pub was called The Chicken On A Pig. Junior levered himself out of his seat and followed the singer, who had disappeared into the bar.

Junior could tell by the stunned looks on the faces of the locals in the packed bar they had never seen a world famous rock star this close up before, never mind his hulking black bodyguard. There was complete silence. Luscious was leaning with his back against the bar, his elbows resting easily on the bar top.

'Hey, killer, you got any money?' he shouted, as Junior ducked in under the small doorway.

'Yeah yeah,' said Junior, pulling out his wallet. He always came prepared to babysit his charges.

'I'll have two large Jack Daniels,' said the American, turning to the barmaid and giving her a full blast of his rock star looks. For a second it looked as if she hadn't heard, so amazed was she to be serving a man who, up until now, had only been a face on her daughter's wall.

'Er, yes, Mr, er, Luscious,' she stammered.

'Call me Luscious, baby,' said the singer, as he leaned over the bar and touched her hand, causing her to blush a deep red. Meanwhile, Junior was taking in their surroundings. This was just the sort of place where a local might think of having a go and getting himself into the papers by starting a fight with a rock star. That, of course, would not be allowed to happen. Luscious turned from the bar, the drinks in his hands, and handed one to Junior, who would only pretend to drink it. Spotting a tiny table free, Junior hustled the American over to it. They sat down and the buzz of conversation started up in the bar once again. There were also a few mobile phones being pulled out as people told their friends who they were drinking in the same bar as, and it didn't take long for the bar to get even more full, as more customers arrived to gawp at the American rock star. A piano started up in the corner.

'This is like being in a fucking movie,' whispered Luscious to Junior.

'Yeah, well, let's hope we don't get eaten by the local werewolf,' said Junior, trying to keep the whole bar in his sight.

'So you've seen hell?' said Luscious, ignoring the stares from the other drinkers. 'Tell me about it.'

'Nothing to tell. I've been in situations which could be classed as hellish; some of those I created myself and some were created by other people, and you really don't want to know about it,' said Junior, trying to get off the subject.

'Oh but I do,' said the singer, his voice now strangely formal, sounding English, Junior observed. 'You see, I've seen hell.'

Junior stared at him, his face giving nothing away.

'And I know it's like nothing you've ever experienced and I know you would not want to go there. But I do know one thing. If you have killed someone, anyone in any situation, you will go straight to hell. That's the law.'

'OK, so I'm going to hell,' said Junior. 'What you gonna do about it? Put a fucking word in for me?'

'Maybe, maybe,' said the singer.

At that moment the blushing barmaid came up to their table. Junior had noticed there had been some whispering going on at the bar. 'Excuse me, Mr, er, Luscious,' she said nervously, 'you wouldn't mind giving us a song, would you?'

The whole bar seemed to be leaning forward in anticipation. Luscious drained his glass, stood up, grabbed the barmaid and gave her a big kiss. She nearly swooned. 'Of course I'll sing,' he shouted, giving a low bow.

The whole bar cheered. Junior sat shaking his head.

Now it is like a fucking movie, he thought.

George pulled himself up on to his knees and fell forward, pain searing through his whole body. He knew Nellie was very badly hurt but she was still alive – just. George had to get help, but how? It was late; there was no one around; he could feel himself drifting out of consciousness. He had to stay awake and help his wife. He could feel Nellie's life ebbing slowly away. He blasted her with 'The Thing', giving her some of the energy that was keeping him awake. Her body jumped and he felt a blinding pain in his neck as he crashed to the floor, barely conscious. He began to concentrate very hard. White light exploded in his head. He had to make this work. He had to get help.

Half a mile away, Big Fat Squinty Bill rolled over in his big double bed. His snores stopped immediately. 'Leeks!' he shouted in his sleep. Mrs Big Fat Squinty Bill punched him, the way she always did when he made a noise in his sleep. He rolled the other way. His feet began to drum up and down on the mattress. 'Leeks!' he shouted again, his feet moving faster. Mrs Big Fat Squinty Bill was beginning to wake up and she wasn't happy. Big Fat Squinty Bill's hands had started to vibrate under the duvet. 'George! Nellie! Leeks!' he shouted. Mrs Big Fat Squinty Bill sat bolt upright in their bed staring at her vibrating husband in the half-light.

'Big Fat Squinty Bill, are you all right?' she said to him worriedly, as she began to shake him gently, naturally assuming he was having a heart attack but hoping it was a bad dream. 'Big Fat Squinty Bill!' she shouted, her voice almost a sob. Big Fat Squinty Bill sat bolt upright too.

'Get your coat, Missus,' he said. 'Nellie and George need

us.' And he leaped out of bed, amazed he had so much energy. I feel like a teenager, he thought. But where would I get one of those at this time of night.

Big Fat Squinty Bill pulled on his big trousers, slipped on his fat man's comfortable shoes and pulled his jacket on over his vest. 'Com'on, man, pet!' he said to his wife as he disappeared out of their bedroom and ran down the stairs.

'Slow down, man, pet!' shouted Mrs Big Fat Squinty Bill at her disappearing husband. 'You'll do yourself a mischief!'

'And bring the little phone!' he shouted back at her.

Mrs Big Fat Squinty Bill was really mystified now. Their son Colin had bought them a mobile phone last Christmas in case of emergencies. And Big Fat Squinty Bill had refused to use it, since the only emergency that ever involved his son was when he phoned them to borrow cash. So this must be a real emergency, mused Mrs Big Fat Squinty Bill as she pulled on her third best cardie and followed her husband down the stairs of their council house.

By the time she had got to the bottom of the stairs, Big Fat Squinty Bill was halfway up the street. She snatched up the mobile from the hall table, wondering briefly whether it would be charged up, but assumed it would be considering they'd never used it. Carefully locking their front door, Mrs Big Fat Squinty Bill followed her husband up the street. He had slowed down a bit now, she noticed gratefully.

'Where we gannin?' she said when she caught up with her husband.

'The allotment,' he replied, gasping for breath. She grabbed him by the arm bringing him to a halt. It was like trying to stop a tanker at sea.

'Why?' she said.

'Because George an' Nellie are hurt, they need us,' he said.

'Big Fat Squinty Bill,' said Mrs Big Fat Squinty Bill, 'are you turnin' into Skippy the bush kangaroo?'

'Aw, divent be daft man, howay,' said Big Fat Squinty Bill seriously. 'We've got to save them.'

'But how de ye knaa, man?' said Mrs Big Fat Squinty Bill to her husband's big back.

'George sent me a telepathic message,' replied her husband.

'You're telepathic now?' said Mrs Big Fat Squinty Bill, impressed. 'Fantastic. We can win the lottery. Come on, let's go rescue your weird mate,' she said, overtaking her husband. The humour disappeared from the situation when the pair reached George's shed. They slowed down on the allotment because it was very dark, but they could see a light burning up ahead in the shed, so they knew something must be up.

Suddenly there was a rustling in the bushes to the right of where they were standing. Mrs Big Fat Squinty Bill grabbed her husband's meaty arm.

'Who's there?' shouted Big Fat Squinty Bill. He was in no mood to be messed around. Suddenly two shadows emerged from the bush and sprinted off towards the entrance. Big Fat Squinty Bill took a step forward but they were gone as quickly as they appeared. Mrs Big Fat Squinty Bill noticed that one or both of them was wearing a very expensive aftershave. That's the sort of thing lasses always notice.

'Bloody kids!' muttered Big Fat Squinty Bill.

'I don't think so, pet,' said his wife, looking into the darkness. 'Anyway, come on,' she said, pulling her husband over to George's shed.

Mrs Big Fat Squinty Bill was the first to reach it and she pushed open the door. It was a testament to just what a strong woman she was that she didn't even scream when she saw the carnage inside the shed and the condition her two old friends were in.

She pulled out the mobile phone from her droopy cardie pocket and immediately dialled for an ambulance. She used her posh phone voice, too, so the operator would understand everything she said.

Big Fat Squinty Bill entered the shed and was also shocked at the sight, but was equally surprised to hear George say, Thank God, though he never saw his lips move.

He moved to help George as he seemed the most badly hurt. A thought flashed into the fat man's mind: Don't touch Nellie, she's got a broken neck!

'Bloody hell, how did I know that?' said Big Fat Squinty Bill out loud.

'Ambulance is on its way,' said his wife. Even now they could hear it in the distance.

Despite the commotion and the shock, there was a little bit of Big Fat Squinty Bill thinking that maybe he could win the lottery with his new superpowers.

'Ye talk shite, an' ye think shite,' said George, before falling unconscious.

It had been a bit of a night in The Chicken On A Pig. Needless to say there was a lock-in. And Luscious sang all night. And the boy could really sing, thought Junior. He sang everything from Ella Fitzgerald to The Rolling Stones and he even knew the words to 'Agadoo', which got the biggest cheer of the night, mainly because no one in the room thought a cool American rock singer like Luscious would know the words to something as tacky as that.

What was just as surprising was that the piano player, a 57-year-old lady who was a cleaner in the pub, knew the songs too. She even knew some of Luscious's songs, but the singer didn't want to sing them. He not only took requests but he performed each song as if he was in front of a stadium audience, prowling around the room, leaping on to the bar and shaking his thang. He exuded sex from every pore and quite a few local lasses and even lads would have taken him home that night. Close up Junior could see just how Luscious had become the biggest rock star in the world.

Every time Luscious sang he poured another Jack Daniels down. Even Junior allowed himself to finish the drink he had started that night. Luscious finally sang his last song which was, curiously, 'Witchita Line Man'. He then leaped from the bar, shouted goodnight and left, quickly followed by Junior with the rest of the audience shouting and clapping. Luscious climbed into the passenger seat of the Ferrari, Junior wedged himself into the driver's seat, marvelling that Luscious had left the keys in the ignition, and the car shot off into the night.

'Nice exit, kid,' said Junior to Luscious – who was now fast asleep.

Even though they hadn't come very far it took a while to find the house, and when he finally got the car up the drive there was a reception committee of Enya and Scooby waiting for them.

'Where the fuck do you think you've been?' shouted Scooby, as Junior stepped out of the car.

'Ask your boss,' said Junior coldly, as he walked around to the passenger seat, yanked opened the door and pulled the singer easily into his arms.

'What have you done to him?' screamed Enya.

'Hey, hey, calm down,' said Junior, trying not to get annoyed at their overreaction. 'He's been showing off. He's had a little too much to drink. Don't get your knickers in a twist.' He had heard someone in the pub say that and thought it was such a stupid thing to say it made him laugh.

'Take him to his room!' barked Scooby. Junior did think about throwing the prone rock star at the fat little manager, but decided that wouldn't be a particularly good career move.

'OK, ladies,' said Junior, moving towards the house. At that moment the singer woke up.

'Good night, eh?' he said as he climbed unsteadily out

of Junior's arms. 'Hey, Mom and Dad you waited up,' he said when he saw Scooby and Enya. 'I'm not grounded, am I?' he giggled.

'No, but your fucking bodyguard is,' said Scooby nastily.

The temperature seemed to drop.

'You'll go before he fucking does!' said Luscious icily. He had completely sobered up. Junior had never seen anything like it. Scooby turned and stormed into the house. Enya didn't know what to do with herself.

'And I'll seeeee yoooooou later,' said Luscious to the girl as he wiggled his fingers at her, the way an adult would say goodbye to a child. She turned and left. Junior was sure she was crying.

When they were alone, Luscious looked into his bodyguard's eyes and whispered, 'I can save your soul.' From the dark grounds behind him there was a sound like the sea hitting a beach. Junior turned to peer into the darkness, instantly on his guard.

When he turned back, Luscious had gone.

The ambulance men wouldn't let Mr and Mrs Big Fat Squinty Bill travel in the ambulance with their friends, so as the ambulance sped off to hospital, its siren wailing, the couple walked back to their house to order a taxi to take them to hospital.

'Are ye still doing yer weird mind stuff?' said Mrs Big Fat Squinty Bill as they hurried through the damp streets.

'Eh, ah divent knaa,' puffed the big man.

'Well, try it, man,' said his wife.

'How?' he replied.

'Well, I divent knaa, you're the one who's suddenly gone aall magical.' She grabbed his arm and they came to a halt. 'Try reading my mind,' she said, staring into her husband's squinty brown eyes. She saw he had been crying silently.

Big Fat Squinty Bill stared at his wife. He scrunched his eyes up. It didn't take much to do that.

Nothing happened.

'Nah, it's nee use, pet,' he said, shaking his head forlornly, 'aall me magical powers have desorted us.'

'Ah, that's all right, man, pet,' said Mrs Big Fat Squinty Bill kindly, 'as long as I can still read your mind, that'll do me. Now come on, let's gan doon the hospital.'

They didn't notice that they had been standing outside Wheelie Billy's shop, or that he was silently watching them from his upstairs window. He hated not knowing what was going on; but he knew he was going down the hospital to find out.

The Big Fat Squinty Bills got back to their house and ordered a taxi. Emily Evans the taxi controller thought it was the funniest thing she had ever heard. Those two ordering a taxi at that time of night.

'Eeeh, are ye gannin' oot clubbin'?' she laughed, as Big Fat Squinty Bill asked for a cab. He explained what had happened, although he didn't really know what had gone on. Emily was shocked. Nellie sometimes babysat for her. Having five kids at the age of 26, a babysitter came in really handy.

'Eeeh, ah'll send a cab straight away, pet,' Emily said to Big Fat Squinty Bill, 'an' ye send them me best.'

The taxi arrived almost immediately.

'All right, Big Fat Squinty Bill. All right, Mrs Big Fat Squinty Bill,' said the taxi driver, as the couple climbed into his cab. 'Ah heard what happened, man. What were they dein doon the allotment at that time of the night, man?' said the driver, watching the couple through his rear-view mirror.

'We divent knaa, man, Ivanhoe,' said Big Fat Squinty Bill, looking nervously out of the window. He had gone to school with Ivanhoe's dad. Ivanhoe had a twin brother called

Santana. Their father had let their mother name them. She died of cancer just after she had given birth to the boys. It was what she wanted. Their father never knew why.

'Didn't George have a big leek on the go? I reckon someone was tryin' to sabotage it. Ye knaa what them leek growers are like, man. They're bloody fanatics,' said the cabbie, as they sped through the empty streets of Byker on the way to the Royal Victoria Infirmary.

'Aye, could be, could be,' said Big Fat Squinty Bill. Neither he nor his wife was in the mood for conversation. Taking their cue, Ivanhoe stopped asking questions.

When the trio finally arrived at the RVI, Ivanhoe refused to take payment for the journey. 'Hey, diven't be daft, man, big fella,' he said, waving away the money. 'Look upon it as a mission of mercy. Send them me best.' And with that he pulled away from the hospital. Ivanhoe's father had told him just before he died that George had once saved his life when he had fallen in the river Tyne. He was going under for the third time apparently when George, who seemed to appear from nowhere, dragged him out of the murky water. It had never been mentioned again. Not taking money for a fare to help George was the least he could do.

Big Fat Squinty Bill hated hospitals. It reminded him of when his dad died. He had been a miner and had lingered on for months after being crushed by falling coal in an accident that had killed seven of his colleagues. In a strange way Big Fat Squinty Bill had been glad when his father had died. He knew what type of man he was and he didn't think he would've been able to live with the guilt of being the only survivor. Big Fat Squinty Bill had been 14 when he saw his father for the last time in this very hospital.

The main thing about hospitals, he thought, was that there was always someone dying somewhere in the building. Everyone was just getting on with their business as if they didn't know what was going on. It made him very sad. He hoped it wasn't his friends who were doing the dying at that moment.

While not being in the same mind-reading league as George and Nellie, Mrs Big Fat Squinty Bill knew exactly what her husband was going through. Grabbing his big paw in her tiny one she led him through the hospital.

'Hello, Fat Squinty Bill,' said a doctor cheerily, as he saw the big man approaching. 'And Mrs Big Fat Squinty Bill,' he said on seeing the big man's wife. The doctor knew them both quite well as Mrs Big Fat Squinty Bill had done a bit of cleaning for him in the past. He really liked the couple, although he had been warning her husband that he should lose weight and he seemed to be taking no notice at all. At first he couldn't get used to calling them a name that seemed like a playground taunt, but they both insisted that's what he should call them. It was as if they wore their nickname as a badge of honour. It was pretty hard to get a badge of any sort where they came from, thought the doctor ruefully. He knew why they were there, that's why he was being so cheerful, trying to make light of a very serious situation.

'So you found Mrs and Mrs Creedy, eh?' said the doctor, the smile dropping from his face.

'Yes, doctor, how are they?' said Mrs Big Fat Squinty Bill. She would never get used to talking to doctors, they were so, well, educated.

'We don't really know yet,' said the doctor, his face giving nothing away, 'but at the moment they're both comfortable and we're running tests on them. Apart from that the police are here and they will need to speak to you.'

As if on cue, two uniformed policemen approached from the coffee machine at the other end of the corridor. They were carrying plastic cups of coffee and both of them looked very tired.

'Ah, officers,' said the doctor. 'This is the couple who found Mr and Mrs Creedy.' The two policemen both nodded and smiled at the couple.

'Shall we go in here?' the tallest policeman said, indicating a small empty waiting room. 'We need to get a few of the facts sorted out.'

The policemen stepped aside as the couple stepped into the room.

Clancy Tree Sr thought he was having a heart attack. The pain was shooting down both of his arms to the tips of his fingers. His chest was tight, his mouth was dry, he was sweating and his face was turning from deep red to purple. Even Satriani's good-looking colleague, who was watching through the office window, appeared concerned at Clancy Tree's appearance.

'Sit down!' said Satriani quietly. Clancy Tree was standing, his body rigid, the veins in his neck standing out, gripping the desk in front of him. He collapsed into his chair like a puppet whose strings were suddenly cut. His forehead bounced once on the desk in front of him, rattling the pencils standing upright in the cylindrical leather pencil holder. He sat there, forehead on desk, completely still. Satriani stared at the back of his boss's sweating red neck impassively.

'Would you like a drink of water?' asked Satriani. Clancy Tree didn't respond. After two minutes of heavy silence Satriani repeated the question.

'No,' said Clancy Tree, without shifting his position. 'I would like you to repeat the story.' Since Clancy Tree's forehead was still resting on the desk, his voice was muffled. Satriani noticed there was a puddle of sweat forming where Clancy Tree's head met the expensive mahogany desk. He took a deep breath.

'We found your son. He was on an allotment with four men. They entered a shed, where they stayed. We heard a muffled shot from a high-powered weapon and two more shots from a lower-calibre weapon. We stayed in position observing. After two hours your son emerged from the shed carrying what we now know were body parts. He buried them all over the allotment. He was completely naked and didn't seem to care who saw him. Luckily the allotment was deserted. He then went back into the shed. There was no more movement until an unidentified elderly man entered the allotment later that night. He appeared to go to his own shed, where he was attacked by one of the men who was with your son. And this is where it gets weird. During the attack, the younger man rose from the floor and stayed there, hovering.'

Clancy Tree looked up now. Satriani saw that his eyes were bloodshot. Clancy Tree cupped his chin in his hands, his elbows on the table. One elbow slipped slightly on the puddle of sweat. He stared at Satriani. It was the third time he had heard the story and he was just beginning to take it all in. His son was a mass murderer and his friend could fly. Fucking great!

'Then,' continued Satriani, 'an old lady entered the allotment and went straight to the shed. The man who was by then, er, hovering too, fell on to her. Then your son entered, picked up his friend and they left quickly. And so did we. We thought it best not to get involved.'

'But you were seen by two people?' said Clancy Tree, his bloodshot eyes narrowing.

'Well, we were,' said Satriani uncomfortably, 'but there is no way we could be identified. It was far too dark. We also tried to get in touch with you every half-hour during the stake-out to find out what our next move should be, but we couldn't reach you.' Satriani had only stuck this last bit in to save face. It was true they had tried to reach Clancy Tree every half-hour; but he couldn't be reached because he was having a very enjoyable day of sex and champagne with Ellen Difford. Satriani suspected this and knew it would make his boss guilty and uncomfortable. Which is just how Clancy Tree felt, but he didn't get to be his age, with his money, without being able to think on his feet. As far as he was concerned there was only one thing to do in this situation.

'OK, enough is enough,' said Clancy Tree, staring hard at Satriani. 'My son has caused and is still causing me pain, heartache and embarrassment. He could quite easily destroy everything I have ever worked for. This is what I want you to do, Mr Satriani. I want you to find my son and his new friend, kill them both and make it look as sympathetic towards me as you can. I think you have the skills and the contacts and I certainly have the means.'

Clancy Tree put his forehead back on to the desk and began to sob for his dead son. Satriani left, closing the door quietly behind him.

'I knew there was something up!' shouted Wheelie Billy, as he pushed himself into the room in the hospital where Mr and Mrs Big Fat Squinty Bill were being interviewed by the policemen. 'Have ye two been arrested. What ye done, like?' He continued, seemingly unperturbed by the amazed looks on the policemen's faces. Mr and Mrs Big Fat Squinty Bill were used to the wheelie man's outbursts, so they just sat while he went off on one.

'Ye haven't murdered anyone, have ye? Eeeh imagine that. You'd probably be the biggest murderer in history, Big Fat Squinty Bill. It's a good job ye divent live in America they'd fry you in an electric chair. Mind you, ye probably wouldn't fit into it, what with yer big arse an' that.'

'I'll kick your bloody arse in a minute,' said Big Fat Squinty Bill.

'All right, all right,' said the older policeman, who was too tired to break up a fight between a big fat bloke and a mad bloke in a wheelchair. He wondered if they had a mental ward in this hospital. Maybe the bloke in the wheelchair had escaped from it. He hoped not. The last thing he wanted to do was to take on a wheelchair-bound Hannibal Lecter. He'd seen the film. He knew what happened to coppers who took on mental people, whether they were wheelchair bound or not. But the policeman's suspicions were unfounded; Mrs Big Fat Squinty Bill was giving the man in the wheelchair mints from her bag.

'Look, can you just tell me who you are?' said the younger policeman. He was in no mood for messing around. He was late off his shift because of this mess and at this time he should be messing around with his new wife. He'd only been married for six weeks. He'd met her in Thailand on holiday and was so taken with her he fell instantly and madly in love. When he married her, his parents were almost as proud of him as her whole village, which the young policeman was unknowingly supporting.

'I'm the newsagent, man,' said Wheelie Billy, as if this explained everything.

'And?' said the policeman.

'Well, I can help you with your enquiries,' replied the newsagent.

'No, you can't. You weren't there. Can you please leave? We are in the middle of an interview.'

'Ah, let him stay, man, he won't do any harm,' said Mrs Big Fat Squinty Bill, stroking the top of Wheelie Billy's head and giving him another mint. Wheelie Billy snorted like a horse.

'Nellie and George have been hurt,' said Mrs Big Fat Squinty Bill quietly to Wheelie Billy. The colour drained from his face. His mouth hung open with shock. The young policeman considered hitting them all with his truncheon.

'All right, you can stay,' said the older copper, sensing the atmosphere in the room change, 'but keep bloody quiet. Right?' Wheelie Billy pulled his right hand across his mouth indicating that his lips were zipped up good and tight.

'So,' continued the older policeman to Big Fat Squinty Bill, 'you have no idea who the two men you saw leaving the crime scene could be?'

'Haven't got a clue,' said Big Fat Squinty Bill.

'They had money though,' said Mrs Big Fat Squinty Bill, absentmindedly feeding Wheelie Billy another mint.

'Hmmm!' said Wheelie Billy urgently.

'How do you know they had money, Mrs Curran?' said the older policeman. Wheelie Billy stopped 'hmmmmming'. He had completely forgotten that his two friends had real names. Curran, he mused to himself. He preferred Big Fat Squinty Bill.

'Well,' continued Mrs Big Fat Squinty Bill, 'they were wearing very expensive aftershave. Most of the men around here hardly bath never mind wear aftershave. You could just tell. And one of them had buckle things on his shoes. I saw them reflecting when they were running.'

'Bloody hell,' said Big Fat Squinty Bill to his wife proudly. 'Yer like Shorlock bloody Holmes, ye.'

Mrs Big Fat Squinty Bill patted her hair.

'Hmmmmmm,' said Wheelie Billy.

'Shut up!' said the younger policeman to the little man in the wheelchair, his hand twitching towards his truncheon.

'But you couldn't identify them,' said the older policeman.

'I can!' blurted out Wheelie Billy, pleased now that all eyes were on him.

'Well?' said the older policeman. Wheelie Billy savoured his moment in the spotlight.

'Those two blokes were Clancy Tree's mates. They've been in me shop asking questions.'

'Have they now?' said the policeman, sitting forward on his seat and clearly interested in what Wheelie Billy had to say.

'Well, Mr, Mr …?'

'Chowdri,' said Wheelie Billy.

Mr Chowdri, thought the Big Fat Squinty Bills at the same time, even though they couldn't read minds. They had completely forgotten their friend had a real name. Chowdri, they mused. They preferred Wheelie Billy.

'Well, Mr Chowdri. How do you know these men are the same men Mr and Mrs Curran saw?'

'Well, your honour,' said Wheelie Billy, now using his posh voice and drawing himself to his full height, which wouldn't have been much even if he hadn't been in a wheelchair, 'I saw them running down my street from the direction of the allotment and even though I couldn't smell them, what with the wonders of double glazing, I did notice one of them was wearing a pair of shoes with buckles on. I wouldn't mind a pair of them myself. Well smart they are. But it's not often you see people dressed posh runnin' down my street. It's normally kids in trainers who are out nickin' stuff. An' I remembered they'd been in my shop asking about Clancy Tree's son. Then I saw them together in a posh car. Hey, I'm a great witness me, aren't ah, man?'

'Aye, ye are,' said the older policeman resignedly.

'But what were you doing up that late looking out of the window?' the younger policeman said.

'Well, ah cannit sleep. I divent knaa why,' said Wheelie Billy. 'I've never been able to. So I just sit up and look out of the window an' dream I could walk an' get a lass an' that.'

Everyone in the room looked uncomfortable and for a spilt second they all tried to imagine what it must be like for a little, crippled Indian bloke living alone in Wallsend.

None of them could imagine just how bad it was. The moment was broken, as ever, by Wheelie Billy.

'So what you ganna de now, copper. Ye ganna get them blokes an' give them a beatin'?'

'Aye, probably,' said the older policeman, smiling.

'So what the fuck we gannin' to de noo, man?' said Albie Donnelly, as he was pulled through the deserted streets by Clancy Jr. Albie looked drunk as he staggered along.

The American stopped. He gripped Albie by the shoulders and looked deep into Albie's good eye. Red gore covered his cheek, his closed eyelid was swollen and blood was still dripping from his ear. Surprisingly for such bad injuries the pain wasn't too bad but that had more to do with Albie's new state of madness and the amount of cocaine he had taken. 'How the fuck did you do that, baybee? The fucking flying?' sang Clancy Jr, into Albie's good ear. Albie looked scared.

'Ah divent knaa, man. One minute I was kickin' the shite out of the auld fucker, next thing I'm flyin'. Ah divent knaa, man. Maybe ah've got superpowers or something.' Albie began to laugh. He had no idea why he had been suddenly hovering above the old man. The fact that it could have been the old man that caused Albie to 'fly' didn't even enter their heads.

'Hmm,' said Clancy Jr, letting go of Albie's shoulders suddenly, so the big man slumped against the wall. The American turned and walked off into the darkness.

'Well, you tell me what the fuck it is,' shouted Albie as Clancy Jr retreated into the distance. The shouting caused his bloodied eardrum to ring. Pus oozed from beneath his eyelid. He took a step forward and fell to the floor. His head hit the pavement with a smack. Albie giggled. Clancy Jr came stomping from the darkness and pulled Albie to his feet by the armpits. He was surprised at how light the big man was. Neither of them realised that they were both losing weight rapidly. They hadn't eaten for a long time and had consumed so much cocaine that it was highly unlikely they would be wanting to eat in the near future.

'Look, you fuck,' said Clancy Jr, giggling at the near-rhyme, 'we have got to find a train station.'

'Why?' said Albie, his body suddenly spasming.

'Because we are going to London.'

'Why?' said Albie again. 'To see the mayor?'

'No, better than that,' giggled Clancy Jr, his lips pulled so far back across his teeth that he looked like a smiling horse. 'No. We, my friend, are going to see Mr Luscious.'

Albie stopped slouching against the wall and stood up straight. 'Luscious?' he breathed as a bubble of blood popped from his ruined ear, causing a fleck of blood to land on Clancy Jr's hand.

'Yes, Luscious,' snapped Clancy Jr. 'So find me a fucking station.'

'Well, why didn't you say, you fucking mad yank?' said Albie as he pulled Bernie's duck cocaine out of his pocket, stuck his nose into the rip and took a massive hit then shoved what was left deep into his pocket. Clancy Jr licked the residue off his partner's nose, not caring about the blood and gore. It looked as though he was feeding from the big Geordie man's face. Albie grabbed Clancy Jr's face in his big hard hands. The American's cheeks squished forward causing his nose to turn up and his eyes to squint. This gave him the appearance of an evil baby.

'I know just the place,' said Albie. 'So fucking follow meeeeee, baybeeeee.' As Albie strode off into the darkness he had a definite Luscious swagger about him. Clancy Jr ran after him like a puppy.

Most sensible people were tucked up in bed at that time of night and would certainly never dream of roaming the streets. The only folk who would be out at that time would be those who were up to no good. But I daresay even the most evil of wrongdoers would have thought twice about stopping Albie and Clancy Jr – they looked mad. They were completely fucked on cocaine and Albie was covered in blood from his exploding eye and lug. Clancy Jr remarked on Albie's state when they stopped in a doorway to snort some more cocaine. Even in his fucked-up state he knew they would have to clean themselves up if they wanted to get to London and Luscious without being arrested. The doorway was to an Oxfam shop and, guessing rightly that the shop wouldn't be alarmed, Clancy Jr kicked the window in and the pair climbed into the musty shop.

'Do people actually throw this stuff away?' said Albie incredulously, as he pulled on a big pair of orange tag stonewashed Levi's, surely the worst Levi's ever released. Albie, of course, thought he looked fanfuckingtastic. Now you see why you shouldn't take drugs. The big Geordie had washed his face in a dirty old sink at the back of the shop. He'd even giggled at his appearance in the cracked mirror, which Clancy Jr found a trifle disconcerting as he dabbed at the blood on Albie's head.

Clancy Jr refused all offers of new clothes from the pile Albie had chosen. Since he always dressed in black, and had the common sense to take off his clothes when he was chopping up the bodies, the little blood he had on him was barely visible. He had managed to get the blood off his new best mate's face with the brown water which was coming in fits and starts from the stained tap, using the back of Albie's old sweatshirt as a flannel. Albie didn't look too bad now in his new crap Levi's and big sweatshirt that said 'Skiers do it on the piste'. Over the sweatshirt he had a donkey jacket that had originally belonged to British Rail, and on his feet he had a pair of beaten-up Nike Air Jordans, which a Japanese collector would have paid good money for. Clancy Jr stood back to admire his handywork.

'Oooh, you look gorgeous,' he pouted, doing a little dance. Albie gave him a scary, coked-up, too-much-teeth smile.

'There's just one thing,' said the American. 'Your fucking eye looks gross, man.' Albie leaned against the sink, his body twitching, his good eye staring unblinking, while Clancy Jr rummaged around the shop. He stood up suddenly from a box he had been bending over.

'Yo ho, fucking ho! Me hearties!' he shouted in an accent which would have made Kevin Costner wince. 'Look what I've found, shipmate!'

He held up his prize for Albie to see. It was a tattered old pirate's costume: a white frilly shirt; a bandana that was fashioned to make a hat; a curly sword; but, most importantly, an eyepatch. 'This is fucking perfect for you, baybeeeeeee!' leered Clancy.

Albie nodded and gurgled enthusiastically and staggered towards his fucked-up friend, snatching the sword and bandana from his hands. He stuck the sword in the cheap plastic belt that held up his jeans and pulled the bandana on to his head.

'Avast, fucking behind, you fat get!' he sniggered.

'Erm, I was thinking more of just using the eyepatch to cover up your fucking evil eye, baybee,' said Clancy Jr. 'I don't think looking like Captain fucking Blood is going to achieve anything.'

'Fuck you!' snarled Albie.

'Ooh aye aye, Captain. Or should that be eye eye, Captain,' giggled the captain's mate. The pair fell into each other's arms giggling like children. Clancy Jr pulled away from Albie and looked him up and down. He resembled a horror movie new romantic. The American thought he looked fantastic. Then he gently pulled the eyepatch down over his head to cover his swollen eye.

'There, there, Captain,' he whispered. 'All shipshape now.'

They took another massive hit of coke, then Clancy grabbed Albie by the hand and led him through the shop and back out through the broken window. Their brains boiled as they set off towards the station and their train to London and Luscious.

'Eee, yer like me now, man, George,' said Wheelie Billy the next afternoon, as Mr and Mrs Big Fat Squinty Bill and Wheelie Billy were allowed in to see George. The old man was sitting in a wheelchair by the window in the ward when the odd trio entered.

'I hope ye haven't brought us any of those grapes from your shop,' said George. 'There always squishy and out of date.'

'Divent be daft, man, George,' said Big Fat Squinty Bill, laughing. 'That would see ye right off, man.' Wheelie Billy didn't even look embarrassed. He knew some of his produce could be little older than recommended, although to be fair he did sell it cheaper. Mr and Mrs Big Fat Squinty Bill were surprised George was out of bed at all after the beating he had taken. She also noticed his wounds were healing very quickly for a man of his age. Even the doctors were astonished at how quickly he had recovered.

'Erm, how's Nellie?' said Big Fat Squinty Bill, his gaze shooting from the floor to George.

'Not too good. Not too good at all,' said George quietly, his face turned away from his three friends. George was making it sound worse than it was, but the doctors had told him to fear the worst. Nellie was paralysed, in a coma and on a life-support machine. Now if she is as bad as they said she was, George had thought, lying in his bed surrounded by experts, how come she's shouting for me right now? Of course, the doctors couldn't hear anything.

'Can I see her?' said George, putting on a frail old man's act.

'Of course,' said one of the specialists kindly. 'We'll arrange it now.'

Later, George was helped into a wheelchair by a nurse, who pushed him over to intensive care to see Nellie. George was shocked when he saw his wife, and as he sat, head bowed, he asked the nurse quietly if she would mind leaving them alone. She disappeared without a sound.

And where do think you've been? said Nellie mentally.

Are you all right, pet? said George, staring at all the electronics that were keeping his wife alive.

Of course I am, pet. Are you all right, though? I've been really worried about you, man, said Nellie.

I'm fine. But I thought you were in a coma an' paralysed an' that, said George, incredulous that anyone could be fine with all those wires and leads coming off them.

Well, technically I am all those things, said Nellie, smiling mentally, *but this is weird, I can feel meself getting better all the time as if me body is rebuilding itself. I think it's ganna take some time, though. Really I should be dead, what with that big fat Albie Donnelly get landin' right on me heed and breaking me neck, but for some reason 'The Thing' wouldn't let us die. Canny, eh?*

Aye, said George, thankful. *Ah knaa just what ye mean mind, cos I can feel meself getting better aall the time. It's like ah'm bein' reknitted. An' when all me knittin' gets done an' I'm a lovely jumper, ah'm ganna kick Albie Donnelly's big fat arse.*

Diven't be daft, man, said Nellie, mentally shaking her head at her daft husband. *He'll be long gone now.*

Ah divent knaa, mind, pet, said George, staring at a point just above his wife's head; he couldn't look at her for too long, it was too distressing. She knew this, of course, and felt sorry for her husband. *I've been interviewed by the coppers an' they reckon he might come back and get revenge. He's a nutter, man.*

Well, we'll just have to watch oot for him then, won't we? Now come over here, Wheelie Georgie, an' give us a kiss.

There were tears in George's eyes as he kissed his wife gently on the lips.

What are you up to? said Nellie, suddenly causing George to go all squirmy in his wheelchair.

Nowt, man, pet, man, said George, rubbing his cheek against Nellie's and pretending to be all innocent, like a puppy.

Don't you give me that, George Creedy, said Nellie. If she could've pulled away and looked her husband up and down with her eyes narrowed, she would have. But in her condition she had to make do with doing it mentally.

Weeell, said George, leaving a gap you could drive a milk float through.

Nellie just lay there, making George more uncomfortable.

George! she snapped.

Ah'm ganna re-enter the competition and win the leek money, said George, expecting his wife to leap on him. She did something even better. She managed to spin his wheelchair round.

Ahhhhhhhh! said George, suddenly coming to a stop.

Say that again, said Nellie.

Nah, man, ye'll ownly spin us aroond again, said George. *Ye can be cruel to an owld bloke. Just wait till you're better, ah'm ganna knack ye.*

Don't you try and make me laugh, George Creedy. You are not entering that stupid leek competition again, it nearly got us both killed, man! said Nellie.

Why no, man, woman, man, The Thing saved us, didn't it? Anyway, I've got to dee it, said George. He could feel Nellie mentally staring at him.

Why? she said coldly.

Because, said George, *I'm not having you staying in this bloody hospital while ye get better. Yer coming home for me to look after, and havin' all that prize money will make it easier. Plus I'm ganna hire a bodyguard to look after us and me big prize-winnin' leek. Now that's the end of it, woman, yer dein' what ah tell ye for once.*

Ah, George, said Nellie, sounding like a schoolgirl. *Yer so romantic, I do love you yer daft owld get. Noo get yem and get growin' that big leek. I wanna come back home to a palace.*

She mentally gave her husband a big hug. George shook his head, tears trickling down his cheeks. They were interrupted by a nurse coming in to say that Nellie had to get some rest, and that George had some visitors. So George kissed his wife goodbye for the time being and allowed the nurse to push him back to his ward. There he was joined by his friends.

'So what's wrong with her then, George, pet?' said Mrs Big Fat Squinty Bill kindly.

'Ah, it's terrible, man, she's on a life-support machine an' paralysed an' everything, man,' said George, 'but the doctors say she'll recover. Ah want to get her home as soon as possible so ah can look after her.'

'Can ah see her, George?' said Mrs Big Fat Squinty Bill.

'Aye, she's through there, pet. Yer not supposed to gan in there, but I'm sure she'd like to see ye,' said George.

When Mrs Big Fat Squinty Bill had left the ward there was an uncomfortable silence like you always get, even with old friends, when they're on a hospital visit. Even Wheelie Billy had stopped talking his customary shite. George decided to put them out of their misery.

'Ah'm ganna win the leek competition,' said George, smiling at the other two men.

'I don't think you can,' said Big Fat Squinty Bill. 'Yer leek was killed. Squashed by Albie Donnelly.'

'How did you knaa?' started George.

'The police have been interviewing everybody, man,' said Big Fat Squinty Bill, 'Ye've been on the news an' everything.'

'Oh,' said George, surprised. 'On the news, eh? Well I'll be on the news again when I've won that money. Your lass'll get her nick-nacks an' all.'

Wheelie Billy looked up expectantly.

'Aye, aa'll reet, Billy,' laughed George, 'I'll buy you a rocket-powered hovercraft wheelchair an' all.' Wheelie Billy smiled, never doubting the existence of such a thing. There was a feeling of great warmth between the friends.

'I'm ganna grow another massive leek an' win the prize so I can look after our lass,' said George, chin jutting out stubbonly.

'I thought you said she was paralysed,' said a voice from the doorway. It was Mrs Big Fat Squinty Bill. She had a big smile on her face. 'Well, if she's paralysed, how come she's just squeezed me hand and smiled at me.'

The three friends got stuck in the door trying to see Nellie. Big Fat Squinty Bill got some nasty wheelchair wheel burns that Mrs Big Fat Squinty Bill had to put calamine lotion on later that night.

Michael Satriani sat on his bed in his hotel room. Spread out in front of him on the table was a selection of photographs. Most of them were of Clancy Tree Jr and had been taken over the years he had been watching him. Michael Satriani hated Clancy Tree Jr and would take pleasure in killing him. The American private detective touched the photographs gently as if the very act would reveal where the spoiled rich kid was hiding. But he couldn't concentrate on the pictures of the man he was looking for for long. His eyes kept straying to the edge of the bed where a single print lay.

The picture was blurred, but Satriani knew what he was looking at. It was a picture of a man flying. Michael Satriani's assistant had taken the photograph as they observed the fight from the bushes in the allotment. If they hadn't been disturbed they could have had Clancy Tree Jr and his new superhero friend. How the fuck had Clancy Tree Jr hitched up with some fat flying fuck? How could he do that? This thing just got stranger and stranger. But Satriani knew that when he found them they certainly wouldn't be killed. He had other plans for them. What the photograph didn't show was George Creedy, as he was on the floor and hidden by the wall of the shed. If Satriani could've seen the golden glow surrounding George he would certainly have been more interested in the old man.

'$15 million dollars,' said a voice from the doorway. Satriani turned to face his partner Jimmy. Not, as Clancy Tree thought, Michael Satriani's lover but his younger brother. Which explained how they were both so good looking. They had been mistaken for gay men on many occasions, much to their amusement. Michael Satriani was always amazed at how vitriolic heterosexual men could be if they were in the company of two good-looking strangers like them. Some people even wanted to start fights with them, which was a very bad idea indeed as the Satriani brothers were very tough boys indeed. And if they ever needed to get really rough with anyone they got in touch with their two other brothers, Simon and Nick, who were even better looking than Jimmy and Michael. Being beaten up by the Satriani brothers was the closest you could come to being attacked by Playgirl magazine.

'Fifteen million, eh?' said Michael, as he gathered up all the photographs.

'Yup, not bad, eh?' said Jimmy, as he picked up the photo of Albie flying.

'How the fuck?' he said, shaking his head.

'Well, that's not for us to find out, is it?' said Michael. 'It'll be out of our hands soon. The sooner we catch our boys the sooner we get our money.

'Both sets of money,' laughed Jimmy, as he flicked the photograph at his older brother's head. Michael caught it and slipped it into his jacket pocked.

'Perfect plan, isn't it, brother?' smiled Michael, as he grabbed his brother in a headlock.

'I'm glad I thought of it,' grunted Jimmy from under his brother's armpit, before throwing him crashing to the floor.

As plans go it was nearly perfect. Over the years the brothers had come across some quite astounding things when they had become involved in certain cases. Apart from the run-of-the-mill stuff, like humans bursting into flames for no apparent reason, ghost sightings, aliens and a dog which could walk through walls (they had the video evidence of that), they had also come across some really scary stuff, like people who could fly, had superhuman strength and, in one memorable case, there were some priests who had managed to conjure up the Devil, which was not a thing the brothers particularly wanted to get involved in again. The thing was, all of these things exist, but up until now there had been no proof. The American government did have a lab in the centre of New York where certain research went on but even they didn't really believe it, they just had to have one because the Russians had one, although the Russians' lab was so old-fashioned all they had in it was a pig who could say one word, and that wasn't even in Russian so it was probably some sort of spy pig.

But when it came down to dodgy spooky and spiritual stuff there was always a nation you could depend on: the Japanese. They had been doing research into supernatural stuff for hundreds of years and had a fine collection of aliens, walk-through -wall dogs, etc. etc. Talking pigs were old news there. But what they really wanted was some superhumans. Maybe then they could breed with them or something and make all Japanese people superhuman.

Over the years, the Satriani brothers had been approached by various Japanese agencies offering them money for anything they had discovered. Unfortunately, the brothers had found nothing until they accidentally came across Clancy Jr's flying friend and had wired their photograph over to Japan immediately, which is why the brothers were now wrestling on the floor of a hotel in Newcastle-upon-Tyne. They were celebrating the fact that not only would they be getting a lot of money for delivering Albie Donnelly to the Japanese, they would also be getting the same amount from Clancy Tree for pretending to kill his son.

Michael Satriani was sitting on top of his brother shouting, 'Who's daddy now?' when the maid started up the Hoover next to his head.

'Apparently you are, pet,' she said in a deadpan Geordie accent, although she was thinking, Ahh, what a shame. Two good-looking lads like that and they're right puffs.

Ellen Difford could barely suppress her smile, although what Clancy Tree had just told her should have stopped her smiling and sent her running to the police. He was going to have his son killed! His own son. Strangely she didn't blame him. Over the last few days Clancy had opened up to her more and more, telling her tales of his son's exploits and how much it had cost him in cash, but more importantly how it had affected the old man mentally. Clancy Tree Jr thought he had kept all his escapades secret, but his father knew about them all: the deaths, the drugs and the debauchery. He even knew what had happened when he had disappeared for two years with the rock singer Luscious, although he had only just started singing and went under the ridiculous moniker of Mr Delicious (he really fancies himself, doesn't he?), all that was to come later.

Clancy Tree had pieced it all together after Michael Satriani had infiltrated the cult and drugged and dragged the youngster back to his father after first shooting Mr Delicious twice in the chest, a wound that would have killed most people. In fact, two people were killed by Michael Satriani, two of Mr Delicious's 'priests' who died protecting their master. Mr Delicious had survived the shooting and the following scandal that had erupted around his cult. He had gone underground and emerged as the rock singer Luscious. If anyone remembered his past, he was now making so much money it was conveniently forgotten.

Ellen Difford was smiling inwardly because Clancy Tree was revealing so much about himself and that could mean only one thing. Clancy Tree really trusted her, which meant he really liked her; and everyone knew really like could turn to really love and really love turned to marriage, and if that happened Ellen Difford would be a really rich woman.

'I feel,' said Clancy Tree, 'that we have grown very close, Ellen, and I'm glad you have let me unburden some of my problems on to you. You have been a great support to me.'

'That's what I'm here for, Clancy, darling,' she said, stroking the old man's hair. She was now talking with a very slight American accent, a fact which her mother had picked up on immediately when Ellen had visited her the Sunday before, although what her mother had actually said was, 'What ye taalkin' aall daft for?' When she had Clancy's money, Ellen thought, she need never see her bloody mother again.

'But we still have business to do here,' said the old man, standing up suddenly. 'I have money to give away and a business to take care of, so let's go down to the site, see how the building is getting on, then go into town for lunch.'

'That's a lovely idea,' said Ellen, standing up and smoothing her tight black skirt down over her thighs. It'll be the last money he ever gives away when I'm his wife, she thought, as they linked arms and left the hotel room.

11 〉

If Clancy Jr had known what Ellen Difford was up to he would've dragged Albie back to his father's hotel and killed the gold-digging Ms Difford and his father with his bare hands. But he had other things to worry about at that moment. Just after they had left the Oxfam shop and were determinedly yomping through Byker on their way to Newcastle Central Station, London and Luscious, Clancy Jr became aware that the buzzing noise in his head wasn't caused by the amount of cocaine he had consumed, it was in fact the noise of a police van which was now following the pair as they half-jogged past the closed shops.

The two policemen in the van, who were just about to come off their shift and were quite used to this sort of sight, at this time of night, in this part of town, were just about to pull past Albie and Clancy and head back to the police station and a cup of tea when, without missing a beat, Albie turned towards the van, pulled out his sword and leaped straight on to the windscreen. Luckily the van was only travelling at a walking pace, or it could've been seriously damaged. The driver slammed the brakes on and Albie was thrown on to the road. He didn't feel a thing. He bounced straight up and renewed his attack on the van. Luckily both doors were locked or Albie would certainly have got into the cab with the officers.

Now these two coppers were old hands at this sort of thing and what they certainly weren't going to do was get out of their nice safe reinforced cab and try to arrest what were obviously a pair of mad junkies. So they immediately called for back-up, although when they called the descriptions through they knew there would be a few laughs at their expense when they described the big one-eyed pirate who was now dancing around the van singing, 'Ho Ho Ho and a big fat bum'. They didn't care. Let someone else take care of it, it was time for their beddy-byes.

'What the fuck do you think you're doing?' screamed Clancy Jr as he grabbed Albie by the arm.

'Ow!' said Albie, like a child, as Clancy Jr's grip caught the loose skin on the big man's upper arm.

'Come on, you fuck,' said the American, as he pulled Albie away from the police van. Just then, the policemen noticed that the smaller of the two men had a big gun tucked into the waistband of his jeans. That certainly got their interest. It also got the interest of the other policemen who were taking their time driving down to apprehend what were obviously two harmless nutters. When the scream 'He's got a gun!' comes over a police radio, you put your siren on and your foot down.

'Fuck!' screamed Clancy Jr, as he heard the sirens in the distance and dragged Albie back the way they had come. They were both running hard through the back streets. Albie had taken the lead, his legs pumping, his pirate's hat hanging down his back. He had lost the eyepatch immediately and blood was once again pouring from his ruined eye and ear. He had no idea what he was running from or where he was running to, it just seemed like a good idea to run. Clancy Jr followed his big friend, not realising he had no idea where he was going.

At about this time something occurred that, had it happened a few months before, would have made the American very pleased. His trousers fell down. He had lost so much weight that they were only being kept up by the added bulk of the gun he had jammed into the waistband. Clancy Tree pitched forward, his chin catching Albie's heel. Clancy Jr's teeth snapped shut, biting the end off his tongue. He didn't feel a thing. Albie tripped over one of his feet and the momentum carried them both head first into a hole left by the local council, who were repairing the drains. Two police cars, sirens wailing, sped into the street, missing Albie and Clancy Jr completely. Oblivious of the pain in his mouth, Clancy pulled Albie to his feet, then pulled up his trousers. He almost laughed. They were both covered in fetid mud. Blood was pouring from Clancy's mouth. The pain hit him like a punch and he collapsed to the floor, where he threw up on Albie's trainers.

Tears were coursing down his face as he pulled the bag of cocaine from his pocket and stuck his tongue straight into the white powder. The pain stopped. He took a big mouthful of coke and swallowed it. He looked up at Albie. The big man's good eye was completely dead and his ruined eye socket was filled with mud. His skin looked as though there were little insects underneath it trying to get out. Every muddy part of Albie that Clancy could see seemed to be twitching. Clancy Jr pushed the bag of coke into Albie's face. The big man took a mouthful, swallowed, then leaped out of the hole and sprinted up the street with Clancy in hot pursuit.

The police were in the next street. The American could

hear them getting closer. Just as it seemed that they were sure to be caught, Albie ran across a main road towards a fence and disappeared. For a second, the small sane part of Clancy's mind thought that maybe Albie really was superhuman, but then he realised Albie had actually run through the fence. Clancy followed his partner straight through the hole and fell 7 feet to the ground. Luckily his fall was cushioned by Albie. Once again they had avoided capture, as the police cars shot past their escape hole. Clancy thought they were getting quite good at this.

The pair lay there; the wind knocked out of them both. Albie was growling like a dog. A sheet of pain shot through Clancy's head and everything turned black. He opened his eyes and found he was seeing everything through a red mist. The pain in the back of his head was so terrible his eyelids were sweating. He was aware of Albie standing up and moving behind him. Clancy couldn't move, and couldn't see where Albie had gone. He could hear Albie growling and grunting and there was a massive pressure on the back of his head. Suddenly the pressure seemed to ease slightly and with that the pain went from being terrible to just bearable. Clancy tried to stand but the weight on the back of his head kept pulling him to the floor.

Where the fuck was Albie? Clancy Jr got to his knees; there was something attached to his head. What the fuck was it? He staggered to his feet and tried to look over his shoulder to see what was behind him, but of course every time he turned his head whatever was now attached to it disappeared from view. 'Albie!' he screamed. He screamed again when he was pulled to the floor by the weight attached to his head. He was dimly away of a figure in front of him. His vision cleared. It was Albie.

'Albie, what the fuck is happening?' croaked Clancy Jr.

'You've got a dog,' said Albie, giggling.

'What?' shouted Clancy, then regretted it as pain shot around into his face through his eyes. Tears streamed down his face.

'A dog,' said Albie simply. 'It's got its jaws locked on the back of yer heed so I choked it, man, now the mad fucker won't let go. It's fucking massive,' gigged Albie.

A dog, thought Clancy. He'd had a dog once but he'd killed it when he was bored one day. Surely it wasn't that dog which had come back to haunt him. Any way he knew they didn't let ghost dogs on flights to England. 'A dog?' he said out loud.

'Yes, man,' said Albie. 'It was guarding the scrap in this scrapyard, but we fell on it so it bit you in the heed, man. It would've eaten you if I hadn't killed it. Hey, I'm a right pirate me, man. Come on, let's go.' And with that Albie disappeared from view. Clancy Jr heard Albie grunt as if picking up something heavy, and felt the weight lift from the back of his head. Although the pain was still appalling he staggered to his feet.

It was a good thing Clancy Tree Jr couldn't see what was going on behind his back. Albie was carrying the biggest dog he had ever seen. When he had first seen it he thought it was a pony with big teeth that had attached itself to his friend's head. Its jaws were locked on to the back of Clancy's skull, inflicting terrible injuries. Flaps of skin and hair hung down off his scalp; bone was showing through and blood was pouring down his back. Albie had choked the dog to death when it wouldn't let go of Clancy. He had tried to prise its jaws open, but when he couldn't do that he figured, quite rationally for a man in his condition, that the dog would have to come with them and he would have to carry the big pooch as it was attached to his mate.

Clancy Jr was standing. Just. He was still aware of the pressure on his head but the pain was so bad he had stopped feeling it. As a matter of fact he couldn't feel anything anywhere on his body.

'How's my leetle dawgie, Albeee baybeeeee?' he croaked.

'Eh, fuckin' fine like, man, c'mon, man, let's get gannin' we're gannin to London to see Luscious.' Albie gave the dog in his arms a little push, which caused Clancy to stagger forward. Albie started to giggle. There were stars exploding in Clancy's eye. The trio weaved their way drunkenly through the scrapyard. Albie didn't even flinch when a rusty bumper from an overturned car ripped deep into his shin; he just kept on carrying the dog. He was wondering what he would call his new pet when it seemed to leap from his arms and bounce out of view. The big man stood rigid, blood pouring down his face and down his shin. He looked down and saw blood seeping over his trainer and into the oily mud. He fell to his knees and scrabbled forward, hands outstretched, trying to find his dog. Without warning he pitched headfirst into the dirty waters of the river Tyne.

By now Clancy Tree Jr was dead. He had once been a strong swimmer. But no matter how many ribbons, cups and certificates he may have won, nothing had prepared him for swimming in an ice-cold river, with treacherous undercurrents, a dead 12-stone dog attached to his head and enough cocaine in his body to keep Mötley Crüe up for a month. When Clancy had hit the water he had instinctively tried to kick his way to the surface. It was then his heart just gave up and stopped beating. He was dragged to the bottom of the river by the dog on his head and swept into the remains of an Austin Allegro. Their bodies were never recovered.

Albie on the other hand was swimming like a fish. The fact he was swimming the wrong way, out to sea, didn't bother the big fish man at all. He was feeling no pain. He had no idea why he was even in the water, he just knew he had to keep swimming and it was all going fine until he was hit by the bag of puppies. It's a sad fact that people still get rid of unwanted pets by throwing them in rivers. Which is exactly what happened to Albie. A plastic bag with three Alsatian-cross puppies hit Albie right on the head mid-stroke. The shock caused Albie to suck in a massive amount of water. There was a splash, he rolled over on to his back and suddenly he too was dead. The puppies, on the other hand, had escaped from the plastic bag and managed to clamber on to the dead man's chest, where they sat whining pathetically until the body bumped into a ferry landing and they were rescued by a welder from Swan Hunters shipbuilders, who took them home and named them Maurice, Robin and Barry after his favourite group, the Bee Gees.

He didn't report the body. He reasoned that if you're in the River Tyne that's probably where you wanted to be. Albie floated out to sea and was never heard of again. Clancy Jr and Albie weren't missed by anyone really. The scrapyard dog's disappearance was a bit of a mystery to the scrapyard owner, but he soon got another dog − from the same bloke who had tried to drown the puppies.

Surreptitiously, Junior had managed to search the house from top to bottom now. He knew almost every inch of it. He had even managed to find the room from where the cameras were controlled, although he wasn't allowed in. He had tried to enter the state-of-the-art control room at the top of the house and was surprised to see two of the crew from the plane leap up and stop him from entering. He hadn't seen any of the crew since they had landed and had certainly never seen them arrive at the house. They jabbered at him noisily in Spanish, and Junior had to put on his I'm-a-big-stupid-old-bodyguard-and-I-got-lost act until they calmed down. He had, for a split second, considered killing them, but he noticed they were both armed so he retraced his steps back to the rehearsal space and watched the band go through their set once again.

Luscious was a hard taskmaster. The band could do whatever they wanted to do in their own time, but when they were working they were his. He had even sacked Kid Mikey the original drummer. Luscious had started screaming at him one day mid-rehearsal, berating him about his timekeeping. Junior thought the singer sounded like a vicious old queen when he got into one of these moods and he usually snapped out of it. But on this occasion he kept on and on. Kid sat there behind his kit, head bowed, until finally he stood up, looked the singer in the eye, said quietly, 'Fuck you, Devil boy,' and walked out of the room. Luscious had merely laughed nastily. As he did two days later when he found out from the television news that the drummer had been found dead in his room in an expensive hotel in Kensington, west London. The TV report said it was a sex game gone wrong.

The drummer's replacement was an Englishman, Eric 'Beano' Reid, who up until recently had been in the second biggest band in the world until the whole band apart from him had been killed in a plane crash. Needless to say he was slightly unhinged. He fitted into the band perfectly. There wasn't really much for Junior to do. Since their night out at The Chicken On A Pig, Luscious hadn't ventured from the house. There had been a bit of excitement when the security of the house had been breached by some of the more determined Luscious fans. Scooby had wanted them arrested but Luscious said no, he wanted to keep them. Junior thought this a very strange turn of phrase and he noticed the worried looks on Scooby's and Fairy's faces. The three fans – two girls and one boy – did indeed stay, although the bodyguard never saw them again.

Junior was no closer to the Luscious entourage than he

had been when they first arrived in the country, although he liked Fairy and was pleasantly surprised to find out that Fairy Flowers was her real name. She was a very serious woman and was constantly on the phone working the press on behalf of her boss. She set up interviews, only to have Luscious cancel on a whim. He had cancelled the last interview because he thought the journalist had a face like a wok. The poor girl was visibly upset when Fairy broke the news to her, as Luscious had made Fairy repeat his words exactly. What he had said was, 'Tell fucking big fat wok face to fucking fuck off.'

Junior had found Fairy sitting in the garden crying. She had ground her mobile into the lawn under the heel of her Jimmy Choos. This didn't really matter as she always had two spare mobiles in a holster slung low around her skinny hips. That had always amused Junior.

'Hey, a crying girl,' said Junior lightly, as he strolled around the corner where two high hedges met and tripped over Fairy, who was sitting on the lawn with her head in her hands. He had, of course, known she was there, as he had heard her sniffles, but he thought it might cheer her up if he fell over her.

'Fuck off,' said Fairy.

Junior picked her straight up from the floor as if she was a child, held her above his head and then threw her on to the top of the thick hedge. The look on her face as she landed was so comical that Junior bent double laughing, the way a giant would, with his hands on his hips and his legs straight. That was the last thing she had expected him to do, and she lay on her back kicking her legs in the air and laughing uncontrollably. The only other person to have done anything remotely like that was her father, who would bump her into the bushes which surrounded their yard in Florida as they played basketball together when she was a kid. The look of innocence on her father's face as she climbed once again out of the greenery always made her giggle. She was glad her daddy was long dead and couldn't see her now.

'Get me down now!' Fairy shouted at Junior, who was standing underneath her with the same 'Who me?' look on his face her father used to have.

'Not until you say sorry,' said Junior, pretending to walk away.

'Fucking sorry,' giggled Fairy.

'That'll do,' said Junior, returning to the hedge. 'Now jump,' he said, extending his big arms. Without a moment's hesitation, Fairy leaped from the hedge and was caught safely in Junior's arms. He placed her gently on the ground just as one of her phones rang. She snapped it to her ear and listened for a second. 'I'm coming now,' she said briskly into the mouthpiece and started towards the house. She suddenly stopped in her tracks and turned towards Junior. 'Leave before next week,' she said urgently, and disappeared behind a hedge.

Junior had been thinking about leaving, but something had happened which made him want to stay, although he was bored and sick of the childish antics of Luscious. One moment he could be charming and the next he would act like a vicious spoiled child. At first Junior had put his antics down to drug abuse, but then he realised there was no way Luscious could keep up his gruelling schedule of rehearsals if he was hoovering class As into his body; and from the very first day at the house Luscious had insisted Junior work out with him at 7am every morning, so Junior saw first hand just how fit the singer was. Luscious had even asked Junior to show him some martial arts moves but when he realised Junior wouldn't show him the moves he could use to kill he lost interest.

Junior had got heartily sick of Luscious's talk of heaven

and hell and how Junior was sure to go to hell because of all the people he had killed. How Luscious knew anything about Junior's past was a mystery to the bodyguard, because he had told him nothing. One morning as they had just finished their daily workout and were leaving the gym, Luscious didn't stop to admire his muscular sweaty torso in the big mirrors that lined each wall as he usually did. Instead he caught up with Junior and grabbed his arm just as he was about to step into the sauna.

'Would you like me to save your soul, big man?' he said in a singsong voice.

'Oh, behave,' said Junior, using an expression he had heard the new drummer use and thought it apt for dealing with naughty children or childish rock stars. Junior pulled his arm away and stepped into the sauna. He scooped some water out of the bucket with a ladle and threw it on to the coals. Steam rose instantly. Junior went to sit down on one of the benches in the small pine room and was shocked to see Luscious there all ready.

'How the fuck …?' began Junior, his body tensing.

'I can save your soul,' said Luscious, his teeth bared, his voice guttural. Junior went to grab the singer and found to his amazement he was frozen to the spot. It was as if the steam was preventing him from moving. Luscious had disappeared. A voice right by Junior's ear said, 'I can save your soul.'

Junior would've jumped if his body had let him. The voice he had heard was so low it wasn't even human, it sounded like an animal. For the second time in his life Junior felt scared. There was cold sweat running down his body. His teeth began to chatter. The coals were burning blue.

'I can save your soul,' said the voice again. Junior was aware the words hadn't been spoken but had been placed into his head. There were icicles hanging from the roof of the sauna. Junior's breath formed clouds in front of his face. Without warning the heat hit him like a hammer. He collapsed. Gasping for breath as the searing air burned his lungs, he crawled across the floor trying not to breathe, reached the door and punched it open. He breathed the cooler air greedily, pulling himself to his feet using the cross bracing on the door of the sauna. He managed to stagger a few yards before falling head first into the Olympic-sized swimming pool which was adjacent to what he now thought of as the pine coffin which he had just dragged himself out of. The warm water of the pool levelled out the extreme temperatures in his body. He let a low moan escape from his lips, the bubbles bursting from his mouth as he kicked towards the surface. Junior swam slowly towards the shallow end of the pool and as soon as he could he let his feet rest on the bottom and he stood in the water breathing heavily. He looked over to the sauna and there stood Luscious. He was looking straight at Junior.

'I mean what I say,' said the singer, before turning and leaving Junior by himself. Junior was too tired to reply. He took a deep breath, put his head under the water and swam lazily towards the deep end.

How could he possibly leave the house after what had happened in the sauna and now that he had been warned by Fairy? He was certainly staying now. Things were just starting to get exciting.

'The last thing your wife needs is any excitement, Mr Creedy. She must have complete rest,' said the doctor, taking Nellie's pulse once again as she sat in the wheelchair, waiting to be wheeled home by George, her overnight bag sitting neatly on her slim knees.

'Is it all right if I tie her wheelchair to the back of the car to get her yem, doc?' said twinkly-eyed George. 'Ye see, ah cannit fit her in the car an' she'll like the fresh air.'

'Yes, very funny, Mr Creedy,' said the doctor, her face showing no sign of amusement. 'I cannot stress how delicate your wife's condition has been, I have never known a recovery like it, and because of that, we're worried she may relapse.'

'Whey, no, man, pet, man,' said George, smiling. 'She can't relapse, she's as strong as a fat binman, anyway she has to get yem and get me tea on, man.'

George began to wheel his wife towards the hospital exit and the awaiting taxi.

'I had to get one of them black cabs like they have in London, pet, to get your wheelchair in,' said George to his wife. 'I had to go to the central station, mind, to get one, so you owe us me bus fare.'

Just get it out me purse, pet, thought Nellie to her husband. George smiled happily.

Which is what the doctor was doing as she watched George gently put his wife into the black cab. The doctor was surprised that either of them were going home at all. How did a man of his age, after the beating he had taken, have the strength to carry his wife in the first place? And how had she made such a miraculous recovery? She should really have been paralysed for the rest of her life, and there she was being taken home in a wheelchair. It almost made you believe there was such a thing as God. As the cab pulled away, George and Nellie both turned to the doctor at the same time, smiled and waved. A shiver ran down the doctor's spine. She looked around embarrassed, as if someone had known what she was thinking, then turned and walked back towards her ward with a quizzical look on her face.

'An' I mean it, mind,' said George, laughing, as they sat

next to each other in the cab. 'Just because yer in a wheelchair doesn't mean you won't be cooking an cleaning.'

Nellie smiled at her husband. It was only a small smile because she didn't really have control of her facial muscles yet and she couldn't speak – although that didn't matter to George and Nellie – but she could feel herself getting stronger every day.

And I'll soon be able to shout at you the way a wife should, she said to George, trying to give him one of her looks. *An' I hope my hoose is tidy, mister, or you're for it, mind.*

George grabbed his wife's hands between his. 'Eeh, it's great to have you coming home, pet,' he said, tears in his eyes.

Ah stop it, man, George, man, said Nellie, her eyes filling up with tears. *Yer just trying to get on me good side 'cos the house will be like a pigsty.*

Pigsty! roared George in her head. *How, man, it's spotless, man, woman. It's had to be cos I've been bringin' lasses back every night. An' not just any lasses either but them supermodels. So ye better watch yer step, pet, ye can soon be replaced.* Nellie laughed out loud in George's head.

The cab wound its way through Newcastle, then down past the Byker wall and on to the Fossway, which took them past Daisy Hill and into Wallsend. Nellie took in all the sights greedily, glad to be going home.

The taxi pulled up at their front door. The street was unusually quiet. George made a big show of getting Nellie out of the taxi. *Stop showing off, man, George, there's no one watchin', man*, said Nellie, laughing as George picked her up and pretended she was far too heavy for him.

'I'll tell you what. I'm going to carry you across the threshold like I did when we were married,' said George proudly.

Eeh, George, you liar, we never got married, said Nellie.

Still holding Nellie, George fumbled for his keys, then

opened the front door. The shout that greeted them made Nellie jump with shock. The whole street was packed into their house to welcome Nellie home. Some folk had even come from as far away as Durham, so you can see how popular Nellie was.

There was a banner strung across the hallway which read 'Welcome Home Nellie Pet'. All Nelly could see were smiling faces. She wanted to touch them all at once. Tears were pouring down her cheeks. Big Fat Squinty Bill ran forward and tried to take Nellie from George.

'Gerrof, man,' said George. 'She's mine, man!' but he finally gave up his wife to his friend. She looked like a little doll as she sat there in Big Fat Squinty Bill's pudgy arms.

'Eeh, it's good to have ye back, pet,' said Big Fat Squinty Bill, smiling down at Nellie, tears running down his big face.

'Where do you want the wheelchair?' said the cabbie, pushing his way through the crowd of well-wishers.

'Put it there,' said George, indicating a spot in front of Big Fat Squinty Bill. The cabbie pushed the wheelchair into position and Big Fat Squinty Bill gently lowered Nellie into it. A big cheer went up. The cab driver coughed.

'Oh sorry, man, kidda,' said George, reaching for his wallet, 'and keep the change,' he said handing him a tenner. 'And yer stayin' for a drink,' said George, shoving a can of lager, which had appeared out of nowhere, into the cab driver's hand. The cabbie, a young lad called 'Dixie Dave' because of his interest in the American civil war, did stay, and had such a good time he asked if his girlfriend, Lorraine, could come down too, which she did. Dixie Dave was so taken with George and Nellie's relationship that he proposed to Lorraine, she accepted and they've now got two kids.

Nellie was overwhelmed by the kindness of her friends. They all wanted to talk to her at once, even though she couldn't answer them. Most of them wanted to tell her how much they'd missed her. A lot of them got very emotional and Nellie had to comfort them in sign language. Nellie put up with all the fuss for about an hour and a half, and then she signalled to George that she was tired and would like to go to bed. George, being the perfect host, shouted at his guests, 'Right, you scroungers, out. Our lass has got to get some kip. She's a very old woman, ye knaa!'

The guests good-humouredly shouted back at him, but pretty soon the party began to break up as all of them knew just how lucky Nellie had been to survive the attack. Even though she looked unhurt, George's face was still black and blue, which reminded everyone what the pair had been through. The last people to leave were, of course, Mr and Mrs Big Fat Squinty Bill and Wheelie Billy, who had taken it upon himself to be Nellie's bodyguard. He was telling everyone who would listen how he was going to show her all the tricks that you could do in a wheelchair and was trying to convince everyone that life was better with wheels. Nellie was glad to be back in the madness.

'How is she really, George?' said Mrs Big Fat Squinty Bill, when at last the five of them were alone in the Creedys' kitchen. Some of the guests had commented on how George seemed to be able to read Nellie's mind, which caused the couple to exchange a wry glance.

'I think she's ganna be fine,' said George, staring at his wife proudly. 'She's tough as old boots, man.'

George, can you put me to bed, pet? I'm knackered, but you stay and have a drink with this daft lot, said Nellie to her husband.

'I'll tell you what,' said George. 'I'm ganna put Nellie to bed.'

'We'll gan then, pet,' began Mrs Big Fat Squinty Bill.

'You'll do no such thing. I'll be back in a minute.'

George picked up his wife and carried her up to their bedroom.

'Get yourselves a drink!' he shouted over his shoulder as he climbed the stairs.

He laid his wife on the bed and gently started to undress her. 'Eeh, yer still a fine figure of a woman,' said George, only to realise his wife was fast asleep. He shook his head, a single tear ran down his cheek and he let out a big sigh. 'I don't know what I'd do without you.' He gently slipped on her nightdress and tucked her into bed. 'I love ye nacked neck,' he said as he bent down and kissed her on the forehead. Then he wiped the tear from his eye and went to join their friends.

'Hey, ah've been dein' some readin',' said Wheelie Billy to George, when he returned to the warm kitchen where he had left his friends.

'Aye, what aboot?' said George, taking a can of Export out of the fridge and slowly pouring it into a glass.

'Well, ye knaa they've cloned sheep?'

'Aye, ah'd heard,' said George, aware that this conversation could be heading anywhere.

'Well, you could have that done to Nellie,' said Wheelie Billy.

'What, have her turned into a sheep,' said George. 'Divent be daft, man, you knaa what she's like with her hair, she'd gan mad if I had her sheared once a month.'

'Ah, man!' said an exasperated Wheelie Billy. 'Ye just divent understand science, man!'

'Ah, that's where yer wrong, though,' said Big Fat Squinty Bill. They were all a bit drunk. 'George does understand science, how do you think he grows his massive leeks, man? Science, that's how.'

'Hmmm,' said George, taking a drink.

'Well,' said Mrs Big Fat Squinty Bill, 'have you started yer massive leek then, George?'

'Of course I have, man. I said ah was ganna win the prize,

didn't ah? But the police have been around and they said ah've got to be careful, like.'

'Why's that?' said Big Fat Squinty Bill, concerned.

'Because,' said George, 'Albie bloody Donnelly's still on the loose with his cronies and they reckon that they might come back and get me an' our lass, because we're the only witnesses. I'll tell ye ah'm worried an' all. Ye knaa how mad Donnelly is. Well, not only can I put him away, but I can grow bigger leeks than him as well. He's ganna be furious, man.'

'Ye knaa what ye need?' said Wheelie Billy.

'What?' said George, expecting the wheelchair-bound newsagent to say something like 'a rocket-powered time-travelling hover robot'.

'A bodyguard,' said Wheelie Billy smugly. The other three around the table looked at him all thinking the same thing: That's the last thing I expected him to say and it's not a bad idea.

'That's not a bad idea, Billy,' said Mrs Big Fat Squinty Bill. Billy smiled as if all his ideas were great ideas.

'Where am I ganna get a bloody bodyguard from?' said George, pouring himself another beer. 'Ah'm not bloody Madonna.'

'Well, there has to be agencies or something, hasn't there?' said Big Fat Squinty Bill.

Wheelie Billy butted in: 'Whey aye, man, what about Charlie's Angels or Minder or ...'

'They're television ... oh never mind,' said George, cutting Wheelie Billy off.

'Anyway, they'll be expensive, surely?'

'Well, I could always ...' started Wheelie Billy, but this time he was cut off by Mrs Big Fat Squinty Bill.

'Well, for the next few days Big Fat Squinty Bill is going to be your an' Nellie's bodyguard,' she said. 'Isn't that right, Big Fat Squinty Bill?' she was smiling sweetly at her husband.

'Eh, aye, er, that's right, pet,' said Big Fat Squinty Bill, sticking up his meaty fists Queensbury style. 'Ah've chinned Donnelly before an' I'll chin him again.'

'Look, man …' began George.

'No, ah'm not having you complaining, George Creedy,' said Mrs Big Fat Squinty Bill. 'Big Fat Squinty Bill is staying here tonight to protect you an' that's that.'

Big Fat Squinty Bill looked stunned for a moment and then nodded vigorously, under his wife's stern gaze.

'Aye, that's right,' said Big Fat Squinty Bill. 'Big Fat Squinty Bill's the name, nacking Albie Donnelly's the game.'

George was secretly glad his mate was staying; even though he and Nellie were well on their way to recovery, he didn't think they could fend off another attack from Albie Donnelly and his cronies. Of course, George was completely unaware that Albie and his pals wouldn't be troubling anyone ever again.

'I can sleep in your Neville's old room,' said Big Fat Squinty Bill. As soon as the words were out of his mouth he regretted saying it. George sagged in his chair.

'Our Neville,' said George, staring into the distance. 'Whatever happened to him, eh?'

'Ah, I'm sorry, George,' said Big Fat Squinty Bill. 'I was getting carried away. Sorry for bringing yer laddie up.'

'No, it's all right, man,' said George, brightening up. 'I know he's all right, I can sort of feel it. I just wish he would get in touch. It would really make our Nellie happy. Come, let's have another drink, man, we're celebratin', man.'

'I don't think so, George Creedy,' said Mrs Big Fat Squinty Bill. 'You are going to bed, yer bodyguard's going to bed an' I'm pushin' Billy here home. Come on.'

Mrs Big Fat Squinty Bill got up and pulled on her coat. She gave her husband a big kiss and George a big hug, and then began to push a protesting Wheelie Billy towards the door.

'C'mon, Billy, I'll take you yem,' said Mrs Big Fat Squinty Bill to the newsagent as she pushed him out the door. 'Who knows, you might get lucky.'

George and Big Fat Squinty Bill could hear Mrs Big Fat Squinty Bill's filthy laugh all the way down the street.

'Thanks for staying, man,' said George to his mate when they were alone.

'Aye, well, this doesn't mean we're courting or anything, mind,' laughed Big Fat Squinty Bill, as he got another beer out of the fridge for George and began to make himself a Sea Breeze.

'This is enormous!' breathed Ellen Difford, when she and Clancy Tree arrived at the site of the newest Big Trees development. Before this, she had only seen it as a model in Clancy's hotel room. It was really beginning to take shape.

'Well be employing 500 people,' said Clancy Tree proudly. 'Should do wonders for the area.'

And for your bank balance, thought Ellen. At that moment the Satriani brothers arrived. Ellen thought them incredibly sexy, but not as sexy as Clancy's money.

'Didn't know you were coming down here today,' said Michael Satriani. As usual his brother stayed in the background, looking bored.

'I didn't know you'd be here either,' said Clancy Tree, annoyed at seeing Satriani because it reminded him of what he'd told the private detective to do.

'We're just about to leave,' said Satriani, clearly agitated. 'Your son's trail has gone completely cold. He's just disappeared. We came up here to check that he hasn't been sniffing around with his new friend. We're flying to London today, then we're going to track down Luscious. We think your son has hooked up with him again.'

'I can't understand how he and his ridiculous flying

friend could have just disappeared,' said Clancy Tree, staring off into the distance. 'Surely they must have been spotted by someone. They'd stick out like a sore thumb back home.'

'Well, that's just the problem,' said Satriani, speaking to the side of Clancy Tree's head. He noticed there was a slight twitch in the old man's neck and a patch of hair that he'd missed with his razor when shaving. 'When I spoke to our police connection about any sightings of two men acting strangely, he said, and I quote, "They're all fucking strange aroond here, every fucking one of them's a heed the baall." Unquote.'

Clancy Tree finally turned to look at Satriani. 'Heed the baall?' said Clancy Tree, his face wrinkling up. 'What's a heed the baall?'

'It means they're all mad,' said Ellen Difford, slipping her arm through Clancy's. A move that did not go unnoticed by the Satriani brothers.

'I'm glad someone can speak the language,' said Satriani, smiling the smile he kept for best at Ellen. He could feel he was losing the old man and he knew if he could charm his new girlfriend he might be able to keep Clancy Tree on his side.

'So we're going to London to see if he's with Luscious again.'

Once again the old man was staring into the distance.

'Keep me informed of everything you see,' he said in a tone that meant their conversation was over. There were an awkward couple of seconds when no one knew quite what to do, then the brothers turned and walked off the site.

'How many of these centres do you have, Clancy?' said Ellen, trying to cheer him up. He didn't answer. His breathing was low and fast, and his eyes wide and staring.

'Clancy!' she said, drawing attention from two builders

who were strolling past. 'You all right, pet?' one of them said, kindly.

'I ... er,' stammered Ellen.

'Twenty,' said Clancy suddenly.

'Yes, we're fine,' blurted Ellen to the builders.

'Yes, twenty Big Trees,' he continued, eyes still staring off into the distance. 'I've made a fortune and I have nothing. Maybe my son is right. Worst of all, maybe Luscious is right.' Ellen was staring up at Clancy. Somewhere on the site someone was stonecutting, the whine of the blade cutting through all the other building noise.

Clancy Tree suddenly shook his head. He turned to Ellen, a serious look on his face. 'The best thing about having so many Big Trees garden centres is that they make me big money, which means I can afford to buy you a big lunch.'

His serious look changed into a big smile and made him look ten years younger. Ellen breathed a sigh of relief. Maybe she would be a wealthy widow after all.

They linked arms and walked off the site.

Junior watched the approaching black van from an upstairs window of the house. He had been on one of his snooping missions and just happened to be outside the camera control room when he heard the buzzer from the front gate go off. He pressed his ear to the door and heard one of the men inside say, 'Good, good, just drive right up to the house.'

Well, they can speak English when they want to, thought Junior, as he walked away to see who the new arrivals were. The van, a Mercedes, wound its way up the driveway, stopped, then did a three-point turn so its rear doors were directly in line with the front doors of the house. Then it just sat there. No one got out and no one came out to meet it. In the distance, Junior could just hear the industrial rumble of the band rehearsing. Four figures dressed as monks suddenly emerged from the hedge either side of the van and stood facing its sides. Junior couldn't see their faces as their hoods were pulled up. He noticed that the robes they were wearing looked expensive, like something Vivienne Westwood might design. One of the monks reached out and touched the side of the van gently. Junior saw that the hand emerging from the heavy sleeve of the robe belonged to a black man. This surprised him. He had thought he was the only black man in the area, never mind the entourage.

As the doors of the van swung slowly open Junior was puzzled to see that they were bulletproof. Whatever was in the vehicle, it was obviously worth a lot to someone. A tall figure appeared from the darkness of the van. He was dressed in the same robes as the others. He stood for a second on the step, then jumped down to join the monks, who were by now kneeling in front of the open door, heads bowed. The new boss monk went to each of them and dropped a handful of seeds, which he pulled from a small worn leather satchel he had slung over his shoulder, on to their bowed heads. He then put his other hand into each of their hoods for a couple of seconds, as if cupping their chins. After he had done this four times the monks stood and faced the open door of the van. The boss monk then climbed back into the darkness of the van. When he reappeared he was carrying what appeared to Junior to be a small cage covered in the same material as the robes. He handed the cage to one of the monks, and then two more cages to two other monks. The fourth time he came out he handed a black metal bowl to the last monk. He then stepped back into the darkness of the van, the doors slowly shut and the van started back down the driveway.

The monks stood watching until the van was out of sight, then turned and walked towards the back of the house. Junior saw that the three monks carrying the cages were walking side by side. The other monk was walking in front of them. He was grabbing handfuls of feathers from the black metal bowl and throwing them up in the air. The three monks behind him were covered in feathers. It would have looked quite comical had the feathers not also been drenched in blood. Junior watched the monks until they turned the corner leading to the back of the house. He waited a few more minutes just in case there was more to the floorshow then went in search of the monks.

As he bounded down the stairs he began to smile to himself. This job was starting to get really interesting and he hadn't even killed anyone yet. It made a nice change. As he turned the corner, he ran slap bang into Fairy who wasn't talking into her mobile. Perhaps if she had been, Junior would have heard her and he wouldn't have sent her skidding across the wooden floor on her skinny behind. Junior pulled out his gun and aimed it straight at Fairy's head. Once again, the look on her face was so comical that Junior couldn't help but burst out laughing.

Fairy was apoplectic with rage and she did what most people wouldn't dare; she attacked Junior. Junior was laughing so hard she managed to get a couple of punches in which made him laugh even harder. Then, in one swift movement, Junior put her on her back. She didn't even see how he'd done it. He hadn't even hurt her. One moment she was shouting, punching and screaming; the next she was lying on her back and Junior had disappeared. She could hear him laughing like a child in the distance as he ran off.

'You'd better run, big man,' she shouted after him. 'I would've kicked your ass.'

Junior would like to have stayed and played, but he really wanted to find out what was going on with the monks. He had no problem finding where they were headed: even the stupidest of trackers could follow a trail of bloody feathers. He followed the trail through the house, but he had a hunch as to where they might be going. He was right. The trail led straight to the Italian part of the house and stopped dead in front of the electronic door.

Junior pressed his palms flat against the wall in frustration. He had to get into the hidden room to see what was going on and he definitely wanted to know what was in the cages. He could feel an electronic throb through the wall. He sensed there was someone behind him. Probably Fairy coming for revenge. He smiled to himself. As if doing a vertical press-up, he pushed away from the wall, turned, pulled out his gun and stuck it straight into the face of Luscious.

Both men had the good manners to keep the smiles glued to their faces.

'Can I help you?' said Luscious, not taking his eyes away from Junior's, who still had his gun pointing into Luscious's face. Junior was sure Luscious's eyes were changing colour and shape. He was mesmerised, and for one split second he thought he saw his boss turn into a big bird. Then the moment passed and, as if realising what he was doing, he put his gun back into his shoulder holster.

'No. I like to make sure everything's safe around the house. Wouldn't want your rich rock star ass to get kidnapped now, would we?' said Junior, trying to lighten the tone. He was beginning to feel increasingly uncomfortable in his boss's presence. The whole house felt different, as if pressure was building up. Junior had put it down to the approaching gigs, but for some reason, here in the Italian part of the house, the pressure was so great Junior felt as though his ears were going to pop.

'Can I help you?' said Luscious again, still not taking his eyes from Junior's.

'Yeah, you can help me,' said Junior, laughing. He could see his breath. 'You can stop fucking about with the temperature control.' Junior's teeth began to chatter.

'I can help you, Junior, baybeee,' said Luscious smiling, his voice singsong. Junior was sure he could hear parrots squawking.

'I will help you save your soul if you trust in me.' Luscious was holding Junior by the wrists. His hands felt hot and dry to the touch. 'I will come for you soon and I will show you what's behind the door.' He let go of Junior's wrists and disappeared.

Junior sagged against the wall, his chin on his chest. The air around him was freezing. He hugged himself, trying to get warm. This was ridiculous, it couldn't be this cold; he was indoors. The last time he'd felt as cold as this was when he'd slipped off an icy roof when he was working undercover in Northern Ireland. He'd been knocked unconscious and had lain out in the open all night. The temperature had gone down to -2 degrees. How he hadn't been discovered and killed was still a mystery to him. Luckily he was found by an army patrol, who dragged him into their van which was attacked itself by locals, who thought the patrol was taking one of their own. He had put up a fight even then and managed to break a young squaddie's arm.

That was cold, real cold, but the cold he felt now was strangely hot and dry. A thought flashed into Junior's head as he staggered back to his room, Can Luscious save my soul? He shook his head and began to smile at himself. Junior was an atheist; had been ever since the age of six, he saw his mother die. She was killed by a hot pie she had baked and his father had thrown at her in the middle of an argument. It knocked her clean out of the open sixth-floor window of their apartment block. It actually said on the death certificate death by pie. Which was strangely poetic because his dad was a maths teacher at the local school. Not that his dad had seen the death certificate. He was in such grief when he realised what he had done he ran out of the apartment screaming and was run over and killed by a Miss Lovely Legs float which was passing through town on a promotional visit. When he was being taken down to the orphanage later that night by a policeman he overheard him tell his partner that the guys on the block watching the float pass by didn't know what to look at, the lovely legs on display, the pie faced dead woman or the squashed dead guy under the float. After that how could anyone believe in God. But when he was with Luscious, Junior got the distinct impression he was with the Devil.

12 〉

Big Fat Squinty Bill was up early. He was taking his body-guarding very seriously. He crept stealthily towards the kitchen. He was sure he had heard a noise there. Shouting his war cry, 'Whey aye, am ganna knack ye!' He threw open the door and assumed his killing stance. He looked like a fat bloke holding up an invisible duvet.

'Morning, Big Fat Squinty Bill,' said George without turning round from the cooker, where he had just put sausage, bacon, mushrooms and tomatoes into a big pan and on to the gas hob. The kettle was boiling. It smelled just like your mam's house used to on a Saturday morning.

'Aw, man, George, man,' said a miffed Big Fat Squinty Bill. 'Ah'm supposed to be yer bodyguard, man, you can't just gan gettin' owt of bed, man, ye could get assassinated, man.'

'Shurrup, ye daft shite, an' get the tea on,' said George.

The back door opened and in wheeled Wheelie Billy.

'What de ye want?' said George. 'It's like bloody Northumberland Street in here.'

'Ah just wanted to see ye were all reet, man,' said Wheelie Billy. 'Ye knaa, make sure ye hadn't been mordered or owt, man.'

'Well, ah haven't, so go on yem,' said George, piling a plate high with all the fried stuff from the pan. 'Haven't ye got a shop to run?' he said, as he put four eggs into the pan.

'I left Bridget in charge, she can dee it aal by herself now. I've taught her everything I know,' said Wheelie Billy, getting his feet and his wheels right under the table.

'Billy, man, it would only take five minutes to know everything ye knaa, man. An' ah should think she can dee it by herself,' said Big Fat Squinty Bill, pulling up a chair and making himself comfortable at the table, while at the same time eyeing up the big plate of food George had been preparing. 'She's been working for ye for ten years, man. Has she got a boyfriend yet?'

'Eh, I don't think so,' said Wheelie Billy, looking suspicious.

'Well, she'd better hurry up, she's not …'

'Hoy, man!' shouted George, suddenly realising the two of them were cosying up to the table. 'What de ye think ye two are dein' like? Ah'm not a bloody café. Come on, oot, the pair of you. I've got an invalid to look after, man.'

'Aw, man, George, man!' Wheelie Billy and Big Fat Squinty Bill said at the same time.

'I'm starvin',' said Big Fat Squinty Bill. 'What with all this bodyguardin'. Anyway, I need to keep me strength up to fend off assailants and that.'

'Aall reet,' said George. 'Ye two stay there. I'll just go an' see how our lass is.' George left the small kitchen with his nurse's face on.

'Ah think ye fancy that Bridget lassie,' said Big Fat Squinty Bill as soon as George had left the room.

'She's not a lassie, man, she's 43, man,' said Wheelie Billy.

'Well, she's the right age for ye, then,' said Big Fat Squinty

Bill. 'Ye should ask her oot, man. Ah would if I were ye.'

'Ah wouldn't knaa how to gan aboot it, though,' said Wheelie Billy.

'Well, yer luck's in,' said Big Fat Squinty Bill, standing up and nicking a sausage from the plate. He stood there, his back against the cooker, holding the sausage like a fine cigar. 'Ye see, ah knaa loads aboot the opposite sex, me.'

'Ye knaa loads aboot shite,' said George, striding back into the kitchen. 'Ye two are in luck. Our lass is feelin' a bit tired. All she wants is some of her special juice.' George began to pull the juice ingredients out of the fridge.

'Dish up then, Big Fat Squinty Bill,' said George to his mate. Big Fat Squinty Bill didn't need to be asked twice. He started laying the table so they could begin their feast. Big Fat Squinty Bill liked to take his time with his food so he could savour every last morsel; the way a drug addict enjoys preparing for his fix. There wasn't much conversation then, as the noise from the juicer effectively cut that out.

George expertly diced carrots, apples, ginger, beetroot, parsley, coriander and whatever other healthy stuff from Nellie's garden was in the fridge. Even though both Wheelie Billy and Big Fat Squinty Bill drank Nellie's juice regularly they never liked watching it be made, in the same way that they knew how to make babies but they didn't want to see one delivered. Surely putting all that healthy stuff into your body couldn't be good for you. Anyway there was a full English breakfast on the go.

'Hurry up, man, George,' said Big Fat Squinty Bill. 'Ah'm dyin' of hunger, man.'

'You start,' said George, and with that he carefully carried the juice to Nellie while his friends tucked into their breakfast.

Ye were right, pet, said George, as he entered the bedroom. *Those two gannets did want feedin'*.

Nellie smiled a small smile. *Ah knew they'd be around*

worryin', thought Nellie to her husband. George helped her drink her juice. She had the use of her arms but she couldn't really grip things. *Ooh that's better*, she thought to George. *You'd better get back down there and have your breakfast pet or they'll eat it all up, mind.*

Aye, okay, pet, said George, wiping his wife's mouth with his hankie. *Do you want the telly on, pet?*

Aye, put Lorraine on, pet, said Nellie. *Let's see what ridiculous outfit she's wearing this morning.*

George pressed the remote and Lorraine Kelly flashed on to the screen of the small television George had installed in their bedroom. They burst out laughing. They both liked Lorraine, but couldn't help laughing at the way she was squeezed into glittery things so early in the morning.

Ah isn't she lovely? said Nelly.

Well, at least she's not bloody Trisha, said George, leaving the room in order to salvage what was left of his breakfast.

When he entered the small kitchen Big Fat Squinty Bill was giving Wheelie Billy his expert opinion on women. He had been with Mrs Big Fat Squinty Bill since they were both 16, so it was highly unlikely Big Fat Squinty Bill knew anything about the opposite sex at all, but that didn't stop him giving his expert opinion.

'Just be nice to her and she'll be nice to you. That's what lasses like. Niceness. Although obviously you've got to be a bit mean sometimes because they like that as well.'

'So I've got to be nice and nasty at the same time?' said Wheelie Billy, looking all confused.

'Errr, aye, that's right,' said Big Fat Squinty Bill, nicking a sausage from George's plate. 'Think Clint Eastwood,' said Big Fat Squinty Bill, grasping at straws.

'Ah, but in what guise?' said Wheelie Billy.

'Eh?' said Big Fat Squinty Bill, stumped.

'Well, do I think of him as Dirty Harry,' continued Wheelie Billy, 'or the man with no name or what about that time he had that monkey?'

'*Every Which Way But Loose*,' said George, sitting down. He didn't want to be part of this conversation but it was like trying not to look at a car wreck; he was just pulled into it. He nicked his sausage back off Big Fat Squinty Bill.

'Or what about that time he was in *Play Misty For Me*?' said Wheelie Billy. 'He wasn't very lucky with that lass. She tried to chop him up with a greeat big knife.'

'No, man, what ah meant was ...'

'What he meant, Billy,' said George butting in before he battered them both to death with a plate of fried food, 'was just ask the lassie oot, man. If she likes ye, she'll say yes, if she doesn't she'll probably push ye doon to the Tyne and hoy ye in and you'll never have lass problems again.' George picked up his knife and fork and started on his breakfast. A serenity descended on the room as the three friends tucked into their food.

'Right, after this,' began George, breaking the contented silence, 'we're gannin' doon to the allotment to have a look at me big leek.'

'Fantastic!' said Big Fat Squinty Bill. 'That's just what you should be doin', gettin' back into the leek saddle, so to speak. The two million poond is as good as ours, man.'

To prove he meant business, Big Fat Squinty Bill speared what was left on his plate – a sausage, a piece of bacon, two mushrooms, half a tomato and some fried bread – on to his fork and ate it all in one go. He took a big slurp of tea, wiped his mouth with the back of his hand and sat back in his chair a contented man.

The back door opened again and in walked Mrs Big Fat Squinty Bill.

'Aal right, pet,' burped her husband as she bustled into the kitchen.

'Ah was going to ask if you wanted breakfast,' said Mrs Big Fat Squinty Bill, 'but I can see you've already had it, you big bloater.'

'The beast is still a bit peckish mind, though, pet, man,' said Big Fat Squinty Bill, patting his stomach. 'Got any Hob Nobs in yer bag?'

'No, come on, you lot, out,' replied Mrs Big Fat Squinty Bill. 'I'm tidying up for Nellie, so you lot get out and do what you normally do. Nowt.' She picked up her husband's coat and threw it at him. George lit up one of his skinny roll-ups and began to clear away the plates.

'No, you too, come on, out,' said Mrs Big Fat Squinty Bill, handing George his coat. 'Nellie needs peace, quiet and a woman's company.'

'Aye, yer right, pet,' replied George, pulling on his coat, smoke from his skinny roll-up making his eyes water. 'Anyway, we've got to gan doon the allotment to see me lovely leek. It's gan to win us aall the money and you will be crowned nick-nack queen. I'll just say ta-ra to our lass and I'll catch ye two up.'

Aall right, pet? said George, as he entered their bedroom.

I feel champion, pet, replied his wife.

George noticed her smile was getting wider. That made him smile even more. *Mrs Big Fat Squinty Bill's come to look after you. I'm just nippin' doon the allotment. Is that all right?*

Whey aye, man, get yourself away, you've got money to win me. George kissed his wife then stood up and pulled on his cap.

Nellie, he said awkwardly. She looked up. *I do love you.*

Nellie beamed. *I know, love*, said Nellie. *I've got 'The Thing' remember? But I do like to hear you say it. And bloody Geordie blokes are the most useless in the world when it comes to love stuff. Go on, get out and see yer leek. Oh and, George?*

Yes, pet, said her husband, turning from the door.

Make sure you tell it you love it.

I will, pet, said George, as he passed Mrs Big Fat Squinty Bill entering the room.

'Right. I'm going to do it now,' George heard Wheelie Billy say as he joined his two friends in the street.

'Do what?' said George, taking a pull on his roll-up.

'I'm ganna ask Bridget out, that's what,' said Wheelie Billy triumphantly.

'Good for you, kidda,' replied George, smiling.

'Aye, I would never have had the courage if it hadn't been for the wise words of Big Fat Squinty Bill,' said Wheelie Billy, nodding his head towards the big lad.

George turned to look at Big Fat Squinty Bill without turning his head. Big Fat Squinty Bill didn't say a thing – he couldn't really, he was eating a Penguin biscuit – but George could tell he thought he was the Yoda of love.

By now the trio had reached Wheelie Billy's shop, and he shot through the door before his courage deserted him. George and Big Fat Squinty Bill could hear him shouting for Bridget as they walked down the street towards the allotment.

'I hope ye knaa what your dein',' said George when they were out of hearing of Wheelie Billy.

'Whey aye, man,' said Big Fat Squinty Bill. 'It's what the lad needs, man. It'll cheer him up. It might stop him from talking such shite.'

'Aye, yer right,' said George, surprising himself by agreeing with his mate.

As the pair reached the allotment, Big Fat Squinty Bill pointed to a poster that was stuck to the allotment members' hut. 'Ye've only got a week to get yer leek massive,' groaned the big man. 'I hope ye can dee it, George.'

'No problem, man,' said George. 'Howay, man, let's go and have a look at what I've grown.'

'Can you smell anything, George?' said Big Fat Squinty Bill, wrinkling his nose.

'No. Why?' said George, striding off towards his shed.

'Something stinks. It's like rotting meat,' said Big Fat Squinty Bill running to keep up with his mate.

'Now that you mention it,' said George, stopping to take a sniff, 'I can smell something. Hoy, get away from there,' he suddenly shouted at a pair of dogs who were digging something up. The dogs just stopped and stared. Big Fat Squinty Bill lumbered towards them and they ran off. He filled in the hole with the side of his boot and pulled a bit of old door over where they had been digging.

'Well, I don't know what that …' started Big Fat Squinty Bill to George, but his friend had gone. He stamped up to George's hut, mud flying off his big shoes.

'George! George! Where are ye, man?' He pulled open the door and saw that George had cleared up the mess from the fight he'd had with Albie Donnelly. Everything was neatly stacked away, but there was no George and no massive leek.

'George?! George?!' bellowed the big man anxiously.

'Shush, man!' hissed George.

Big Fat Squinty Bill spun around. His friend was nowhere in sight. 'Where are you?' whispered Big Fat Squinty Bill; it was catching.

'I'm over here in Trevor's shed,' said George.

Big Fat Squinty Bill looked over to Trevor's shed and sure enough there was George peeping out from behind the open door.

'What are ye dein' in there, man?' said Big Fat Squinty Bill, rushing over to where George was standing. George pulled open the door and dragged him in. It was very shadowy inside Trevor's shed.

'Trevor'll gan mad, man,' said Big Fat Squinty Bill, massaging his big arm where George had nipped him again.

'No, he won't,' replied George. 'Trevor said I could have it. He reckons I've got more chance of winning the leek money than him. So I've taken over his shed. Albie Donnelly's so stupid he'd never think of looking somewhere else for me leek.'

'Bloody hell, George, you've done it again,' said Big Fat Squinty Bill, looking over George's shoulder at a shadowy shape lying on a workbench. 'That's a massive leek!'

'That's a carpet,' said George. 'The leek's over there.'

'Oh, aye,' replied Big Fat Squinty Bill sheepishly. 'Well, if you'd put some lights on.'

George flicked a switch and a weak yellow light lit up Trevor's shed. He wasn't a great gardener old Trevor, so his shed was a bit of a mess. But there, in the corner, in a small trough, proudly stood George's new leek. It was tiny.

It gave a little squeak. Luckily Big Fat Squinty Bill couldn't understand leek.

'Is that it?' said Big Fat Squinty Bill. 'It's tiny, man, George. That'll never win you two million quid, you've only got a week left.'

'That's plenty of time, man,' said George, stroking the little green vegetable tenderly.

Big Fat Squinty Bill looked behind him. He could've sworn he heard a kitten purring.

'C'mon,' said George. 'Let's go for a walk and see how everyone else's leeks are dein'.' George flicked off the light and the pair went for a mosey around the allotment to size up the competition, although for the first time Big Fat Squinty Bill didn't think there was any competition. He couldn't see how they could possibly win.

Junior couldn't help applauding. The band rocked. He

looked around at the other people in the room and they were all smiling and applauding too. A girl in a wheelchair pushed herself forward and handed Luscious something. The singer smiled, took it from her and rewarded her with a kiss. She grabbed him by the neck and wouldn't let go. For a split second Junior thought about giving his boss a hand. He'd once seen a middle-aged midget dressed as a little girl kill an undercover FBI man who had been dressed as Santa Claus. The midget had got up on to Santa's knee and pushed two Hello Kitty pens into his eyes.

Junior realised he was taking the job just a bit too seriously as the wheelchair girl's smiling parents quickly stepped up and prised their daughter's arms from Luscious's neck. The singer stood up laughing and joking with them. The girl's parents stood the way all parents do when suddenly face to face with someone ridiculously famous who also happens to be their daughter's idol. The mother turned into a giggling 16 year old and the father, who felt like he was a giggling 16-year-old girl, kept a manly, smiling silence, one arm draped casually over his daughter's shoulders. They were smitten.

The day had been organised by Fairy to give Luscious maximum publicity. It was the final day of rehearsals before the gigs, and the press had been invited down to watch, as well as a few competition winners and members of the fan club. It was obvious from the reaction of the small audience that they adored him. The British press in particular had always been kind to Luscious, although he very rarely featured in their pages. He hardly ever did interviews and was never pictured falling out of nightclubs with a model on each arm. Although they tried, the tabloids didn't really understand him. The music was too loud and hard. It was far easier to write about the latest banal pop poppet than to delve deep into Luscious's lyrics. But judging by this performance Luscious had won them all over and he was preparing himself for the press conference. Fairy had done a good job. All the tabloids, most of the broadsheets and all of the rock magazines were there, plus some specialist magazines like *Tattoo* and *Bondage*. Of course, the mainstream journalist couldn't wait to chat with the two ladies from *Bondage*, who were dressed up for work.

All the journalists were being plied with food and drink and, interestingly, it was the tabloid hacks that refused the alcohol. Everyone else steamed in, especially the lads from *Kerrang!*, who were putting away bottles of Cristal as fast as the Luscious look-alike waitresses could deliver them.

It wasn't like any of the other press conferences Junior had attended. Luscious happily mixed with everyone present, slinking through the throng like a cat and giving his full attention to anyone he was particularly attracted to. He had changed into an expensive black suit, but combined with his long blond dreadlocks, heavy silver jewellery, ripped T-shirt and biker boots he looked like a wicked aristocrat. No matter what Luscious wore, he gave off SEX. Junior watched his boss work the crowd and had to admire him. Everyone he talked to had a big smile on their face. As he spoke to them he touched them gently on the face or stroked their hair, and they all became like lovestruck teenagers.

'Easy fucking job for you, eh?' said a gruff voice at Junior's shoulder. Junior turned and looked down into the squashed-up face of Scooby. 'What would you do if someone pulled a fucking gun on him, eh?'

'I'd throw you at him,' smiled Junior. 'Now fuck off, I'm working.'

'Yeah, yeah,' said Scooby. 'Listen, tonight your boss wants you to join him in a little celebration, and guess what? You're gonna be the guest of honour. You'll love it. I'll come and get you, tough guy.' And with that Scooby wobbled off through the crowd giving his shark-eye to everyone he passed.

Enya passed by and Junior grabbed her by her skinny arm. He felt as if he was holding just bone. She wobbled on her high-heeled boots. Junior looked into her face. He hadn't seen her around for a while. She looked dreadful: eyes sunken deep into their sockets; skin pale and papery. She was shaking like a cold puppy.

'Hey, Enya,' said Junior.

She stared at him, her eyes dull.

'Oh, hi, Junior,' she said. She was trying to smile, but her lips seemed to be sticking to her teeth. Her tongue was poking out slightly; Junior could see it had a blue tinge to it. Whatever this girl had been doing it wasn't doing her any good, thought Junior, but in this state she might open up to him a bit.

He smiled at her. 'Are you coming to the party tonight? Apparently I'm to be guest of honour. I hope a naked lady isn't going to jump out of a cake. I hate that naked lady cake stuff.'

Enya's eyes focused on his face, her pupils were the size of pinheads. She began to laugh. She sounded like an old man.

'Yes, yes, tonight is the night. Yes, we'll all be there. And so will he at last.' Enya staggered and was caught by Fairy. She whispered something into Enya's ear. Enya actually went paler than she already was. Junior was just wondering where all her blood could possibly be going, when Fairy ground her heel into his foot. He looked down at her. She was dressed as usual, just like Luscious, but strangely enough she wasn't as sexy as Luscious. Not that Junior would be admitting that.

Although she was smiling, Fairy's eyes were hard. 'Do not go tonight. Leave now,' she said through her smile. She turned and was immediately collared by a drunken woman who, thinking Fairy was a waitress, demanded a drink. Much to Junior's amusement Fairy pushed her away and told her pleasantly to fuck off. The indignant looks on Fairy's and the journalist's faces made Junior laugh, although he stopped when they both glared at him. What is it with glaring woman? They can make the toughest man feel like a little lad.

Time to do some work, thought Junior, as, smiling, he threaded his way through the crowd. He was wondering to himself what the collective noun for a crowd of journalists was (a lie? an expenses? a drunk? a think-you're-the-best-writer-ever-to-put-finger-to-keyboard?), when he felt a muscular arm slip through his.

'And this is the most important member of my entourage,' he heard Luscious say. 'This is Junior.'

Luscious was slurring his words but Junior knew he wasn't drunk. He was playing to an audience. And they loved him.

'And what do you do, Mr Junior?' said a very serious girl wearing a badly fitting suit.

'Junior,' continued Luscious, 'is my bodyguard. He's killed people, you know.'

'Have you really?' said the serious girl, her eyes shining. The other journalists craned forward smelling another story. Junior smiled in a he's-had-far-too-much-to-drink way and the moment was broken.

'Don't worry,' continued Luscious, 'because tonight I will save him.' Luscious began to dance with the serious girl.

She looked at him the way a bacon sandwich looks at a hungry fat builder before it's eaten. Terrified.

Soon the party was winding down as the journalists had to get back to London. It was obvious from their disappointment that the girls from *Bondage* had expected they would be invited to stay, but even they were ushered out of the door and into the waiting cars. Junior wandered around the grounds making sure none of the guests had got lost, then returned to the house. It was very quiet, but the air was still thick with smoke and the smell of drink. The waitresses, who had changed out of their Luscious costumes, were tidying everything away.

He climbed the stairs to his room. He should leave, that was obvious. He felt it in the house. Something was going to happen tonight. But what could they possibly do to him? Luscious was a rock singer, for fuck's sake. What was the worst that could happen? They could kill him. Junior thought he deserved to die anyway.

'What you doin', you daft old get?' said Big Fat Squinty Bill, as he pushed his way into George's kitchen and found George on his hands and knees, head under the cooker.

'It's her, man,' said George, indicating Nellie, who was sitting at the table with a it-must-be-around-here-somewhere-and-if-it's-not-it's-your-fault look on her face.

'She's lost her bag an' she's blaming me, man.'

'I'm not blaming you,' said Nellie, although it sounded like 'Amotlaminoo'. She only said it out loud for Big Fat Squinty Bill's benefit.

'You can speak,' said Big Fat Squinty Bill.

'Aye, an' I wish she'd shut up,' said George. 'She's never bloody stopped all morning.'

Big Fat Squinty Bill ignored him. 'That's great, Nellie, man,' said Big Fat Squinty Bill, his eyes slightly less squinty than they normally were, which was a sure sign he was impressed. 'That means yer getting' better, man. I'll put the kettle on to celebrate.'

'Aye, I thought you might,' said George. 'Look, pet, I cannit find it anywhere. It must be in the hospital.'

Ah but, George, it had all me photographs and everything in, man, there was some lovely photos of you. I'd hate to lose them, said Nellie.

Big Fat Squinty Bill didn't hear that, of course, but what he did hear was George replying with, 'Well, I can understand you not wanting to lose any photos of me. I'm a good-looking man. I'm very photographic me, man, pet.'

Big Fat Squinty Bill turned from the cooker, which was a place he loved to be standing as it gave him both heat and food. 'What are you talking about, George?' he said.

'Look, man,' blustered George. 'When Nellie came out of hospital she had an overnight bag with her.'

'Turkey,' said Nellie.

'She bought it in Turkey,' said George, translating, 'when we were on holiday over there. It's always been her favourite. Anyway, when she was in hospital I filled it with some of the things she needed, like her nightie and washbag and things she likes, you know, family photos and that, and took it up for her. Well, now we can't find it an' she's blaming me, but I've looked everywhere and I can't find it. She had it when we came out of the hospital, but ...'

'You've left it in the taxi,' said Big Fat Squinty Bill, getting the milk chocolate biscuits out of the cupboard without a by-your-leave.

Nellie and George made faces and you're-an-idiot noises at each other.

'Of course, man,' said George, clicking his fingers. 'The taxi. I'll go up and get it later.'

It was just at that time that the brick came through the window. It narrowly missed Big Fat Squinty Bill, bounced off the grill and landed on the table. Although the three of them were showered with glass, they were unhurt. They all froze, looking at the brick. There was a note tied around it.

'Are you all right, pet?' said George to his wife. She nodded, although he knew she was before he had even asked the question.

'The postman always was a bit rough round here,' said

George, getting up and looking out of the broken window. The street was deserted

'Are you gonna open it?' said Big Fat Squinty Bill.

'Nah, it'll just be a bill,' said George.

'But,' began Big Fat Squinty Bill.

'Course I'm gonna bloody open it,' said George, picking up the brick and weighing it in his hand. 'Could've bloody killed someone.'

George untied the note. It was attached to the brick with gardener's twine.

'Be careful,' said Big Fat Squinty Bill. 'There could be fingerprints on it.'

'Aye,' said George. 'I'll be careful before I hand it over to Clarice Starling.'

George flattened out the note on the table. The letters that made up the words in the note had been cut from a newspaper, the way you see it done on the telly. It said: 'KEEP AWAY FROM THE COMPETITION OR YOU'RE DEAD'. The note-writer had neatly cut out a full stop and an apostrophe to make sure it was well punctuated. They had only used upper-case letters and they were all in the same font. George thought the brick-thrower was a bit anal to go to all that trouble, and the fact he had used punctuation at all meant the brick hoyer, to use the local patois, was one of the older members of the leek club. George certainly wasn't scared of a bunch of old granddads.

'Bloody Albie Donnelly!' said Big Fat Squinty Bill angrily.

'Nah, it can't be,' said George. 'He wouldn't go to all that trouble. He'd just come around and bash us. It looks like we've got even more enemies. I think I might have to move me leek from its secret hiding place. What do you think, pet?'

Nellie let loose a stream of angry noise which basically meant: We will not be terrorised in our own house and if I could get my hands on them I'd kick their fat arses. George translated for Big Fat Squinty Bill. Although he left out some of the swear words as George thought his mate had had enough shocks for the day.

'Well, at least me bodyguard was here, eh, Big Fat Squinty Bill?' said George, slapping his mate on the shoulder.

'Divent ye worry, man, George, man, I'd take a brick for you,' said Big Fat Squinty Bill seriously, taking a big slurp of his tea.

'You knaa, I think we could do with another bodyguard just to make sure you're really safe,' continued Big Fat Squinty Bill.

'Divent be daft, man, I'm not the bloody president,' said George.

'What about my bag?' said Nellie.

'Right, this is what I'm going to do. I'm going down to the allotment to get me leek. While I'm away I want you,' said George, pointing at Big Fat Squinty Bill, 'to fix the window.'

'But will you be safe by yourself?' said Big Fat Squinty Bill.

'Whey aye, man,' said George. 'Anyway, I'm ganna stop by Wheelie Billy's an' take him with us, he's mad enough to keep anyone away and I can put me leek trough on his wheelchair. The only downside is that he's ganna be talkin' shite for the whole journey. Then I'm ganna come back here an' settle me leek in the living room in front of the telly. It'll be like that *Ground Force* is on, and then I'm going to find Nellie's bag'

Surprisingly Nellie agreed with everything George said and she told him as much. But they also had both noticed a change in each other. It was as if their injuries had made them stronger. Nellie knew George would have his trouble antenna up and would not allow himself to get into a position where he would be hurt. The only reason he was taking Wheelie Billy was because Nellie had insisted. She wanted to find out about the little newsagent's love life.

'Right,' said George, finishing off his tea, 'I'm off to the allotment to pick up the bairn. There's glass for the window under the cupboard, ye knaa where it is.' George gave Big Fat Squinty Bill a stern look and Big Fat Squinty Bill had the good manners to look embarrassed.

Big Fat Squinty Bill had broken their window fourteen times, basically because he is big, fat and squinty. Mrs Big Fat Squinty Bill reckons he has broken everything in their house at least twice. George always kept spare glass under the stairs in case of accidents. It was one of the only times the phrase 'In case of emergency do not break glass' could be used.

If there was one thing George Creedy enjoyed, it was pulling on his cap and coat, lighting a roll-up and heading off to the allotment. Which he did after giving Nellie a kiss and Big Fat Squinty Bill a lecture on how to look after Nellie, not that she needed looking after. Big Fat Squinty Bill asked for a kiss all the same.

And don't forget Wheelie Billy, flashed Nellie into George's head as he was halfway down the street. It had crossed George's mind to do just that, but Nellie could read him like she could read the big book of mind-reading with extra large print. Easily.

All right, man, woman, I'm goin' for him now, replied George, pretending to be irritated. *But if he starts talking about love stuff I'm pushing him under a ... Hang on love*, said George suddenly. He stopped abruptly and pretended to look for something in his pockets. George was being watched, he could feel it.

I'll speak to you later, pet, said George to Nellie ending their conversation and beginning to concentrate on his surroundings.

There were three of them, thought George, as he carried on up the street towards the newsagent's. Two were behind him and one was in front. He wasn't worried at all. He could sense by their thoughts that they were men as old as he was. They had more of what George thought of as 'dignity' in their thoughts. Not like the youngsters' heads George sometimes got into. Their heads were just full of nonsense, just wanting a fast fix of pleasure without earning it.

George suddenly sprinted forward. He knew that one of his pursuers was hiding in a garden up ahead. It didn't really take mind-reading to do that; George could see his tartan cap above the hedge. He ran in to the garden and crept up to the man who was hiding there.

'What the bloody hell do you think yer doin', Norman?' said George over the man's shoulder. Norman fell to the ground clutching his chest.

'Bloody hell, man, George!' gasped Norman. 'Divvent creep up on us like that, man, you could give us a heart attack.'

'Well, what you watchin' us for?' said George, thinking about how ridiculous it was asking Norman Sewell that question, as he wore the thickest glasses anyone had ever seen. He was technically blind but was just too vain to admit it as he thought he was a bit of a ladies' man, which was precisely why he never had a lady.

'Err, well, you see ...' began Norman sheepishly, but he was cut short by the noise made by the two other men running into the garden.

'He went this way,' one of them shouted before he was stopped dead in his tracks by the sight of Norman on his knees in front of George.

'I might have known it was you two,' shouted George to the new arrivals.

'Has he hit you?' said the second man as he stopped behind the first.

'Grow up, man,' said George shouting. 'Of course I haven't hit him, mind you, ah should after he threw that brick through the window.'

'Eh, sorry about that, George,' said the first man who looked, sadly for him, like Mavis Riley out of *Coronation Street*, only with a beard. Which is why he had grown it. Of course, people called him Mavis. The fact he was as deaf as a post saved him from most of the embarrassment his nickname would have caused him and it was why George was shouting.

'Norman didn't realise you were in the kitchen. I knew I should have done it. He's blind as a bat,' said Mavis.

'No, I'm not,' said Norman indignantly.

'What?' said Mavis.

'W,W,W,W,Whey aye you are, m,m,m,m,m,an,' stuttered the third man, Harrison Ford, not the real one, obviously. Norman wished he was called Harrison Ford. They all patiently waited for Harrison to finish. 'Ye c,c,c,c,could ... h,h,h,h,h,have k,k,k,k,k,k,killed someone.'

'What?' said Mavis.

This could take forever, though, George.

'Right!' he shouted, so Mavis could hear. 'Norman, tell me what's goin' on, before I bash the lot of you.' George could have as well, since they had all been at school together and they all knew that George had been a bit of a hard case.

'Well, we want to win the leek money,' began Norman, 'cos we wanna gan on a cruise, like, an meet lasses an' that. Cos we're aall on our own now.' George remembered that Mavis's and Harrison's wives had died a couple of years ago on the same day and the three of them, who had been mates since all of them were kids, had got together for company. What George saw in front of him were three lonely old men. Which is what he would have been if he didn't have Nellie.

'An' we reckon we could win, well, if you weren't in it. So we thought we'd try an' scare you off. Sorry, George.'

'What?' said Mavis.

'Look,' said George, 'this is what I'm ganna do. I'm gonna win the leek prize. An I'm ganna pay for your cruise and anything else you want, ye daft old gets. Just stop hoyin' bricks through me window an' followin' me around, OK?'

'Ah thanks, man, George,' said Norman and Harrison together. Mavis didn't say a thing, but he could tell by the look on his friends' faces something good was happening.

'Hoy, what about me?' said a voice above them. George, Norman and Harrison looked up. Mavis followed their gaze.

'What about you?' said George to the woman who was hanging out of the upstairs window. They all knew her as well. Once you went to school in this area you tended not to move very far.

'Well, you lot have ruined me garden with yer tramping aboot, so I think I deserve something, too.'

'What would you like, missus?' said George exasperatedly.

'Weeell,' said the woman. Her first thought was to say, Can that bloke with the specs on come in for a cup of tea? She quite fancied him and anyway if he was wearing specs that thick he might fancy her. Unless he had unfeasibly sensitive hands and could 'feel' what she looked like. But she was an old-fashioned woman from a time when women didn't do the asking out, so what she did say was, 'It's not for me, you understand, but you knaa what we need aroond here?'

'What?' said George resignedly, expecting her to say something like a puppy-powered rocket launching pad. He was sure talk of the leek money had made folk dafter than they normally were.

'A baker's shop,' she said.

The four men looked at her. 'What?' said Mavis.

'I miss having fresh bread and nice cakes. So could you open a bread shop?'

'Anything else?' said George sarcastically.

'A fish shop would be nice,' said Norman. 'I like a bit of fresh fish, me.'

'That's a good idea,' said the woman.

'I,i,i,i,it is,' said Harrison.

'What?' said Mavis.

'All right, all bloody right,' said George holding up his hands in surrender. He never thought he'd see the day when he'd have a conversation that was more ridiculous than one with Wheelie Billy. 'If I win the competition, I'll send the three wise bloody monkeys here on a cruise and I'll open up a bakers an' a fish shop. Now I'm goin' to me leeks.'

'Thanks, George, you're a saint,' they all said, apart from Mavis who said, 'Five past one.'

I'm ganna have nee bloody money left at this rate, thought George as he stamped up the street to see Wheelie Billy. He didn't have far to go, because coming towards him was Billy himself. He was with Bridget. They were holding hands, which meant Wheelie Billy could only push with his right hand which meant his wheelchair kept hitting Bridget's legs and knocking her off the path and into the road. They both had big smiles on their faces.

'Hello, George,' simpered Billy and Bridget.

Oh bloody hell, they're in love, thought George.

'All right, Billy, Bridget,' said George. 'Where you two off to then?'

'We're going to have a look at bathroom suites,' said Wheelie Billy. Bridget smiled.

George couldn't take it any more. 'Well, enjoy yourselves. I've got to get down me allotment. See you later.' And George hurried past the lovesick pair.

I caused that, thought George, me and my bloody advice. Well, at least they're happy. But how am I ganna get me leek home now?

13 >

The knock, when it finally came, was very quiet. So quiet, in fact, that Junior decided to ignore it. He hated wimpy knocking. It came again, more insistent this time. Junior got up from the floor, where he had been passing the time doing some stretching exercises, and pulled on his jacket. He was wearing a black, lightweight Prada suit, black Grenson Chelsea boots and a grey v-necked cashmere sweater. He was carrying his full complement of weapons. He hadn't eaten for a couple of hours, which always made him feel light and dangerous.

He pulled open the door.

'What the fuck do you think you are ...?' said Junior to the sight that greeted him. He was playing dumb. He knew from the uniform the small, slim man in front of him was wearing that he was one of the Pope's own guard from the Vatican. It would be as weird for you as going down to breakfast one day to find it being served by a Beefeater.

The man spoke quickly in Latin, then turned away from

Junior and walked quickly down the corridor. Junior followed warily. He felt like Alice in Wonderland. The uniformed man didn't look around, he just carried on walking. He had strange little mincing steps. Junior had to trot to keep up. The man wasn't going the way Junior had expected, he was walking away from the Italian part of the house.

'Hey Pinocchio! Shouldn't we be going this wa ...?! Obviously not,' shouted Junior, when he realised the man was heading for the gardens at the back of the house. The uniformed man didn't slow down or look around.

Two of the band members were sitting at the breakfast bar in the large kitchen as the uniformed man, followed by Junior, entered. They both had big fat spliffs. There was an open bottle of gold label tequila in front of them and they had just had a shot each when they spotted the new pair. They stared at each other trying not to laugh.

'Fuck!' said one one of the musos. 'Is it gay pride already?' They gave each other high fives and doubled over laughing, the way only spliff can make you laugh. As Junior left the kitchen he heard one of the musicians say through his giggles, 'Did we really see that?'

Junior was now in the garden and he could see the Vatican guard was heading towards the lake. 'Right,' he said under his breath as he broke into a jog, 'I'm sick of this.' But the man in front of him, as if anticipating what Junior was going to do, broke into a jog too and pretty soon they were both running at full pelt. The uniformed man's mincing steps had turned into the strides of an experienced runner and he was running straight for the lake. Junior was by now about six feet behind him and gaining, his Chelsea boots throwing up little divots of mud as he thundered after his prey. Junior's outstretched fingers touched the robe of the guard's uniform just as he threw himself head first into the lake.

Junior followed him in and landed on the guard's back,

crushing him beneath the water and instinctively grabbing the man around the neck. The weight and impetus of the two men took them straight to the bottom of the lake to a depth of about four feet. Junior tightened his grip, but the man suddenly threw his head back, catching Junior on the chin. He tasted blood in his mouth as his lower gum split. Junior hardly felt it. What he did feel was a hand, a child's hand, grab his ankle. He looked over his shoulder for another attacker. No one. He felt a tentacle curl around his wrist. There was nothing there, although he could see the blood floating up from the welts on his arm where the suckers had been. He was aware of the man wriggling in front of him. Junior looked at the back of his head only to see a face. If Junior had been watching British television for the last ten years he would have immediately recognised the face. It was Felicity Kendal.

Junior supposed it was meant to frighten him, so he punched her in the mouth and Felicity disappeared. The big American managed to get his feet on the muddy bottom of the lake and he stood up dragging the uniformed man with him. He was absolutely furious; his clothes were ruined. Junior spun the man around and punched him hard in the chest. The man fell back into the water stunned. He picked him up and threw him over his shoulder. It was then that the lake floor opened beneath Junior's feet. If anyone had been watching from the shore they would have seen the two men instantly disappear as if sucked under the water. In fact, someone was watching from the shore, although they would never have been spotted by even the most accomplished of observers. If Junior had been anywhere near the Italian part of the house he would have heard a big cheer go up from behind the concealed door.

In a tangle of arms, legs and water, Junior and the uniformed man were dropping down a stainless steel pipe.

There were small lights recessed into the walls, which gave off a fluorescent glow. Even as he fell, Junior wondered who could have created such a feat of engineering and why.

The pipe changed direction. Instead of falling vertically they were now travelling down a small incline and they appeared to be slowing down. Junior was on his stomach and he felt as though he had the guard on his back. There wasn't much water in the tunnel, so Junior assumed that whatever door had opened to cause them to drop into the lake floor had closed again. Suddenly the pair shot through an opening and into more deep water.

Junior kicked his feet and swam to the surface and to the sound of loud cheering and clapping, and loud rock music was playing. He shook his head to clear the water from his eyes and ears. He seemed to be in a massive tank of water like a fishtank. The sides were made of reinforced glass. Junior lay in the water with his arms over the side of the tank as if relaxing. In front of him were about fifty people applauding, and Luscious was leading the applause. Junior pulled out his gun and pointed it straight at the singer. Luscious didn't even stop clapping and seemed to be looking over Junior's shoulder.

The bodyguard heard a strange gurgling noise behind him and spun around, gun raised. There was the small uniformed man, who had regained consciousness and was swimming towards Junior, a look of absolute terror on his face. A black fin broke the surface and was heading straight for the pair of them. The uniformed man reached Junior, climbed straight up his body and threw himself out of the tank. He dropped ten feet to the ground and landed with a sodden squelch. The cheering and applause started up again. Junior dropped below the waterline and grabbed the approaching dolphin around the neck. It carried him to the centre of the tank then nudged him on to its back. It then proceeded to swim around the pool showing off for the audience.

As Junior passed a metal ladder fixed to the side of the tank he slipped off the big fishy, grabbed the ladder and hauled himself out of the water. He had lost his gun. Luckily he still had two more. Junior dropped to the floor. He was at the back of the tank. He considered trying to hide but realised that the audience could see him through the glass walls and clear water of the tank. He turned and looked at their distorted images through the tank. He thought about pulling out one of his hidden guns and firing at the glass walls that would shatter and, hopefully, cause the audience to be drowned. There must be tonnes of water in the tank, he thought, but he couldn't do it. He liked dolphins. He could see there were three of them swimming around the tank. Junior decided to go and grab Luscious, find out what the fuck he was up to and then kill him.

Junior squelched around to the front of the tank. The audience had broken up and were milling around drinking champagne and chattering noisily. Junior saw he was in a big room. It was like an art gallery: marble floor and pillars; expensive paintings hung on the walls, all in some way depicting Christ's fight with the Devil. Junior recognised many of them. There were comfortable settees and chairs scattered about. Waiters served food and drink. There were four recesses in the walls, covered by red curtains. In front of each of these stood one of the priests Junior had seen carry the cages down from the black van.

At one end of the room opposite the dolphins there was an altar. Resting on that there were four smaller altars. The whole room was lit with a low light and because of the smoking and drinking there was the atmosphere of a sophisticated party. As Junior walked around, people smiled at him as if they knew him. And many of them did. Some of the most famous people in the world were at the party, some of them Junior had even worked with over the years. There was the politician who Junior had saved from assassination in Jakarta. Junior had killed the assassin.

There was the squeaky-clean pop star who Junior had saved from OD-ing in a toilet in Los Angeles. Junior had killed the only witness, a junkie prostitute. There was the racing driver who was being blackmailed by his gay lover, who happened to be a famous American basketball star. Junior had killed the basketball star and made it look like an overdose. It was beginning to look like a look-who-I've-killed *This Is Your Life*. Junior saw at least twenty people who he had killed for. He was now beginning to feel really uncomfortable, and it wasn't just because he was dripping wet. He was beginning to feel haunted.

'Would you like a towel, baybeeee?' said a smooth voice at Junior's ear. Junior was expecting this. He didn't even turn around as a warm cotton towel was draped over his shoulders. Luscious appeared in front of Junior. He was smiling.

'Enjoying yourself?' said Luscious with a big grin, as he stared hard into Junior's eyes.

'What the fuck is this all about?' said Junior, his face giving nothing away. He had been toying with the idea that he may have been drugged.

'It's all for you, baybeee. I'm going to save your s,s,s,soul,' stuttered Luscious mockingly, 'and you will be with me forever.'

'What happens if I don't want to be with you f,f,f,fucking forever,' replied Junior.

'Ha ha ha.' Luscious laughed like it's written. 'You have no choice, baybeeeee. Would you like me to explain?'

'I'd love it,' said Junior sitting down on an empty settee and pulling off his boots.

Luscious sat up close next to him. 'Let me get you a

change of clothes,' said the singer. An exact replica of what Junior was wearing was placed down next to the bodyguard by a small, slim man, who could easily have been the Vatican guard's twin brother.

'I'm OK with these,' said Junior, pointing to his wet duds, realising that if he took his clothes off his weapons would be revealed.

'Oh we know about your guns,' laughed Luscious. 'And they're no use down here, you cheeeeeeky monkeeeeeeee.'

Junior bent down and unbuckled the holsters at his ankles. He threw them to Luscious, who caught them and threw them over the back of the sofa. They hit the Minister of Education for Kenya, who was laughing at something a muscular transvestite was saying. Still sitting with his back against the settee, Junior wriggled out of his clothes. He was acting embarrassed, although no one in the room batted an eyelid at a big black man taking off his clothes. Junior towelled himself dry then slipped on the sweater. His knife was hidden again.

Let's see if the clever fuck knows about the knife? thought Junior. He pulled on dry underwear, not his normal brand but the same shape and size, then stood up and put on the rest of the clothes. While this was going on, a table had been put down in front of them and a selection of food put out. Even though Junior was starving he resisted the food. He wanted to stay light and dangerous. Luscious picked at some fruit.

'You see, Junior,' began Luscious, putting on his idea of an English schoolteacher's voice, 'you have killed many innocent people.' He couldn't keep the accent up so he lapsed back into his normal black American bastardised rock star patois. 'Because of all the bad things you have done, the Devil will take you for his own and you will burn forever in the fires of Hell. When Satan comes back to take his rightful place as ruler, and God is driven beneath his path you will continue to be tortured because you didn't turn yourself over to him. But if I save you, and you turn your body and soul over to be a disciple of the dark one now, you will reap vast rewards.'

Luscious said this so matter-of-factly that Junior thought he was joking. Luscious realised this and shouted to a man who was standing just behind them, beckoning him to come over. Junior saw it was a big movie star, famous for big macho blockbusters. He came and sat in between Luscious and Junior.

'Waddya want, ya fucking rock star,' said the movie star good-naturedly.

'I would like you to explain to our guest here how you feel about Satan,' said Luscious softly.

'Fucking A,' said the movie star. In one fluid moment he pulled out a tiny gun from inside his jacket and shot himself in the mouth. The gun was so small there was only a tiny pop as the bullet came out of the top of his head and embedded itself in the ceiling. Junior pushed himself away from the dead man who fell face down into a tray of miniature hamburgers. Blood, bone and brain had sprayed a young girl in the crowd. She had a Dalmatian puppy on a lead. It now had red and black spots.

'Fuck,' said Junior, 'I guess he liked Satan, but what fucking use is that now he's dead?'

'Ah, but he isn't dead, Junior, baybeeee waybeeee,' smiled Luscious. 'You see he's just joined him in hell, and that's where he's gone because that man was a very bad motherfucker. Much more evil than yoooooou. And soon the Devil will return and give him his earthly body back so he will live in two places: the heaven of hell; and Earth. Lovely, isn't it?'

'So the Devil's coming to the party, eh?' said Junior,

smiling. 'Hope he brings a bottle. I'd like to taste some of that hell wine.'

'You will,' said Luscious. 'And you will adore him. Let me explain.'

'I'm all fucking ears. Unlike him,' said Junior, pushing the dead man on to the floor.

'You see,' said Luscious delicately peeling an orange, 'we need people like you, very baaaaad killing people. There's nothing our black lord loves more than murderers. Which is what you are and once you've met him you will give your soul to him and thou shalt be saved.'

'Well, let's meet the big black fucking Devil then and stop fucking about. You Devil-worshipping lot put on a mutherfucking good show, but I haven't seen any big fat Devil ass around the place. So come on then, let's fucking do it, I've got a soul that needs saving, baybeeeeeeee,' Junior said, in a Will-Smith-taking-the-piss tone that was getting to the singer, he could tell.

'Hey,' shouted Junior to the other people in the room, 'has anybody seen the Devil, 'cos I's in need of some souuuuuul savin', maaaan.' Some of the people raised their glasses and hollered back at Junior.

'It's time,' whispered Luscious in Junior's ear. The singer walked towards the altar. The noise in the room got louder. Junior stood and moved to the back of the crowd. He was a head and shoulders taller than most people there, so he could see everything that was going on. He had to stifle a giggle. 'This is serious Devil-worshippin' shit,' he shouted.

He could see glasses being raised. 'Hail Satan!' someone shouted. Junior laughed out loud. His foot caught on something. Junior looked down and saw his guns lying there; the Dalmation puppy had been chewing on the holster. Junior took his guns out carefully, he hated puppy slobber. He slipped the guns into his jacket pockets, though he had never liked carrying guns like that – it ruined the line of a good suit.

When he looked up he saw Luscious was standing with his back to the altar. The four priests carried the cages towards him. As each priest passed, Luscious touched the covered cage gently. They were then placed on the mini altars.

Junior moved forward, as he wanted to get a better look at what was in the cages, it had to be some sort of horrendous beast from hell. He was looking forward to seeing what the Devil's pets looked like. Junior wasn't surprised to see Enya, Fairy and Scooby walk up on to the altar. They got a big cheer from the crowd. It was like being at one of Luscious's gigs. Enya looked dreadful. All of Junior's staff were there but Junior wouldn't have recognised them in their Devil-worshipping robes. The four of them moved behind each of the cages and placed both their hands on to the cage. Then, with one movement, they whipped off the covers. As one the crowd inhaled, then began to applaud.

'Hang on! Hang on!' shouted Junior as he pushed his way up to the altar. 'What the fuck are these?' he said as he pointed to the cages.

'Budgies,' said Luscious.

'I can see they're fucking budgies,' snapped Junior, 'but what the fuck have these got to do with the fucking Devil. Shouldn't they be … I don't know lizardy-type monster, beast things?'

Someone in the audience laughed. Another shouted 'lizardy-type monster, beast things, yeah!' This crowd were extremely drunk and having a laugh. It wasn't your normal conjuring-up-the-Devil do.

'No,' said Luscious, as if talking to a small child. 'Budgies are the Devil's chosen animal. They're even mentioned in the Bible. And these four birds are the direct descendants of the bible budgies. My disciples and I have spent millions of pounds and years of research searching for these royal birds and now we have the four of them together we can bring our black lord to be the true ruler.'

'You rock, Satan!' shouted someone in the audience.

'Oh just … grow the fuck up!' said Junior. 'Beelzebub's fucking budgies, my ass. What's God got? A gerbil?'

'You're not taking this seriously, are you?' said Luscious, his eyes glittering dangerously.

Junior could hear champagne corks popping; there was a smell of dope in the air.

One of the budgies said, 'Oranges.'

'No, I am not taking it fucking seriously. I'm going home. I'm sick of you lot and your childish shit.' Junior turned to walk away.

Someone in the audience shouted, 'Oooh get her.' Junior recognised the voice. It was a world-famous American film director. He was very stoned and very giggly. He had chocolate on his beard.

'You can't go,' said Luscious quietly and Junior was suddenly frozen to the spot. He couldn't move a muscle.

'You see,' said Luscious, approaching the bodyguard, his voice sounding miles away, 'this is how we bring Satan on to this earth, baybeeeee. While I am singing an ancient incantation, we sprinkle the blood of a recently killed murderer on to the heads of the budgies. This channels the dark lord's power and he joins us on this earth. We then give up the body of the deceased to our master. The dark lord can grant the dead person immortality, for they have offered themselves up to him. But if they have been killed against their will, renouncing Satan, they are eaten in hell for the rest of eternity, and that's got to hurt.'

By now Luscious was whispering into Junior's ear. Junior could feel warm saliva against the side of his head.

'Ha fucking ha!' Junior managed to whisper.

'I have decided you will be the sacrifice,' shouted Luscious angrily.

There was a sudden screaming from the altar. Luscious turned to see where the noise was coming from.

'No, no,' screamed Enya, rushing towards Luscious. 'You said it would be me. It's what I was in training for!' She threw herself at Luscious, teeth bared. The singer knocked her to the ground and began kicking her. She was still screaming as Luscious rained blows on her fragile body. Junior staggered, he was free from whatever had been holding him. The audience watched and cheered as if they were watching a theatre performance.

Junior pulled out one of his guns and fired at Luscious's back. The singer dropped suddenly and the bullet caught him in the shoulder, spinning him away from the prone girl. He was thrown against the altar. The priests pulled out guns from their robes. Junior shot them all without thinking. One of them fell on to a chair and smashed it to bits. Some wood splintered off and blinded a teenage soap star in one eye. She began to scream. Luscious pulled himself to his feet and rushed at the bodyguard. Junior shot him in the chest and the singer did a backward somersault over the altar. The audience were roaring with laughter and cheering their support for Luscious. An action-movie star, who thought what he did on screen was real, grabbed Junior from behind, his thick arm around Junior's neck. Using the impetus of the untrained man, Junior rolled forward dragging the man with him. The movie star was catapulted over Junior's head. Junior pulled out his knife and stabbed the movie star three times in the heart. 'Your movies were shit,' he said to the dead man as he wiped the knife on his sweatshirt.

With a knife in one hand and a gun in the other, Junior stood up. He was covered in blood. The audience watched him: laughing, applauding and drinking. He could see priests moving through the crowd towards him. He shot two as they approached, their bodies folding up over their wounds as if they didn't want to be seen to be hurt. He then noticed the film camera, so he shot that as well, neatly, down the lens. Luckily for the cameraman he was having a quick line of coke off a flight case; not so luckily for the soundman he was having a quick peek at the action. He crumpled to the floor, his boom-arm hitting the cameraman on the back of the head and pushing his face into the flight case and the straw up his nose. His nose was numbed by the coke, but it really bled.

Junior heard a noise behind him. He spun around. It was Luscious. He had pulled himself upright and was staring at Junior. 'I can save your soul,' he said, blood running out of his mouth. Junior pulled the gun level to Luscious's face and pulled the trigger. It clicked on an empty chamber.

'Oranges,' said the budgie again.

Luscious made a grab for Junior. Junior stabbed him in the outstretched palm. The power of the blow forced back Luscious's hand, the knife passed through bone and muscle and pinned the singer's hand to his chest and he dropped from sight. Junior turned, pulled out his other gun and fired into the crowd.

He had expected more of a panic but they didn't even seem that concerned. Some of them even poured another drink. Without thinking, Junior grabbed the nearest budgie cage and ran into the crowd. Something smashed into his shoulder. He recognised the all-too-familiar feeling, as he was thrown forward on to a table. He'd been shot. He turned to face his attacker. It was Scooby, who'd picked up the small-calibre weapon the suicidal actor had shot himself with and shot Junior. As Junior turned his body he instinctively managed to shot Scooby in the mouth, rearranging his big white false teeth and driving them into his brain.

Picking up the budgie cage he staggered forward trying to find a way out, then something smashed into the back of his head. Now what? he thought, as lights exploded in his eyes. He fell face down on to the floor, breaking his nose. He was still grasping the budgie cage. Surprisingly, the budgie was remaining incredibly sanguine about the whole thing.

Enya straddled the unconscious bodyguard. She had a chair-leg in her hand and had no idea where it had come from, but she did know that Junior had ruined her big fucking chance to become immortal. Well, fuck him, because she was going to kill him, get the budgie back and get the fucking Devil here herself. She raised the chair-leg again. She had noticed there was a screw sticking out of the end. All she had to do was drive it through Junior's head and it was bye bye, Junior, baybeeee. Unfortunately for Enya, to use an English phrase she wasn't familiar with, he was 'As tough as old boots'.

Waking up and feeling the weight on his back, he bucked like a horse. The girl was thrown forward, her forehead hitting the budgie cage and splitting it neatly in four places, where it connected with the bars. Blood began to pour down her face. The budgie quietly watched her with one beady eye. If you're the Devil's budgie this sort of thing probably happens all the time. Junior jumped on to the girl's back and punched her in the neck. The pain was so severe she passed out from shock, her body spasming.

Junior sat there on top of Enya, head bowed, regaining his strength. He could feel a cool breeze on his neck. As he turned his head, rockets of pain shot into his face. He thought he was hallucinating, as the whole side of the room had disappeared behind the altar. He could see trees and the lake. The party was carrying on outside, although a few people were milling about inside as if nothing had happened. Junior stood up. Pain from his shoulder, head and broken nose got together and decided to have a big party of its own. It was so bad Junior began to retch, but because he hadn't eaten, a thin sliver of watery blood and bile escaped from his lips and splattered on to Enya's expensive boots.

'Fuck,' he said under his breath.

'Oranges,' said the budgie, as a shot rang out, the bullet narrowly missing Junior and ricocheting off the cage into Enya's ear, effectively ending her quest for immortality.

Junior dropped to the floor and rolled behind a heavy chaise longue, his body crackling with pain, bullets whistling above his head. Junior had the comforting thought that because all the shots had missed him the attackers must be amateurs. He risked a peep around the posh French settee and was horrified and astounded to see Luscious staggering towards him, flanked by four priests all carrying pistols. He was now in trouble.

He watched their approaching feet from beneath the chaise longue.

Fuck it, he thought, I might as well try and take a couple with me. He lay there waiting for the moment. He could hear the sound of the party getting more raucous. He looked around for a weapon. The only thing close enough was the budgie cage.

'Oranges,' said the budgie. Junior took this as, 'Why don't you use me and my house as a club to batter Luscious with?'

He took two deep breaths, grabbed the cage and launched himself over the back of the chaise longue, brandishing the last thing Luscious and his gang had expected. He barrelled into the cage, catching one priest on the side of the head and sending him sprawling. At the same time, he punched Luscious in the throat, knocking him into the other priest, their arms and legs flailing. Their guns were going off but missing their intended target completely. Junior had landed on his feet. He ran towards the altar, flung himself over it, bullets flying over his head, made a crouching run and joined the party outside. He ran through the partygoers battering them with the budgie cage. Up ahead was the garage block. Junior could see the cars sitting there, waiting to drive him to freedom. Bullets were screaming past his head; he looked back at his pursuers. There were at least ten men, including Luscious, all armed and rushing towards him. Without warning, four priests, two either side of Luscious, fell to the ground, blood erupting from wounds in the sides of their heads. The priests took protective covering stances either side of Luscious. Shots rang out from the foliage. Luscious grabbed a handgun and, holding the gun sideways like a movie 'gangsta' homeboy, began to fire into the trees and shrubbery. A man dropped out of a tree and hit the floor with a dull, shoulder-breaking dead man's thud. The second man who had been firing at Luscious and his gang of priests would've remained unhurt if he hadn't run out of a hedge screaming and shouting, 'The fuckers have killed my brother.' It was the largest number of words he'd said in company in a long time.

Luscious shot him twice through the forehead. The good-looking Satriani boys were as dead as the career of a British soap star going to America to break into movies.

'That's for shooting me,' screamed Luscious at the dead men.

The first car Junior reached was the Ferrari he had driven on the night Luscious and he had visited The Chicken On A Pig. He flung open the door, threw the budgie cage into the passenger seat, threw himself into the driver's seat and prayed that Luscious had kept his habit of leaving the keys in the ignition. Junior laughed out loud when he found he had, and gunned the engine. The driver's door slammed shut as the car shot off down the driveway. A bullet smashed into the back window and Junior instinctively ducked. He heard the sound of other engines exploding into life over the whine of the Ferrari. Checking his rear-view mirror, he saw he was being pursued by another Ferrari and an Aston Martin. (If this is made into a movie, I'm definitely going to watch this bit being filmed.)

The Ferrari's engine was screaming as Junior slid into the main road. He grappled to gain control, then shot off up the winding road away from the house. He didn't turn the headlights on until he was at least two miles further on, which caused some consternation to the oncoming drivers, who let him know what they thought of his driving technique by blaring their horns.

'Oranges,' said the budgie.

'You got that right, brother,' replied Junior, smiling, which caused more blood to trickle out of his nose.

The car shuddered as it was rammed from behind by the second Ferrari. The wheels screamed on the tarmac as Junior grabbed the wheel hard and dragged it out of a skid. He pushed his foot to the floor and the car leaped forward into the darkness. He saw a roundabout up ahead, the right exit leading to London. He slammed his brakes on and the car fishtailed left and right as he skidded around the roundabout. He kept his foot down as he drunkenly careered along, the effort of keeping the car under control causing his wounds to start bleeding again. In his side mirror, he saw the other Ferrari edging up to him. Waiting until its nose was level with his passenger door, he swung the car to the left.

There was a screaming of both metal and human, and the pursuing Ferrari shot off the road, through a hedge and into a field. Because it was travelling sideways, it rolled over and kept on rolling until the two priests inside it were nicely tenderised. Then it burst into flames and cooked them. They would have made a lovely meal for a hungry cannibal or a serial killer. Junior stuck his foot down and headed towards London.

'I think,' said Junior to his budgie passenger, 'that this lot don't really care about little old me. It's you they want.' The budgie said nothing.

Just then, the Aston Martin pulled up next to them. There were four priests jammed into the car, but no Luscious. Surely the singer had to be dead by now, thought Junior. He was heartened to see they looked worried. He decided to check just how worried by pushing the Ferrari up to 120. The priests appeared very apprehensive indeed as they pulled back, but they made sure they were always in sight of their quarry.

At this rate we'll be in London in thirty minutes, thought Junior, but of course there was no way they could travel at this speed, as almost instantly the traffic got heavier, causing Junior to slow down to a modest 90 and then 70, until he was dodging through the traffic at a quite respectable 40mph. The Aston pulled up level again, and one of the priests pointed a handgun at Junior. He slammed his brakes on, causing the car behind to lean on his horn. Junior hit the gas and shot ahead of the Aston Martin and weaved in and out of the traffic. They were on the M40 now, heading past Shepherd's Bush. The other road users were shocked to see the powerful cars racing past them.

'Where are the police when you need them?' whispered Junior to the budgie.

'Bananas,' said the budgie, looking out of the window at the sights. He had never been to London before. The Ferrari shot past Baker Street and past Madame Tussaud's. Junior knew he would have to get off the main road and dodge down a side-street to lose the pursuing priests. What he would like to do was wait until they drew level and then shoot them, but all he had as a weapon was his budgie in a cage and Junior's experience in warfare told him that budgies in their cages could not compete with guns. The Aston Martin was three cars behind him. He would have to make his move soon. He saw a gap appear behind him, he pulled on the handbrake and the car slid across the road to a halt, completely blocking it off. The traffic behind ground to a screeching halt. Junior grabbed the budgie cage and leaped out of the car. The car drivers behind him stopped their shouting and swearing and suddenly found the British Library very interesting when they saw just who was getting out of the car. Junior ran across the road and leaped the safety barrier and on to the pavement. He looked back and saw the priests in hot pursuit.

He was running hard now and was feeling no pain. Up ahead was King's Cross station. He increased his speed and ran into the main concourse. Quickly scanning the departure board he saw there was a train leaving now. He sprinted down to the platform. A guard thought about stopping him but then remembered he had a wife and kids. Junior ran up to the train. It was just pulling out as he flung open the door and fell into the carriage. The door slammed shut behind him. He lay there catching his breath as the train picked up speed. The budgie cage was lying next to him.

'In a hurry, are we, pet?' said a voice. Junior looked up. An old woman was standing there looking as if a big, blood-covered, black man carrying a budgie cage falling at her feet was an everyday occurrence for her.

'I had a budgie like that once,' she said. 'It was called Joey. What's he called, pet?'

'Oranges,' said the budgie.

'Nice name. Sort of citrusy,' said the woman, as she left Junior to go back to her seat.

'Excuse me, lady,' said Junior, trying to make himself look as unthreatening as possible.

'Yes, pet?' said the lady kindly.

'Where is this train headed?'

'Newcastle-upon-Tyne, pet,' smiled the lady. 'We'll be there in about three hours.'

Junior had no idea where he was going.

14 〉

'Alreet, leek?' said George, as he crept into his secret shed. The leek squeaked its reply. George was pleased to see it had grown at least a foot since he'd last been there.

It's a good job Big Fat Squinty Bill's not here, thought George. He'd be rushing aboot the place all excited. A picture of Spinny Dog flashed into George's head. That's what Big Fat Squinty Bill reminded him of sometimes: a big daft puppy, although he and George were nearly the same age. Of course, thoughts of Spinny brought back thoughts of Neville. George sat down heavily on an old office chair and lit a roll-up.

'Divent have kids,' said George to the leek. 'They break yer bloody heart.'

'Squeak,' said the leek.

George let out a thin stream of smoke as he looked sadly up into the rafters of the shed. A spider looked down at him and waved.

'Ah know our Neville's OK,' continued George. 'Ah just wish we knew where he was. Mainly for his mother, mind, she still worries about him like he was a babby. She never lets on to me, mind, but ah knaa.'

The leek lay and stared at him. George stood up and crushed his cigarette underfoot.

'Right, you're coming with me,' huffed George as he picked up the leek trough. 'We can't have a prize leek like you living like this. Ye should be livin' in a castle. That's why yer coming to my hoose,' laughed George. 'You'll like it there. Sorry you can't have the spare room, Fat Squinty Bill's in there but ye can sit in the living room where the telly is, you'll like that.'

George had found an old pram tipped over outside the shed. It was just the job for doing some leek transportation. He placed the leek trough gently on to his new leek taxi. The leek squeaked. George could have sworn it snuggled down. He locked up the shed, put the key in its secret hiding place where no one could possibly find it – under a brick to the left of the shed door – and began to push his prize leek home.

'Aye, ye'll like it in my hoose an' ye'll be safer there than here, man,' said George to the leek. The leek must've gone to sleep in its pram because it wasn't saying much. It might have been big but it was still only a baby.

As George passed Wheelie Billy's newsagent's he heard someone shout his name. Mrs Fat Squinty Bill's came bustling out.

'Are you going back to your house?' said Mrs Fat Squinty Bill.

'Nah, I think ah'll take me leek ice-skating. Wanna come?' said George, indicating the pram.

'I can't, George,' said Mrs Fat Squinty Bill, laughing. 'Me skates are in the cobblers. Which is what you talk, George Creedy. C'mon.'

She slipped her arm through George's and hurried him and his leek along the street towards home.

'I've got some fish an' chips for us all,' said Mrs Fat Squinty Bill as they pushed through George's gate. Mrs Fat Squinty Bill went straight into the kitchen. George could hear Big Fat Squinty Bill's happy chat as his wife got out the fish and chips. George had already warned Nellie in advance that they had another visitor.

George picked up the leek trough and carried it into the warm kitchen. The smell of fish and chips was fantastic.

'Are you havin' some, George?' said Mrs Fat Squinty Bill as she dished out their supper.

'Whey aye, man, I'm starvin'. It's hard work pushing leeks all over the place. I'll just settle it in though, man.'

George carried the leek through to the front room and put it gently down on the table by the window. He made sure it could see the telly. 'Right, I'm just going to have something to eat. You'll be all right here.'

'Squeak,' said the leek, as it grew a bit more.

'Right,' said George as he entered the kitchen, rubbing his hands together, 'I'm going to have me fish an' chips then I'm going up the central station to see if Nellie's bag's there. Ah think that young taxi driver who was here would've handed it in he seemed like a nice lad. Can you pass the tomato sauce, missus?' The last bit was to Mrs Fat Squinty Bill, and she handed him the ketchup.

Thanks, pet, said Nellie, whose speech was much easier to understand. George looked up and smiled. She was tucking into her fish and chips and thoroughly enjoying them. *I would hate to lose those lovely photos of me lovely husband*.

Mr and Mrs Big Fat Squinty Bill saw the way George and Nellie were looking at each other and smiled themselves. If George wasn't careful he was going to became all soppy.

'Right, I'm off for your bag. I'll not be long,' said George, finishing off a forkful of chips and pushing himself away from the table. He hadn't taken his cap and coat off so he was ready to go. 'I'm taking the car. I haven't had it out for ages and it'll do it good to give it a little run out.'

'Be careful,' said Nellie as her husband kissed her goodbye, 'and don't drive like a joyrider.'

'Aye, OK, pet,' said George as he waved himself out of the warm comfortable kitchen and took the car-keys off the window sill.

It was true. George and Nellie hadn't been out in their old Vauxhall Viva for a long time. It was parked in some garages behind their house. George paid £6 a week for the privilege. George had always liked driving but like most northern men would always walk if he could. George unlocked the garage and pushed up the up-and-over door. There stood the car, its blue paintwork and chrome gleaming. Nellie had always liked to keep it looking nice. George climbed in. He turned the ignition. The engine fired up immediately and off he went. Well, not straight away. He got out and shut and locked the garage door. If he didn't his garage would be full of teenagers of both sexes, smoking, drinking and flirting by the time he got back. He could never figure out how they found out about open empty garages so fast.

George had long ago given up any idea of keeping anything of real value in there. Nellie reckoned that some of the teenagers in the area had trainers that were worth more than their car.

This shouldn't take long, thought George, as he drove through Wallsend, past the cranes standing in Swan Hunters, then up the Fosseway towards Byker. He hadn't been along here for ages. Although there wasn't much to see, he enjoyed the drive. Especially since there was hardly any traffic on the road. By now he was driving past the Byker wall.

There was a film crew all lit up filming a scene with that Geordie actor. What was his name? He was in *Auf Wiedersehen, Pet*. His wife was in *Coronation Street*. Tim Healy, that was it. They'll have to be careful filming down here, thought George, smiling to himself. Some of these kids are right tearaways. Wasn't their fault. There just wasn't anything for them to do. Those other lads who were in *Auf Wiedersehen, Pet* did all right as well, he thought. That Jimmy Nail and him that was in *Morse*. Lewis. That's him. They were never off the telly those two.

'Aye, it's a canny life doing that acting lark,' said George aloud to himself. By now he was winding his way past the Tyne Bridge and down towards the railway station. He pulled past the Royal Station Hotel and into the carpark. There was a taxi rank at the end. George got out of his car and locked it up.

'All right, pet. Can I get you a taxi?' said the friendly moon-faced woman, as George approached.

'Eh, no thanks, pet,' said George. 'It's just that our lass left her bag in the car when I picked her up from hospital a few days ago and I was wondering if anyone had handed it in, like.'

'Have you any idea who the driver was, love?' said the lady.

'I do actually, pet,' said George. 'His name was, er, Dixie Dave, I think.'

'Ahh, so you're the bloke who got him drunk when your wife came out of hospital,' said the lady, laughing. 'Well, you're in luck. He has found your bag. He was going to return it but couldn't remember where you lived. Must've been some party. He's due on in half an hour. If you hang about you'll catch him.'

'Thanks, pet,' said George, smiling. 'I'll just go for a walk. I'll be back in half an hour.'

'OK, love,' said the taxi lady. 'He wants to see you anyway. I'll tell him to wait here.'

George decided to have a walk around the station. He hadn't done that for years. He liked to watch people travelling off to exciting places and other folk coming home to their loved ones. He walked into the main concourse and looked at the departure board. There were trains heading off everywhere. He had always liked the journey to Scotland. The scenery was so raw, nothing like England.

George bought some mints from a kiosk and wandered over the footbridge to the other side of the station. He stopped and had a look down the track. He could see a train in the distance. It was coming in from the south. For no reason at all he decided to go and meet it. He had this ridiculous nagging thought that Neville would get off the train.

It would be nice if I was there to meet the lad, thought George.'You're going senile,' he said to himself, which caused two passing teenagers to agree with him.

George got on to the platform just as the train was pulling in, and he was immediately engulfed by alighting passengers. The old man stood with his back to the wall, craning his neck to see if his long-lost son was finally coming home. But the platform quickly emptied leaving George standing by himself.

'Stupid old fool,' said George under his breath. 'Getting yourself all worked up.' He was walking to the back of the train. This was its final stop so all the doors were open waiting for the cleaners to get on. He passed the guard on his way home.

He was just about to turn back when something bounced out of the open door of the carriage in front of him. It was some sort of cage. George looked around, but the platform was empty. He walked up to where the cage was lying, rolling gently backwards and forwards. There was a budgie clinging quite happily to the bars of the cage. As George approached, it said, 'Oranges,' which made George smile.

He bent down, picked up the cage and stood it upright.

'Well,' said George, 'what are you doing here? I think you'd better come home with me.'

'It can't,' said a voice from the door. George jumped. There stood a big black man in the doorway. It looked like the doorway was the only thing holding him up. He was covered in dried blood. The sleeve of his black suit was torn off, the knees in his trousers were ripped and he had a makeshift bandage on his shoulder. There was a heavy silver chain around his neck. It was Junior. He was terrifying.

'I'm sorry, I didn't realise he was yours,' said George. 'Are you OK?'

'Been shot,' said Junior, his voice slurring lazily. 'Guarding the bird. No police. They'll find us. Kill me. Bring back Devil.'

'Have you been drinking, son?' said George sternly.

'Oranges,' said the budgie.

Junior fell off the train, colliding with George. They both fell to the platform. George dragged himself out from beneath Junior and sat next to him. The big man was lying on his side breathing heavily. Blood was running slowly from his nose, across his top lip and into his ear. George's cap had come off.

'Well, whoever ye are, man,' said George, 'I think ye've taken a right batterin', man. So I think you an' your little budgie mate had better come home with me. Our lass will enjoy the company.' Junior opened one eye and smiled at the old man. He had no idea what he was talking about.

George jammed on his cap and got his hands under Junior's shoulders. Junior shuddered as if he'd had a sudden electric shock. His eyes shot open. George pulled him upright. The big man groaned but managed to get to his feet. George could feel the muscles rippling under the ruined suit. Because of his build and American accent George thought the man might be an athlete, maybe a boxer or a sprinter, but why would he be all beaten up and getting off a train from London with a budgie? He was probably a gangster. George tried to get into his mind but got out straight away when a bolt of pain shot across his forehead. This man was badly hurt. But he was hiding it well. Tough as old boots, thought George.

George had the man supported on his shoulder and the budgie cage in his hand. Hopefully the police wouldn't stop them, although he had no idea what he could be arrested for. Ever since the budgie riots in Newcastle in 1784, anyone was allowed to carry a budgie on their person in the centre of the town.

Hang on, thought George, what you doing, you daft get? This bloke could be anyone. You should hand him over to the police now. But George knew he wouldn't. The stranger had met his son. George was sure of that.

He half-carried, half-dragged Junior across the station concourse. 'Why don't you two get a room,' someone shouted drunkenly. George looked straight ahead, ignoring everyone.

'Is that your son?' said a little old lady standing at the taxi rank as they came out of the station.

'Eh, no, pet. Just a friend,' said George, hurrying past.

'He spent the whole journey in the toilet. I think he's ill. Oh and his budgie's called Oranges,' shouted the little old lady to George and Junior, as they reached George's car.

'Er, thanks, pet,' said George as he forced Junior into the little car. He stuck the budgie on the back seat and rushed around to the driver's side.

'George! George!' he heard someone shout. George looked up and there was Dixie Dave running towards him holding Nellie's bag.

'Sorry I didn't bring the bag down, George,' said Dave as

he reached George, out of breath. 'Lily in the office told me you had been in. Here it is.'

'Thanks, son,' said George, taking the bag out of Dixie Dave's hands and throwing it on the back seat next to the budgie.

'Is yer mate ill, then?' said Dixie Dave, staring at Junior slumped in the passenger seat.

'Aye, too much to drink, son,' said George, thinking to himself that a big, blood-covered black man should draw more attention than this.

'Ah well, I've gotta gan to work. See you soon, George. I hope yer mate gets better.' And with that, Dixie Dave was gone.

George was incredulous that their walk across a brightly lit station had gone without a hitch. But he was saddened that no one apart from Dixie Dave had asked if either of them were OK. No one even asked about the budgie. When did people stop caring? George shook his head and stuck the key in the ignition, started up the little Vauxhall Viva and pulled out of the carpark.

He didn't realise they were being watched.

'Ah bloody hell!' said George out loud as he stopped the car suddenly. 'How am I ganna explain ye?' Junior stirred in the seat. He had been slumped against the passenger seat door. He turned his head and looked at George.

'Could you possibly speak a bit slower, brother?' he said, then leaned his head back against the seat. The exertion of talking had tired him out.

'Well,' said George, trying to speak slower and a bit posher. 'You see, son. I only came out to pick up my wife's bag an' look what I'm bringing back. You and a budgie. I can't exactly say you followed me home, can I?'

Junior smiled. He liked this old man. 'Why not?' he said.

'Well, son. No disrespect, mind, but if you were followin' me home I'd make sure you didn't catch me. If you know what I mean, like.'

Junior let out a throaty laugh. 'I know exactly what you mean, brother,' he said, 'doesn't your wife like budgies then?'

George stared at Junior for a second then burst out laughing. 'I think she'll like you, son. I think she'll like you,' he said, as he started up the car and pulled out into the traffic.

'So, er, what happened to you then, kid?' said George to Junior as they drove through the centre of Newcastle.

'The budgie got out of its cage. It's a vicious little thing,' said Junior deadpan.

'Oh I know, son,' said George, without taking his eyes of the road. 'But if you'd stop talking shite for a moment, I know a bullet wound when I see one. And your nose is broken, and you've got a big lump on the back of your head. It wasn't the police, was it? 'Cos our lass has never liked me bringin' home fugitives from the law, especially if I don't know what they're called.'

'I'm Junior,' said Junior, holding out his hand.

'I'm George,' said George, taking Junior's hand and shaking it. Luckily all the blood had dried up, but tiny flakes stuck to George's fingers.

'It wasn't the police,' said Junior. 'But I would be grateful if I could get lost for a couple of days. You see, I don't think the people who are after me appreciated me taking their budgie.'

'Must be a bloody good budgie. What does it do?' said George, taking a look at the bird sitting quietly in its cage. 'We had one once. It didn't do anything. Until one day it just fell off its perch. Dead. I'd hate to be a budgie. What's its name?'

'Oranges,' said the budgie.

The two men looked at each other. There wasn't much they could say. So they drove on in comfortable silence. The budgie was a bit put out by that. He was normally the centre of attention.

The two men finally pulled up at George and Nellie's

house.'I think you'd better stay here, son,' said George, leaning over to the back seat and grabbing Nellie's bag. 'I may have some explaining to do.'

'It's OK, I understand,' said Junior. 'Not many wives like surprises like me.' George climbed slowly out of the car.

'George,' said Junior. George bent down and looked into the swollen eyes of the big black man. 'Thanks,' he said.

'Ah, stop yer slavver,' said George, slamming the door. 'Ye'll wanna kiss us next.'

'What have you done?' said Nellie to George as soon as he walked into the front room. She and Big Fat Squinty Bill were up watching the late-night movie. Mrs Big Fat Squinty Bill had gone home to do some ironing. The film was *The Big Easy*, a favourite of Nellie and George's. George was very pleased to see Big Fat Squinty Bill sitting in his chair drinking his beer and eating his crisps.

'Well, I've got your bag for one thing,' said George to Nellie. 'And for another thing you can stop eatin' an' drinkin' us out of house and home,' he said to Big Fat Squinty Bill as he tried to pull the glass out of his hand. Big Fat Squinty Bill had a very hurt look on his face. He'd been practising it while George was out.

'Don't try and change the subject, George,' said Nellie sternly. 'You're up to something. What is it?'

Big Fat Squinty Bill turned away from the television screen, his mouth covered in crisp crumbs. He enjoyed seeing his mate get a hard time.

'Weeeeell,' began George, 'you know how you like pets?'

'Have ye bought her a helper monkey?' said Big Fat Squinty Bill enthusiastically. 'You can get them if you're not able to …'

'No, I haven't got her a bloody monkey,' said George, cutting Big Fat Squinty Bill off. He couldn't be bothered with this at this time of night.

'I've got you a budgie,' said George calmly.

'Ah like the leek budgies,' said Big Fat Squinty Bill as if it all made sense.

'Er, that's right,' said George, grabbing on to anything to soften the shock of what he had to say. 'I thought I'd get you a budgie to keep you and the leek company now you're in the house together.' The three of them looked over to where the leek was sleeping. If it could have, it would have been sucking its thumb.

'Ooh, yes that makes sense,' said Nellie sarcastically. 'Now what have you really got to tell me. And you'd better tell the truth, mind.'

'Weeell,' said George, 'you see the budgie's got a little friend with him.'

'And that friend's me,' said a voice from the kitchen.

'Err, you'd better come in, Junior,' said George.

'Bloody hell,' said Big Fat Squinty Bill as Junior fell to the floor, a cloud of dust rising up from the carpet.

'I think you'd better put him in the spare room,' said Nellie calmly.

'Er, aye, I will, pet,' said George as he began to pull Junior to his feet.

'But, George,' said Nellie, 'where's me budgie?'

'Eeh, man, woman,' said George, carrying Junior, 'Can ye not wait until ah've put the lad to bed, man.'

'Well, hurry up, man. I'm missing the film,' said Nellie.

'I'll tell ye what,' said George to Big Fat Squinty Bill, 'can ye nip oot an' get the bird. It's in the car.'

By the time Big Fat Squinty Bill had got back with the budgie, George had explained everything to Nellie, Junior was in the spare bed, Nellie had got some birdseed from the back of the cupboard for their new feathered guest and had started juicing up a drink for their new injured guest. She was shooting around the kitchen like a ball bearing in a pinball machine. There was nothing Nellie liked more than looking after people and animals. She, like George, had tried to get into his head but had got an immediate blinding headache. 'He feels haunted,' she whispered to her husband just before he carried the big man upstairs.

'Hello, darling,' said Nellie, as Big Fat Squinty Bill carried the cage into the small kitchen and placed it on the table. Even though the bird was starving and very thirsty it still managed a quick 'Oranges', as Nellie filled up its feeding cups with seed and water.

'Funny cage,' she said, as the budgie tucked into its grub.

'You'll have to sleep on the settee tonight, Big Fat Squinty Bill,' said George to his friend, as he stepped back into the small kitchen. His jacket was off and his sleeves were rolled up. Nellie could see his hands had been scrubbed clean. He had obviously been treating Junior's wounds, although they didn't really have that much in their small bathroom cabinet.

'That's all right, man, George,' said Big Fat Squinty Bill. 'That lad must've taken a right hammering. Where'd ye find him?'

'Oh never mind that,' said Nellie, changing the subject. 'I think I should go up and have a look at the lad. Then we should all turn in.'

'Aye, yer right, pet,' said George picking up his wife to carry her upstairs.

'Don't forget the budgie,' said Nellie. Big Fat Squinty Bill picked up the cage and rested it gently on her knees. It never stopped eating.

'Err, I think I'll watch the end of the film,' said Big Fat Squinty Bill suspiciously.

'The only thing you're ganna see the end of is my beer and crisps,' said George.

'You are a suspicious man, George Creedy,' said Big Fat Squinty Bill, smiling and closing the living room door on Nellie and George.

Nellie, George and the budgie climbed the stairs and went into the spare room. Junior lay on the bed, wearing only underwear. George had cleaned up the blood from his face. He looked at peace. His shoulder had been tended to. The bullet wound was really just a graze, but George had cleaned it and put a fresh bandage on it. Old scars covered Junior's well-muscled body.

George put Nellie down on the bed then took the cage off her lap and put it on a small bedside table next to the bed. Junior opened his eyes and looked at them both. He smiled. 'George,' said Nellie, 'can you nip down and get me some juice. I've just made some. It's in the fridge, pet.'

George was back almost immediately, carrying the glass. He held it to Junior's lips and he drank it down greedily. Then he fell back on the pillow fast asleep.

'He reminds me of Neville,' said Nellie.

'That's what I thought, pet,' said George. 'But how?'

'I don't know. I can just sense him,' said Nellie, her eyes filling up with tears.

'Howay, spooky lass,' said George, picking up his wife. 'Let's gan to bed.'

They left the room, Nellie giving Junior one last look, and switched off the light the way she had for her long-lost son all those years ago.

'Oranges,' said the big fat replete budgie in the darkness.

A few miles away Ellen Difford stared at Clancy Tree lying next to her in bed. She smiled to herself. The way things were going it looked like she could end up a rich girl after all.

'I want no more fucking excuses,' whispered Luscious. The rock singer was lying on his bed, he wore only his black leather trousers and heavy biker boots. Like Junior he too was covered in scars. He was being bandaged by his doctor.

The medic was always amazed at Luscious's recuperative powers. The singer should be dead.

Around the bed stood four priests and Fairy. She looked dreadful. She had just come back from having bodies incinerated in the grounds. Two of them were Scooby and Enya and while they weren't exactly friends she had known them a long time. It was the morning after the party.

'The gigs are in four days' time,' said Luscious, pushing the doctor aside and jumping up from the bed. For a man who had been shot, stabbed and hit with a cage full of budgie, he was in pretty good nick. He began pacing around the room. 'Which means our black lord must be here by then, you fucking retards,' he winced as pain shot through his stabbed hand. It would be healed completely in time for the shows. The singer was confident of that.

'So where the fuck are Junior and the bird?' said Luscious, sitting down behind his desk.

One of the priests stepped forward and cleared his throat. He had a heavy African accent. Junior had shot his brother through the nose, so he in particular wanted to catch up with the bodyguard. He hoped that Luscious would allow him to be the one to kill him. He would make sure it took a long time.

'He is in the north-east of England,' said the priest. 'We followed him into the centre of London. He managed to evade us. It took us a while to realise he had got on a train. I personally never travel on the trains in this country, they are so appalling.'

'Our master Satan will see that the trains run on time,' said Luscious, smiling. He was glad they had found Junior, and a chase made it all the more fun and worthwhile. He was looking forward to seeing Junior beg for mercy.

'I don't think the Devil himself can fix British trains,' said the priest. The atmosphere in the room had lightened up.

'Junior was seen being rescued by an old man,' continued the priest. 'He is in the old man's house now.'

'But why would the old man rescue him?' said Luscious, his brow furrowing. He was gently stroking the wood on his desk.

'It has to be,' said another priest.

'Why?' said Luscious.

'Because our Lord Satan is on the way to his rightful place,' said the priest. 'So God has to perform tiny miracles to help anyone who is against the Devil. It's the least he can do. But will it be enough?'

'Ha, God is weak and he'll be dead in two days,' smiled Luscious. He looked like a little boy.

'Me and my three brethren will go to the old man's house, kill everyone there and bring the bodyguard and the bird back here for you and the ceremony,' said the African priest.

'I've got a better idea, priest man,' said Luscious, pulling on a ruffled silk shirt and leaving it calculatedly untucked. 'We will all go to the old man's house and perform the ceremony there. It'll save time. And it will be the last thing Junior expects. Oooh woooo, a trip out. It'll do me the world of good and we get to kill people. I think we should take a picnic. Have they got an airport?'

'Yes,' said the African priest.

'Excellent,' said Junior, clapping his hands. 'Well, we've got a plane. We'll leave right away. Come and get me when everything is ready.'

The priests and the doctor began to leave Luscious's enormous bedroom.

'Fairy, you must entertain me until we go,' said Luscious, his eyes sparkling.

The girl, noted the last priest out as he closed the door, looked terrified.

George woke up to find Nellie gone from their bed. He checked the bedside clock, whose old hands told him it was 8 o'clock. George never slept this late. Then he saw the wheelchair.

Aw, ah hope she's not flyin' again, thought George, as he dressed hurriedly. He was pulling on his old cardigan as he passed the spare room. The door was slightly ajar. George peeped in. Junior and the budgie were gone.

'Nee body tells me nowt,' grumbled George as he trotted down the stairs. He pushed open the kitchen door.

'Havin' a party, are we?' he said at the sight which greeted him. Nellie was standing at the cooker. By the smell George knew he was in for a fantastic breakfast. Around the table there was Mr and Mrs Big Fat Squinty Bill, Wheelie Billy, Bridget, Junior and the budgie.

'Isn't it great?' said Mrs Big Fat Squinty Bill. 'Your Nellie can walk. It's a miracle.' While she said this, George noticed she never took her eyes off Junior.

'Well, I'm usin' a stick though, pet,' said Nellie, pointing to a walking stick hanging over the cooker. 'It's the one you used when you sprained your ankle showing everybody you could jive.'

'Why didn't you get me up, man, pet?' said George, giving his wife a kiss and changing the subject. He could jive, it was just that the floor was too slippery on the day he was giving his demonstration.

'Ah, you looked so lovely lying there, pet, like a big old baby. I thought I'd let you sleep for a bit. You're not young, you know, pet. You've got to keep your strength up.'

'Aw, get me breakfast on,' said George, giving his wife's bum a good-natured slap.

'And what are you lot doing here?' said George, turning to everyone sitting at the table.

'Er, I think that's my fault,' said Junior, who hadn't felt this comfortable for a long time.

'How can it be your fault, man, son? You don't even know this lot,' said George.

Big Fat Squinty Bill cleared his throat and looked down at his plate.

'I might have known it was you,' said George, shaking his head as he looked at his mate. 'Come on then, what happened?'

'Well,' began Big Fat Squinty Bill, 'Junior needed a change of clothes, and none of yours would fit him. So Nellie asked me if he could borrow some of mine, what with us bein' the same athletic build and that. Anyway, when I got home I mentioned to our lass that you had an American visitor.'

'We have no secrets from each other,' butted in Mrs Big Fat Squinty Bill. The couple smiled at each other. Big Fat Squinty Bill patted her hand.

'So,' continued Big Fat Squinty Bill, 'she said she would come down and help Nellie.'

'And on the way here,' said Mrs Big Fat Squinty Bill taking up the story, 'I popped into the newsagent's and mentioned it to Wheelie Billy and Bridget, and they decided to come down to give you a hand too, after all you're not young.'

'Aye, all reet, all reet,' said George exasperatedly. He wished he'd never asked.

'And when we all got here, there was Nellie nearly back to normal and you lying in your pit sleeping. It's a good job we came around to give her a hand,' Mrs Big Fat Squinty Bill admonished, 'what with you not lifting a finger to help the poor crippled woman.'

George sat at the table and looked around at his friends. He knew he would get the blame for something, and the amused look on Nellie's face told him it was pointless arguing.

'Give us me breakfast,' he said resignedly.

So Nellie, Bridget and Mrs Big Fat Squinty Bill began

serving up the food. This was the north-east. You didn't
think the men were going to do it, did you?

'I wondered why you were wearing that,' said George,
pointing at Junior's chest with the sausage that was stuck on
the end of his fork.

'Er, yes,' said Junior sheepishly. 'It was the only thing that
fit.' Junior was wearing a massive T-shirt that had seen
better days. On the front it said, 'Toon Army terrors of
Tyneside' above a picture of Kevin Keegan with the body of
a lion and his curly hair looking like a mane. It was
hilarious.

'What does it mean?' asked Junior. The hilarity had
passed him by.

'It's our football team, man, pet,' said Mrs Big Fat
Squinty Bill.

'Toon Army!' shouted Wheelie Billy. Bridget looked on
fondly.

'Oh,' said Junior, none the wiser, 'but what's Leo Sayer got
to do with it?' Wheelie Billy was about to get indignant so
George thought it wise to change the subject.

'Did he give you those tracksuit bottoms as well?' said
George, looking under the table at Junior's legs. He was
wearing shellsuit bottoms. They were so big he had to hold
them up with a belt. Added to that he was wearing his own
boots. The king of tramps would've turned down the chance
of wearing such an outfit. Junior felt ridiculous but
appreciated their kindness.

'Yes,' said Junior, 'Big, er … Fat Squinty Bill has been very
kind.' Junior had been in some very odd situations over the
years. He had killed more people than he cared to
remember, but nothing had prepared him for calling
someone Big Fat Squinty Bill. The name was perfect,
though, because that's what he was. He couldn't call Mrs Big
Fat Squinty Bill by her nickname, however. Luckily he

hadn't had to, as all she did was stare at him and say completely unintelligible things then laugh. What he did know was that these were very good-hearted people. He liked it here.

'So how do you know George, then?' said Mrs Big Fat Squinty Bill slowly. She was fascinated by Junior, as they all were. None of them had ever met anyone so exotic. It was as if someone had brought a tiger into the house.

'Well, I had a little accident on the train yesterday and George very kindly helped me out,' said Junior, trying to avoid eye contact with everyone.

'What happened, like? Did the train run you over?' said Big Fat Squinty Bill. He was the only one apart from Nellie and George who had seen the state Junior was in when he arrived at the house.

'Er, I had a little fall,' said Junior. 'I think I had too much wine.'

'Aye, that'll happen,' said Big Fat Squinty Bill, both cheeks filled with sausage and beans.

'So what've you got a budgie for?' said Wheelie Billy.

George knew this question was coming. 'Howay, man, let the lad have his breakfast, man, he's starvin',' said George, changing the subject once again.

Silence descended on the kitchen as they all tucked into their breakfast. Mrs Big Fat Squinty Bill missed her mouth twice so engrossed was she in Junior.

'Eeeh, you Americans eat just like us,' she said amazed.

'Especially when the food's as good as this, ma'am,' said Junior, smiling down at Nellie who was sitting next to him.

'Eeh, he called me mam,' said Mrs Big Fat Squinty Bill. 'An' ah'm not even his mam.'

'Oranges,' said the budgie.

'So what've you got a budgie for?' said Wheelie Billy again. He wouldn't let up.

'It's for a competition,' said Nellie. Her speech hadn't really been that good so there was a stunned silence when it came out perfectly.

Junior stared wide-eyed at Nellie. 'Er, that's right,' he said haltingly, 'I'm entering Peaches in the best budgie competition.'

'In Sunderland,' said Nellie, knowing that none of them would know anything about a budgie competition, especially in Sunderland.

'So it's called Peaches, then?' said Mrs Big Fat Squinty Bill.

Why did I say that? Junior thought to himself. I'm panicking, he thought. I never panic.

'That's right,' he said.

'Oranges,' said the budgie.

'It's *a little joke we have between us,*' said Junior, in italics, while staring hard at the budgie hoping that it would understand what he was trying to say, the way wives do at dinner parties when their husband have had too much to drink and they're chatting up the hostess's teenage daughter.

'You should ask George about budgies,' said Big Fat Squinty Bill. 'He knows all about them.'

'Do you, George?' said Wheelie Billy. 'I thought it was just big leeks? Mind you, George could grow you a massive budgie. Now that would be handy. You could train it to fly you all over the place. I'd definitely get rid of me wheelchair and get a budgie. Obviously you'd have to wear some sort of harness, though. That'd be cushty. So do you get prizes for big budgies, Junior? What do you get, a cup or something? George is ganna win us aall two million poond, ye knaa?'

Junior's head was spinning. This was worse than being interrogated.

'A cup. Yes, a cup,' spluttered Junior. 'Peaches gets a best budgie cup if he wins. He's won quite a few cups. He's a very special budgie.' (I'm beginning to sound like them, he thought.)

'That's 'cos it's American,' said Wheelie Billy knowingly.

'Why's that?' said Big Fat Squinty Bill, fascinated.

'Well, it stands to reason, doesn't it?' said Wheelie Billy, nodding his head as if all the clever stuff in his brain was making his head too heavy. 'If they can send a man to the moon and invent Disneyworld, they can certainly make a superduper budgie,'

Bridget nodded her head loyally.

A lot of people in the area thought the fact that Stephen Hawking was in a wheelchair and was dead brainy was down to the fact that he didn't have the use of his legs, as if all the goodness from his legs had been squashed into his head, in the same way that blind people have more acute hearing. So they naturally assumed Wheelie Billy was cleverer than a fox with a degree. They were wrong.

George and Nellie were looking around the table at their old friends talking shite and Junior and the budgie trying to keep up. *How come this always happens to us?* George flashed mentally to Nellie. *One minute were having a nice quiet life the next min...'*

Nellie looked up, startled, just as the back door splintered off its hinges and shot across the room, hitting Big Fat Squinty Bill on the back. Junior stood up knocking his chair over. The only weapons he had were his knife and fork. Everyone else sat in stunned silence as two priests stepped into the room. They stood either side of the door. Luscious stepped in between them.

'Neville!' said George and Nellie in unison.

'All right, Mam. Dad,' said Luscious. He was smiling nervously like a kid who's had his first drink and doesn't want his parents to find out. He even had a slight Geordie accent. The priests gave their boss a sideways glance.

Everyone else stared at George and Nellie and back to Luscious.

'Ah wondered when you'd turn up,' said George, annoyed. 'Yer mother's been worried sick.'

'Don't start, Dad,' said the singer. He was in danger of turning into a teenager again.

'But where have you been, pet?' said Nellie. 'Are you hungry? I'll make you your favourite. Do you want a Kit-Kat?'

'Maaaaaam,' said the singer.

'It is. It's bloody young Neville,' said Big Fat Squinty Bill. 'Eeeh, ah never realised you were that Liquorice bloke.'

'Luscious,' corrected the singer irritably. He was. He was turning into a teenager.

'Aye, him an' aall,' said Big Fat Squinty Bill.

'We've come for the bird and you, baybeeeee,' said Luscious to Junior.

'What you talking like that for, Neville?' said Mrs Big Fat Squinty Bill.

'Shut up!' said Luscious.

'You always were full of shite,' said Mrs Big Fat Squinty Bill.

'Can I have your autograph?' said Wheelie Billy.

'Oranges,' said the budgie.

The leek in the front room wondered what all the noise was about.

'Shut up!' screamed Luscious. He pulled out a gun from the back of his leather trousers and shot Junior through the forehead. The bodyguard stared wide-eyed at the singer. He smiled, then his face became calm. He fell forward on to the breakfast table, smashing it, splinters and food flying across the room Wheelie Billy was sent spinning across the room. The budgie cage spun up into the air and came to rest on the draining board. If the budgie survived this it really was going to need some budgie therapy.

Bridget began to scream hysterically. Two more priests ran into the room and grabbed Junior's body. One of them was carrying a medical bag. He flipped it open and pulled out a glass bottle. The other held Junior's head off the ground. Very carefully the first priest began to fill the bottle with Junior's blood.

Mrs Big Fat Squinty Bill stood up and punched Luscious in the side of the head. In his weakened state the singer staggered into one of the priests just as Big Fat Squinty Bill hit him. The priest dropped to the floor poleaxed. Mr and Mrs Big Fat Squinty Bill gave each other high fives.

Bridget screamed.

Wheelie Billy picked up a teapot and threw it at the priests bending over Luscious. It hit one of them on the back of the head, sending hot liquid down the back of his robe. The priest ignored it.

George and Nellie stood as one. It was unspoken that they would have to kill their son. Tears streamed down their faces as they stared hard at what their little Neville had become. They summoned up every last reserve of power they had, and directed all their force at their son. Nothing happened.

'Stop!' shouted Luscious, his trained voice cutting through the pandemonium. Everything stopped. Even Bridget stopped screaming. He looked at his parents. 'You can't kill me. I am stronger than you. I always have been,' he said.

'But what are you doing, Neville?' sobbed Nellie. 'Why?'

'You know why, Mam,' spat Luscious, his accent getting stronger. 'You gave me these powers and now I'm going to show you why we've got them. You two never used them properly. But I have travelled and learned from many different cultures. I found out that the reason we have been blessed with our gift is to bring the dark light back into the world. We were given these powers by Satan himself to help us bring him back.'

Everyone in the room was stunned into silence by the exchange between George and Nellie and their son. Even the priests, who always assumed Luscious had no parents.

'I always thought we were given these powers by God,' said Nellie, staring hard at her son.

'You were wrong,' said Luscious. 'And I am going to show you how wrong. I'm bringing back our black lord. Here. Now.'

'So can I have your autograph, then?' said Wheelie Billy.

'Shut up!' screamed Luscious once again. It was always like this, he thought. Everyone talking stupid inconsequential nonsense. Well, he was about to change that.

Just then, Fairy stepped into the kitchen. She was carrying an Uzi, although by the look of her and the bruising and scratches which covered her face and arms she hardly looked strong enough to carry herself.

'Are you all right, pet?' said Nellie in a quiet voice.

Fairy smiled. 'I'm sorry,' she whispered. 'Are you really his mother?'

Nellie nodded.

'Shut up!' screamed Luscious. He hit Fairy across the face with the back of his hand, knocking her back out through the door. She landed in the garden and lay still.

George started towards his son but was stopped by Nellie.

'Why don't you try and hit me boy?' said George to Luscious. 'Or can you only hit lasses?'

'Don't start with me!' shouted Luscious. He had actually wanted to say, 'Don't fucking start with me!' But even now, as Satan's true representative on Earth, he couldn't swear in front of his mam and dad.

'You don't understand, man, Dad, Man,' he said, sounding like a 12-year-old.

'Ah think ah do, son,' said George. 'Why don't you just leave, eh?'

'I can't, man, Dad. It's gone too far,' said Luscious.

'But, Neville, pet …' began Nellie. She was crying quietly.

'Stop!' screamed Luscious, recovering his composure. 'I am no longer your son!'

'We're ready,' said one of the priests by Junior's body.

'It is time,' said Luscious quietly, head bowed.

The two priests dragged Junior's body out of the kitchen and into the hallway, closing the door behind them.

'You lot against the wall and on your knees!' shouted Fairy. 'Please,' she added quietly when she caught the distraught look on Nellie's face.

'Can I still sit? You see I can't really kneel what with me legs an' that an' …' began Wheelie Billy.

'Just sit there and shut up,' said Fairy, the gun coming to rest at a point between Wheelie Billy's eyes.

With a cracking of joints Nellie, George, Mr and Mrs Big Fat Squinty Bill and Bridget knelt. Bridget was leaning against Wheelie Billy's chair. She was sobbing to herself. Wheelie Billy stroked her hair gently.

Two more priests entered the room. The kitchen was starting to look like the Vatican. They were carrying a small lightweight transportable altar, a bit like a fold-up picnic table except that it was for summoning up the Devil. The priests set up the altar in front of where everyone was kneeling, kicking debris from the breakfast out of the way. Their heads were visible above the altar.

Big Fat Squinty Bill snaffled a sausage that had suddenly spun his way. Well, if he was going to die he wanted to go with a full tum.

The two priests exited and another priest entered and covered the altar in a heavy white cloth. The edges were trimmed with lace and pearls. There were four rings sewn into the cloth in white silk. As everyone watched, three priests entered one at a time and placed three cages on to the altar and into the rings on the tablecloth. Finally another priest picked up the cage from the draining board and placed that on the altar too. All the other cages were gleaming and polished. Junior's budgie's cage looked as though ... well, you've read the book. The budgies looked at each other. They were sitting in the centre of their perches. George noticed that the carrying handle on each cage was also a funnel. He was soon to find out what it was for.

All but one of the priests left the house. Fairy stood against the back door. She was exhausted. The gun was pointing at the floor. Rain had begun to fall. It was a miserable day.

Luscious began to sing. It wasn't his normal style. He sang quietly but strongly, the words tumbling together as if trying to get away from each other. He was singing in Arabic, Latin and Hebrew, the clashing sounds creating a rhythmic pulse. All the words rhymed. Some of them hadn't been spoken for 10,000 years. Luscious's body sagged, his chin was on his chest. The words were falling from his mouth, they appeared briefly in the air and hung there before disappearing. Some of them weren't words but tiny pictures that shattered, as soon as they fell, covered in spit, from Luscious's lips.

The remaining priest stepped forward to the altar. In his hand was a vial, filled with Junior's blood. He tipped the blood into the funnels at the top of the budgies' cages. The budgies' heads were splashed with Junior's blood.

'Urrrrrgh!' said Mr and Mrs Big Fat Squinty Bill together. Bridget squeezed her eyes tightly closed, tears popping out on to her lashes like fat grapes. Wheelie Billy was lost for words. Nellie and George couldn't take their eyes off their son.

The budgies didn't say a word. Blood dripped down their feathers and on to the floor of their cages. The priest stood away from the altar. Luscious stepped forward. His head was thrown back. He wasn't actually speaking any more but the words and pictures exploded from his mouth and nose like thick noisy smoke.

There were four loud bangs as the budgies disappeared one by one. Luscious fell to the floor. The words had stopped.

Silence seemed to be pouring into the room. There was no Satan.

Luscious looked up. He was on his knees. His forehead had been touching the worn lino. The smile on his face vanished as he realised they were still the only ones in the room. There should have been someone else there. Maybe sporting a full complement of horns and hooves. Where was his master, his black lord, his saviour? Luscious stood up shakily. He was wide eyed and panicked.

From the front room there was a cough and then a voice said, 'I'm in here.' Everyone in the kitchen looked at each other, puzzled. Surely this wasn't how it was supposed to be. Luscious staggered out of the kitchen into the front room. The room he had spent his childhood in.

Standing in the middle of the room was a small, bald fat man. He was wearing a T-shirt that was too small for him. His belly hung over the waistband of his shorts and he was wearing flip-flops. In the movie it's Danny de Vito.

The new Danny De Vito bloke was smoking a skinny roll-up the way George did, cupped in his hand. Smoke was coming from his shoulders as if he'd recently been singed. An identical-looking man, although dressed slightly differently, was standing behind the Danny De Vito bloke looking bored. He was wearing a Ry Cooder British tour '89' T-shirt, old Levi's and Nike trainers. He stepped up to man one and slapped at his T-shirt, extinguishing a flame that had suddenly sprung up.

'Ow,' said the first man.

'Oh, stop with your whinging,' said the second man as he sat down on the settee, picked up *Bella* magazine and became engrossed in the crossword. By now everyone was crowding around the door staring at the new visitors. They were all avoiding looking at Junior's corpse.

'Who is it?' shouted Wheelie Billy from the back of the scrum.

'Come on in,' said the little fat man, beckoning to them with his tab-holding hand. He sat next to his identical twin on the settee.

'Four down is "cupboard",' he said, looking over his shoulder at the crossword.

'I knew that,' said the other twin, annoyed.

They all crammed into the tiny living room. Luscious was at the front, Wheelie Billy was next to him, Nellie and George sat in their favourite armchairs, Bridget was behind Wheelie Billy, and Mr and Mrs Big Fat Squinty Bill were in the doorway, which annoyed the priests because they couldn't see what was going on, but they certainly weren't going to argue. Fairy had collapsed on the floor in the kitchen.

'Who are you?' said Luscious.

'Who do you think?' said the man sarcastically. 'Have you forgotten all the stuff with the budgies and the murderers and the blood and incantations? Oh, you got some of them wrong. You set me T-shirt on fire. It's me favourite as well.'

'It's about time you got another one,' said the other man, without looking up from his crossword.

'Yeah, maybe I could get a Doobie Brother T-shirt, like you,' he replied in a whiney, taking-the-piss voice.

'You're the Devil?' said Luscious incredulously.

'Yup,' said the Devil.

'Fuck off!' said Luscious. His mam and dad didn't flinch.

Big Fat Squinty Bill sniggered. Mrs Big Fat Squinty Bill nudged him. The Devil shot him a look. Big Fat Squinty Bill shut up and looked at his feet, though he still had a smile on his face like a naughty schoolboy.

'Well, if you're the Devil. Who's that?' said Luscious, pointing at the other man.

'Hoy, a bit more respect,' said the other man, raising his eyes from the crossword.

'Oh that old hippy,' sneered the Devil, 'is my brother, God.'

'Don't start,' said God.

The silence was so shocked it couldn't keep it up.

'Aw, make us walk, God, man,' said Wheelie Billy.

'Sorry, mate,' said God, 'it's not my call today, it's his. Who plays Jack Duckworth in *Coronation Street*?'

'Bill Tarmy,' said Bridget. She'd often spoken to God, but not face-to-face.

'That's it. Thanks, love,' said God, clicking his fingers and filling in another clue.

'So what do you want?' said the Devil to Luscious.

'Well, I've brought you back so you can wreak revenge on God and take your rightful place as ruler of all things.'

'Ha!' snorted God. 'I'll kick his fat arse if he starts with me.'

'Do you want some?' said the Devil, turning to his brother.

'Oh I'm really scared,' said God, pretending his knees were shaking. 'Just shut up and deal with your daft disciples. Tell them what we've got planned and let's go. I haven't got all day.'

The Devil thought about arguing then decided his brother was right.

'Well, you see,' said the Devil, 'it's all very kind of you to bring me back and all that. Well done on the budgie thing, by the way, no one ever gets that. But it's not how it seems. You see, me and God, well, we're brothers so we get on OK, really.'

'Apart from when all the good-looking girls fancy me,' said God under his breath.

'Look, am I doing this or what?' said the Devil.

'How come all your followers are thick?' said God.

'Will you zip it?' said the Devil, making a zipping motion across his mouth.

'Hmm,' said God.

'You see,' began the Devil, 'throughout history as we know it, but not human history, obviously ...'

'Human history isn't history,' said God. 'It's just a speck of time.'

'All right!' said the Devil pointedly.

The leek squeaked.

'Thanks,' said God to the leek, and filled in another clue.

'You see, throughout history,' began the Devil again, 'the Devil and God must be related. That's the only way to get a true balance on existence. But every now and again the existing Devil and God pack it in and someone new takes over. The new people have a different perspective on things, you see. It would be a boring old place if it was the same person running things all the time, wouldn't it?' Everyone in the room nodded, but they didn't know why. 'So that's why God and me are retiring and handing the reins over to you.'

'What? I'm going to be God?' stammered Luscious.

'Don't be stupid,' said God, putting down the crossword. There was still one clue still to be filled in. 'You can't be God, you haven't got the right qualities.'

'But you do have the right qualities to be the Devil,' said the Devil. 'Neville the Devil. It's got quite a ring to it.'

'I'm called Luscious,' said Luscious.

'Of course you are,' sniggered God.

'But I haven't got a brother,' said Luscious.

'So?' said the Devil.

'Well who's going to be God?' said Luscious, puzzled.

The Devil and God looked at George and Nellie. George and Nellie looked at them.

'Oh no!' said George. 'I'm not being God. I hate all that do-gooder stuff. Anyway I like me beer an' me tabs.'

'Who said it was going to be you?' said God.

'Well, who else could …?' George stopped and stared at Nellie, shocked. 'What, you mean our lass is God?' blurted George.

'Nah, I'm just joking. You're both God,' laughed God.

Nellie and George looked at each other.

'How can we both be God?' said Nellie.

'Well, why can't you both be God?' said the Devil. 'Do you really think you got all those powers for no reason. We've been watching how you use them and you've come through with flying colours. Your son, on the other hand, just wants to do the usual daft things like rule the world. It's OK, though, when he sees the bigger picture he'll understand.'

'That's a result, George,' said Big Fat Squinty Bill. 'You can put a plague of locusts on the other leeks in the competition. We'll easily win the two million poond noo.'

'But where are you two going?' said George. 'Isn't there some sort of training course or something for new Gods?'

'Or Devils?' said Luscious nervously.

'Nah, you'll be fine,' said God. 'You pick it up pretty quickly. All you have to do is keep things ticking over. And remember the Earth isn't the only place you're looking after. Here you might need that.' God pulled out a dog-eared book from his back pocket and handed it to George. On the front cover it said *God's A to Z*.

'So that's it then,' said George. 'You go off to … Where are you going?'

'Holiday.'

'Holiday,' said George. 'Where do the Devil and God go on holiday, man?'

'Birmingham,' deadpanned the Devil. God sniggered.

'Look,' said God, 'it doesn't matter where we go, you wouldn't understand anyway now. But as soon as we leave this room, you'll be God and you'll understand everything.'

'And we can do all the God stuff?' said Nellie. 'Like bringing people back to life ...'

'Making poor cripples walk,' butted in Wheelie Billy.

'Winning leek competitions,' finished Big Fat Squinty Bill.

'Giving people bigger breasts?' blurted Bridget. Everyone stared at her. She flushed scarlet.

'Aye, ye can dee aall that,' said God, speaking in a Geordie accent, which is quite a difficult accent to do, but when you're God you can turn your hand to most things.

'But these are all very trivial things ...' said God.

'The breast thing's quite import ...' began Wheelie Billy, but he was cut short by a look from Nellie. And he certainly didn't want to start annoying the new God.

'Look we've got to go,' said the Devil, shaking Luscious's hand. 'Have a good time, and don't do anything I wouldn't do.' The Devil thought he had a sense of humour. Behind him his brother rolled his eyes.

God grabbed one of Nellie's hands and one of George's hands. He looked into their eyes. They felt as though they were being enveloped in beauty. 'You'll be fine,' said God. 'You have been chosen.'

'Come on!' shouted the Devil. 'You've always got to make a big thing of it.'

And with that God and the Devil left the house, leaving the new God and Devil in their place. There was an awkward silence.

'Do I have to curtsy to you now, Nellie?' said Mrs Big Fat Squinty Bill.

'Only if you want your arse kicked,' said Nellie.

'Well I'd better be off,' said Luscious, embarrassed. 'I've got Devil stuff to get up to.'

'Well, give your bloody mother a kiss before you go,' said George.

Luscious grabbed Nellie and gave her a big hug.

'Bye, Mam,' said Luscious.

'Bye, pet,' said Nellie. 'Shall I make you some of your favourite sugar sandwiches before you go?

'No, it's OK, Mam,' said Luscious. 'I'm the Devil. I'll just nick something on the way.'

'OK, pet,' said Nellie proudly. 'Eeeh, who would've thought it? Our Neville the Devil.'

The new Devil turned to leave.

'Son,' said George quietly.

'Yes, Dad, er, God, er, Dad?' said the Devil.

'You're me son and I love you,' said God, 'but don't get up to too much mischief. Or me an yer mam will nack ye.'

'I'll try, Dad. Bye.' With the priests following, Luscious walked out of the house. He left Fairy behind. He could sense she wanted to stay with his mam and dad.

A voice boomed out of nowhere. It said, 'The Devil has left the building! The Devil has left the building!'

'Cheeky bugger,' said George, smiling.

'Well, we'd better get on with some God stuff,' said Nellie, rubbing her hands, 'But first we'd better tidy up.'

'Can we give you a hand?' said Mrs Big Fat Squinty Bill.

'No, thanks, pet. We can manage. After all, we're God now,' said Nellie, smiling.

'I'll tell you what. We'll see you in the club later,' said George. 'We'll have a bit of a celebration. It's not every day ye get to become God, ye knaa.'

'Aye, yer right there, George,' said Big Fat Squinty Bill, pulling on his coat. 'We'll see you later in the club.'

Their stunned guests wandered off one by one. As soon as they left the house they forgot everthing that had gone on there. Well, you wouldn't want your mates to know you were divine beings, would you? They might start treating you differently. George and Nellie decided they were going to keep it quiet about them being God. They were going to be like Batman and Robin.

It didn't take them long to tidy up their little house or 'heaven' as they now called it. They considered bringing Junior back to life, but Nellie said no, as he seemed much happier where he was.

George and Nellie quite like being God, and are actually very good at it. Although they have had to tell Neville off a few times, they do see a lot more of him than they used to. He's even got a girlfriend.

Big Fat Squinty Bill went on to win the leek competition. He'd completely forgotten he'd been growing a leek. He gave most of it away to charity and him and Mrs Big Fat Squinty Bill are very happy.

Modern medicine came along in leaps and bounds and Wheelie Billy can now walk with a stick. He married Bridget and they've got two kids. They got married in December and there was freak weather that day. It was hot and sunny.

Ellen Difford married Clancy Tree and she's very happy.

George and Nellie have even had a word with everyone who was killed in the telling of this story and they all seem very contented.

Just a thought, though. Next time you pray to God, no matter what religion you are, just remember, to me they're a little Geordie couple from Wallsend, a small town just outside Newcastle-upon-Tyne. To you, God's just like your mam and dad, and they know stuff.

The End.

Now phone your mam and dad before they phone you.